EVEREST 1292

A Collection of Contemporary Turkish Literature

AHMET ÜMİT

Born in 1960 in the city of Gaziantep in southern Turkey. He moved to Istanbul in 1978 to attend university. In 1983, he both graduated from the Public Administration Faculty of Marmara University, and wrote his very first story. An active member of the Turkish Communist Party from 1974 until 1989, Ümit took part in the underground movement for democracy while Turkey was under the rule of a military dictatorship between 1980-1990. In 1985-86, he illegally attended the Academy for Social Sciences in Moscow. He has one daughter, Gül. Since 1989, Ümit has published one volume of poetry, three volumes of short stories, a book of fairytales, one novella, and fourteen novels. One of Turkey's most renowned contemporary authors, Ümit is especially well known for his mastery of the mystery genre, as reflected in many of his bestselling novels and short story volumes. Drawing upon the unique political and historical background of his home country, Ümit delves into the psyches of his well-wrought characters as he weaves enthralling tales of murder and political intrigue.

ELKE DIXON

Born in Tacoma, WA in 1969. From 1988 to 1994, she studied Art History and Literature in Washington State and Puerto Rico. After numerous visits to Istanbul between 1990 and 1996, she settled there more permanently, and has since been involved in a variety of projects, from translations to visual arts.

WHEN PERA TREES WHISPER

Ahmet Ümit

Translated by
Elke Dixon

§

Publication No. 1292

Contemporary Turkish Literature 23

When Pera Trees Whisper
Ahmet Ümit
www.ahmetumit.com
www.twitter.com/baskomisernevzat

Original Title:
Beyoğlu'nun En Güzel Abisi

Translated by Elke Dixon
Cover Design by Füsun Turcan Elmasoğlu
Cover Photo by Nazım Serhat Fırat
Page Layout by Hülya Fırat

First English Edition: May 2014

ISBN: 978 - 605 - 141 - 738 - 7
Certifacate No: 10905

Printed by Melisa Matbaacılık
Certifacate No: 12088
Tel: +90 (0212) 674 97 23
Fax: +90 (0212) 674 97 29

EVEREST PUBLICATIONS
Ticarethane Sokak No: 15 Cağaloğlu/ISTANBUL
Tel: +90 (212) 513 34 20-21 Fax: +90 (212) 512 33 76
Distribution: Alfa, Tel: +90 (212) 511 53 03 Fax: +90 (212) 519 33 00
e-mail: info@everestyayinlari.com
www.everestyayinlari.com
www.twitter.com/everestkitap
facebook.com/everestyayinlari

Everest is a trademark of the Alfa Publishing Group.

To the precious memory of the people who were forced to leave these lands...

Love keeps life from being ordinary.
Murder saves death from mediocrity.

Darkness... Darkness made much heavier by the cold. From a distance, songs reach his ear, the jovial shrieks of women, exaggerated drunken wails. Someone is cursing, perhaps to the heavens. Perhaps someone is sobbing, and just maybe someone is dying in the midst of this cacophony, this uproar. He doesn't give a damn. He's shed it all off; there's just the rage... Rage that permeates every inch of his being and shakes him from head to toe. Possibly he's not even conscious of this dark street or the ancient quarter he's passing through. Nor this timeworn neighborhood left over from the city's more glamorous days, nor this forgotten street, nor this cold, nor this night. He walks without knowing where he is going, engulfed by hatred. That green-eyed monster, jealousy, has clutched his heart in its steely claw and is squeezing away.

Women, says a voice from the depths of his consciousness. *Women. You cannot play around with them. You think you are playing with them but then the next thing you know, you've become the toy.* In the street appear the faces of the women he's had in his life. Their images fall at his feet one by one. All of them with heads hung and eyes filled with grief... All of them heartbroken. He brushes it off, passing over and stepping on them like puddles, but the images fall onto the ground once again. *Women,* the voice says again. *You can never escape them; their spirits will haunt you for the rest of your life.*

9

He takes a deep breath and chases the voice from his mind. The images of the women disappear along with the voice. The heavy smell of coal filling his lungs makes him cough. An expletive rises from his throat, but he refrains. What good would it do? He picks up his step a bit. Despite not knowing where he's headed. And knowing full well it's no solution. His long strides are strained, his fists are clenched, his right eye is twitching. It's all he's aware of. And perhaps that is why he flies into a rage. This right eye of his, which he never could manage to get under control, always twitches when he loses his temper. How is it that humankind is so pathetic?

If he could get out of this darkness, reach Istiklal Avenue's frenzied rippling crowds... maybe the colors, the lights and the sounds would pull him out of this well of despair he'd fallen into. If he were to throw himself into that mob of pleasure seekers celebrating the arrival of the new year... Perhaps it would end, this jealousy, this hatred, this emptiness that gripped his soul. Maybe the damp wind would pick it all up and carry it away. Maybe things would go back to the way they were in his youth, in Zurich... Like the nighttime walks he took on the lake's shore. Before he'd come to this godforsaken city...

Just then he heard the sound. Footsteps reverberating on the cobbled pavement. He can't be sure of it with all the noise. Could it be from his feet? He's all ears now, though he doesn't slow down. He listens to the street, the darkness, the night. The sound echoing off these houses which have already lived out their lives, their walls like rotted tombstones. The din of menacing footfalls from someone stealthy and sinister. There is someone behind him, all right. Matching him step for step without missing a beat, a shadow synchronized to his shadow, breath synchronized to his breath.

Had that day come? Was this when his nightmares became reality? Now? At this moment? Strange as it seems, there's a flutter of contentment inside him. Yes, he clearly feels the delight rising in his chest. And why not? Maybe it was for the best. And so it would come to an end, this torment that had dragged on for years. And as such he'd be at peace, his sins atoned for. It appeals to him, this sense of surrender

10

that suddenly grips his entire soul when he least expects it. As if he's experiencing his killer's approach as he cocks his gun and places a finger on the trigger. There's a bang and he feels himself double over. He can even taste the blood in his mouth. But this acceptance is fleeting and his will to live comes back in force. Jealousy, anger, and the remorse he feels over love quickly return him to life. No, not yet. It is still too soon to die. He suddenly remembered his uncle's words. Those words murmured in a peculiar voice as he stroked his handlebar moustache. "Let it be his mother who cries, not mine."

He calmly unbuttons his jacket and his right hand reaches for his belt. The assuring chill of his pistol grip reunites him with the anger he's recently overcome. As always, it is loaded. All he need do is turn and fire. Calmly though, without his hand shaking or confusing his target... Like he's done so many times before. "Let it be his mother who cries, not mine." He has a firm hold on the grip and gently pulls out the pistol. He spins round but doesn't even manage to take aim. A sharp wind strikes his left side. A silent but powerful gust. He looks in its direction. Someone is standing there in the darkness. Someone he knows all too well. He attempts to smile at this killer in the dark. "I knew it," he says before he crumbles onto the cobblestones. "I knew it."

"Looks like the killer acted faster"

It is a policeman's nightmare, New Year's Eve. That night when everyone else is laughing and having a ball, happily dancing away, means some horrific hours for us; a dark, bloody, never-ending nightmare that starts in the afternoon and goes on till the first day of the year grows light. There's always an incident; it never fails. Somebody always fires a gun, somebody draws a knife, somebody murders somebody... Up to now it has always been like this, and it will be like this forevermore. This is the reason holidays have been revoked and the whole force is on edge. While some people are out living it up in fancy restaurants and night clubs, or others at home with their families and loved ones, we police will greet the new year with our so-called little celebrations in our boring stations, all of us in bad humor, or worse. All of us hypervigilant due to the announcement that will come over the radio. Strangely enough, tonight the time has flowed by without any noteworthy incidents save the occasional injury, or one of those disgraceful molestations seen every New Year in Taksim. Maybe tonight would be an exception and no one would kill anyone. Maybe the murderers would put their business on hold for tonight... Just as hopes were beginning to rise, the announcement came, as Ali, standing, was nibbling at the last crumbs of the raspberry cake left forgotten on the table and I sipped at my coffee... Right at that moment, the transmitter relayed the New Year's first murder. A male body had been found in Tarlabaşı.

It was difficult to make out the details on the street, lit as it was by the pale light of a moon that appeared and then disappeared from among white clouds. If it weren't for the blue and red flashing lights of the patrol car, neither the body nor the two policemen posted at its feet would be visible. A few steps closer the scene became clearer; the corpse was lying below an unlit sign reading "Tarlabaşists Club" in front of one of these tired, crumbling Beyoğlu buildings. On the left side of its chest, right where its heart was positioned, a bloodstain spread like a massive flower on its pale coat. The silver veneer of a Beretta held tight in its right hand shone indistinctly in the light of the patrol car. Noting our arrival, our two uniformed fellow officers were already standing at attention, but Ali ignored them as his gaze was locked on the gun in the man's hand. With no explanation, he leaned towards the body, planted his hands on the ground and, without touching the gun, sniffed at its barrel.

"He didn't get a chance to shoot," he mumbled without looking up. "Looks like the killer acted faster." Now he was looking over the bloodstain on the slain man's chest. "They finished the job in one go."

It was far too early to reach these conclusions. I turned to the officer standing over the victim. "Were you the one who found him?"

"We did." It was the skinny one who spoke; he had taken a step forward. "We found him, Chief Nevzat." So he knew me. "An hour ago... We were patrolling the area. Last New Year's there was a rape so... lest we have another incident this year... We saw it when we were making the rounds. We thought it was a drunk who'd passed out but... When we got closer we realized he was dead."

I kept scrutinizing the victim as I listened to my colleague's explanation. A dark liquid, blood or saliva I couldn't say, had oozed out the side of his mouth and down to his neck. He was a handsome guy: straight nose, thick shapely eyebrows, dark moustache and a broad chin adorned with a stubbly beard. I turned from the body's ashen face to our officer's tired eyes.

"Did you see anyone with him?"

"No, we didn't. And we didn't see anyone fleeing the scene either. Who would be here anyhow at three in the morning?"

He laid down his words one after the other without thinking or even taking a breath.

"What about there?" I said, pointing at the first floor where the Tarlabaşists Club sign hung. "Wasn't there anyone there either?"

"No..." Again, despite not having been here at that time, he spoke without hesitation like someone absolutely certain of what had gone down. "The club closed at one o'clock tonight."

"What is this club?"

"Just a club..."

He was trying to look relaxed but the nervousness in his voice was giving him away.

"Yeah, I got that. But what do they do there?"

Our skinny colleague swallowed; he'd lost his former confidence.

"You know... The neighborhood residents get together in the evenings. For fun, I mean. They play bridge and whatnot..."

"Bridge, poker..." said my assistant, having his own fun with it. "Gambling. Just spit it out."

It was my turn to add something.

"You turning a blind eye to gambling?"

The wimpy police was tripping over his tongue.

"Of course not, Chief. What gambling?"

"It's not gambling, Chief," said his tall friend, coming to his aid. His body had odd proportions. His legs were short and his chest broad, but the appendage that really upset the balance was his head. With the uniform cap he wore making it larger, his head was so enormous that it gave the impression of having been plunked down between his shoulders after the fact. "They were playing just because, for kicks. You think we'd allow it if it was gambling?" As he spoke, ash-colored steam puffed from his dark mouth, which opened like a little cave.

"Would you?" Ali persisted. He must've been cold, as he'd stuck his hands in the pockets of his navy blue coat.

14

"We wouldn't." The officer with the big head held his gaze without blinking. His composure was calculated; he wasn't shy like his colleague who would have been knocked down if you blew on him. "Why would we allow that, Chief?"

My assistant had been itching to start something, but when an excuse finally fell at his feet, he was thwarted by my next question.

"Have there been any similar incidents at this club?"

"Like murder? No, Chief. There haven't. There's the odd skirmish of course, like everywhere else. But gunshot wounds and the like, especially resulting in death, have never happened."

His words didn't seem believable but I was in no mood to push the issue. I turned to look at the lifeless body again.

"Do we have an ID?"

"Yes, Chief." The skinny officer spoke up again; he must have relaxed. He held out a worn identity card with protective lamination. "Engin Akça."

"Did you know the man?" I asked, taking the card.

They paused, swallowed and exchanged glances, but didn't offer an explanation.

"I mean, he never landed in your station or anything?"

The bigheaded guy was the first to regain his wits.

"No. Or if he did, I don't remember it. This is Beyoğlu, Chief. You have been stationed here, you should know. It's a madhouse, the things we deal with every day." For appearance's sake, he asked his friend, "Do you remember him?"

"No. Maybe he's a robbery victim or something... and they killed him for his money?"

"So what about this gun then?" Ali had taken his hand out of his pocket and was pointing at it. "Was it just for decoration?"

"How should we know?" The officer who never lost his cool had an answer for this too, of course. "Who the hell knows why he was packing?"

As Ali was finally about to explode, this time it was a ruckus from the other end of the street that stopped him. The sound of a darbuka and a violin... An entertaining song pouring from the mouths of a lively if deficient ensemble:

15

"Oh boy, mother-in-law, what'd you do to us... what'd you do to us... you see, we're running away... you see, we're running away..."

They must have come out of a nearby *meyhane*. It looked like a customer who'd got carried away with the New Year's celebrations had dragged the musicians out with him, wanting to carry on the party in the street. But the fun didn't last long; when they saw the patrol car, the instruments went quiet and the song petered out. They'd noticed us. No, it was no customer, but rather three street kids about sixteen or seventeen years old... One was swimming in a coat at least two sizes too large, curly-haired and with a violin in his hand. There was a darbuka under the arm of the one who wore nothing but a baggy sweater that came down to his knees, and the one with the red leather jacket had no instrument, yet he had the most interesting appearance: the black patch covering his right eye was every bit as striking as his red jacket. The eye must be blind. Or maybe not, and he just wore the pirate patch as an accessory. He might have been the small group's vocalist, but like his two friends he'd also fallen into a deep silence. Even on New Year's it was no pleasant thing to be caught in an alley by the police as you are singing and dancing at three in the morning. They froze in their places like spooked rabbits caught in the headlights. The voices of the people still having a wild time in Taksim Square became a buzz that was carried into the street by the harsh, frosty wind. But the stillness didn't last long and the teens slowly began to stir again. The one with the red jacket was the bravest; setting his one good eye on us, he gingerly came our way, and his friends followed. The red jacket was in front but it was the violinist who first noticed the corpse. He wasn't afraid, but on the contrary made his way over with visible curiosity. As soon as he saw it though, he shouted out in surprise.

"Engin! Hey, it's Engin Abi..." He turned to the darbuka drummer in a panic. "Keto, man, look! They killed Engin Abi!"

Keto shook his head resolutely. "It's not him. You think it's that easy to hit Engin Abi? Nobody can touch him."

The officer with the huge head glowered when he saw the children. "Huffers!" he spit out. "That's all we're missing."

Not even bothering to ask me, he put his hands up and said, "Oy! Don't you come into this street, kids. Go on, get lost. Scram!"

They ignored his warning.

"I'm talking to you. You hear me?"

I put a hand on his shoulder. "Let them over. Maybe they saw something."

He looked at me with surprise. "What could they possibly have seen, Chief? Look, they've been sucking down paint thinners and are high as kites. They don't know which way is up."

"So be it," I said decisively. "I still want to have a chat with them."

Seeing me stand up for them, the boys came right up to the corpse. "Holy shit," barked the one named Keto. "It's true, man. It's Engin Abi, all right!"

Although his swearing and surprise were genuine, it didn't seem that authentic coming from his mouth.

"Well, fuck me," he uttered, wiping his nose with the sleeve of his sweater. "They shot Engin Abi, for real." He looked with disappointment at his friend. "Man, Musti, I thought you said he had an amulet... with a protection prayer in it, you said. A *Cevşen* prayer... You said he couldn't die, huh? That he was bulletproof?"

Musti hung his head, looking guilty as though he had killed Engin Abi with his own hands, then suddenly looked over at me. "How did they kill him?"

"With a knife," I answered, in order to open a dialogue with them. "Someone stabbed your Engin Abi."

He breathed a sigh of relief like a suspect whose name had been cleared and hollered to his friend. "Did you hear that, Keto? They killed Engin Abi with a knife. The charm was written against bullets, so it had no affect on blades..."

"So you know him." My tone of voice was neither bossy nor admonishing; it was confused and sad, like theirs. Perhaps that was why they had no qualms answering my question.

"Yeah, of course we do." Swallowing, Keto took the darbuka from under his arm. "He was like a big brother, a father to us. He..."

"He was a sound guy," Musti concluded. "There'll never be another like him."

"Who would have stabbed him?"

They recoiled and looked me in the face as though waking from a long sleep. They eyed us over, starting with me, then moving on to the uniformed officers next to me. As they studied the officers, their eyes clouded over with something akin to fear and reservation.

"Look kids, my name is Nevzat. Chief Inspector Nevzat, from homicide. I have no beef with you. I just want to catch the guy who murdered Engin. So seeing as how you were on such good terms with the man, you need to help me. Otherwise, your 'big brother' will have died in disapppointment."

All three of them stared into the glassy blue eyes of the victim lying there on the ground.

"Those bastards," Keto snarled. "They ambushed him, Engin Abi."

Musti nodded his head angrily. "They came at him from behind, the pansies. They couldn't have lifted the knife if they looked him in the eye."

It sounded like they knew who the killers were. If so, it meant we'd lucked out.

"Who are you talking about? Who couldn't lift a knife?"

They all looked at the uniformed cops again as if they'd agreed to beforehand. The one called Keto came over to me. He reeked but I ignored it. He stood on his toes and whispered into my ear, "Abi, aren't you a cop from this 'hood?"

"No, I'm not," I murmured in a reassuring voice.

He seemed relieved by my answer but kept a wary eye on the patrolmen.

"Come on. Let's take a walk," I said, indicating the direction they'd come from. "We'll be more comfortable talking over there."

As the tension in the kids' faces disappeared, an uneasiness settled into the eyes of the officers, but I ignored that too and said to Ali, "You stay here. Şefik from CSI will turn up with the prosecutor in a bit. Watch that they don't mess up the crime scene."

"When in fact these kids had no homes, no hope, no future."

※

As I walked with the trio, a strange feeling overcame me. I felt like I was their father. My daughter Aysun would have been their age if she hadn't died. I looked sadly over at these three kids walking side by side next to me. In fact, they didn't look so out of place. They were like a piece of this musty smelling street and the decrepitude of old apartment buildings which leaned back to back barely managing to stay standing. But not just the street. They were like a piece of this city that shattered your conscience, this New Year's night where joy mingled with violence, this contradiction-riddled human condition...

"You got a cigarette?" asked Keto, his voice scattering my thoughts. "I'm really jonesing, Chief."

I had a mind to tell them I don't smoke and they shouldn't either, then thought better of it as I realized how trivial the comment would sound. I took a twenty from my pocket, which Keto deftly snatched out of my hand before I could hold it out.

"Appreciate it, Chief! God bless you."

"Hey, that money's all of ours."

It was the kid with the pirate patch who had taken issue; he'd grabbed Keto by the wrist and was shaking him. Keto fought back, despite his frail body.

"Let go of my hand... I said let go, Piranha, or you'll be sorry."

19

Piranha didn't look the type to wimp out so easily.

"You can't just steal it like that. The loot's all of ours, boy. The chief gave the money to us all."

He had the determined look of someone who believed the righteousness of his case.

"Your friend's right," I said, backing up the trusting street urchin. "The money's all of yours, but before the cigarettes, you'll go get some food in your stomachs."

"You heard him, right?" Piranha shook him again. "Look, if you pocket it again like last time, I'll fuck you up..."

His one eye gleamed savagely like a wild animal's, impossible to tame.

"Stop swearing!" I snapped. "Can't you talk like a grown man?"

Caught in the act, his one eye blinked.

"I can, Chief, but you don't know Keto..."

"What is there to know, boy? Anyone who hears you would think I fu..." He swallowed the word at the last second. "... would think I did something bad to you. We're not bad to each other, and if we were it would be by mistake. So stop going on about it. The money is all of ours."

The issue had finally been smoothed over, or at least so it seemed. We stopped under a street lamp in front of one of those dilapidated buildings in Tarlabaşı that probably used to be home to one of our citizens of Armenian or Greek descent but had since gone to ruin.

"Yes." The three of them gathered around me as though they'd been given a command. "Yes. Now tell me, who could have killed Engin?"

Keto answered without hesitation. "Who else, Chief? Ihsan, of course."

The other two nodded in agreement.

"Yup, Dice Ihsan."

"And who is this 'Dice' Ihsan?"

Keto tucked his darbuka between his legs and blew into his cold hands.

"You don't know Dice Ihsan? He's the dirtiest gambler around. A real scumbag. And a coward."

"Whereabouts is this Ihsan's joint?"

With a filthy hand, he pointed to the building in front of which the corpse was lying.

"There it is, the Tarlabaşists Club..."

"And why would Ihsan murder Engin?"

All three of them eyed me condescendingly.

"You don't know a damned thing, Chief." It was Musti who had plunged into the conversation like this. "Engin Abi was a Genuine Tarlabaşists Club man. I mean, Black Nizam's..."

I was confused.

"Just a sec, just a sec. Wasn't the club called Tarlabaşists?"

They all three laughed in unison.

"There are two clubs, Chief," said Keto, supposedly trying to clarify the situation. "Dice Ihsan's club's name is 'Tarlabaşists'. Black Nizam's is 'Genuine Tarlabaşists'. Black Nizam opened his just to mess with this prick Dice."

"Why? What did Ihsan do to Black Nizam?" As I was asking this, I felt some cold flakes settle on my face. Looking up, I was met with a sky covered in pure white clouds. From the edges of the clouds, the barely visible flakes were falling over us.

"Snow!" the exuberant boys cried out. "It's snowing, man, snowing!"

They began to jump up and down with joy. I was also filled with an irrational excitement along with them. And yet a murder had been committed, and these children had no homes, no hope, and no future. However, even if only for a moment, I was overcome with the pleasure of the snow; for a moment I let myself get caught up in the children's enthusiasm. Only for a moment though, because just beyond us lay a corpse whose murderer was still uncertain.

"Anyhow," I said, putting an end to their joyous cries. "Let's get back to our work now."

"Our work?" a surprised Musti repeated. "What is *our* work?"

Piranha nudged his friend with his elbow.

"We're solving a murder, moron. Didn't you get it yet? We're helping out the Chief here."

"You're helping, of course. Now tell me. This Black Nizam, why was he at odds with Dice Ihsan?"

"Problems over women, Chief," Piranha continued. "This one woman was playing the two old Tarlabaşı mobsters against each other. But she wasn't just anyone, man, this was one foxy lady..."

God knows how much older than him was the woman he referred to as 'foxy lady'. He must either have thought his big talk ingenious, or else was putting on a tough guy act in a show of power.

"She's foxy, you say, but the woman is a slag." Keto spoke as though challenging him. "First Dice, then Nizam... Your average whore, in other words... Anyhow, what is it they say? You can't trust Istanbul's weather or its women..."

"Whose are we going to trust?" Piranha said, laughing. "Worry about the sluts where you're from first."

I noticed Keto clench his teeth and puff up his chest like a fighting cock.

"What about the women where I'm from, boy? What are you trying to say?"

Something was up, but god knows what.

"What's going on, kids?" I intervened. "What the hell are you doing?"

Piranha bared his dirty teeth and sneered.

"It's nothing, Chief. Just, this guy's mom is a working woman and... She's employed in the city brothel."

Keto wasn't as impressed as I was.

"At least we know who my mother is, boy. More than we can say for yours. Seeing as how you're such an asshole, must have been queers that gave birth to you."

The word 'whore' was bad enough, but the word 'queer' made them even crazier.

"You're the queer, man," Piranha said, moving to attack. But Keto was ready; he jumped back and took the opportunity to bring the darbuka in his hand down on his friend's head.

"Ow!" Piranha cried out, but then quickly recovered. "I'm gonna fuck you up!"

He was about to jump on Keto, who stood on guard waiting for the coming attack, but I grabbed his arms.

"Knock it off," I scolded them both at once.

22

"What the hell are you two doing? Look, don't piss me off or I'll haul the both of you in."

"But Chief, he threw the first punch..."

"Look, still yapping away..."

Although they eyed each other angrily, they both backed down when they saw I was serious.

"Listen up," I growled. "I don't want any more bullshit. All right? I ask, you answer. Kapish?"

Apart from a drunken shout from the side streets, no other sound could be heard.

"I said, kapish?"

"All right," said Keto, as he leaned down to pick up his fallen darbuka. "All right, Chief."

Musti, seeing what had happened to the darbuka, got scared and stuck his violin inside his coat before agreeing with his friend. "All right."

I turned to Piranha, who was scratching at the ground like a mad bull because he couldn't hit Keto.

"I didn't hear you."

"All right," he muttered, defeated.

I looked the three over, in turn.

"Good, then we have a deal. Now tell me, who seduced whose wife?"

Piranha sniffled.

"Not his wife, Chief, his friend, his bitch... The woman was with Ihsan first, then Nizam. But you know, Nizam's an old man so she took up with the other one again. The truth is, Black Nizam did Ihsan a lot of favors. He sent a lot of customers to his gambling den..."

I pretended to be hearing about it for the first time because I wanted to learn the details. "What gambling den is this?"

"We told you, Chief. Tarlabaşists," Keto quickly put in. "What do you think they're doing in those clubs?"

"Gambling?"

That condescending look appeared on the three faces again.

"Big time! Some people leave their whole fortunes there in one night and walk away." He looked accusingly down to the other end of the street, at the policemen standing anxiously beside Ali. "And your cop friends know this. Didn't they tell you?"

I didn't have it in me to blame my colleagues.

"Anyhow," I said, skipping over the subject, "let's just get back to this murder. Do you know the name of this woman Ihsan seduced?"

"A whore named Çilem..."

Piranha had emphasized the word 'whore'. Keto's hanging his head didn't escape my attention.

"I thought we agreed not to swear," I shot back. "Careful with the language."

"Okay Chief, okay. So then that woman Çilem, she was sneaking around with Ihsan. But Black Nizam is sharp and he caught on. One night he snuck up on them and emptied all his bullets on them. But he didn't manage to get them. Ihsan's no fool himself, of course. He also had a finger on the trigger. They wasted two rounds each without anyone getting killed or injured. Anyhow, that night Ihsan saved his skin. But then they were enemies, of course. After that, Black Nizam opened the Genuine Tarlabaşists Club on the street below, opposite Ihsan's club. Lots of fights break out. I saw with my own eyes only a week ago, Dice Ihsan himself fired his gun in front of the club."

"I don't get it. Why did Ihsan fire his gun? He stole Nizam's lover from him. What more could he want?"

The three of them were falling over each other to speak, but it was Keto who won out.

"Because Çilem dropped him and went back to Black Nizam three days later. We told you, yeah Chief? The woman is a vixen..."

Things were getting increasingly interesting.

"So did Nizam take the woman back?"

They averted their gazes in shame, as though they had done it themselves.

"If it were me I wouldn't have, Chief," Piranha finally said. "Now you'll get all angry again but word is this Black Nizam has some gay tendencies..."

"Don't say that!" It was Musti who objected. "Black Nizam is a nice guy, that's why he forgave Çilem..." He must have

24

thought his words weren't convincing enough because, after checking the violin under his coat, he raised his voice and continued his explanation. "He loves the woman. What's he supposed to do, man?"

Rocking back and forth where he stood, Keto agreed.

"He's telling the truth, Chief. There was nothing else Black Nizam could do. The man was in love with Çilem. He forgave her so she wouldn't wind up on the streets. And Engin Abi gave him a bit of advice..."

Piranha was upset that his two friends took sides against him.

"Man, you go on and on about Engin Abi, anyone who hears you would think he was a saint. But really he was just any old son of a bitch, wasn't he?"

"Take that back, boy," roared Keto again. "Engin Abi wasn't that kind of person."

"What, is that a lie? Wasn't your Engin Abi that pedo barber's best friend? Yes, I'm talking about 'Skinny' Ziya. And he was taking you to Skinny's shop, too..."

"Stop being so ungrateful!" This time it was Musti who rebuked Piranha. "How many times did Engin Abi slip you some cash? Or get you some soup? He wasn't that kind of guy. And that ponce Ziya couldn't touch a hair on our heads when Engin Abi was around."

"Don't listen to these blockheads, Chief. Just because Engin threw them a bone, they aren't telling you the truth. He wasn't that precious a man. This bravery and whatnot is bullshit, too. I saw Dice Ihsan spit in his face with my own eyes and he didn't make so much as a peep..."

"That's a lie," Keto cut in. "Didn't Engin Abi just beat the shit out of some man with that queer Ihsan two weeks ago in front of that liquor store? We were right there."

Piranha sighed irritably; steam spewed from his wide nostrils.

"We were there, but it wasn't your Engin Abi, it was Nizam's nephews who beat up Ihsan and his men. Okay, Engin may have thrown a punch or two, but that's it."

He turned his one good eye on me.

They're making shit up, Chief. Engin wasn't like he seemed. There was something else going on with that guy. Don't ask me what, but there was something."

"Where did this Engin live?"

"On the other side of the street," said Piranha.

"There are hundreds of houses over there."

"I'll tell you, Chief." Keto was pointing to the end of the street. "You walk that way and turn down to the right. Go down into Dolapdere. Behind the church... It's the third street I think. Building number 1."

"Yeah, number 1. But it doesn't go through. It's a dead end." Musti laughed. "And the name is really funny. Kadın Çıkmazı: Lady's Dead End."

"Did you go to Engin's house often?"

"We didn't go at all. He would feed us and give us cigarettes but we never went into his house."

Piranha guffawed. "Go on, tell us. It's exciting."

The other two children ignored him but I had to ask. "So how do you know his house?"

"When the club closed, we'd walk with him to his door."

"Why?"

"We had fun talking to him. Engin Abi would tell us everything that happened to him."

"That's a lie, Chief," Piranha spit out. "Engin gave these guys money." He stared at his two friends with an expression of disdain. "They say they didn't go in or whatever, but that's a lie, too. Sometimes they wouldn't come out till morning. Tell him the truth, boy..."

I noticed that Keto was shaking, not from the cold but from anger, or perhaps shame.

"Yeah, man," he shouted. "Yeah, we went to Engin Abi's house. Like you didn't go to Barber Ziya's? Is that a lie, man? Engin was like our big brother; he never laid an eyeball on us. But you were Barber Ziya's rent boy, weren't you? Before your eye popped, of course, when it was still shiny. Ziya, with you in his lap..."

He couldn't finish his sentence. Piranha, taking advantage of my letting my guard down for one second, planted a fist squarely in the kid's face.

26

"Who's sitting in whose lap, jackass?"

The punch landed in an awkward spot and his darbuka fell to the ground again.

"Ow!" he said, grabbing his nose. "Screw you!"

He was doubled over, the blood between his fingers beginning to trickle down to his wrist. But not even the blood would calm Piranha's anger. He was preparing to attack again.

"That's enough!" I said, smacking him upside the head. "Enough of that!"

I must not have known my own strength I guess, as Piranha crumbled over to the left. It was a sad sight; the slap had caused his patch to slide off and a black hole appeared where his right eye should have been. He hurriedly readjusted the eye patch while Keto tried to stop the bleeding with his hand and Musti, whose condition was just as bleak, had begun to shiver in fear where he stood. I felt like a fiend. I took pity and held a hand out to Piranha.

"Come on. Get up."

His lone eye stared at the extended hand with hatred, then in one agile movement he stood up and without even waiting for me to ask what was up, he shot down the street like an arrow.

Ali had also heard his footsteps.

"Chief," he shouted out from behind. "Chief?"

He looked tense. He was having difficulty holding back and not chasing Piranha. "Stay there." I said, signaling for him to keep calm.

The lamp that swung from the rusty electric post didn't put out sufficient light to make it worth chasing that dauntless child, who had disappeared into the dark street. It would make more sense to try and stop Keto's bleeding.

"Are you saying this was some kind of duel?"

※

The street was beginning to be covered in a blanket of white. It seemed a bit lighter out now, not from the snow starting to stick but from the strong glow spreading from the headlights of the ambulance that had come to collect the corpse. As the young prosecutor Oğuz took notes near the victim, the CSI team's plucky Inspector Şefik stood under the light a few meters back from the dead man, swinging his right hand into the air as though throwing a knife. While the chubbier of the two men whose plastic suits made them look like nuclear plant personnel scanned inch by inch around the corpse with his flashlight, the short one took photos of the crime scene. In this state, with Şefik at their head, the group resembled an inharmonious three-man orchestra. I shook off the snowflakes collecting on my shoulders and approached the orchestra's conductor.

"What're you doing, Şefik?"

He flinched as though waking from sleep.

"Uh, well, Chief... I was looking at the uh..." He was pointing down to where he was standing. "The murderer must have stood here. More or less, I mean. I think he took a swing from back here." He turned to look at the Beretta resting unfired in the victim's hand. The falling flakes melted away as soon as they touched the barrel of the gun, leaving the shiny metal faintly moist. "Helluva gun," he murmured. "A knife against this gun. It's hardly fair. The gun should've won. But would you look at this; knife beat gun in this affair, it seems."

He was talking about a possibility that had never occurred to me.

"Are you saying this was some kind of duel?"

"You could call it that, Chief, but they can't have faced off one with a knife and the other with a gun. If so, the gun would've prevailed. The guy with the knife blindsided the guy with the gun. Maybe the man's back was turned and the killer called out from behind. The man turned round and grabbed his gun but was too late. The killer had already swung his knife. Right on target."

He walked quickly to the victim. The two cops saw the detectives come over and stepped back from the corpse. Şefik leaned over the victim and pulled an imaginary knife from the left side of a coat which didn't quite cover his belly.

"He must've been pretty composed," he mumbled as he straightened up. "He doesn't panic after he hits the guy, doesn't try to run away... He comes up, takes the knife... And when he's sure nobody's seen him, he vanishes."

I stomped my frozen feet trying to warm them up.

"So you mean it was a professional. Only a hit man could pull this off so flawlessly."

"Why not, Chief? It's pretty clear from the gun in the victim's hand that they were a bad bunch. And it says something that the incident happened on these streets, anyhow. The murderer really knows how to use a knife. He preyed on the guy from a distance, not giving him the chance to pull the trigger."

"How do you know it was from a distance?" The objection came from Ali, who stood back a step. "What if the killer was right next to him? If he suddenly pulled the knife out and stabbed the victim?"

Şefik calmly nodded.

"That's another possibility, of course." He leaned in again. "It's just, his coat's quite heavy. The knife ripped through the cloth and sank in deep. Probably into his heart. It'll be clearer at the autopsy, but if the killer were beside the victim, the knife wouldn't have sunk in so deep. The killer must have swung from back here. At that speed, it plunged deep." He pointed to where the bloodstain was darkest. "If the killer had stabbed from a close proximity, he would have had to twist the murder weapon in until the man died. We'd see ragged cuts where the knife entered the coat when in fact, look, the cut is really clean. Can you see that?"

What Şefik said made sense, but of course Ali wasn't convinced.

"I see that but... what if the murderer is someone really strong? If he killed the man with one stroke? He wouldn't have to twist it in that case."

Şefik didn't insist.

"It's possible of course. We'll know for sure after the autopsy, when Inspector Zeynep gives us the results." He looked around like he'd just remembered. "Where is she, anyhow?"

"She was off tonight. For New Year's, you know..."

"Good," he said, smiling sincerely. "If nothing else, let her spend New Year's with her family." His gaze slid back to the dead man. "That's some bad luck. While other folks are off into the new year, you are headed off to the other world."

Ali shrugged. "What difference would it make if it was some other day? What is New Year's anyhow, Şefik? Just a regular night. Someone came up with the idea to say the year starts today and people went along with it."

The reactionary talk probably came from his not wanting to recall all the New Year's he celebrated in an orphanage. Now any attempt to explain New Year's connection with Pagan culture, Christianity or the like, would seem out of place. Besides, he wasn't so off the mark. Şefik agreed with him, anyhow.

"You're right, Ali," he said. "There's too much fuss over New Year's..." He pointed towards the din still coming from Taksim. "And these guys. Crammed in like sardines until morning. They never get tired." He shouted louder, as though they could hear. "Enough already. Enough!"

His voice came out tired and cracked. Maybe his complaint wasn't with the people celebrating but rather his occupation, which had him following the trail of a killer on a day like this when he should be with his loved ones. Just then my mobile rang. A number I didn't know. I picked up.

"Hi, Chief! It's Zeynel... The kid's nose is fine. Just tissue damage, the doctor says. Anyhow, the bleeding's stopped."

It was the huge-headed cop. When Keto's nose started bleeding, I'd bundled the kids into the patrol car and sent them off with the two uniformed police to Taksim Emergency Hospital.

"Did they take an x-ray?" I asked. "They didn't just give him a sloppy onceover, did they? They're pretty frenzied tonight."

"Of course not, Chief. The children have us with them. They saw to him pretty good. X-rayed him like you ordered and examined him all over. And anyhow, he knew the kid. He came to the hospital twice before. Once he was injured with a switchblade, once he was burned." He took a deep breath. "Really, Chief, what are we gonna do with these kids?"

"Just let them go. But first find out where they live. We want to be able to find them again. We may need another statement. You got that?"

"Got it."

He was trying to be respectful but his voice was tense, wondering where these pains in the ass had come from. And now they would have to find out where these hooligans slept, at this time of morning, in this weather...

"Zeynel," I warned. "You be nice to those kids, you hear me?"

"Of course, Chief."

No emotions could be read in his voice anymore. It was monotone and soulless like the noise from a machine. I knew that despite my warnings they would verbally abuse the kids. Now that we weren't with them they'd ask them what we'd talked about, and they'd definitely berate them, but at least they would no longer presume to rough them up.

"We're about through here, Chief," the young prosecutor said as I put my mobile in my pocket. "Our friends have finished their work. Let's get the body up now if it's okay for you."

"Sure, Oğuz Bey." I signaled to two orderlies who stood beside the ambulance watching us disinterestedly. "You can take him."

31

The orderlies sprang into action and enthusiastically threw open the back door. They had the stretcher down in a heartbeat and very competently placed the poor man's body on it. With the same dexterity, the same skill, they loaded their unfortunate cargo into the vehicle. Perhaps they were still hoping to catch the tail end of a party they'd left at the hospital. By the time Şefik's second puff of grey smoke wafted up from the cigarette he'd lit, the ambulance, with the prosecutor's official car right behind it, had already pulled out of the street.

"Come on," I said, turning to our men. "Let's all go for some soup over here. It'll warm our insides."

Şefik spread his hands in helplessness. "We should go, Chief. There's this equipment..."

"Have your boys take it."

He looked forlornly from the men to me.

"No, I should go, too. Some other time."

He was a good cop; he didn't want to leave his men alone. I had to respect it.

"All right, then see you at the station tomorrow."

"See you, Chief."

As Şefik and his two-man team got ready to load the equipment into the CSI minivan, we started walking off in the direction the prosecutor's car had gone. A wider, better-lit street greeted us as we rounded the corner. A long street that opened into Tarlabaşı. It was one of those streets situated in the heart of Istanbul, in what had once been among the most decent neighborhoods. But years ago after people had got all worked up thanks to some provocateurs, and these barbarians attempted to plunder the shops and raid the houses of our Greek, Armenian, and Jewish neighbors, it had been slowly abandoned, and as it was, a strange desolation and deprivation had settled over it. One of those dilapidated streets where over time people had taken refuge, those who had been chewed up and spit out and struggled to keep on their feet, poor women and men from far away fields and villages tossed all the way up here to this fallen neighborhood. Naturally, it was a place where drugs were sold, a meat market decorated in gaudy colors where people trying to stay alive sold their own flesh, a cesspit where all forms of crime shot up... But whether it was because it was under snow or what, it seemed more beautiful to me. Gloomy but more sedate, more tranquil. The celebrations had ended early in this street. Lights shone sporadically in the houses, maybe some TVs were on, but the only sound to be heard was the buzz of that crazy crowd partying it up in Taksim Square. It was so desolate that if we hadn't known someone was murdered fifty meters beyond, we could've even believed in this fake tranquility where drifting snowflakes blew about under the yellow light that filtered from the streetlamps on either side. But then a brash laugh came from a hanging bay window as we passed by and spoiled the artificial serenity.

"Hey boys."

We turned our heads and were met with the come-hither look of a woman who was sixty if she was a day, displaying her shriveled breasts on the windowsill despite the falling snow. The make-up on her face was so heavy that it was sadness more than sexual desire she roused.

"Hey, I'm talking to you," she said.

We both kept walking in silence.

"Hey, you! Up here!" she repeated

"What is it?" Ali snapped. "What do you want?"

"Don't get mad, my handsome. What're you getting all busted up over? Don't you want to have some fun?"

"Really, auntie? At this ungodly hour, in this weather?"

At this ungodly hour, in this weather, business must be pretty bad if the poor woman was on the lookout for random pedestrians to pick up for customers.

"How about it?" the woman insisted. "It's New Year's Eve and everybody's having a good time. Would it be so bad? While everyone's sliding into the new year, you can slide into me..."

The woman's bluntness made Ali blush, the same as it did me.

"Shit," he grumbled. "We are police officers, for god's sake. Go back inside."

It bounced right off her; she just shrugged.

"Even better, you'll relax a bit. They wound you pretty tight tonight."

My assistant was using all his strength to keep from losing his cool.

"Come on, lady. Back inside," I said, sweetly but firmly. "You won't get bread on the table from us. Find someone else."

Who could say how many rejections she had had tonight. She slammed the window shut in a rage, though not neglecting to loudly complain first.

"Everyone in the world has gone gay. The police are gays, the drunkards are gays, the drug addicts... Isn't there one real man left in this city?"

"The love old men feel is brutal, Chief"

※

Although there were only a few hours till morning, Tarlabaşı Boulevard was still packed with people. The street was full of cars lined up side by side and one on top of the other as though in a heap. People hanging out car windows and whooping, groups on the pavement boisterously singing, drunks struggling to stay standing... I wasn't surprised by any of those, but when a phosphorescent-white clad clown astride a black horse passed in front of us, that I couldn't believe. As it moved away, the black horse disappeared, and the clown in white garb swayed rapidly back and forth as though on the wind. This place had become a circus in every sense of the word. And of course our Chef Mehmet's place, "Zest", would see its share of this pandemonium.

I used to frequent this small restaurant back in the years I was stationed in Beyoğlu. At the entrance to a stumpy street which emptied into Tarlabaşı Boulevard, there in its usual place just opposite that other joint that was a cross between a bordello and a taverna, it had unostentatiously welcomed its customers for many years. The sleepless night owl residents of Beyoğlu. We ducked into the low doorway of the restaurant under its unpretentious sign, completely unchanged since who knew when, and were hit with the smell of anise and alcohol from raki, mixed with food and cheap perfume. After the outside cold that stole your breath away, it really wasn't disagreeable at all, this heavy air. In fact, even the blinding,

35

raw light wasn't entirely uninviting. The real problem was trying to find somewhere to sit. Two girls had taken the small table at the back. They were both fairly buxom, you know, chubby so to speak. One had obstinately green, obstinately shiny eyes, the other looked around all tired out. They both had overdone it on the make-up. My father used to say there was no escape for these unfortunates from the bad paths they were headed down. Whatever path that was. The girls had no appetite; they kept picking at their baked pasta with their forks. At the next table two punks shamelessly ogled them, but the girls knew there was nothing to gain from these dirt poor boys, so they didn't even acknowledge them. At the table to their right, four musicians from Dolapdere, sporting identical black jackets, impossibly white shirts and red ties, ignored everyone and were busy chowing down their food without hardly coming up for air as though someone were about to snatch their plates away. Behind them, three buff young men who probably worked the door of a local bar sat calmly and quietly waiting for their order to arrive. Two tables had been put together near the window. There sat the restaurant's most entertaining people, a group of six transvestites in flamboyant outfits with plunging necklines and crazy-colored hair. Showing no signs of fatigue, as though they hadn't been on the street all night, they animatedly debated something on the one hand while hungrily spooning up their soup. I noticed Ali prick up his tail and prepare to growl like a dog who'd encountered a clutter of cats. In fact, I didn't suppose this small unconventional gathering would be terribly thrilled with our Ali either. Something unsavory could happen at any moment; perhaps it'd be best to leave the place as quietly as we'd come in.

"Chief!" a voice said, preventing that. "Chief..."

A big beefy man called to us from one of the tables. At first I didn't recognize him, but as I looked closer I figured it out. The man was the neighborhood's most notorious pimp. Süleyman, otherwise known as Harem Süleyman, a moniker he came by for having four wives, and for peddling those four wives out himself. He called out insistently, his tiny moist eyes trained on me from behind the handlebar moustache dyed raven-black that covered half his face.

"Come on over, Chief. Over here..."

Everyone rubbernecked as they heard the word Chief, especially the trannies in their flashy clothes, but eventually they all returned to their own worlds. There was no leaving the restaurant now, and we made our compulsory trek over to Süleyman's table. A woman sat opposite him, neither beautiful nor ugly, but old before her time. A tired, very tired woman. She was asking him with drooping eyelids why they didn't go home and sleep. Süleyman stood and buttoned his jacket as we approached. I'd forgotten just how big he was; in the face of his magnificent bulk I couldn't stop myself taking a step back. His enormous head nearly brushed the ceiling, his arms were long enough to wrap around a table. Not even Ali could hold back.

"Whoa!" he mumbled. "What the hell is that?"

But I'll be damned if he didn't bow in front of me, even with all that mass. "Okay, okay, Süleyman," I said, barely managing to rescue my hand from being kissed. I gave his shoulder a friendly pat, this man who was at least a head taller than me even. "It's been a while, hasn't it?"

"You said it, Chief. We used to see you once or twice a week in this joint. You haven't checked in on us since you left Beyoğlu. That's the last we heard from you."

His words were full of reproach, but the smile that bared his gold tooth said otherwise.

"You know how it is in our line of work, Süleyman."

He shook his head meekly. "Tell me about it, Chief. It's a tough trade, God help you."

"And this here is Ali," I said, indicating our addlebrain, who still stood there dumbfounded, studying Süleyman's bulk. "We work together."

Süleyman stood at attention again. "Pleased to make your acquaintance, Inspector Ali."

"Likewise," said Ali with an amused smile. "Likewise, Süleyman."

I turned my gaze to the woman, who hadn't so much as batted an eye despite having three men looming over her talking away.

"Hello..."

Her black eyes were so wide in her palm-sized face that it warmed my heart. Not sure why, but a vision of those old horses with their beautiful eyes that pulled the horse buggies on the Princes' Islands came to mind.

"Hi, sir."

"You remember Naciye, don't you, Chief?"

I gave it my best effort and came back to life. "Of course I do. How are you, Naciye Hanım?"

The woman opened her bored, weary hands. That was it; no word, no excitement, nor any sign of familiarity. Her heavy eyes had already instantly returned to their previous state. Süleyman was annoyed with Naciye's lack of interest and he gestured towards the empty chairs with exaggerated courtesy.

"Won't you sit, Chief?"

"Don't let us disturb you..."

"We were just getting up." He glowered at his wife. "Naciye is sleeping in her seat, anyhow."

Naciye didn't take the least offense at her husband's reproach. She'd long since forgotten how to be offended. Whatever they said or did she didn't give a damn. She'd become so hardened to the world in which she lived, she accepted everything without any objections. Maybe it was because she knew objections would get her nowhere that she'd become so quiet, so unmoved, so indifferent.

After taking off our coats, Ali and I plunked down in opposite chairs. The table was full of the leftovers from the humble meal: four emptied plates and two glasses, one half full of water, the other filled with cola. A few broken toothpicks rested conspicuously on Süleyman's empty plate.

"What's up, Chief?" Süleyman sincerely wanted to know. "What brings you to Beyoğlu?"

"Nothing good, I'm afraid," I said, tearing my eyes away from the details of the table. "Some guy was murdererd on the street down there... over near the Tarlabaşists Club."

His broad face grew taut and his handlebar moustache trembled. "Who was it?"

That's when it dawned on me that Süleyman wasn't such a stranger to gambling. Maybe he could even help us.

"A guy called Engin. Engin Akça."

His face lit up as though he'd just had some great news.

"Engin the German Turk?"

"I don't know whether he's German... He was Black Nizam's man."

"That's the one! Did they shoot him?" Without waiting for a response, he brought his right sledgehammer of a fist down onto a left palm so wide it resembled a baker's oven spatula. "It was bound to happen, of course."

Getting information on a murder in a restaurant we'd come to fill our bellies in... Now that would be a stroke of luck. My assistant started digging in the dirt like a miner who'd chanced upon some treasure in a cave.

"Why do you say that? Did Engin have a lot of enemies?"

Süleyman's thick, dyed eyebrows furrowed. "He sure did. He was always hitting on everyone's wives and daughters."

For a second my gaze slid to Naciye. I wondered if... No way, it was a ridiculous thought.

"Whose wife did he hit on?" asked Ali, continuing to poke. "Anyone you know?"

Süleyman shrugged his broad shoulders. "Dice Ihsan's, for one. And for that matter Black Nizam's. The man couldn't keep his zipper up."

"Wait a sec..." I interrupted. "What we heard is there's a love triangle involving Ihsan and Nizam."

"You mean this thing with Çilem? "He laughed softly. The raw fluorescent light flashed on his gold front tooth. "Dice Ihsan supposedly stole the girl from Nizam..."

"Is it a lie?"

He gave me a look.

"What difference would it make? Who do you think brought Çilem to Nizam in the first place?"

Things were getting interesting.

"Engin?"

He nodded slowly, certain he was right.

"Engin, of course. The guy's a real looker, right? He drives the ladies crazy. Of course Çilem isn't exactly some girl from a nice family who's never known a boy's touch before. She was Dice's mistress. I mean they were both up for it. The girl knew Dice would amount to nothing and she saw a future with Engin. She thought to herself that maybe he'll marry her, get her out of that dump, but instead he'd sink her straight into the depths of a cesspool. He already had. After Engin, Black Nizam comes onto the scene. Ever seen Nizam, Chief?"

"No. He's an old man, isn't that right?"

"Not that old. But ugly." He grimaced. "They say a man can be neither pretty nor ugly, but boy can they, Chief. Nizam is truly ugly."

"The man was ugly and that's why Çilem cheated on him with Ihsan?" asked my assistant, hurriedly wrapping it up when he could wait no longer.

"If that were all there was to it... But Çilem was also running around with Engin. Cocaine, group sex parties and so on... They even asked me for a girl once. Figure that out. Çilem never let go of Engin. While she was with Ihsan and while she was with Nizam, there was always Engin, too. The way I see it, it's why Ihsan dumped the woman."

"What?" we both said, reacting in unison. Ali shut up and I continued.

"Didn't she walk out on him? Was it Ihsan who gave Çilem the boot?"

"It was Ihsan, of course. He was caught with an unlicensed gun at the club and landed behind bars. While he was locked up, she started sneaking around with Nizam. When Dice got out, he picked up on it. He beat the shit out of her and threw her out on the street."

"Didn't Nizam know all this?" asked Ali, putting the thing that was eating at me into words.

"Of course he did. But he was in love with Çilem. The love old men feel is brutal, Chief. The most feared man in our world, this ruthless Nizam, set aside his pride and his honor and took her in, turning a deaf ear to his nephews' objections."

"There's something I don't get," I said, getting the first word in this time. "Okay, Nizam was in love with her, so then why did he keep Engin on with him?"

Süleyman narrowed his eyes as though faced with a problematic question.

"I swear, I gave that a lot of thought myself, Chief, but I couldn't work it out."

Did he not want to say or did he really not know?

"And you didn't get wind of anything?" I persisted. "What's the word on the street?"

"There are plenty of rumors... Some say he was secretly Nizam's partner. Supposedly he brought a load of cash from Germany and that's how he partnered up with Nizam. There's some major construction being done around here now. All these dilapidated buildings left over from the Armenians and Greeks are being renovated. They say they went in on that business together. Others say there's no such thing. They say Engin saved Nizam's life. That what he did is a favor that can't be repaid. And some say Engin had ties higher up."

"Higher up?"

"I mean in the mafia. Whether it's the Kurdish mafia or the Laz mafia, that I can't say, but Engin had something solid to lean back on, for sure. Nizam wouldn't let him live otherwise."

"Maybe he didn't," I was about to say, when a hand on my shoulder shattered my train of thought. Standing over me was the twig thin body of 'Cutlets' Mehmet, the restaurant's owner.

"Shame on you, Chief," he lambasted me straight away. "Why are you hiding out back here in the corner? You didn't even say hello. Or were you planning to sneak out before I saw you?"

I was sheepish, of course. "Hi, Mehmet Usta," I said, shaking the outstretched hand. "We just got here. I looked at the cashier's desk but you weren't there. So we saw Süleyman, and sat ourselves down here and got to talking," I explained hoping he would leave us alone, but he didn't go.

"I was back in the kitchen," he said. "I have to keep an eye on that, too." Before looking around, supposedly for an empty chair, he threw Süleyman a look that implied it was time for him to get up. Süleyman, probably the biggest person among all the revelers on Istiklal Avenue, let alone those in this restaurant, got the message.

"You come sit here, Mehmet Abi," he said, jumping up. "We were just leaving anyhow." He turned to look at his wife before we could object and said, "Come on, Naciye my darling. Come on my love, let's call it a night."

She was neither pleased nor excited about it. Her tired eyes just parted slightly. She held her tiny waist and quietly stood up. After pulling her shiny silver coat over a black dress that exposed her shapeless legs, she hung her huge knock-off bag on her frail shoulder and looked fixedly at her husband. "All right," she said in a cracked voice. "All right, let's go."

"There's no such thing as an 'old-style' or 'new-style' bandit."

✕

As Süleyman passed through tables full of the weary night crowd, he hooked his skinny wife Naciye's arm through his. She was having difficulty even standing, let alone walking, in the heels she was wearing.

"Even the best steed sometimes stumbles," Cutlets Mehmet mumbled. "I knew him as a boy twenty years ago. The toughest kids around didn't dare cross his path. He was so brave, so fearless and strong. I've seen him run off five people after they attacked him on this very street. He was practically showing off to the big guys. And look at the state of him now..."

The three of us looked over at this strange couple again. Swaying gently with his wife like the sad dance that accompanies a song of defeat, this once notorious tough guy, Süleyman, left the restaurant.

"He's selling that woman, isn't he?" Ali asked, although he already knew the answer. Perhaps he couldn't get his head around it.

Mehmet and I both held our tongues.

"What a shame, and he seems like such a nice man..."

Cutlets Mehmet preened his Clark Gable moustache. "He was a good man. Maybe he still is. He's never done me any harm."

"Me neither," I agreed. "But does that make him a good man? I don't know." I leaned back in my chair. "Anyhow, forget about Süleyman. Who are we to judge?"

Mehmet's exhausted face lit up. "You're right, Chief. We shouldn't be kicking the man while he's down. Now, what'll you have?" he asked hungrily, as though he himself had an appetite.

"Soup." I looked over at my assistant. "Or did you have something else in mind?"

"Naw. Soup is good. You have lentil, don't you?"

Mehmet seemed thrilled.

"Of course! The best lentil soup ever, not just in Beyoğlu but all of Istanbul, as the Chief can attest."

Before waiting for me to confirm it, he called out to the young black waiter taking food over to the three bouncers' table.

"Namadi, son, look here..."

Namadi smiled, showing a row of perfect white teeth.

"Okay, Mehmet Abi. I'm coming."

His Turkish was a bit broken, but he understood well enough. My assistant copped a derisive attitude.

"You employing Kunta Kintes?"

This Ali of ours was completely hopeless. I was just wondering if I should give him a serious scolding right here at the table when Cutlets Mehmet made a more decorous job of it.

"Please don't talk like that. Namadi is a good kid, not to mention handsome. Just look at him. They even wanted him for a TV show. Some director came into the restaurant last week and made him an offer on the spot. The kid is so loyal that he didn't just jump on it but asked me first if he could do it. I told him to go ahead. But I warned him these jobs were just temporary. I told him not to quit the restaurant, that I'd give him the day off when they filmed. He was delighted. These immigrants have a tough life, Chief. They're even worse off than our poor. The jackals in the area are always after them. Dolapdere druglords and that sort always trying to coerce the poor guys into the drug business. And while there *are* those who go down that path, most of them have integrity, and are hardworking, too. Every one of them I've taken on has turned out to be sound." He turned towards the youth, who had dropped the bouncers' food off and was by our side in a flash. "Hey Namadi, can you take these plates away first?"

The same bright smile appeared on his face again.

"Sure thing, Mehmet Abi. I'm on it."

At least six feet tall and athletically built, the youth had all the plates on the table stacked in one vigorous movement.

"Good on you, Namadi. And give it a nice wipe down, will you? Now, we'll have two bowls of lentil soup, don't forget the lemon, and uh... Oh look, there's no pepper flakes left. Go on, son, the Chief is starving."

Namadi winced at the word 'chief'. It didn't escape Ali's notice, and our rascal turned into a busybody again.

"What's up, Namadi? Why the hesitation?"

The young man's black eyes grew wide with fear.

"No reason, sir. It's nothing."

"Leave him alone," I said, putting a hand on Ali's.

I turned to the boy, whose unnerved eyes contemplated us.

"It's all right, Namadi. Go on, you get the soups."

As he grabbed the empty plates and quickly walked away, Ali tried to explain himself.

"Sorry, but you saw it too. When the boy heard the word 'chief' he panicked..."

"You're a cop too, right?" said Mehmet, the question interrupting my assistant's jabber.

"Yes." He was in his 'so what if I am?' mode, the wretch.

"Deputy Ali is my assistant," I said, trying to smooth over his bad manners. "We work together."

"I see," muttered Mehmet dismally. The solemnity of a man who has been around the block settled into his expression. "Let me explain something, Inspector Ali. One of these boys you call Kunta Kinte died in jail last year. Your people claimed the man had tried to pull his gun, but the other African migrants weren't swallowing that account. They believe their friend was killed on purpose. That's why the kid flinched when he heard the word 'chief'. But he's not doing anything against the law. I can vouch for him in every respect."

The table's mood was broken. "But really," I said, bringing the subject back round to Harem Süleyman in an attempt to fix it, "just how is it that Süleyman suddenly hit bottom like this? His fame and glory were intact when I served around here."

Mehmet sighed deeply as though he was the one who'd taken a plunge.

"It's been seven years since you left, Chief. That's a long time. It didn't just happen overnight, anyway." At least Mehmet's mood was returning. "The harem went slowly, like the fall of the Ottoman Empire. His old power and strength failed too as he got older. And when these new kids showed up lacking a conscience, or any compassion..."

Ali, aware of his blunder, must have been well pleased with the change in subject, as he eagerly jumped into the conversation.

"He was one of the old tough guys, Süleyman, wasn't he?"

"He sure was, maybe even the last of his kind. Whatever he had, he would always spread it around. He had a reputation as a father to the poor. That must have a little to do with why he never moved up." He turned back to me. "You would know that world better than me, Chief. That old-style tough guy is a thing of the past. The new kids don't comply with the old methods. They've forgotten all about courtesy, loyalty, respect..."

It was true I knew that world well, but Mehmet and I had a difference of opinion. I hated when anyone tried to paint a pretty picture of those old tough guys, as though they were a boon to society. I never understood this country's admiration for brutes. And anyhow, almost everything said about them was a bunch of malarkey. Taking from the rich and distributing it to the poor, shows of bravery and great heroism and such... All mostly lies. And what difference would it make if they *did* spread it round, those things that they took by force to begin with?

"There's no such thing as an 'old-style' or 'new-style' bandit," I objected. "What the both of them do is still just bullying. Let's drop the fiction already. What is there to respect in domination that's gained by a fist, gun or knife? It's fair play we should look up to, not power."

Mehmet's expression looked dubious.

"You're right but, when the state backs away from fairness, it's these bandits that fill the void."

He did have a point. We left the door ajar and these bandits dove in headfirst.

"Regardless," I said irreconcilably, "this business is wrong, Mehmet. It was wrong before and it's wrong now. The real heroism is what you do. How many years have you been here? How many years have you been carving out your livelihood from this little restaurant? With all these dogs, these bloody degenerates around. Yes, that is what you call real bravado. The others are lies. There's no enviable side to it, either. They're a pitiable bunch, actually. They live in fear, always with the expectation of betrayal. They either succeed in making a new life for themselves with the money they have, or at least manage to emancipate their children if not themselves, or they wind up dead. Otherwise, they just fall into disgrace, like Süleyman."

Mehmet rapped his knuckles on the table three times.

"I wouldn't wish that on anyone, least of all Süleyman, Chief. Even dying at the hands of your enemy has honor and integrity. Naciye will most likely be sleeping on the streets when she dies."

Just then it occurred to me. "Doesn't this Süleyman have three more wives?"

Ali nearly jumped out of his seat.

"You gotta be kiddin' me. He's selling four wives at a time?"

Mehmet chuckled. One of those vulgar, cynical laughs we men have.

"The others are not actually wives. They used to be that campy Femme Yahya's prostitutes. You remember Femme Yahya, Chief? He was running a brothel on Küçük Bayram Street? Anyhow, Nebil from Kasımpaşa was always terrorizing them, trying to steal his girls away. That's when Süleyman stepped in. For a certain amount of protection money, he became Yahya's guardian. So when Femme Yahya was stabbed to death at a cocaine party in Nişantaşı, the girls were left to Süleyman. Some said the women went over to Süleyman voluntarily, others said he held them by force. Let that be on their heads if they say it. But those were Süleyman's glory years. He didn't answer to anyone. His word was law, and on these streets whatever he willed was instantly carried out. But then Dice Ihsan took the wind out of his sails. He challenged Süleyman to a fight and, daredevil that he is, he went alone. Ihsan and his men beat him to a bloody pulp back there near the Assyrian Church. It scared the living daylights out of him. Still, he didn't fall straight away. Dice Ihsan is a bastard, but he must have a little humanity in him because he didn't take the women from him. And that's how Harem Süleyman became a four-whore pimp. But he didn't hang up his gloves, although they wouldn't have left him alone even if he had. Anyhow, Süleyman was itching for trouble. He went back to his old ways, namely gambling. Put down one take back ten, you know. Of course, the opposite happened. One night at the table they got his four women, too. They left him Naciye, though, because she couldn't keep customers."

"Was it Dice Ihsan who did it?" Ali cut in.

Mehmet slowly shook his head with its wavy, graying hair. "No. Black Nizam... Or rather Nizam had a henchman; it was him."

"Engin Akça?" The same name spilled from both our mouths.

Mehmet, our restaurateur of the year, realized something was up.

"How do you know Engin?" He trained his light brown eyes on me. "Seriously, Chief, what are you doing here in Beyoğlu at this time of night?"

What harm would there be in telling him?

"Engin's been murdererd."

He didn't show any surprise; he just sniffed noisily.

"He who lives by the sword... So he died by it then." He went quiet as though trying to process this and then, without any sign of emotion asked, "Who killed him?"

"That's not clear. Who do you think?"

He pulled his hands down from where they rested on the table. "Could be anyone. Yep, just about anyone could have murdered Engin. Dice Ihsan, his own boss Black Nizam, even Harem Süleyman or any number of people..."

"He was a ladies man, always coming on to people's wives and daughters."

"So they say. Handsome, arrogant, lacking in conscience... Everyone was leery of him; everyone hated him. It's not good to speak ill of the dead, but I didn't like him either. There was something very disagreeable about that guy. His face was decent, but those blue eyes were disconcerting."

"When did Engin come to Beyoğlu?"

Mehmet's lashless eyelids opened and closed; he looked away and then back again.

"I don't know, but he's been around one or two years. Always with Black Nizam though, like his right arm. Some people said he was finding Nizam some skirt. It's possible. The guy is a looker. And he has a shiny new car."

"Was he living alone?"

He scrunched up his narrow brow.

"I don't know about that, but recently I was seeing him with a young girl. A girl with a fresh face who you'd never picture mixed up in this kind of racket. You'd reckon she's an angel."

"Çilem?" Ali threw in.

"No. I know Çilem. She's with Black Nizam. They came here in the middle of the night once to have soup. The four of them I mean: Nizam, Çilem, Engin, and that girl. Maybe he was living with her."

"He was in Tarlabaşı, right?"

"Near Dolapdere... He got sick once, and Black Nizam sent him food. We took it over three days in a row, morning and evening... down there by the Greek church. He was living in one of those ramshackle old buildings. At the top of a dead end. I never understood that either. He could have lived somewhere much nicer."

The words ramshackle building brought the construction to mind.

"We heard something about him forging a partnership with Nizam. There's some urban renewal here?"

His shoulders dropped and his mood fell.

"Don't ask, Chief. They're destroying everything, turning the whole place upside-down under the pretense of returning it to its previous state. They are going to toss folks out onto the street. It won't be long before they toss us out too. I've been a tenant here for thirty years." He looked hopefully into my eyes. "Really Chief, can't you do something about it?"

I'd come across requests like this hundreds of times in this line of work, and not all of them were quite so innocent. But even if he was right, these problems were beyond my control.

"What can we do, Mehmet?" I said, hanging my head. "We're all just plain old civil servants. We can't do a damn thing. If you spoke with the municipality, maybe they'd relocate you."

His bottom lip pouted. "We did, Chief, but it didn't work. There are so many shopkeepers in my position. 'Which one are we supposed to help?' they say. The orders come from the top. Huge commissions are being thrown around. Everyone is trying to grab up a building. Some people are even closing up entire blocks at a time. Television actors, celebrated rich people, big hotel chain owners..."

Cutlets Mehmet was in a bad way, but I had a murder to solve.

"You mean Engin and Nizam could have gone into this business together?" I said, getting back to the subject. "Since there's that much money flying around?"

"Why not, Chief? The money's whet everyone's appetite, so it probably got Nizam's attention, too. If he had Engin with him... Or maybe Engin lured him in... The best thing to do would be to speak with Black Nizam. If he'll talk, that is."

"If I hadn't shot him, he would have shot us."

By the time we'd left Cutlets Mehmet's restaurant, the hordes had diminished a great deal. Even if there were still cars on the street, the bottlenecks had ended and the clusters of people on the pavement had thinned. It wasn't snowing anymore, just frosty. Maybe it was the freezing cold that got rid of the fiery crowds on the street. Yes, the fun was over and the celebration had broken up. All that was left were the shiny paper hats, the scattered confetti, trampled flowers, empty bottles and food scraps. In a short while the garbage collectors would begin to crop up, and as the last signs of New Year's were collected, this old neighborhood would return to its previous state. Yes, Beyoğlu was getting on in years now. And it wasn't aging gracefully. People hadn't looked after her well. They'd done their best to turn this unique area, once described by foreign travelers as the world's most captivating woman, into a prematurely crumpled old crone. With a greediness befitting only barbarians, they had knocked down hundred-year-old buildings, put the elegant streets through the wringer, and filled the already small squares with hideous apartment buildings. That the area managed to keep its charm, or even stay standing, was a small miracle.

We didn't bother to stop by the Beyoğlu Police Station on the corner of Kalyoncukulluğu Street, one of those historic buildings of which only a trace remained. I was dead certain it would be teeming with lawbreakers. Our colleagues would be in no state to even scratch their own heads, let alone deal with us, poor things. We hit the bottom of the Kalyoncukulluğu slope. Cutlets Mehmet had said it was possible the dead man's girlfriend had lived in the same house with him and we wanted to knock on the door and try our luck. Maybe the girl would say something that would help us solve this murder. In fact, if we'd done things by the book, we would have got permission from the prosecutor's office, but this meant losing time. Also, if we did find the girl there, we may get a chance to glimpse the victim's belongings or some documents, which would be invaluable to the investigation.

Where Engin lived was behind the Saint Constantine Church, a relic from Beyoğlu's days of old. Back when I worked this area, I had grown to know Dolapdere like the back of my hand. And it was that, not Keto's and Musti's perfect directions, that helped me to easily find Kadın Çıkmazı Street where the house was. I had a very bad memory from this Kalyoncukulluğu Street. In the first month I was on duty in Beyoğlu, on Düğün Street, opposite this bend turning into Kadın Çıkmazı Street, they had burned down a house with a young woman, a man, and two children inside. The man was a drug dealer and his name was Habib. He'd come here from Anatolia. They had holed up in the derelict house, whose original owners had migrated to Greece who knew how many years before. At first they'd taken on odd jobs, but it was difficult to feed a family living hand to mouth. Then they saw the boys with gelled hair posted on the street corners and couldn't figure out why these street urchins always seemed to have money in their pockets despite just bumming around all day. But it didn't take them long to work it out. Yes, there was a way to get easy money: selling weed, pills, even heroin. Habib, who was bone-weary from always being broke, dove in head first without giving it a second thought. For a while he sold the neighborhood middleman's goods. He was a sharp cookie and could tell a plainclothes cop from their eyes, and light-footed as well, stepping out of the darkness and then vanishing. In the evenings there in Dolapdere, he couldn't keep up with the demands of the addicts who sat in their cars with their lights out. Finally he began to put food on his and his family's plates, but it wasn't enough. He'd got a taste for money and was questioning why the middlemen should get a cut, so he started to buy the goods directly. He wasn't even aware that he was violating a rule that could get him killed. But he was brave, and fearless, Habib. Like Harem Süleyman he was big, and he knew how to fight. Witnesses who gave written statements spoke of him saying, 'I trust only my god, my fist, and my knife.' The poor guy had no idea what could happen to him in this black hole in the heart of Istanbul. If he had, he would have scrammed at the first warning. He didn't, even after the middlemen set two kids with sticks on him to give him a nice beating and send him on his way. Because he'd got rich, and had slowly started to make plans for the future. Maybe he himself could rule supreme in these parts. Why not? What did the slouching, dark, wimpy men who ran this show have that he didn't? With his towering build and his strength – he could squeeze water from a stone – he would instill fear in everyone and in no time be sitting at the head of the neighborhood trade. But that didn't happen; one night they set him and his wife and two sons blazing. In front of the entire neighborhood to boot, while they screamed to the heavens. Yes, the killers had aimed for everyone in the house to die. They had wired up the windows and doors so no one could get out.

By the time we arrived at the scene of the fire, the house had been reduced to a blackened shell. We found Habib's charred remains in the living room doorway, a knife still clenched in his fist. His wife was in the bedroom, tangled up with the two small bodies of her sons. Not one person in the neighborhood would tell it like it was. They had all agreed to the same story and spoke of a blood feud. We put the pressure on them but got no results. We learned the truth six months later, from a narcotics officer who'd infiltrated a drug ring. But due to insufficient evidence, we were never able to catch Habib's killers. In those days I was up and down this street numerous times, and that's why it wasn't difficult to find Kadın Çıkmazı Street this evening.

As I got to the entrance of the dead end street, I thought I saw a shadow slip past. I couldn't be sure though; maybe I was wrong, because the only light in the street was on account of the snow. I looked the stubby street over carefully; there was no one. Most likely my weary eyes were playing tricks on me. Ali, who had fallen behind as he was cleaning the snow stuck to the bottom of his shoes, finally caught up with me. He stopped in front of a wall with a red sign, its puffy white letters reading 'Kadın Çıkmazı'.

"Interesting where this guy lived," he mumbled with weary amusement. "A classic playboy and he comes and lives on Kadın Çıkmazı, a street with a name like Lady's Dead End..."

It was funny all right, but I was busy staring at building number one, where Engin had lived. It was one of those three-storey Tarlabaşı apartments built in typical Greek architecture. I was startled as I neared the door. Was it open, the wooden door at the top of the four stone steps? Or did it just appear that way in the dusk? I looked down at the ground and saw a pair of large footprints in the snow, extending towards the building. Fresh prints... There was not one flake of snow in the voids left by the shoes. Whoever the prints belonged to must have just gone inside. So then the shadow I'd seen was real. It could be they noticed someone coming, panicked, and didn't even close the door. More interestingly, the footprints clearly belonged to a man. Could it be Engin's murderer? But that was ridiculous. It was a known fact that some killers returned to the scene of a crime, but for a perpetrator to visit the house of a man he'd murdered elsewhere, he'd have to be an absolute fool. Or else there was some evidence that needed removing.

"The door is open," my assistant whispered. He had also noticed the footprints. "Someone's inside."

For a second we came eye to eye and then with a habit formed of years, we pulled out our guns and quietly loaded them without a word. With our guns in hand, we took position and moved slowly and surely towards the door. We were keeping an eye on both the door and the dark windows, but there was neither movement in the half open door nor light from behind the dark drawn curtains. We had our backs against the walls, with Ali to the right of the door and me passing to the left. There was not a sound, just the faint crackling of snow. Ali, with his usual impatience, kept signaling that he was going in. With my free hand I signaled back for him to wait, then gently pushed on the door. It creaked open as though to spite us. We leveled our guns and pricked up our ears. No, there was neither a movement nor a sound... Could we be wrong? Ali, his patience stretched to its limit, squeezed slowly through the door without waiting for a go-ahead. Then, while half his body was still outside, all hell broke loose. Someone was pulling a trigger over and over.

"Ali, pull out!" I shouted, but the maniac plunged inside headlong. I counted five revolver shots. The last two were from our thrill-seeker's gun. And then a small squawk, "Ah!" which put my heart in my throat. After which came a loud clatter. Someone must have fallen to the floor. Then silence... Was it Ali? I dove in without thinking twice. Darkness; it was pitch-black inside after the glow from the snow. The pungent odor of gunpowder burned my nostrils. I blindly pointed my gun back and forth; if it was Ali who was shot, it was only a matter of time before the man's bullets rained down on me.

"Over here, Chief," said Ali, subduing my panic. "I'm here to your left."

At last I could make out my assistant, lying there spread out on the doorstep with his gun trained on some point.

"You okay, Ali?"

"Yep, Chief. I'm all right."

So then the other guy had been hit. My eyes, adjusting to the darkness, searched for a light switch on the wall behind the open door. And here it was. It was one of those old-style switches that you twist rather than flick. Yellow light squeamishly lit up the interior. Slumped in front of the stairs leading to the upper floor was a silhouette that caught my eye. A bundle of cloth the color of rat fur. But underneath this pile of fur, bright red blood was spreading across yellow linoleum. I slowly approached the silhouette. With every step, the wooden floorboards under the linoleum screeched as though in pain. However it was that he'd fallen, the man Ali shot was now curled into a ball, his dark grey coat covering his entire body. He was motionless, but not to be trusted.

Keeping my gun on him, I gently pulled the coat back with my left hand. He seemed to be face down, but his forehead wasn't to the ground, the right side of his face was. He was curly-haired, with a young unwrinkled brow, wide open eyes the color of chestnuts, and crooked, nicotine-stained teeth bared between thin parted lips. A gun, a Glock, rested just beyond his right hand. The red stream spreading out under his motionless body encroached on his assault weapon. "Is he dead?" Ali asked, as I nudged the Glock with my foot.

His voice had gone hoarse, but his gun was still pointed at the man lying on the floor. I put two fingers of my right hand on the man's left wrist. There was no pulse.

"Looks that way."

Ali couldn't take his eyes off the fallen man. That quarrelsome, impulsive police officer had disappeared without a trace.

"It's not your fault," I said, and that was the truth. "He fired first."

He didn't hear me. He just kept looking at the man on the floor. In fact, he'd been in countless clashes, shot plenty of men. But it wasn't easy, taking a person's life. No matter who it was, no matter how justified you were, killing someone meant taking the weight of the world on your shoulders. 'Playing God,' an old friend of mine used to say. 'That's what killing someone is.' My assistant was facing the consequences of playing that role.

"Ali, son, are you okay?"

Again he made not a sound. His wide-open eyes were still swimming in the blood he'd spilled.

I walked over to him but he wasn't seeing me. I grabbed him by the shoulders and shook him.

"Snap out of it now, Ali." I stood up.

"What?"

The remorse in the depths of his eyes diminished, but didn't completely go away.

"You had no choice. If you hadn't shot him, he would have shot us."

He swallowed, blinked, took a deep breath and put his gun in its holster.

"You're right, Chief," he said, his voice still creaking. "If I hadn't shot him, he would have shot us."

"Love is the best excuse in the world."

As the weak winter sun melted the ice on the dirty station windows, the mystery of the man in Engin's house also began to shed some light. The computer spit out all his deeds one by one. His rap sheet was rather bulky. His name was Tarık Seberci, but he went by 'Tidy'. A hired killer whose name made everyone quake in their boots. To date, no one on his list had survived. He worked for nobody; he was his own man. Money was his only boss. He killed for whoever paid the highest price. He was a principled man though, and he never left a job unfinished. He hadn't always been the hunter of course, twice he'd found himself staring down the barrel of a gun. The first incident, he made it out with only a few scratches. In the second, he nearly met his maker. After a week in a coma, he opened his eyes and then enjoyed another month's holiday in the hospital. He'd been taken into custody as a murder suspect four times but had only once been convicted, for killing Hızır Cevdet, the owner of a Turkish folk music bar on Balo Street. That was a mistake he'd made that didn't vibe with his nickname; he'd left a muddy left footprint on the edge of the carpet of the man he'd hit in a single shot to the forehead. He'd paid the price for not being meticulous at that murder site, receiving a twenty-five year sentence, though thanks to a general pardon he got out after only three years twenty-seven days. It's a beautiful tail that leads a fox to its death, so the saying goes. Tidy Tarık's huge feet were what ruined him. This time it was the footprints he left in the snow, rather than muddy footprints, that lead to his ruin. And this time it wasn't a trip to prison, but one to that happy hunting ground in the sky.

When Ali realized the man he'd shot was a hitman, he relaxed, if only a little. Prosecutor Oğuz had said it was "obvious self-defense" and he began to feel like himself again, whatever the judgment handed down would be. But whenever Zeynep walked through the door of my office, that was when he would completely recover his old joy, the rascal. And he tried to hide the trauma he'd been through, as if he hadn't experienced that wooziness from the blood or been influenced at all by the event.

"It's nothing, Zeynep. It's beyond question that the man opened fire on us. And I fired back. He got hit is all."

Our criminologist was anxious; her pretty face still carried New Year's exhaustion. Though the danger was over, even the possibility of Ali's being shot was enough to ravage her nerves.

"Oh man, Ali," she said, keeping her eyes on him. "You dodged a bullet." She suddenly remembered me and quickly turned round. "Hope you're feeling better too, Chief. You also had a narrow escape."

I didn't take it to heart, her forgetting about me; love is the world's best excuse.

"Thanks, Zeynep. But Ali was the one who was in real danger." I shot our hobo a disapproving look. "Jumping through a door without stopping to think about it first..." I took a deep breath and shook my head. "Thankfully nothing happened to Ali. Would've been better if the man hadn't died of course. Better in every respect. We could have learned a lot about Engin's murder from him. It's a shame."

"It's a shame," Zeynep murmured, still standing there. "You're right. It would've helped the investigation if he lived."

Ali, thinking we were blaming him and at a loss for how to handle it, got up out of his seat and unconsciously took a couple steps.

"There was nothing else to do," he said, throwing his hands up. "I pulled the trigger blind. It really was dark. You saw that too, Chief. I aimed in the direction of the gunfire. If I could have seen the man, maybe I would have shot him in the shoulder and just wounded him, and we could've apprehended him. But it was dark, really dark..."

Zeynep squinted, her small mouth opened; it was like she was feeling the tension through her entire soul, as if she herself had lived that moment of conflict. "Ali, you are okay, aren't you? Now, I mean." Her tone of voice was gentle. "This is not an easy thing. You shouldn't be afraid to ask for help. You can't handle this alone. No one can... Look, I..." Once again she remembered her supervisor. "I mean we, are here. We're with you." As she spoke, the compassion in her voice deepened, laying bare the affection she felt. "If you're not okay, just say so."

Ali chewed on his lower lip. His eyes looked watery; he wasn't used to all this attention. How many women had given a damn about him up to now? How many people? If he let himself, he might fall to pieces and start sobbing. But of course he didn't.

"I'm fine," he said, averting his eyes. He tried to sound confident. "Why wouldn't I be? This isn't the first run-in we've had... We've been through all this before. The man fired on us and I fired back. Guns went off and someone died. That's all."

Zeynep knew that wasn't all there was to it.

"Maybe you should see a psychologist. Look, Ayten Hanım is really good at this. Maybe you'd better talk to her. If you suppress it now, it'll be a bigger trauma in the future."

"What psychologist? What trauma?" our hardened officer interrupted. "I said I'm fine, Zeynep. Stop blowing it out of proportion. I'm all right." I also should have insisted he see a psychologist, but it wouldn't have amounted to anything. He wasn't the reasonable type. Maybe if I pushed him he'd go but he would never tell a psychologist what he thought or felt. "We couldn't find the knife," he said all at once. In his own way, he wanted to change the subject. "The house keys turned up. After seeing the Glock, I thought we'd find the knife on him too." He noticed his girlfriend's indifference and tried to explain. "I'm talking about the knife that killed Engin. Glock makes combat knives as well, you know, Zeynep. You remember last week, we saw some in their company catalogue? The fighting knives? With the gun and the knife, I thought maybe the man had a weapons set from the same company."

"I don't remember any knife," Zeynep snapped. She stood opposite Ali, her feet apart like she was ready to fight. "Maybe it's time you stopped thinking about it too. You just cheated death. And not only that, but you killed somebody. You are in no shape to assess the situation properly."

My two closest colleagues, or should I say my two closest friends in life, my family, were in a standoff. It was their love for each other that drove them to argue, but I still worried that one of them would say something wrong and they would hurt each other in a way that would be irreparable. Then Ali did something I wasn't expecting. He slowly leaned over and took Zeynep's hand.

"I know you are just thinking of me," he said, in a voice sweet as honey. "Thank you. You're right. I'm not doing so great. But it'll be worse if I don't get back down to work." He was speaking softly, but his resolve could be perceived straight away despite the gentle manner. "Please, let me be."

Our wise girl didn't know what to say; her eyes got emotional, her head cocked slightly to the right, her shoulders slumped and she pulled her hand back helplessly, but she didn't give in.

"You say something then, Chief, to this guy," she appealed. "Can't you see he's on his last legs?"

Having witnessed time and time again that these kinds of problems were never solved by making too much of them, I tried to look like I didn't care.

"Okay Zeynep, don't make an issue," I said, placing my hands on my desk. "Our work is just about done here anyhow. We've been on our feet for twenty-four hours now. We'll be passing the torch to you and going to get some shut-eye in a bit. You prepare a file on both Engin and Tarık while we're resting. All right?" I turned to Ali, who eyed me skeptically as if he was being set up. "We'll get together tonight and plan out our road map. Okay?" He stood looking me over, not sure what to say. "Don't give me that look, Ali. You are going straight home. I need police who are mentally alert, not walking around like zombies. Do I make myself clear?"

He reluctantly agreed to my cliché remarks. "Yes, Chief. As a bell."

"Good," I said, turning back to our criminologist. "Now Zeynep, let me fill you in on what happened."

"Şefik enlightened me a bit while you were speaking with the prosecutor. The man Ali shot..." She realized she'd chosen the wrong wording and immediately corrected it. "I mean, the man who engaged Ali in conflict, was he the one who murdered Engin in front of the Tarlabaşists Club?"

I saw an image of Tidy Tarık in his rat hair coat, fallen face first in the middle of the ever-darkening blood.

"We don't know that, Zeynep," I said, chasing away the unpleasant image. "It's questionable, actually. Why go to a man's house when you just murdered him hours before? It's not professional. Wouldn't you worry about running into someone else in the house? Or that the police would go to the house after learning about Engin's murder? A mistake like that wouldn't be easy for an experienced killer like Tarık. Let's say he was after some vital document and that's why he went to the house. Why would he fire on us without first trying to see who we were?"

"Honestly, Chief," said Ali, scratching his neck, "I can't be sure, but I reckon Tarık was waiting for the house owner so as to kill him. Remember what your restaurant guy said? Everyone was Engin's enemy." He looked at Zeynep with a half-formed smile on his lips. "The man was the supreme playboy. Always hitting on everyone's wife and daughter..."

I didn't think the matter was that simple.

"I'd take what Cutlets Mehmet says with a grain of salt. He knows these people from a distance. There could be some other reason besides women."

"Don't get me wrong, Chief. I'm not insisting it's about women. Mehmet also said Engin was cruel. He caused people a lot of pain and suffering. And this urban renewal thing is also interesting. They say he brought money back from Germany? Maybe it's for the construction in Tarlabaşı. You know, there are massive profits to be had in those deals."

Now he was making a much more reasonable case for murder. Despite the tough guy attitudes and all the talk of face-saving shows of honor, in the underworld, just as in the world above, it was money that mattered most. Yes, it was more important than love, or courage, or esteem. Because money meant women and a comfortable life, and more importantly, staying on your feet. Money meant buying off officials when you needed to; it meant power in the true sense of the word. You lose money, you lose everything. Just like Harem Süleyman once did...

"Yes, it might be land grabbing and buy-to-rent profiteering behind Engin's murder." Ali's words had interrupted my train of thought. "Could be why he hired Tidy Tarık."

I turned to Zeynep, who was trying to get down to work.

"Ali's said issue of urban renewal is not to be taken lightly. They say the construction sector is the only thing keeping the country's economy afloat. To that extent, I mean. While you are looking into Engin, see if he has anything to do with the construction in Tarlabaşı. The German outfit is important too, of course. Poke around a bit and see if you can come up with Engin's connection abroad. Then there's this Black Nizam guy whose name keeps popping up. He's also from that world, and Engin was working for him. And a guy called Dice Ihsan. A gambler. He and Black Nizam are rivals. They've had some run-ins and such. Over a woman, so they say, but it'd be great if we could get to the bottom of it."

"As you wish, Chief. I'm on it."

My gaze went back over to Ali. Despite not even having blinked all day and although he'd just killed someone a few hours before, he seemed completely over his guilt complex and looked ready to get back to work. Of course he wasn't going to do that; still, I was pleased with his condition. I guess the team had pulled itself together.

"You have a point too, Ali," I said, not feeling the need to hide my pleasure. "Tarık may have shot at us after coming for Engin. Interesting that the house key turned up in his pocket. It would mean whoever hired Tarık was close enough to Engin to get his key. Yes, Tarık must've been waiting for his victim. He probably thought you were Engin, and didn't even notice me. That'd be why he started firing before asking questions. As such, it's very unlikely that Tarık was the murderer. Anyhow, the knife that killed Engin wasn't on him, which further supports this likelihood."

"It makes sense." Zeynep gently tossed back the auburn hair that fell onto her face. That sparkle in her brown eyes that I knew so well had settled in. Yes, she was on this case body and soul now. "So Tarık wasn't Engin's killer. Tarık had a Glock. Why would the man use a knife when he had a gun like that? Especially when Engin had his gun pointed at him..." She paused as another possibility occurred to her. "That is if Tarık is not a master knife thrower. You know, Chief, men like these have a bizarre psychology. Maybe he enjoyed killing with a knife."

The objection came from Ali. "But he never used a knife in any of his previous hits, always a gun. It's written in his criminal record. A pistol was used in every murder he was accused of. And they were all Glocks... Nine millimeter bullets."

Zeynep's face went pale. I suppose the thought of him being shot was running through her mind again.

"What if those bullets had found you?" she fretted, heaving a sigh. "Heaven forbid, Ali..."

He grinned like a Cheshire cat, the scoundrel. "The bullet that can hit me hasn't been cast yet, Zeynep." I gave him a look as if to say 'you're hopeless', but he shrugged it off.

"Is that a lie, Chief? Tell me, have I ever been shot?"

"The graveyards are full of young officers who felt like that, Ali," I answered, looking in his eyes. "The majority was braver, faster and more skilled. And unfortunately, they will never hear the answer to that question."

"Because some facts were of no benefit to anyone."

⚒

The worst thing about sleepless nights spent on the street is returning to an empty home. When I got to the door, even our street's carefree dog Bahtiyar was nowhere in sight, whereas he usually waited on the doorstep for me. I had spread an old carpet under the bay window ledge so that he wouldn't get cold. Maybe some charitable soul had taken him into their home. I interpreted it positively and went inside.

Silence, sharper than the cold; the silence that greeted me was almost tangible. But I knew whispers were hiding in the muteness of the furnishings. As soon as they found the chance, they'd begin to fill my ears, the grim voices of the dead that never went away. These painful memories mostly appeared at moments like these when I was overcome with exhaustion. There was no way out; whenever I was seized by these dark emotions, the torture would last until my mind had given over to sleep. The point was to shorten that time between wakefulness and slumber. It loomed large right now, that undetermined slice of time. I should probably have walked straight out of the house, occupied my mind with this murder and abandoned myself to life's frantic tempo again. That way I might escape this loneliness, this coldness, this cruel emptiness... My mind and body needed to be tired, so tired that I had no strength left to remember, feel, or think. Which was fine, but how fitting would it be to go back to the station after haranguing poor Ali so much? If I was to go somewhere else? But where? Evgenia... Yes, I could go to her of course. Why had I come to Balat anyhow when I could have gone straight to Evgenia? Tatavla would have closed late. After all, it was New Year's Eve. Perhaps they'd even stayed open all night. She was probably just heading home to sleep as well. It was like I could smell that scent of lavender rising from her warm skin. No, there was no need to torture myself. This was my life, and I couldn't live it running away. With determined steps, I climbed the stairs. I washed my hands and face, went over to the wardrobe and looked myself over in the mirror. A tired, worn-out old man. Even undressing was a chore, but undress I would. Whatever I'd done up to now, I would keep up that same routine. I would put on my pyjamas, climb into the freezing bed, and try to get to sleep. I would go through the motions of all those little habits that kept us alive. I got out of my clothes. Shivering, I headed towards the pyjamas sitting folded at the end of the bed. A habit left over from Güzide. I couldn't have kept it up alone, of course. I had Havva, my cleaning lady, to thank. Evgenia had sent her. She went to her place twice a week, too. Evgenia had said she was an honest woman, thorough and hardworking. And that she was. It worked out well, as I was off the hook from doing housework. She told me she would also do the cooking, but I was afraid to sign up for all that. My days and nights weren't so fixed. How should I know where I'd be eating any given night? All that lovely food would just go to waste.

The bed was like ice. I regretted not turning on the heating but it's hard to sleep in the heat, too. As I was wondering whether to stop being lazy and get up, the old-fashioned telephone at the bedside started ringing. Evgenia? There weren't too many people who knew my home phone number. I picked up the receiver, hoping nothing was wrong.

"Hello?" said a familiar male voice. "Hi, Nevzat."

It was a warm, friendly voice, which I knew very well but couldn't quite put my finger on.

"Hello...?"

He sensed my hesitation. "Shame on you, Chief. So then you've forgotten us..."

"No, I mean…"

Luckily, he didn't carry on too long. "It's me. Cemal."

The shining grey-blue eyes, the grizzled moustache yellowed from smoking, the amber worry beads that never left his hand… always elegant, always sincere… Yes, that was our Cemal. 'Swank' Cemal… An old tough guy I'd been fraternizing with for years. But there was no tough left in the guy anymore. In his words, he'd 'hung up his gloves', even if he did occasionally put on a show. He had a coffeehouse in Hacopulo Passage. When I was working in Beyoğlu I'd dropped by pretty frequently. We'd smoke hookahs and play backgammon. And I must say, he was a big help to me. He was never an informant and he never sold anyone out. But the stories he told were very useful in solving the world of crime.

"Wow! Cemal!" I said cheerfully. "Sorry, I couldn't place the voice for a minute. Must be getting old."

"What do you mean old, Nevzat? Would Beyoğlu's Finest Big Brother ever get old?"

A pain seemed to insidiously creep into my heart, that familiar knot in my throat… The dark eyes of a young corpse flashed despairingly in my memory.

Cemal wasn't aware of the state I was in. A hoot of laughter broke out on the other end of the line.

"You remember, don't you? Who called you that?" Cemal asked impatiently, his words rubbing out the cheerless face in my mind. "It was Madam Anahit, friend. She was the first to use that moniker."

He was mistaken, but I didn't want to burst his bubble, because some facts were of no benefit to anyone.

"How could I forget? Madam Anahit!"

"May she rest in peace. I'll never forget the day, either. We were there at Gentleman Cavit's. You know he passed away, too? Anyhow, we were having our lunchtime drink, raki."

The pang in my heart subsided and the warmth of beautiful memories revived me.

"Yes," I said, leaning back on the bed's wooden headboard. "In Huzur Restaurant."

"Gentleman Cavit was standing over us. 'Get His Excellency a drink!' he was just saying, when Madam Anahit gestured

66

toward you and corrected him. 'That's not His Excellency, that's Beyoğlu's Finest Big Brother.' Then she tapped her accordion's keys and came up with a little tune in your honor. You'd sorted out some problem for her or something..."

Really, what was it I'd done for her anyhow? I must have rescued her son. Or no, her friend's brother. An old woman had been murdered in one of the apartments in Ömer Hayyam Street. The boy had been taken into custody. He was Armenian, as was the dead woman. He'd been doing her shopping and whatnot. Our numbskull police officers had suspected this kid. He was in and out of the house with such ease, you know. They whipped the soles of his feet and when he couldn't take it anymore the poor thing shouted out 'I killed her!' and accepted all the blame. I think his name was Isa. And like his namesake the prophet Jesus, he had an angelic face. We took another look at his file, and as we probed and reviewed it, the truth came to light. The murderer had been a telephone repairman. He'd gone in to fix her phone, somehow seen the money she'd been saving up, and strangled the poor woman. He might have got away with it if he'd only taken the money, but he got greedy and collected everything he could get his hands on. We caught him selling an antique set of silver in Çukurcuma. That's where Madam's debt of gratitude had come from. And thus the compliment...

Again the sharp knife, again the forgotten pain... Again that vague knot in my throat.

"Not all good deeds end in positive results," I thought of saying. But I didn't. Cemal was sincere, and he really liked me. There was no sense in making either him or myself sad.

"Don't exaggerate, Cemal," I said, trying to banish the bad memories from my mind. "I was just doing my job. So, what's up with you? How've you been since last we saw each other?"

"I'm fine, Nevzat, just fine. Be even better if my friends called to check in."

His scolding wasn't without merit. How many times had the man rung me? And every time I told him all right, I'll stop by soon, and then forgot about it. Not out of disloyalty mind you, but lack of time.

"I'll stop by soon, Cemal. I will. There were some incidents in Tarlabaşı tonight and I wanted to talk them over..."

As the remark left my mouth, I realized I'd put my foot in it. I'd just told the man I was coming to visit him because I needed a favor. I started to apologize when he said, "That's why I called you, too." I relaxed and listened intently to the old tough guy.

"Dice Ihsan was not responsible for Engin's death." Here we go; Cemal dove straight into the subject. I gave him my attention and hoped for the best. "Yes, Ihsan is innocent. There was a big set-up. Murdering Engin there in front of the Tarlabaşists Club was all a ruse. They wanted to frame him."

"Who?"

"That I don't know. Whoever has issues with him."

"Your Dice had issues with him," I answered back straight away. "They fought..."

He laughed nervously.

"Don't say that, Chief. How is he 'my' Dice?"

"I know you, Cemal," I said, my voice tense. "You wouldn't call me about a murder for nothing. And before the victim's blood has even dried... You have some connection with Ihsan. Or at least you talked to him."

He didn't bother to hide it.

"It's true. Ihsan came to the coffeehouse an hour ago. He was panicking. 'Man, you are the only one who can help me,' he said. 'They're setting me up. It's a conspiracy. My head's going to roll.' I told him to calm down and sat him down next to me. He explained it all in detail. There's bad blood between him and Black Nizam. First because of the venue, and then this problem over a woman entered the equation. Nizam sicced this Engin on Ihsan every time. But no matter what they did, they couldn't scare him. So now Nizam has rubbed out his own man and is trying to pin the blame on Ihsan."

Even if there was some truth in what he said, Ihsan's accusation was fairly dubious.

"Why would he do that? I heard Engin was a valued employee. In fact, I think they had some partnership or something."

"Ihsan said that as well. They were collecting buildings in Tarlabaşı. You know how the neighborhood's being rebuilt... Engin had some connection to Germany. I guess he was bringing over some big money. He didn't explain much, but it sounded like drug trade to me. 'Maybe that's why,' is what Ihsan said. If Engin had screwed his boss over, Nizam would be killing two birds with one stone. He'd be taking out the man who'd betrayed him while at the same time putting the blame on Ihsan."

That was a possibility, but it was also possible the gambling den proprietor was lying in order to save his own skin.

"Can Ihsan prove what he says?"

"How could he?"

I already knew he couldn't. If he could have, he'd have come straight to us instead of Cemal, but my real aim was to shed some light on the dark spots from last night's murder.

"The incident happened outside his venue. Didn't they see the murderer? The club was open after all, while the murder was taking place, wasn't it?"

He didn't realize I was just sounding him out and confirmed as much with his usual frankness.

"It was open. But no one saw it. That time of night sees the most heated moments in gambling. All kinds of evil tricks run through the gamblers' minds. Everyone's eyes are on the table. Who's going to get curious and look outside? One of the customers saw Engin's body as they left to go home. He notified the club. And they called the police."

"Ihsan called them?"

"No, Ihsan was in a brothel in Talimhane. It's New Year's so you know, he was out with friends, and some foreign ladies as well. They'll testify to that, if you want. It must have been Ihsan's men who called your guys."

Our guys... I drew up a mental image of the two officers we'd run into the night before. That huge-headed Zeynel and his wimpy little friend... I was certain Ihsan was bribing them. I knew it wasn't possible to control scandals like this; once again we'd just write it off as this vocation's corruption, so long as it wasn't relevant to the murder of course. I wanted to dig deeper to understand.

"But when we arrived, we didn't see anyone from the Tarlabaşists Club. Just two officers with the victim."

There was a brief silence. I suppose Cemal was trying to deduce what Ihsan hadn't told him.

"Beats me, Chief," he said, though his voice was faltering. "I'm just passing along what Ihsan said. The call is yours, as always."

Was he offended? I didn't want to hurt his feelings.

"Thanks, Cemal. You were a big help actually. This cleared up some questions in my head. So, what kind of man is this Ihsan?"

"He's not a bad guy, actually. I knew his father well. Osman was a gambler, but he was good to me. He stood by me in my darkest days. Ihsan is following in his father's footsteps, as I'm sure you guessed. He used to have a venue in Tarabya. With the raids and whatnot, your usual issues, he couldn't manage to hole up there. So now he's in Beyoğlu..."

"How'd he find out I was the one dealing with this situation?"

Again silence. I guess Cemal realized he'd hit a snag and had already begun to regret speaking to me, but it was too late for him to take a step back.

"I would suggest the men saw you, but you say they didn't. How he knows you, I honestly can't say. I'll have to get back to you on that. I'll ask around and find out."

"Thanks, Cemal. I'll swing round later today or tomorrow. It's been a while since we've rattled some dice."

"I'd like that, Chief. It's been a while since I've smoked a hookah, too. We'll share a puff in your honor."

The old warmth had returned to his voice. With peace of mind, I hung up. My eyes had started to burn. As I rubbed them, I fell asleep.

"Please just stick to the murders in your novel."

✖

Maybe it'd be better if I hadn't slept; I felt much more tired now. I was disoriented, and felt like my eyelids each had a millstone on them. The smell of rot, the taste of must in my mouth, was of the sort that could only be found in the basements of Tarlabaşı's century-old buildings... The foul smell didn't leave me when I got out of bed, either. I took a warm shower, shaved and brushed my teeth, and the smell disappeared, at any rate. But my head was still dazed. I made coffee, the strong black sort without sugar, but it didn't help at all. I got dressed, thinking it best to just dive back into normal life. Or dive back into running after grisly murders, I suppose I should say. Yes, that was the reality; the very actions that brought lives to an end were for me life itself. This was no contradiction; it was my job, murders... Where the killer's job ended, mine began. I felt better when struggling with these murders, humanity's dark side, that is. The worst thing was trying to get used to it. 'You get hardened to it,' is what Commissioner Rauf told me years ago when I first started this line of work. 'Facing dead bodies becomes easy in the same way a teacher gets comfortable starting new classes. You'll take a look at a man's scattered brains and then go eat dinner.' I had in fact started to do at least part of what he'd said. Like last night, we'd gone from the scene of a murder to eat soup plenty of times, though when I was with a victim I

71

never felt like a seasoned teacher starting a new class. Even if there was an educational side to murder, death was always tragic. Even more horrific, it was contagious, and you could never protect yourself from that. Last night it had infected Ali. It had presented him with such a cruel dilemma, having to kill or be killed.

My gaze slipped over to the photo of our daughter, smiling at her father as if she'd never died and was about to open her bedroom door and wish me a good morning. Yes, it had crept all the way to our house, death. It had taken my wife and daughter from me. As if the grim reaper was saying that anyone who messes with him will pay. 'You shouldn't have wandered so close to me, Nevzat!' The worst part being it was no longer possible to escape him. 'Let's leave this city and go to Gökçe Island,' Evgenia coaxed me. 'We'll start a quiet, peaceful life, from scratch.' I couldn't explain why I wouldn't accept. That calm life, that for her meant growing old to the sound of waves under the warm, sea-moistened wind, would be hell for me. The nightmares I managed to control in the real world would, during the lazy days and long nights of that quiet life, take hold of not only my mind but also my subconscious. I was dead certain of it, because I'd been through it before. Though not every morning, I often woke up with nightmares. I would make Evgenia's life hell too, not just my own. The only way to cope with the nightmares was to face them while awake. And with that thought, I left my house.

Our faithful old neighborhood dog Bahtiyar's house, which I'd improvised from a cardboard box, was still empty. And the food I'd put out the previous morning was just as I'd left it. Where had that mutt gone?

"Bahtiyar's with us," a voice said, startling me. On the narrow sidewalk, wet with melting snow, stood the owner of the voice. "It's so cold, Nevzat Bey. We were worried he'd freeze. I fixed up a little place for him in our greenhouse. Our grandson also loves it. He can make do with that until the cold spell passes."

It was that detective novelist speaking. With an index finger, he pushed up the glasses at the tip of his nose and then finished his sentence.

"If that's okay with you, of course..."

"It is," I answered, smiling reluctantly. "That's good. At least the poor creature won't get sick."

This detective novelist was an odd one. He'd bought our deceased neighbor Mihael's place, two buildings up from ours, and restored it. In his defense, he had done the building properly, sparing no expense. And he was extremely respectful towards me, beyond respectful, actually. He was always staring at me fondly as though we were close. Not with love, but understanding rather, as if I was his best friend or a member of the family. On previous occasions I'd caught him watching me as I left the house, immersed in thought and counting my steps, his right hand on his grizzled beard like an artist looking at a painting he'd completed. He was never embarrassed to see I'd noticed him; he just waved at me with a bold smile that bared his white teeth. There was something strange about this man all right, but I couldn't put my finger on it. It's not that I thought he'd do me any harm. Besides, he had a very nice wife, polite, cheerful and considerate. But the sweetest member of their family was their grandson, Rüzgâr. He was the cutest little thing, bless him. I never saw his mother and father; I guess they didn't come round much. Perhaps they were wary of our peculiar novelist. But the grandson was at their house every weekend. Once we ran into Rüzgâr in our local grocer Recep's shop. "Are policemen the good guys?" he'd asked. I didn't know what to tell him. I mumbled something like, "It depends on which policeman." My thoughts had already gone back to the writer. The man had even told the boy about me. Consider the relevance! Evgenia noticed it as well. "Maybe he'll write your novel, Nevzat," she said with her usual optimism. "Would that be so bad? Everyone would know you. They'll learn what a real man is." But I didn't want everyone to know me. And I knew these author types; they always exaggerated people and events. More blood than there really was, more intrigue, better heroes, worse villains... Events that never happened in real life, people that never existed... And how was someone else supposed to explain me when I didn't even fully understand myself?

"How's the investigation going?" asked the author, scattering my thoughts. "Have you arrested any suspects?"

He was doing the same thing again. Ruffling my feathers, asking questions about the details of my day as though he knew every minute of my life. I shot him a chilly look.

"What investigation? I don't know what you're talking about."

He didn't take it personally. He assumed his usual sympathetic manner again. And his insistent approach, of course.

"I'm talking about the Tarlabaşı murders. You are the one who's investigating the incident, aren't you?"

His arms were crossed on his chest and his head rested slightly to the right in that overconfident stance of his that so ruffled my feathers.

"How do you know about the Tarlabaşı murders?" My voice came out sharp as a gust of winter wind.

"From the TV... The news bulletins have been going on and on about the murders all morning. They even said the two murders are connected. Is that true?"

In fact, I'd never openly rebuke the man. I should've told him to keep his nose out of this business, but he was my neighbor and we were face to face, so there was no way.

"The media is being irresponsible," I said, holding my anger in check. "They're waiting in front of the morgue for someone to kill someone so they can make it news."

"You sure are on edge."

What was this man on about?

"I don't think you feel that way about the press. You're the empathetic type of officer," he said, answering the question as though he'd heard my thoughts. This was too much.

"How do you know I'm empathetic? You think you know me?"

He gently raised his hands. "I'm sorry. I guess I've overstepped my boundaries." I had no intention of backing down. I dropped the neighborly courtesy.

"Yes, you did a bit. You can't go making presumptions about people you don't know. And even if you do, you shouldn't say it to their face."

74

"You're right. I just..."

No, I wasn't listening to him. I'd waited for this chance for a long time and I was going to give him a piece of my mind, this so-called author who stuck his nose in everything.

"No justs about it, sir. I am not a character you created, no more than these murders were constructed for your novel. There are real people here, real deaths, real pain. Please just stick to the murders in your novel. You wouldn't be able to handle the ones in real life."

I was speaking quite severely but no matter what I did, he somehow couldn't manage to wipe that empathetic smile off his face. Whatever I said, the man didn't get angry. Even with my daughter Aysun, I hadn't shown such patience. He was an odd one, all right. They say writers are half mad but I never believed it; looked like it was true.

"I'm aware I couldn't handle real murders, Nevzat Bey," he said in a voice devoid of so much as a spark of anger. "And I know how difficult your job is. I just asked out of curiosity."

No, not curiosity. He had other motives, however, which I failed to understand. I was considering having Zeynep check him out. And at that moment, my phone rang.

"Anyhow, don't let me keep you," he said, choosing to sneak away after hearing the phone. It was good timing, too, or I might have got even nastier. Still, he couldn't go without getting the last word in. "Tough job. A complicated case with two deaths for you to solve... Good luck to you."

Good luck, he says. Look at this guy, as if he were my superior. As if anyone was waiting for his good wishes. I looked down at my phone without thanking him. It was Ali. And with my frayed temper, I answered it. "Yes, Ali. What is it?"

He paused. He wasn't expecting such curtness from me.

"Umm... Chief, I'm disturbing you, I guess?"

I watched the writer trudge away and answered. "No, Ali. You aren't. I was just arguing with some tactless person."

"If you want I can call you later."

"I said it's all right, Ali. I'm listening..."

He got straight to the point. "They've attempted to burn down the Tarlabaşists Club."

"Dice Ihsan's place?"

"That's right, Chief."

"Things are heating up."

"They sure are, Chief. This must be Black Nizam's doing. Looks like he's trying to take revenge for Engin."

Or he's trying to make it look that way, I thought to myself. But I couldn't help asking, "Were the perpetrators caught?"

"No, Chief. The street was quiet at that hour. There were no witnesses. Someone threw a Molotov Cocktail."

Molotov Cocktail? This was the first I'd heard of mafia using a Molotov.

"Any dead or injured?"

After having killed someone the night before, he'd become more sensitive, our musketeer.

"Fortunately not," he said, his voice betraying his delight. "The building's janitor came away with minor injuries, is all."

I wasn't as optimistic as he was. It looked like we were in for a bloody settling of the score. Two dead, one injured... Let's see what came next.

"I see. It's time we stopped by Black Nizam's place."

"I already tried, Chief, but the Genuine Tarlabaşists Club is closed. They left a sign on the door saying 'At a funeral'. That's all."

"All right. Where are you now?"

"At the scene... I mean, the Tarlabaşists Club." He wasn't such a slowpoke as his boss, of course. He'd gone to Tarlabaşı as soon as he heard. "Okay, Ali, I'm on my way."

"There was something magical about this woman."

⁂

It looked like this initially backwards day was going to trickle along with more setbacks. This time it was my faithful old Renault getting all coy. I was used to him moaning in extreme cold like this, but whether it was because I'd got irritated by that author or what, I had no tolerance for my old friend being such a spoilsport. I would try one last time and then go straight to Hanifi on the street below. He would understand our little guy's trouble. Luckily it didn't come to that. "Come on boy, don't cause me trouble," I said, banging on the steering wheel. And it started running. Who knows, maybe after all these years we'd spent together it'd started to appreciate all I'd done for it and learned to not let its friend down. As the smell of petrol in the car filled my nasal, I gently stepped on the pedal and set off across this city settling into night. The snow that hit last night was only on the rooftops now and there wasn't so much as a puddle in the streets. I proceeded parallel to the Golden Horn, which under the last rays of sunlight had become a golden pool. Just seeing this view was enough to cheer a person up. But like a pleasant dream, the view was gone in the blink of an eye without giving me a chance to appreciate it. My phone began to painfully ring. I didn't recognize the number. I wondered if it had to do with last night's murders.

"Hello, how can I help you?"

"Hi, Chief. It's Erdinç, from Feraye."

That's right. I was having dinner with Evgenia. We always met on the first day of the year not in Tatavla but in a different *meyhane* each time. Neither of us had the luxury to enjoy ourselves or see each other on New Year's Eve. So we celebrated it one day later than everyone else. And so this was our tradition; what could we do? Naturally, I hadn't forgotten I was meeting her. I'd called a week in advance to book a table with Erdinç but the things I'd been through since nighttime had muddled my mind. If Erdinç hadn't called, no doubt Evgenia's call would have come along a little later. It was even strange she hadn't already called. Was she angry at not hearing a peep out of me? I should have acted faster and told her I'd got us a place, but I'd wanted it confirmed first.

"You're getting our spot set up I guess, Erdinç?" I said to my friend on the other end of the line. "You got us the bay window, right?"

"Of course, Chief. Just like you asked. And the heating is sorted as well."

"That's great, thanks! It's important. Evgenia always gets cold."

"Don't worry," said Erdinç confidently. "It'll be warm and cozy. Evgenia Hanım will be able to fully appreciate the charm of the bay window."

The overhanging oriel window was truly the nicest spot in Feraye Meyhane. All of Istiklal Street lay at your feet. People passed by in the lights reflected from shop windows; people from the city, the country, and the four corners of the earth... Every night, every single night without exception, they strolled past, growing in number, in this possibly most crowded street in the world. Every race and every color, men and women arm in arm and hand in hand from every culture. Most of them drunk but some sober, usually well-dressed but sometimes unkempt, some half-naked, others in headscarves... They were mostly happy, occasionally angry, and sometimes deep in thought. Sometimes groups would sing football anthems but more often there were groups protesting the government. Sometimes hopeful, sometimes forlorn, sometimes kissing, sometimes fighting... Every state

78

of mankind would pass before our eyes. You could sit here every night of the week watching people pass by and never get bored with the sight. This is why I chose this place, so that Evgenia could see this river of color made up of people. "Thanks so much," I told Erdinç, who was still waiting on the line. "We'll be there around eight."

"We'll expect you, Chief."

I didn't put the phone in my pocket after hanging up; I had to call Evgenia right away. I pulled the car over, but before I could dial my phone began to ring again. Maybe Erdinç forgot something? No, it was our criminologist ringing.

"Yes, Zeynep?"

"Hi, Chief. Look, I'm in the victim's house. Engin Akça's... in Tarlabaşı, in the apartment building on Kadın Çıkmazı. Just where Tarık Seberci resides hasn't come to light yet. He left the Ataşehir apartment he's registered in three months ago and now he's not registered anywhere."

That was no surprise. It just meant our hitman had a secret life.

"So what did you turn up in Engin's house? We didn't search it after Tarık was shot."

"We found a steel safe, Chief, on the second floor. It was one of those mounted inside a wall, not the big kind. But we couldn't find a key. I wondered if anything resembling a safe key turned up on Engin last night."

I didn't remember any key. "Could it be in one of the evidence bags? Did you have them take a look?"

"Yes. They looked but it wasn't there."

"Must mean it's hidden somewhere else. Somewhere more secure. Maybe in the building."

"We looked, Chief. It's not here either. I hope the murderer didn't take it after he killed Engin."

Maybe that was why Tidy Tarık had gone to the house, to get his hands on some valuable documents or money in the safe. And when he saw us... But why wait so long? There'd been a window of a few hours between Engin's murder and when we went to the house on Kadın Çıkmazı.

"So I guess there was nothing like a safe key found on Tidy Tarık?" I put in.

"Nope. Just the house keys." My enthusiasm faded as quickly as it had come on. So then it wasn't what I thought, and Tarık hadn't come for the contents of the safe. His sole motivation would have been Engin's death. Perhaps Black Nizam had the key, seeing as how Engin did his dirty business for him. I should talk with these street kids. They knew everyone Engin consorted with. I suddenly remembered what Keto had told me. How he'd mentioned a *Cevşen* prayer. These *Cevşen* prayers were usually carried on one's person. I wondered where Engin had kept his?

"Zeynep, can you remember?" I said, my interest returning. "Did you come across a necklace or anything, around his neck or maybe in his pocket?"

"Sure. He had a necklace with a big silver triangle round his neck. Not a pendant but a locket. One and a half, maybe two inches in length and less than an inch thick. There was a *Cevşen* prayer or something inside it."

"Did you open it up and take a look?"

The light bulb suddenly went on in Zeynep's head.

"Oh... No, Chief. I'm afraid we overlooked that," she said sheepishly. "At that point we didn't know about the safe. I'll call the station immediately and have them check. You're right; the key may be inside that silver box."

"It's possible, Zeynep. If whatever's in that safe is important, he wouldn't have let the key out of his sight. I'm already on my way to Tarlabaşı. Don't leave the building; I'm coming to you."

I pulled into the street again and stepped harder on the gas. There was something wrong here. I couldn't predict what was going to happen but, with the two bodies in one night, some issue big enough for a killer to be hired, and somebody wanting to burn down a gambling den... I supposed we'd landed ourselves in a gambling mafia war. These men would tear each other to bits. And it didn't bode well that Swank was in it deep enough to have to call me. I was afraid the murders wouldn't stop here. Swank hadn't, in fact, explained the big picture. Although to be fair, he may not be able to see it yet. Maybe he needed me to ask him the right questions before he figured it out. My phone started ringing again before I'd even

80

come to the old Cibali Tobbacco Factory. Evgenia! Yes, I'd just stopped to ring her. Zeynep's call made me forget all about it. I answered the phone, embarrassed.

"Hello, Evgenia. Happy New Year. I'm sorry I couldn't call you last night."

"Happy New Year to you too, Nevzat." Contrary to my expectation, her voice was cheerful. "Don't worry. I couldn't call you either. Not couldn't, but didn't. You remember last New Year how when I called you, you were standing over a dead body in Kocamustafapaşa? I didn't want to have a sloppy, distracted conversation like that again. So I waited till today."

I relaxed. She wasn't sore.

"You're right, Evgenia. It was pretty bad this New Year's too. But never mind, I won't go into it now. I'm guessing you were also busy. Was it really crowded, the *meyhane*?"

"Extremely. It was packed. Standing room only. Old customers, newcomers... But it was a lot of fun. My Greek relatives made a surprise appearance. My cousin came from Athens. Angeliki... with my Aunt Fofo."

I was hearing the names for the first time. "Wow, that's great! Are you close?"

"Very. Haven't I mentioned them? Angeliki is like a sister. She was born after my Uncle Niko and his wife Fofo emigrated to Greece, but she still loves Istanbul. We've known each other since we were very little. My father used to take me to Athens every year before he died. Angeliki is an angel, as her name suggests. But Aunt Fofo is the real attraction. She's one of a kind, Nevzat, I can't even tell you. She's going on eighty now but she still runs around like a teenager. She was knocking back the raki last night, I swear. By midnight poor Angeliki was three sheets to the wind, but Fofo didn't even seem tipsy. It was the middle of the night and the woman started dancing the Greek *syrtos*. Can you imagine, Nevzat?"

There was such unbridled excitement in her telling of it, she must really have been happy last night. And I was happy for her.

"It wasn't the alcohol but rather the gaiety she was carried away by," Evgenia continued. "I'm an idiot. I was trying to protect her but I really put my foot in it. 'Raki's not like ouzo, it'll go to your head,' I told her. She frowned, with those painted black eyebrows of hers, and scolded me. 'Who do you think you're lecturing about drinks? Your Uncle Niko and I were clinking glasses all over Pera before you were even born. And yes, he always called Beyoğlu by its old name, Pera,' she said. What could I do? I just shut up and sat there. But nothing happened to Aunt Fofo. It was like she'd been drinking water all night rather than raki. Then at three in the morning she stood straight up, wished us all a good night, and was off home to bed as if it was nothing."

As Evgenia spoke, her good cheer spread to me and I felt better. There was something magical about this woman. Something that made you feel like the world was a place worth living in. I could be staring into her green eyes or just talking on the phone like this without even seeing her face, whenever I heard her voice I was filled with joy, and all the dark thoughts in my mind would just up and leave.

"And up early in the morning..." she continued. "Yes, while Angeliki and I were still fast asleep. She put our poor doorman Remzi Efendi to work. Sent him to the shops, the greengrocer, the delicatessen, to complete what was missing from the house. She made breakfast. And not just a slapdash spread, but a meal fit for a king. Omelets, all kinds of cheeses, salami and sausages, jam, clotted cream... everything but bird's milk, if you know what I mean. She doesn't eat that much herself but the woman sure takes pleasure in preparing it and feeding those around her. Imagine that, Nevzat. At that age she has more of a grip on life than we do. Incredible, isn't it?"

"It's incredible, all right. But the way you explain it," I said, smacking my lips exaggeratedly, "is making me hungry. How am I going to wait till eight?"

There was a brief silence. Evgenia, who had been chirping away, suddenly clammed up.

"Nevzat..." she finally said.

"Yes, Evgenia. What is it?"

"Umm... I wanted to ask. Would you be very upset if we postponed our dinner tonight?"

I got the picture. She wanted to set tonight aside for her guests. I should have been happy. I had a difficult investigation ahead of me; Ali was waiting for me in the Tarlabaşists Club and Zeynep in the victim's house. It was doubtful I would even make it to Feraye on time, and yet it felt odd. I hadn't realized it, but this dinner was really important for me. Not the dinner as such, but seeing Evgenia. It had been a week since I'd seen her. We were meant to meet at Tatavla on Monday, but I had some documents to send to the courthouse involving the case of an American woman whose body was found in Sarayburnu, and I couldn't make it to the *meyhane*. I suddenly realized I really missed Evgenia; the lavender that on her skin became another scent entirely, her warmth, that peculiar light that appeared in her eyes when she looked at me. No more murder investigation, no more friends waiting for me... it all disappeared. I thought to tell her all right, we don't need to meet this evening, but let me come see you, if only for a minute. If only for a minute let me hold you, breathe in your scent. But I immediately changed my mind. Evgenia was with her relatives and the meeting I envisioned would never take place in front of them. No, I had no right to feel this way.

"Why would I be upset, sweetheart?" I tried to make my voice sound indifferent. "You have houseguests once in a blue moon. And they're from Athens no less. We can see each other later."

There was another silence.

"Your voice says different." No, you couldn't keep anything from this woman. "We don't have to postpone if you'd rather not. I don't have to go with them. They're going to a *meyhane* in Asmalı Mescit. The owner is a childhood friend of Aunt Fofo's. She's insisted that I come, too. But I can get out of it. I mean, it's not absolutely necessary. You know I would never want to make you sad."

I kept up the facade of course.

"Why would I be sad, Evgenia? We'll meet tomorrow. Or if not then, some other time. There'll be other days. You can look after your guests with a clear conscience."

No, my words didn't comfort her. "Are you sure?" The disappointment in her voice was audible.

"Yes, I'm sure. I'll go to dinner with the kids. I've been thinking of taking them out for a while now, anyhow."

Not a sound came from the other end of the line.

"I mean it, Evgenia," I persisted. "It's no problem for me. If you're happy, I'm happy." I emphasized this and put an end to it. "All right?"

"All right." She knew it wasn't all right. She probably regretted saying we should postpone but it was too late now. "Thank you, Nevzat, for being so understanding."

The strong Nevzat should look unfazed, and that's what he did. "Have a wonderful New Year, Evgenia. We'll talk later."

"Happy New Year's, Nevzat."

After hanging up, a sadness swelled inside me. Some sense of abandonment. It seemed like the sun that was reflecting off water had been extinguished and the blue of the sky had got the deeper. How quickly night fell over the city!

"Around Beyoğlu I'm humbly known as Flea Necmi."

There was no sign a murder had been committed on this street last night; the water from the melted snow had washed away the blood in front of the Tarlabaşists Club leaving not so much as a tiny stain on the ground. If not for a workman reprimanding his poor apprentice as they changed the club's window, we could say it was quiet. In the daytime the street looked more ramshackle, its buildings more run-down and tired. I'd once read that night was 'a black velvet cloak covering the flaws of old cities' but I couldn't remember from which book or which author. Well, we were also reaching a ripe old age. My memory was at least as tired and worn-out as these streets. The building where the Tarlabaşists Club was located looked worse in the daylight as well. The paperbag brown paint was chipping away and the bricks underneath were laid bare in places. Bits of the triangular pediments over the narrow windows had fallen off and the small ornamental sculpted women's heads were in pieces. There was a slab of marble in the wall to the left of the entrance of this once glorious building. It had been painted over in bone white, but the chiseled Greek letters still legibly displayed the name of the Greek architect: Vasilaki Kiliantis. The apartment was crumbling, but apart from the two broken windows on the Tarlabaşists Club floor, there was no evidence to suggest a fire had broken out. A vague burnt smell hit me as I walked through the enormous iron door, but the heavy smell of mold from down below overpowered it. I continued up the corridor under fluorescent lights and came to a marble staircase. The bordeaux carpet on its steps had begun to disintegrate around the edges and in the corners evoking shoddiness rather than flamboyance, but I doubt those who came to gamble noticed the flaws. Who really gave a damn about this beautiful city's history anyhow, that gamblers should try to protect these true gems of buildings? Worse yet was the reddish steel door at the top of the steps. If the architect saw this, the poor man would probably turn in his grave. The functionality of the impassable steel door in keeping uninvited guests out would no doubt be beyond him. As it was, the moment you laid eyes on this metal heap you realized you weren't in such a safe place. That was not a problem for the clientele of course, because everybody who knocked on this door knew exactly why they'd come here. I pushed the metallic buzzer under the entry phone. From inside came a succession of canary tweets. A bell with the voice of a canary... in a gambling den? But then why not, in this cultural stewpot of a city. A shadow landed in the peephole on the other side of the door. A husky voice could be heard in the entry phone.

"Who is it?"

"Chief Inspector Nevzat."

No more questions, but there was the immediate sound of a lock and then the door opened. So they'd been expecting us. With the jarred door came an increased burnt odor and that husky voice hit my face.

"Welcome, Chief. We've been waiting for you."

But what's this? I was expecting a hulk of a man, but in front of me stood one no more than five feet tall. There was no hair or beard to speak of, just a bright shiny head, a handlebar moustache and bushy eyebrows. As if a master calligrapher had written a carefully crafted script on a human face. Yet his body was well-proportioned, his shoulders broad and his muscles in place, and he stood up straight in front of me without the least bit of a complex. I was stifling a fit of laughter, but the runt with the handlebar moustache was utterly serious.

"Come on in, Chief. I'll take you this way, to Ihsan Abi's office."

We passed from the hall with the blue lighting into a room with high ceilings. The large room was made smaller by the nonsensical plaster of Paris archways and layers of ceiling trim. Cutesy bulldogs looked out from a dozen wooden frames they'd gone to special pains to hang on three of the walls. The only wall that had no photos hung had been set aside for shelves of alcohol. A wooden bar top ran the length of the shelves where multicolored bottles lined up, from raki to vodka, whiskey to wine. On the bar were two glass pitchers. Maybe they'd tried to put out the fire with them. Three behemoths sat on long-legged stools in front of the bar. They stood up respectfully when they saw us. With a hand signal from the pocketsize Hercules next to me, they sat back down in their places. How could these giants have a boss like this shorty next to me? It looked like I'd have to take our friend, who was little better than the biggest of the seven dwarves, more seriously. In the vast area between the broken windows and the three goliaths sitting at the bar were six tables draped in green felt covers. The only table missing a cover was the burnt one near the window to the left. Looking closely, I saw the green cover lying half singed on the floor. Both the tablecloth and the honey-colored parquet floor were soaked.

"I guess there wasn't much damage?" I muttered. "I was expecting worse."

He scrutinized the room as though seeing it for the first time himself. "God protected us; it was a close call, Chief."

"I think someone was injured?"

"Yes, Nazif Efendi. He looks after the kitchen. He was doing some cleaning inside. If it weren't for him the fire would have spread. Thankfully, we got off light. It's when he went to put it out that he burnt his hands. Well, gasoline fires don't go out so easily of course. But it's not serious; the doctors didn't even keep him. He'll be better within a week."

As the trinket-sized bodyguard spoke, my gaze went over to the glass in front of the window. A brown-haired worker who hadn't seen us come in was spreading putty round the window frame on the one hand, while continuing to swear at his apprentice on the other.

"Man, if I hadn't got here in time that huge glass would have gone down just like that. What am I going to do with you? What would the boss say? I told you how the man counts his pennies. And what if someone was walking past and it fell on their head? They'd throw the both of us in jail. Nothing would happen to you 'cause you're young, but they'd throw the book at me..."

The apprentice was barely fourteen years old. His face was ghastly pale but his eyes were fidgety. He was blocking his head from any sudden punches.

"Would you look at this idiot," said the worker, raising his right hand as if to smack him. "He has the gall to glare at me."

The apprentice immediately drew his head back. The worker's hand still hung in the air as he considered whether or not to slap him.

"That's enough," growled the gambling den's strong-arm, noticing the situation. "Lay off! You've been nagging away since you got here. We've got the Chief here. It's disgraceful. And anyhow it's evening already and you still haven't finished."

The worker dropped his hand straight away. His face went three shades of red. "Okay, brother, but..."

"Don't you 'but brother' me. That's enough. Stop giving the kid such a hard time. The glass didn't fall. And these things happen. Come on, get it in and then off you go."

The worker shot the apprentice a rancorous look, as if to say 'look what we go through thanks to you' and then, after a deep sigh, began to labor with the glass.

"Sorry, Chief," said the runt with the handlebar moustache, turning to me. "He doesn't know his place. He has no grasp on just who comes in and who goes out." He wore the smile of an indulgent supervisor.

"Don't worry about it. What's your name?"

"Necmi." He put his right hand on his chest and gave a small bow.

"I didn't quite make it to the neighborhood during your time, but maybe you've heard of me anyhow? Around Beyoğlu

I'm humbly known as Flea Necmi. I know Cemal Abi very well. I was under his instruction. If you need a reference, I mean, you can ask him, Chief."

A smile of satisfaction with his nickname appeared on his face.

"Flea Necmi, eh?" I repeated. "Flea Necmi... No, I don't recall. Must mean you have no prior incidents."

Though he tried not to show it, his smile slowly faded, as though I'd made a defamatory remark. Still, he had the foresight to say what had to be said.

"God forbid, Chief. What incidents? We're just trying to make a living here. We've got some soup on the boil here and we're just working to keep the stove lit, so to speak."

This Flea Necmi was speaking confidently, like someone with nothing to hide. Like he was sure no harm would come from me. Did he think I was one of these cops who accepted their bribes? Maybe Dice Ihsan had told him not to worry. That Swank Cemal had spoken to me and everything was fine. It'd be worth playing along. If that's what he thought, I may as well take advantage of the misconception.

"Were you here last night, Necmi?"

He paused. Of course he was here, but what was he supposed to say?

"Sorry, Chief? I didn't understand."

"Last night, I said. Were you here?" I planted myself there as if to say I'd stand there till I got an answer. "You were open late."

His black eyes flickered.

"You know, someone was murdered outside your door?"

"I know," he finally managed to say. "It happened after we closed."

"What time did you close?"

"In the new year," he said jokingly. "After midnight, I mean," he continued, getting serious when he saw I wasn't smiling. "Must have been one thirty or so."

"Was it you that closed up the club?"

His Bobo doll face got a look on it like he'd upset the apple cart. Worse still, he could no longer deny it.

"Yeah, but I didn't see any corpse or anything on the street." He averted his eyes. "They sorted Engin out after we left."

I was getting him where I wanted him.

"So then, you knew the victim?"

His expression soured as though he was picturing something foul.

"Everybody here knew him. He wasn't exactly a revered friend. Just your average cheap letch. You know, one of those assholes who lives under a girl's skirt."

I wondered if Engin had also pulled a fast one on this mini tough guy.

"Did he mess with your girlfriend, too?"

I expected him to get angry but he laughed quietly, like I'd touched on an amusing subject.

"His type knows who they can and can't mess with, Chief. He wouldn't have lived quite so long as he did if he'd made that mistake."

Whether he was being candid or just talking tough was hard to say. I kept poking.

"You don't seem too sad he died."

He gently threw up his hands, no bigger than a child's.

"I'm not going to lie just because he's dead, Chief. Okay, I wouldn't go congratulating a murderer, but Engin wasn't exactly well liked around here."

"And you've fought, I guess."

"He was a degenerate man, Chief," he murmured arrogantly, like a cocky teenager. "Hanging around degenerate places. All kinds of trouble can find a person in that case. Being with Black Nizam is a problem in itself, for one. Although there is a bright side to it; at least everyone can see what he's made of. Anyhow, after that we stopped doing business with him."

He'd played right into my hands. "And what business was that exactly? Gambling?" I immediately asked.

The candor in his expression shattered like the window of the gambling den had when hit with the Molotov. He was wondering just how wrong he'd been about me, or if Dice Ihsan had given him bad information. But he recovered quickly enough.

"No, Chief. What gambling? This is a clubhouse. With men, women, and whole families that come here. People play cards for fun but nobody places bets. We wouldn't allow it." A sardonic light shone in his dark eyes. "And even if we tried to, your colleagues wouldn't give us room to breathe."

He was openly taking jabs at me. *But we know what you are made of, despite all the talk,* is what the impertinent light in his dark eyes said. I pretended not to understand of course, for the time being.

"And this Molotov cocktail incident? Who would want to burn down this innocent den of recreation?"

A broad smile spread through his already wide mouth, such that his handlebar moustache nearly brushed his earlobes.

"How should I know, Chief? This is Beyoğlu. The devil's bed and the djinns' dining table. Thieves and hooligans, pimps and... pardon me for saying it... poofs. You name it, we've got it here. Not two days ago on that back street over here, an old man was beaten so badly he was hospitalized. For twenty lira, no less. Any breed of psychopath you could possibly want, they're all here. Maybe we didn't let some son of a bitch in and he took it personally and flung the bottle." He nodded towards the red light in the dim corridor. "I should show you to Ihsan Abi now. Maybe he'll know who threw it. He and Inspector Ali are waiting for you, in any case."

"Black Nizam is buying up Tarlabaşı block by block."

In the narrow corridor lit with a dim red light were three beige doors. The one on the left was wide open, and as such the kitchen with its white furnishings were visible. As for the door immediately opposite, it had been closed up tight as though there were treasure inside and was probably locked. The door at the end of the corridor was slightly ajar. The light that filtered out had formed a long, thin cobalt blue angle on the floor. As I stepped onto the tip of this blue spot, I heard my assistant's voice.

"Couldn't see? The windows are big as donkeys; all you gotta do is stick your head out and the street's right there in front of your eyes."

Ali was in form again, all thunder and lightning.

"He couldn't look out, Inspector. The man's too old."

The speaker's voice was gentle. He wanted to settle things without any trouble. He must have known that golden rule that anybody who wants to exist in the underworld has to keep in mind: Whatever you do, don't get on the cops' bad side.

"I told you, he was trying to put out the fire at that point. It never even occurred to him to look out. And the poor guy didn't know how it started. He thought the tablecloth caught fire from a butt that fell out of an ashtray. He really panicked."

"Okay, so what do you say? Who did this?"

With Flea Necmi's stubby fingers knocking on the door, he had to put off the answer Ali was waiting for.

"Come on in," he said softly.

Necmi opened the door and stepped aside respectfully. I fell into the middle of the blue light. It was like I'd walked into a night club rather than an office. As soon as Ali saw me he ceremoniously stood to his feet. After a moment's bewilderment, the man sitting opposite him took my assistant's lead, an exaggerated smile settled on his face.

"Ihsan," he said, extending a hand. "It's an honor, Chief Inspector."

His thick brown hair had begun to grey around the temples. Eyes the color of cinnamon looked out from under thin eyebrows with superfluous congeniality. He was at least as handsome as Engin. I hadn't actually pictured Dice Ihsan like this. Don't ask me how I'd pictured him, because I couldn't say, but not like this.

"Hello, Ihsan," I said, shaking the proffered hand, which was as soft as a woman's. "Nice place you got here."

My words pleased him and his eyes shone with satisfaction.

"Thanks to you, Chief."

I gave him a look to ask why 'thanks to me' but he didn't catch it. He gestured almost blithely to a leather chair behind a mahogany desk.

"Here, Chief. You come sit here."

Aside from the ordinary bootlicking, he didn't seem anything like the venue owners we were used to. He wore a dark brown suit and a short necktie tied round the collar of a light yellow shirt. He looked more like an insurance salesman than a clubhouse owner. A huge picture behind the desk he'd pointed to screamed out for my attention. A bulldog the dark brown of Ihsan's tie lay sprawled out with five sweet puppies climbing over each other to suckle on the milk-filled teats of its chubby belly. The serenity on the face of this dog, with its sagging cheeks and googly eyes, was worth seeing; the darling picture may have won me over but that didn't mean I was going to sit where Ihsan had indicated.

"That's your chair," I said, adopting the role of understanding cop. "I'll sit opposite Ali."

"I can't let you do that," he tried to insist.

When I ignored him and sat where I wanted, he was forced to concede.

"Okay, Chief. If you say so."

Before settling back into his black leather chair, only slightly larger than ours, he asked, "What'll you have to drink?" demonstrating his intent at unfailing service alongside his unfailing respect. "If you're hungry I can arrange for something."

"No thanks, I just ate. And I had a coffee before I left my house. Maybe later."

"As you wish, Chief." He turned to look at Ali. "What about you? I still can't get you anything?"

"I'm fine like this," our surly friend grumbled. "I've had my fill of tea and coffee today."

Ihsan turned to the pocket-sized Hercules standing in front of the open door. "See that we aren't interrupted, Necmi."

"Sure thing, Ihsan Abi."

As Necmi went out, I eyed our crackpot. He looked like a bundle of nerves. Seems he hadn't shaken off the night's events. Our eyes met.

"How's it going?"

He immediately pulled himself together.

"Fine, Chief. Really good."

No, he wasn't trying to hide it. He'd gotten over the trauma; otherwise he wouldn't have smiled like this.

"Great," I said, my voice compassionate. "Looks like the rest did you some good."

His smile grew, spreading across his face.

"Thanks, Chief."

I looked back at the picture on the wall. Drowsy with contentment, the bulldog continued to nurse her puppies, oblivious to family planning.

"It's our Mualla," Ihsan explained. "The little minx has puppies every year. They're purebreds. We can give you one if you're interested."

"So you like dogs, eh?"

"Love them, Chief." He relaxed and spread his elbows on the table. "Such loyal animals."

The words fell tenderly from his lips, as though petting the dog in the photo, but his fond recollection was interrupted when our obtuse Ali cut in. "Çilem not loyal enough then?"

Ihsan recoiled as if receiving a whopping slap in the face. But it didn't last; he recovered.

"What's it got to do with Çilem?"

"What do you think? The man was killed outside your place. I mean Engin. Çilem was his ex-lover."

He didn't give a damn about Engin's death, but just hearing Çilem's name shook him up. His body slackened and his eyes seemed dreamy.

"Not Çilem, Hacer. Yes, her real name is Hacer," he emphasized unhappily. "Her father used to work with us. 'Machete' Ragip. That was ten years ago. He was my now-deceased father's right hand man. He looked after everything. Then three years ago he got caught in the middle of a street battle. He was shot in the back and ended up paralyzed. From that day on Ragip has been bedridden. He has three children, Çilem and her two brothers. My father and I gave him all the support we could, of course. And that's how I met Çilem." He sighed deeply, relapsing into the old memory. "I took her on, as a secretary. She was a smart girl, and not a bad worker, but then something terrible happened. Right here, yes here in this very room, a gun was mysteriously found in this drawer here. And of course I took the fall for it. I already had an old case against me and I was arrested for possession of an unlicensed firearm. And that's when that maggot Engin seduced the girl. He was an expert at that. When I got out of prison, the situation was explained to me and I sent her packing."

He'd got emotional; was it possible he still loved her? Even if so, my antsy assistant just wanted to solve this murder ASAP and was in no mood to pay tribute to this bygone love.

"That's not what we heard. We heard Çilem went to Nizam of her own free will. That she left you."

The words injured the already wounded Ihsan's pride.

"That's a lie! I sent Çilem away because she was spying for Engin. I think they were seeing each other before I went to jail. She may have even had a hand in that unlicensed gun. Am I that stupid that I would allow an unlicensed gun to be discovered in my club, in the desk in my room no less?"

"So you pummeled the girl?" Ali didn't beat around the bush. He weighed up the clubhouse owner with half-mocking eyes. "No, not you. Let's be fair, you don't seem the type to beat up chicks. Did this little half pint of yours do it? I mean the bulbhead that was just in here?"

I thought he'd deny it but he didn't.

"That was a mistake," he said, regret in his voice. "I was so sorry later. I'm not saying that to absolve myself. Anyhow, what's done is done. Let's just call it a momentary fit of rage."

Ali didn't miss his chance, of course.

"What if these jackals in the other room here were overcome by a 'momentary fit of rage' and killed Engin? Isn't that possible? If the bosses can't control themselves and bust up a young girl's face, what's to say they'd have no qualms sending any man they perceive as an enemy to the next world?"

Ihsan whipped his hands off the table as though he'd touched a hot stove.

"No, they didn't do anything of the sort. If they had, I would know about it. He noticed our still dubious stares. "Or do you suspect me? Come on. Why would I have Engin killed?"

Ali waved his right hand animatedly.

"Ooh, you're looking for a reason? There are heaps. Engin was Black Nizam's man, for one. And Black Nizam is your nemesis. Isn't he?"

"Really, just what is it between you and Black Nizam?" I asked, joining in the amusing banter. "You got on fine to begin with. How did you two sour?"

He didn't immediately answer. With the air of someone betrayed, he leaned back in his chair.

"Nizam was my father's friend, Chief. I didn't know him that well, to be honest. But he did stand by me. Our club used to be in Tarabya, back in my father's day. Four years ago when business started lagging, we came here. I won't deny it; it was Nizam who found us this place. 'Your father was a good man, you're like a nephew to me, blah blah blah,' is how he put it. But you can't judge a book by its cover, so they say. The man's calculations, his intentions, were different. When business picked up, he asked to be a partner. And I didn't accept. Two acrobats can't walk one tightrope. And what's more, Nizam's greediness is legendary. He wants it all to himself and he's a very involved man. He's got a finger in every pie. If you've checked his records you'll know that. From murder to robbery, shady property acquisitions to drugs, there's no dirty business he hasn't dipped his toe into. I loathe drugs, those who use them and those who sell them. But anyhow Chief, when I refused him, all hell broke loose. The threats, the beatings, the shootings outside the club and what not... It didn't work, of course. I wasn't born yesterday. So now he has opened up the Genuine Tarlabaşists Club down there out of spite. And put this Engin in charge."

"And you had Engin killed," said my assistant, hitting the point home.

Dice stared at him with eyes full of innuendo.

"Why don't you think it was the other way round? What if Black Nizam killed him?"

"Why should he?" I said, putting my right elbow on the table. "Why would he want his own man taken out?"

He gave me a look like I still didn't understand.

"Because Engin had his eye on Nizam's place. Yep, he wanted to be boss. That was his intention, to be head honcho. Nizam was his target, not me. That's why he got his hooks into Çilem, as well. To set us at odds. To pit Nizam and me against each other. That way the arena would be left to Engin."

"But Nizam picked up on it," I teased. "And that's why he had Engin killed. Is that what you're trying to say?"

He didn't notice the implication in my voice. He was too excited.

"Yes, exactly! The bastard had his own man killed and tried to pin it on me. Who is Engin to me, anyhow? He's not even my enemy. Grappling with him would be beneath me."

"And yet everyone says a couple weeks back, you two had a fight," I reminded him. "There are witnesses."

His brown eyes narrowed. While he thought about what to say, Ali openly provoked him.

"Not a fight, Chief. More like our friend here beat Engin to a pulp," He glared at Ihsan. "Is that a lie? In fact, you even had another one of your men with you."

He furrowed his brow and his chin trembled in anger.

"For starters, nobody beat up anybody." As he spoke, he got louder. "There were others there besides me and Engin. It shouldn't have happened but it did. We had a go at each other. Well, we've been clubhouse owners for years. We aren't picking apples, for heaven's sake. If things come down to it, we know how to protect ourselves."

The brutal mafia boss underneath the polite words and smart suit was finally coming out. He took a deep breath and tried to calm down but it didn't help; he turned his fiery eyes on me.

"Didn't Cemal Abi call you, Chief?"

"He did," I said calmly. "Really, just how is it you know Cemal?"

He was relieved, if only a little, by my interest in the man who was backing him up.

"He was my father's friend." He was trying to bring his voice back under control. "He was a part of my childhood, Cemal Abi."

"Seems everyone was your father's friend," I said, to stop him getting too comfortable. "What was your father's name?"

"Osman." Seeing no sign of recognition in my face, he clarified. "More often known as 'Dice' Osman."

The name didn't ring any bells, but Ali started to laugh.

"Dice Osman's son, Dice Ihsan. So you're the second generation in the gambling business? Or is it the third? Was there another generation before your dad's? Say, Dice Salman? Seriously, do you have a grandpa like that?"

Ihsan's shiny face went three shades of red. "You're funny, Inspector Ali," he said, overcoming his anger. "I'll tell you something else, although you won't believe it either, but I've never touched dice in my life. That's the god honest truth, Chief. Just ask Cemal Abi if you won't take my word for it. Not dice and not playing cards..."

The man was looking me in the eyes and lying. Knowing full well we were savvy to his lie. He was just incredibly audacious and couldn't see the harm in keeping up the game.

Ali had had enough and was ready to say something but Ihsan continued, cutting him off. "All right, I'll admit my father was a gambler, Chief. He loved the dice. He used to say he couldn't live without the rattle of the things. That's how crazy his addiction was; figure that out. You wouldn't believe the apartments, the land he lost at the tables. My poor mother cried her eyes out. Mine's a little bit of a reaction to that. I swore to her that I'd never gamble. And thank God on high, till this day I have not."

There was no trace of the nervous man from before; an illusionist had come sat in his place. The funny thing was, he believed his own lie. Despite the murder outside the club and the Molotov attack inside it, he'd almost managed to finish the day in peace when our Ali hit him with another reality check.

"Maybe *you* didn't sit at the table, but you sat other folks down there."

Ihsan swallowed again; every time Ali opened his mouth, the blood went straight to Ihsan's head. Still, you had to give him credit, he was stubbornly fighting not to show it.

"What, Inspector? I don't understand."

"You know exactly what I mean," said my assistant, putting an end to the buffoonery. "You yourself didn't play, but you played others, and bled them like chickens."

Ihsan laughed to cover up his rage.

"Listen, Inspector, you're looking at this the wrong way."

I didn't let him continue.

"Actually, you listen, Ihsan," I said, my tone authoritative. "It's no skin off my nose whether you play or not. We're homicide, not the gambling and morality department, understand? And our goal is not to prove whether or not you gamble. It's to find out who murdered an individual by the name of Engin Akça. This is serious stuff. And you know all too well that murdering someone is not in the same ballpark as shooting craps. You can't wriggle your way out of this so easily."

All the cards were on the table now and his face fell. The courtesy was left aside, as were the mask and the tricks.

"I swear on my mother's good name I had nothing to do with it," he said. "It was Black Nizam that set Engin on us. But I had no part in that murder. Not me and not my men."

"So why did you close the club?"

For one minute he thought to lie, but then he realized it would be senseless.

"Damn that cue ball Necmi! He panicked, the animal. They closed down the club and bolted."

"Without asking you?"

He nodded with regret.

"He called. We were celebrating the New Year, though I wish we hadn't been, in the Şiribom Nightclub in Talimhane. How was I supposed to hear my phone with all that commotion?" Again with the pleading voice. "I didn't have Engin killed, I swear it. I told you, they are trying to frame me. And this fire is all part of the conspiracy. You don't realize, there's a massive fight going on here over this land grabbing. Black Nizam is buying up Tarlabaşı block by block." He sniffled as though he were crying and took an imaginary pen in his right hand. "Look, I'm writing it down right here. He had Engin killed. Possibly because of this rentier business. It's all a ruse, Chief. That's why I called Cemal Abi. Otherwise, why would I bother you?"

"To get a guarantee for yourself." Ali could be much harsher than necessary. "You're in cahoots with the police here, yeah? Well, to form a bond with us too."

The club owner nervously threw his hands up.

"No, Chief, I swear it. Why don't you believe me? I'm swearing in God's name."

"Stop waving your hands around," Ali warned. "And don't raise your voice."

He pulled his long neck in. The flicker in his light brown eyes had all but gone out.

"All right. I apologize for any wrongdoing, but I have nothing even remotely to do with this murder."

"Fine, do you know Tidy Tarık?"

First he was startled and then his face took on a thoughtful expression, but he didn't string us along.

"Of course I do. Who doesn't? Everybody in the gambling world knows him. He's a real sicko. A modern hangman. He often stopped by here and I couldn't very well tell him not to. No sense in making more enemies." He went quiet. He looked at Ali, then at me. "He's dead too, isn't he? And now if I tell you I'm not sorry, you'll say I had him killed too."

"Who told you Tidy Tarık was dead?" I turned my suspicious gaze on him. "It happened in the small hours. How'd you hear about it?"

He gently threw his head back as though offended.

"Please, Chief. This is our neighborhood. If a window breaks or a cat is run over on the street, we know about it. The only thing I don't get is why Tidy was in that house."

"Engin was hanging around some innocent-looking, clean-faced girl. She was staying at his house."

"I really have no idea, Chief. A lot of girls came in and out of Engin's house. Who the hell knows which one it was. What's weird is that Tarık was there. They didn't like each other, so what reason would he have to go there?" His bottom lip sagged. "And Tidy's killer wasn't caught, was he? Or did this girl you mentioned kill him?"

Did he really not know Tarık was shot by a cop, or was he pretending? We'd find out, but not now.

"Where did this Tarık live?" I asked, changing the subject.

"He stayed in hotels. A different hotel every night. The man's a hired killer. He hurt a lot of people and he knew one day someone would hurt him too. It wasn't in his best interest to stay at any known address. But he only stayed in hotels he was certain had security cameras at the doors. Nobody wants to shoot anybody in front of those cameras, as you well know."

"Why didn't you have a security camera?"

Ali's question once again put Ihsan in a tight spot.

"What can I say, Inspector Ali?" He swallowed, this clubhouse owner who'd sworn off gambling. "The customers... they didn't want one."

Ali was happy as a cat playing with a cornered mouse. "Why not?"

The other wore a smile that begged understanding.

"We get all types here. Former MPs, retired prosecutors, vice governors... even a former cabinet minister, so help me. People don't want to be filmed."

Ali chortled.

"Funny customers you got. Why are they so shy? You'd think people were gambling here or something. But it's just a clubhouse. At most you've got your bingo, isn't that right? Who gets embarrassed by bingo?"

Ihsan grinned impertinently.

"Of course they're not embarrassed, but what can I say? The customer is always right. Who am I to object?"

"NO! to Tarlabaşı Land Grabbing!"

※

With nightfall, the snow started back up. I shivered as I left the Tarlabaşist's Club. We turned up our coat collars and, watching the white snowflakes blow about in the air, headed down Sakızağacı Street. The urban renewal was well underway; the old apartments and masonry buildings on the boulevard going towards Dolapdere had been evacuated and covered up in sheets of shiny tin. The empty houses that had lost their lights stood silently in the darkness like sick people in quarantine waiting to die.

"Were there Greeks living here at one time, Chief?" asked Ali, peeling his eyes away from the gut-wrenching appearance of the buildings. "Gözde used to be from this neighborhood, didn't she, before?"

I loved the way my assistant asked questions with the genuine curiosity of a schoolchild.

"Yes, Ali. Mostly Greeks, but some Armenians too. In fact, it's not such a rich neighborhood. The people who worked in the shops in Beyoğlu lived here. You know, what we call the working class. The shop owners lived more around Istiklal Avenue, and Tarlabaşı was where the middle class resided."

His brow wrinkled up and his eyebrows furrowed.

"But aren't they foreigners then?"

This simple fact that none of us were able to wrap our heads around had also tested our young inspector's intellect.

"No, they weren't foreigners. They were the honest-to-goodness locals of this area. The roots of our Turkish 'Rum' Greeks trace all the way back to the Romans. These people were already living here when the Ottomans came."

The questioning look in his eye seemed to diminish.

"So they were the ones Sultan Mehmet the Conqueror took the city from?"

"You could say that, although they later became Ottomans themselves. The word 'Rum' that we use for these Turkish Greeks comes from the word 'Rome', in the same vein that Mevlana was called 'Rumi'."

I wasn't sure that he understood, but he nodded meekly and looked back at the buildings.

"Wow. The people who've come and gone," he muttered. He seemed moved. "What lives were lived in these houses, huh? And now they're in the hands of the dregs of society. Dice Ihsan on the one hand, and Black Nizam on the other. It's a crying shame."

"By the way, just what did you think about what Ihsan said?" I asked while I had the chance.

Before answering, he gave it some thought.

"To tell the truth, it struck me as logical. Engin really could have been killed by his own boss. If Nizam found out his man had ulterior motives. And there could have been some jealousy between them. Didn't Harem Süleyman say Çilem had a relationship with the victim? If Nizam also realized..."

It was possible, but there were still some pieces missing. For example, we had no idea what the hitman Tarık was doing in Engin's house. If he were waiting there to kill Engin, which was probably the case, then who was it that hired him?

"And there's this issue of the unfairly acquired properties." My assistant continued with his allegations, steam issuing from his mouth. "Maybe Engin tried to screw Nizam over in their scheme. Maybe that was the last straw."

There were more possibilities than just the ones Ali listed. Enough to confuse us. If we ran after all of them, we risked losing sight of the truth.

"What I don't understand," I said, putting my hands in my pockets, "is how Çilem would have the guts to put that gun in Ihsan's drawer. What is she, the Mata Hari? Isn't she even a little afraid of Ihsan? The men are mafia, after all. How much could a woman be worth in that world? They'd kill her without batting an eye."

My young assistant watched me with an officer's interest, wondering where the conversation was headed.

"Meaning?"

"Meaning I think Dice Ihsan is lying."

He stomped his cold feet on the ground rapidly.

"I don't know about that, but I'm pretty sure the guy is still in love with that woman. Every time the name Çilem was mentioned, his face went all funny. And this thing with her being beaten up really upset him."

He couldn't finish his sentence; a taxi suddenly appeared in the dark street and was bearing down on us. At the last second, we jumped aside and saved ourselves. The yellow cab brushed past the buttons of our dark coats.

"Slow down, you beast!" Ali shouted. "There's people here."

The beast didn't pay him any heed; he just quickly disappeared up the narrow street.

"You see that, Chief? Those are the real murderers. And I didn't get the guy's license..."

As Ali grumbled, looking for any opportunity to have a go at someone, I heard a hum. A melody from the depths. What was this? A folk song, a dirge, an anthem? When I turned to look in its direction, I noticed some silhouettes coming up from the bottom of the hill, walking slowly up from the darkness towards the light. As they approached, I made out a woman at the head of the crowd. She'd left her wavy hair to the wind and was climbing up the narrow street with determined steps. The others kept pace behind her. If by chance the woman stopped, it seemed they would all suddenly be standing still. That's how perfectly congruous they were. The crowd behind her was carrying cloth banners, paper posters and little flags. 'NO! to Tarlabaşı Land Grabbing!' read the dark letters on one of the white cloth banners. Another, with yellow paint on a red background, defiantly stated 'They Can't Have our Bread or our Homes!" They must be the people of the neighborhood who were suffering the consequences of building demolitions, like Cutlets Mehmet, the owner of Zest Restaurant. For a moment my eyes searched for Mehmet among the crowd. Because, you know, shouldn't the man who'd wanted our help in saving his restaurant be at a demonstration like this? I couldn't see him, though. Among all these people and especially in the darkness, it would be very hard for me to pick him out, but even then I really doubted he'd joined in. There was such a thing as 'shopkeeper mentality'. They'd have chosen to solve their problems by pulling strings with influential people. As for these kinds of demonstrations, they always kept their distance. I soon realized just how wrong I'd been in my sentiments. Alongside colorfully dressed transvestites, Kurdish women in white headscarves, and black migrants hurled in from African countries, were greengrocers in blue aprons and butchers in white, barbers, musicians with traditional stringed instruments, violins and clarinets in hand, mechanics, laborers from the workshops where mannequins were made... and all their children.

"Now I understand why that taxi sped by us in such a rage," Ali, caught inside the crowd, grumbled testily. "Waiting behind these protest freaks must've been a royal pain in the ass for the driver."

The people he referred to as 'protest freaks' were those poor people who faced losing their houses, who struggled with the helplessness of not knowing where they would go, where they'd live if they left here. My assistant was looking at them with such bitterness. Why? I'll tell you why, because he compared himself to this hapless lot. Or more precisely, this community of the dispossessed reminded him of himself. Of his solitude and abandonment growing up in an orphanage. That's why he hated them, these people he'd never even met.

"They're blocking the road, Chief. Look at them. As if this street was their fathers' property. I agree with the taxi now. What's he supposed to do, with them pouring onto the street like city bandits?"

I didn't feel like arguing with him, not at this time of night, in this cold, and in this crowd.

106

"Never mind, Ali," I said, patting his shoulder. "Just forget about it. Come on, let's get walking."

He met my request and we began to inch along the side, which was tough going of course. Two girls with purple placards popped out in front of us and we were forced to give way to them.

"This is downright occupation, for god's sake," Ali jeered. "It just won't do. Hey, I'm talking to you. Look, you're impeding your fellow citizens."

The girls must not have wanted to mess with us, so they just passed on by without answering back. But once our 'upholder of the law' got started...

"Well that's just great; go find eighty, a hundred people, and pour into the streets. And they've got their excuses handy. Losing their houses..."

The crowd had begun to shoot daggers, but of course our country's spokesman, who can do no wrong and doesn't give a damn about anything, would soon begin to openly rebuke everyone.

"Stop it, Ali!" I scolded. "That is enough."

Whether he didn't hear me or couldn't get his head around my reaction, he turned to me in surprise.

"What's that, Chief?"

I lowered my voice as much as possible so they wouldn't understand we were arguing.

"I said that's enough. Now knock it off!"

He swallowed and we came eye to eye, but he was so sure of himself that he didn't avert his.

"I'm not doing anything." He was beginning to act like a nitwit again, the inspector. "I don't know what you mean. Are you saying these people are right?"

I cut him off.

"Yes, I'm saying they're right. Put yourself in their shoes. What would you do if you lost your house?"

"I haven't got a house," he said. He smiled wickedly, the lout.

"That's exactly what I'm saying. You should understand these people better than anyone."

He threw his hands up in desperation.

"Don't you see, Chief? It's not about houses and whatnot; these guys' intentions are bad. They're just trying to stir things up. Look at this lot. They're not so innocent."

From this group of not-so-innocents, a woman with a headscarf caught my attention. With a slight limp in her left foot and a five-year-old girl by her side, she was struggling unsuccessfully to keep up with the crowd.

"So that poor little old lady is guilty?" I muttered sarcastically. "Let's take a closer look. Seeing as how you can read people by their faces so easily, maybe you could also tell me what she's guilty of? Don't hold back. Take a good hard look. I hope she's not that serial killer who murdered all those children, this woman wearing summer shoes in the dead of winter. Maybe she's the Eyüp monster who keeps eluding us."

He understood he'd blundered and changed his tune.

"You misunderstood me, Chief. That's not what I meant. I'm not saying everyone here is guilty, but you know what goes on around here. The things our guys went through before we managed to clean out all the criminals. And it's not over. Narcotics can't even come in here without special forces backing them up."

The crowd was beginning to thin. Three young black boys were the last to pass by us. The short one in the middle had a sign with the slogan 'Festus Okay was Murdered by Police' written in huge letters.

"See, what did I tell you?" Ali said, raising his voice again. "Now these guys are all over us, as if we didn't have enough problems already. Whatever drifters and lawbreakers there are, they are all here."

"And whose fault is that?" I said, my voice sterner than I'd meant it to be.

No, he really didn't get it. The police academy desperately needed a class to train our young friends to have more empathy and a better conscience. Unable to find the guilty party, Ali squinted and asked, "Who, Chief?"

I took a deep breath of the cool air in order to gain some calm.

"Okay, so let's rephrase the question: Is it the fault of these poor, powerless people that this neighborhood's becoming a dump, or is it the government who is responsible?"

A light went on in his dark eyes as he'd begun to catch on, but he didn't answer.

"Look Ali, we just came out of a gambling den. We both know plain and simple they are gambling for money. But if our people weren't always turning a blind eye, would Dice Ihsan still be able to sew up Tarlabaşı? Would there be drug gangs holing up in Dolapdere if our guys were determined?"

Listening carefully, he stared down at the snowflakes that melted away as soon as they touched the asphalt.

"No, Ali, you've got it all wrong. These poor people, even children, out here on the street in the snow in wintertime to have their voices heard... They're not the enemy. You're right. This place is a dump. And all right, it's mostly places like this where crime is growing. But these are our people. Even if we don't like them, we have to understand."

I couldn't find the necessary words. My eyes roamed the windows of those faded houses that still hadn't been emptied out.

"What I mean is, in the same way a farmer has to know the soil in order to raise wheat, we have to know these impoverished people really well in order to fight crime. But to assume them guilty from the start would be wrong. They are no different from us. Don't look at me all surprised like that. How many people in the crowd we just passed through are well off, do you suppose? Okay, and how many rich people in our police? How many of our friends say 'actually my dad's got millions but I chase after killers out of curiosity'? What salary are we on, for heaven's sake? Never mind us, how much does a Chief of Police from the upper echelons even make? How much compensation are the families of our martyred officers getting? No, son. You're looking at this all wrong. These people are not to blame. If you are looking to blame someone, you have to go deeper."

I knew I'd gone on a bit too long, or worse, it sounded like I was sermonizing; I'd nagged our boy like a father scolding a child. Anyone else, maybe I wouldn't have cared so much. After all, most of the country shared Ali's mentality. Even though they were exactly the same way themselves. There was nothing I could do for them. But when my closest friend, someone who was like a son to me, made the same mistake, I lost my temper.

Not a single word came from Ali's mouth. Was it out of the respect he had for me? I couldn't say. Was the silence a good sign? I wasn't sure about that either. Had he accepted what I'd said or did this really mean he would never agree with me? It was impossible to understand. For a moment it occurred to me to ask, but then I changed my mind. There was no point in pushing the subject; he had the right to think as he wanted. We stuck our hands back into our coat pockets and, watching the snowflakes whirl about, walked to Engin's house on Kadın Çıkmazı Street.

"Who are these women?"

※

The blood where Tidy Tarık had fallen was darker, taking on a deep rose color. The two of us stared at the dark stain. It spread beyond the white lines drawn to determine where the body had been before its removal a few hours earlier and stretched to our feet.

"I didn't want it cleaned till our work was done, Chief."

Raising my head, I met the tired eyes of our criminologist, who stood planted on the wooden steps.

"Hi, Zeynep."

Her placid face lit up.

"Hi, Chief." That was sufficient for her old supervisor. The real attraction for her was standing next to me. "What's up, Ali? How've you been?"

Our yokel's answer to her loving attention, that sweet voice that would have turned many a male head, was a mere curt, "Fine." He'd pulled his eyes away from the bloodstain, but his expression was still shadowy. So then even seeing Zeynep didn't restore his mood. "I'm fine. You know how it is."

Was he upset about the lecture I'd just given him? I gave him a look out of the corner of my eye to see if we were okay. He caught it.

"It's nothing to do with you, Chief." He looked back at the bloodstain, like a massive carnation on the floor. "I just felt funny coming in here."

111

He was right. It was normal to be affected. But he couldn't keep living with these feelings of guilt, he had to get over it and get on with things.

"That matter is behind us, Ali," I said firmly. "Come on, let's get down to work." I addressed Zeynep again. "Yes, so what have we got?"

Our criminologist was also pleased with my resolute approach. The clouds of worry forming in her brown eyes quickly dissipated.

"Come on up," she said with enthusiasm. "It's all here."

We moved towards the stairs, careful not to tread on the bloodstain. With me in front and Ali behind, we climbed the creaking wooden staircase.

"It's hard to believe Engin wasn't married," Zeynep continued. "The house is so clean, so organized, you would think it wasn't a gambling den bouncer who lived here but some persnickety old woman."

I got the same impression when we came here this morning, but we hadn't looked around the building much due to the corpse lying on the floor. As we got to the step where Zeynep was standing, I explained my hunch.

"Maybe this new girlfriend of his was doing the cleaning. This girl whose name we don't know."

"Maybe, Chief." With agile movements, Zeynep climbed the few stairs in front of her and got to the landing. "But Engin's personal effects were also tidy and everything was filed. It's like the man was an archivist. So much paperwork in the safe, it's surprising."

It looked like I was finally in for some good news.

"You got the safe open?"

A triumphant grin adorned her lips.

"We did, and you were right. The key to the safe was in the *Cevşen* prayer locket hung round Engin's neck. The man was carrying it on him." A mysterious gleam flashed through her dark eyes. "It was that important."

"What came out of the safe?" I asked, as soon as I reached the landing. But Zeynep wanted to savor her victory. With her gloved right hand, she gestured towards a room with a wide open door.

"Come on in. It's all out on the table."

The room she showed us was like a small sitting room. Just like downstairs, it was furnished in an obstinately modern style counter to the old building's character. A machine-made carpet with red and white geometric shapes was spread on the wooden floor. In the middle stood a large table, also red. Yes, whatever the man's tastes, he'd plunked a red table down in the center of the room and two small side tables in the same color. There was a set of furniture consisting of a sofa and two armchairs in beige, and an LCD television on the wall that looked like a black hole.

"The safe was hidden behind the TV, Chief."

I went over to the wall Zeynep was indicating. In the middle of the dingy beige wallpaper was a conspicuous safety deposit box, about one foot high and a foot and a half wide. The cover to the safe was hanging open.

"Look, they made a metal cover for it the color of the wallpaper that opens downward with a light touch.

The television was hung so that it could move back and forth a foot and a half in either direction. Engin could easily open the safe whenever he wanted.

"Who are these women?"

It was Ali who'd asked. He was bent over the table scrutinizing two photos.

"Must be the victim's girlfriends," Zeynep answered. "We know the man was a ladykiller."

I went over to the table, covered in files, deeds, promissory notes and similar documents. I placed my spectacles on the tip of my nose and looked at the photographs sitting side by side on a black notebook. They weren't turning yellow yet. In both photos Engin looked into the camera with the same cold smile, the same expression in his eyes, not revealing his feelings. In both, he had a woman next to him. The woman in the first was younger and prettier, but she had too much makeup and tacky clothes. Yet the look on her face was so innocent it made one want to help her, to protect her. In the photo, her wide black eyes looked shyly out from within the dark mascara.

"This must be his new lover."

"You're right," Ali confirmed. "She fits Cutlets Mehmet's description."

The woman in the second photo was also pretty, if past her prime. Her makeup was understated, her clothes impeccable, her hair quite tastefully dyed platinum blonde, and a peculiar pride could be read in her eyes, which were green or hazel, it was hard to say.

"He was seeing both women at the same time." Zeynep showed him the dates on the digital photos. "Look, both photos were taken last August. There are three days between the dates. I wonder if the women were aware of this?"

I knew what Zeynep was thinking.

"Are you suggesting a murder over jealousy?"

"Why not?"

All three of us looked back at the photo again.

"I don't think so," said Ali, raising his head. "No woman would be bold enough to try and kill a man like this."

Zeynep shrugged.

"Why? We don't know these women. Maybe they're a part of this world, too. Isn't that possible? Okay, let's say the young girl couldn't do it, but this woman? You remember Henna Meryem? You know, the one from the Assyrian murder..."

Ali didn't deem that likely either.

"We'll see." He pointed at the files on the table. "What are those?"

"Deeds." Zeynep picked up the registry on top, opened the blue cover, and laid nine similar documents out in front of us. "Title deeds to nine detached houses in Tarlabaşı, all of them in Engin Akça's name. And all bought within the last six months."

Ali's eyes shone like a miner who'd struck gold.

"Would you look at that! So it was Engin who was buying up Tarlabaşı parcel by parcel, not Black Nizam."

"Maybe he was buying them for Black Nizam," I started to say, when Zeynep interrupted.

"No, Chief. Black Nizam has already bought up a lot of houses here in his own name. Twenty-two deeds with his name on them." She saw us looking around, expecting her to show us those deeds as well, and she smiled. "His aren't here.

114

I found out about it this morning. You told me to look into him? Well, we came up with that info right away."

I gazed at her admiringly and asked, "So who is this Black Nizam then?"

"Your typical modern mafia boss. He's involved in every messy business there is, from mugging to extortion of checks and title deeds and illegally collecting fees in the street parking racket. Dozens of criminal records, dozens of complaints against him: murder, assault, aiding and abetting... He got into drug sales too, for a while. He was even mixed up in a big shipment of heroin that was caught in Naples, although he got off due to a lack of evidence. Tarlabaşı is his latest interest. Maybe his point of contention with Dice Ihsan and the Genuine Tarlabaşists Club is just an excuse, and the real problem is this buy-to-rent land grabbing. Oh, and by the way, his surname is Black. I mean he's Nizam Black, not Black Nizam."

"Black Nizam is more appropriate, in my opinion," said Ali, grinning sweetly. He was beginning to lighten up, the rascal. "It may be that Black Nizam killed Engin over these nine deeds he'd hid from him. Because he was up to something behind his back, just like we talked about on the way here. Or more importantly, to prevent a now rich Engin from overthrowing him and taking his place as boss. I think Dice Ihsan was telling the truth, Chief."

"Yes, Dice Ihsan," said Zeynep, nodding. Ihsan Yıldızeli is his real name. He's a second-class mafia man. He's going the way of his father. And he doesn't just gamble; he employs all manner of tricks and cheating to land rich people in debt at the table, then makes a killing by swiping their property and possessions. And if they don't willingly hand it over, he breaks their legs of course. Ihsan has a pretty long rap sheet as well. He's been in and out numerous times for robbery, assault and battery... the usual abuses. However, he never got messed up in other business. His crimes were all gambling related."

I turned to look at the documents on the table again.

"What else was there in the safe?"

Zeynep took a bordeaux passport out from under the blue file.

"Well, there's Engin's passport. He came into Turkey two years ago." She flipped through its pages with her long, gloved fingers. "He lived abroad for years, mostly in Italy. There are heaps of entry stamps for Italy, but the exit stamps are mostly from Switzerland."

So he'd been in Turkey two years then. "He hasn't been back to Italy?" I asked, to make sure.

"No, Chief. He hasn't left the country in two years. Not to Italy or any other country."

"You saying it was drug trade?" Ali had caught on to my line of thinking.

"Why not? His connection with Black Nizam could be drug related as well. The man was shipping drugs to Naples by freighter. Maybe Italian narcotics police had started to watch him and so he escaped to Turkey and joined Black Nizam. Perhaps Nizam proposed hiding Engin in return for a partnership in his drug business."

Zeynep was still skeptical.

"It's possible of course, but the drug shipments to Naples were three years ago. Since then, Black Nizam hasn't been accused of anything drug related. It seems like he never got involved in that business again. And then there's this, Chief." From under the blue file, she took a straw-yellow A4 sized envelope, removed another photo and a white sheet of paper with drawings on it, and held it out. "There's a diagram and a third woman's photo inside."

My eyes slid to the photograph first: a woman, her wavy hair spilling onto her shoulders, her determined eyes looking out from beneath sculpted eyebrows and a wide forehead, and behind her, people..."

"It's that woman, isn't it?" Ali launched in excitedly. "Yeah, that woman walking in front of the crowd just now..."

I squinted. It was the same woman leading the demonstration, all right.

"Must have been taken at another protest," I agreed. "And there's a banner."

He stuck his nose into the photo. "Yep. It was taken at a protest... It's the same banner we saw today. Look Chief, it says 'No to the Tarlabaşı Land Grab'."

116

However close I looked, I couldn't make out the letters.

"I see the word Tarlabaşı but I'm not so sure about 'land grab'. Still, you're right; it has to be a protest rally. Do you see the anger in the people's faces?"

Zeynep got curious and was also trying to see the photo and that's when the two young people's hair touched. My assistant immediately pulled his head back and grumbled as he tried to hide his excitement.

"Okay, but what is this woman's photo doing here at Engin's?"

I turned to look at the white paper in Zeynep's hand.

"You say this is a diagram? Can you see what it's for?"

"Yes. It's a building. The entrance doors, windows, a fire escape that was added, and the back service door... The building's name is written here, too. She looked down at the paper to make sure she hadn't misspoken. "Ferhat Çerağ Culture Center. Look. It's the building on the corner of Sakızağacı and Tavla."

It was only a few streets away. We would have passed by it on our way here.

"Ferhat Çerağ Culture Center," Ali murmured. "That must be where the group gathered a bit ago. Yes, there's bad blood between them, Chief. The woman's obviously putting a spanner in the works. Probably they were thinking to scare her. Or maybe kill her? Maybe Engin called Tidy Tarık to his house for that."

I pulled a face.

"Nobody calls a hired killer to their house, Ali. Least of all someone embroiled in this business like Engin was. Not to mention Tarık had just got to the house when we arrived. You'll remember the door was ajar..."

That's when we noticed the police officer coming up the wooden stairs. It was the fat one of the two cops on duty at the door. Even climbing these few steps had worn him out, the poor guy.

"There's a man here, Chief," he said, trying to control his breathing. "He wants to come in. I said he can't, but he's insisting. He wants to talk to you."

Dear lord, who could this be? It couldn't be our Swank Cemal?

"What's his name?"

"Nizam... Nizam Black. He was friends with the victim."

"If you don't want to give the angel of death ammunition, you have to limit the number of loved ones you have in this world."

✳

If the glory in ugliness were to be explained, I suppose it would be enough to show the face of Black Nizam. He had dyed black hair, spiky as a hedgehog and reaching half way down his narrow forehead, two thick briar patches for eyebrows, beady black eyes eddying in their deep pools, a flattened, small aubergine of a nose, a shapeless mouth like an incision transecting his face, and skin as pockmarked as a stony field. In the middle of all that were his unaccountably contrasting stark white teeth, smooth as pearls. His sparkling smile. The man grinned, and was no longer ugly or repulsive.

"What'll you have to drink?" he asked with propriety. "The Turkish coffee here is excellent. Even better than Mandabatmaz's."

It was quite an assertion. By far the best coffee I'd drunk to date was at Mandabatmaz in Olivia Çıkmazı. And that was even better than what Evgenia made. Still, best not to be biased.

"All right then, let's have one of your coffees, black."

"Nothing for me," my assistant put in before Nizam asked.

Just under Kadın Çıkmazı Street, at an intersection between long crooked streets and shorter squat ones, we settled into the best seats of the coffeehouse, which looked onto a small, squalid open area. Eight people at two tables, one group playing rummikub, the other spades, were the only other customers. The chubby waiter took our coffee orders and, as he made his way back to the hunchbacked cook at the stove, I thought of those days I'd served in Anatolia. This unkempt, haphazardly organized space reminded me of the public squares of forgotten Anatolian towns. There was a grocery store, a barber, a carpenter that made cheap furniture, a hardware store which wasn't reluctant to display its goods outside on the pavement, a string of intercity coach ticket offices with names no one had ever heard of, and of course this requisite place for men to doze off, the large coffeehouse that was the center of it all. We'd come to this place at my request, rather than at the insistence of the ugly old tough guy with the beautiful smile. It wouldn't suit to let Black Nizam and his two nephews into Engin's house.

In the chair just opposite mine sat Black Nizam. He leaned back against the brown wall, where a massive photo of barren slopes and whatever gushing river graced their homeland hung, and attempted conversation. As for Ali, he sat in a chair to my right, in such a way that he could see both the door and the two guards. Nizam's nephews, who were also his protection, sat at the table to our left, their faces turned away from us. The two swarthy brothers were the spitting image of each other. And when I say spitting image, it's no exaggeration. The two nephews, Medet and Kudret, were actual twins. If that weren't bad enough, they wore identical dark green anoraks with fur-lined collars. The sight of them was beyond funny, yet the way they sat there so serious made it impossible to laugh.

"We've never had the good fortune of meeting before," said Nizam, continuing the conversation. "Our office was in Laleli when you were stationed here. But I know you by reputation through Cemal. Swank Cemal, that is, he talked about you the most. Our relationship has soured a bit I'm afraid. But anyhow, he used to tell me 'Chief Inspector Nevzat is nothing like the other police you know'."

Petite as a woman's but hairy as an ape's, his hands fidgeted on the sky blue tablecloth as he spoke, like two furry prehistoric animals.

"How did you hear I was heading this investigation?"

My voice had come out cold and suspicious.

"Tarlabaşı's a small place, Chief," he said almost pertly. "This is our neighborhood. If a window breaks or a cat is run over, we hear about it..."

I couldn't stop myself laughing.

"Dice Ihsan used that exact line," I explained. "Word for word... Must be a popular catchphrase in Tarlabaşı these days."

It turned the color of charcoal, that uncontrolled face of his. I must have hit a raw nerve.

"He got it from us, the crook. And to think we were the ones that got that murderer into Tarlabaşı."

I was on the right path. I had started to rile him.

"Murderer?" I repeated, emphasizing my ignorance. "Who did Ihsan murder?"

He pulled his furry hands quickly from the table.

"As if you don't know. Who do you think? Engin..." He looked from me to Ali then grunted with helplessness. "Of course, he had Cemal call you. To cover up the murder... Swank Cemal, I mean. They're thick as thieves. His father, Osman, was a close friend of Swank Cemal's. When Osman was on death's door, Cemal promised him he'd look out for his son. Now, whenever his back is against the wall, the punk wastes no time knocking on Cemal's door."

"What do we care about Cemal?" Ali reamed. "You think we're taking requests for who the killer is and will decide from that?"

"No, please," our modern marauder pleaded, not expecting to be slapped down. "You got me wrong, Inspector. I mean, you wouldn't, but that bastard..."

He couldn't have made my assistant listen if his life depended on it.

"This is a formal investigation we're conducting here," he retorted. "So keep the 'bastard' comments to yourself."

Nizam sat up straight in his chair.

"Excuse me. I meant no disrespect, but it's obvious Ihsan is lying to you."

Ali was having a field day.

"So what you're saying is we're idiots, we don't understand, and you need to show us the way?"

What could the man say now, I wondered.

"No, Chief, I'd never be so bold. I thought I might be of help."

I stepped in with my calm, almost sympathetic approach.

"What makes you think Dice killed Engin?"

He appeared to relax. He put his hands back on the table, though his fingers kept fidgeting.

"Engin beat the living daylights out of him, that's what. He couldn't show his face in public for days. And not so long ago, just ten, maybe fifteen days is all."

I feigned interest, as though I were hearing it for the first time.

"Why? Why would Engin beat up Ihsan?"

He glanced over at our crackpot to make sure he wasn't out of line again before hungrily launching into an explanation. "Engin had a lover. Jale Hanım... Very polite. Rich, too. This lowlife Ihsan was talking shit about Engin. Calling him a dog, a scumbag, a disgrace and so on. So the woman left Engin. It hurt him, of course. And I won't lie; he didn't go alone." He nodded his head towards his two nephews at the next table. "He took Medet and Kudret with him. Believe it or not, the thrashing they gave Ihsan right there in front of everyone was so bad, if it were me I'd never show my face in public again."

I took out the evidence bag I'd brought with me from the victim's house and placed it on the table. I showed him the three separate photos of the three women, who stared out at us from under clear plastic.

"Which one is Jale?"

As he went to pull them in front of him, his hand slipped inside the bag.

"Better not touch those photos," I warned him.

His hand hung there.

"You can touch the outside of the bag; I'm just telling you not to take the photos out. We haven't dusted for prints yet."

His face drew taut with doubt like he was expecting an unpleasant surprise, but he didn't balk at pulling the evidence bag over. His eyes settled on the photo of the woman we'd seen among the demonstrators.

"This one's not Jale, it's Nazlı. Crazy Nazlı. The woman who heads the anarchists. They have some buildings just up here and are doing everything in their power to stir up trouble. Fighting with cops, occupying buildings, threatening average citizens and assaulting them... And they're not afraid of anyone. Not the government, not the people, not even God. They're on the streets day and night, bottles of gasoline in their hands. Burning and busting things up whenever they get the urge."

By gasoline bottles he undoubtedly meant Molotovs.

"Just a minute," my assistant butted in. "You mean to say it was this woman Nazlı's gang that attacked Tarlabaşist's Club and not you?"

His tiny eyes grew wide with surprise.

"They attacked Dice's joint?"

"Don't try to tell me you didn't hear about it," Ali grumbled.

"I didn't. I'll swear on whatever you ask me to, but I really didn't know."

A mocking expression appeared on my assistant's handsome face.

"What happened to knowing if a window breaks in your neighborhood? Some men throw a Molotov in broad daylight and you are completely oblivious to it? How does that work?"

Nizam looked embarrassed. With the impotence of a man who had failed to carry out his duties, he struggled to explain.

"I was out of Istanbul for a few days, in Uludağ, for personal reasons. I actually planned to stay longer, but naturally I came running back when I heard about Engin. I've only been back in Tarlabaşı a few hours now. That's why it's news to me. Still, I'm telling you, if there's a Molotov or anything involved, it'll be the work of this Nazlı."

Ali wasn't going to let it go of course.

"That's not what Dice is saying."

"Of course it isn't," Nizam exploded, without waiting for the end of the sentence. "He's covering up the murder he committed."

The argument was about to go off the rails.

"Anyhow, let's move on," I said, pointing to the second photo in the bag as I tried to bring things back under control. "Is this Jale?"

But Nizam was charged up and kept grumbling as though he hadn't heard me.

"No, let's not move on, Chief. Who knows what that miscreant has been saying about me."

"We'll get back to that, Nizam." It was the first time I'd raised my voice. Even the two nephews turned to look. "But first answer the question. Is this Jale Hanım?"

He shied away as though trapped.

"That's Azize," he said, looking at the photo. His voice was tight, his speech choppy and terse. "She's a good girl. A *konsomatris* or umm... nightclub hostess. She sings, too."

"Where is she hostessing, Azize?"

"At the Neşe Pavyon... I say *pavyon*, but it's more of a dive than a nightclub, actually. Azize is the only flower in that dump."

There was a twang of sarcasm in his last remark.

Would Ali let the opportunity slip?

"So you are belittling the girl because she's ugly?"

He caught the implication and his face turned red.

"Perish the thought, Inspector! I'd never belittle any of God's creatures. And anyhow, Azize is not exactly ugly. What I mean is... Forgive me, Chief, but you know how some women have that way about them, that stops you in your tracks? The girl doesn't have that. You can't tell if the poor thing's a woman or a child. Chest like a board, all skin and bones... Okay, her voice is kind of nice. Not nice, but touching. But just for her voice..?"

"Apparently, Engin doesn't share your sentiments."

"He had some strange tendencies, your deceased." He shook his head mournfully as if remembering. "Actually, the ladies loved him. He was a good-looking bloke. He made the rounds with a number of women and girls. I didn't know most of their names even. But he was stuck on this Azize. He took an interest in her that he never took with the others. Affairs of the human heart are such a mystery."

So now we'd found the lover with the innocent face, but we needed details.

"Was the girl living in Engin's house?"

He seemed to find the question odd.

"Engin lived alone. He didn't want anyone around. He was used to living alone, from Switzerland."

This business abroad was another point that needed clarifying, but I asked about the woman in the last photo so as not to get off topic.

"Okay, so who is this?"

"That..." He tapped the photo twice with a stumpy index finger. "...is Jale Hanım. The woman who drove a wedge between Engin and Ihsan."

"We didn't hear it like that." Ali took the stage again, with that uncompromising attitude. "It was Çilem who drove a wedge between them, not Jale."

The moment Nizam heard Çilem's name, his dark face went white as a sheet. But he knew how to control himself and he held his tongue.

"What's wrong? Cat got your tongue? Don't you know Çilem?"

The lines on his narrow forehead folded into layers but he didn't avoid the question.

"I know her," he said, with utmost solemnity. "Not Çilem, Hacer... Hacer Hanım, she's my wife."

It was our turn to be bowled over. Nobody had said anything about any marriage. Was Nizam lying? He certainly didn't seem to be. He'd dropped that smarminess he'd maintained from the start and was extremely convincing. He was giving my assistant a defiant stare as if to say he wasn't afraid of him. His glorious ugliness was for the first time daunting, but Ali had met dozens of men like this in his occupational life and he didn't even react.

"Of the unrecognized religious type, by imam?" he asked, making no concessions in his mockery. "How many wives have you got?"

"One." His eyelashes flicked, his eyeballs completely disappeared into his sockets and his gruff voice sounded ready to explode. "How many wives can one man have?"

Thanks to his raised voice, his nephews also noticed the tension between us and their right hands slid slyly down towards their waists, supposedly without our noticing. They were trying to limit the distance between their fingers and their guns. Naturally, our rascal also understood the situation, though he didn't care. He relished these dangerous moments.

"Any normal human being would have one, of course," said Ali, continuing to needle him. "But nowadays some individuals take four wives, thinking that makes them real men.

"Well, I'm not one of them." Nizam leaned back. His left hand was still on the table but his right hand, like those of his nephews, had gone gently down to where we couldn't see it.

"Congratulations," I said respectfully. There was no sense getting into unnecessary conflict with the men. "May God grant you a long, healthy marriage."

These were not words Nizam was expecting to hear. The lashes of his squinty eyes parted and his eyeballs reappeared, although only as thin flames. He weighed the words over and in the end believed them.

"Thank you, Chief."

It was plain to see that he wanted no trouble with us either.

"You must have got married quite recently."

The icy look on his face melted and he nearly laughed.

"We got married yesterday." He'd forgotten the unpleasantness between us and his tense face grew emotional. "Yep, just yesterday. In Uludağ. As I said, if they hadn't killed Engin, we would have stayed longer."

Just when I thought calm had been restored, Ali's words shook up the table again.

"I know I shouldn't ask, but what number wife is this?"

Nizam shot my assistant a look that said he was out of line.

"That's none of your concern. My personal life is none of your business." He turned ambitiously to me. "I have plenty of respect for you, Chief, but if you two carry on like this I'll be forced to continue the conversation with my lawyer present."

He was right, but I wasn't about to reprimand my assistant in front of him.

"It's not our aim to offend you, Nizam. You're right; your personal life is your business. The questions the inspector is asking are to do with the murder. We have no intention of judging your relationships, and anyhow we have no authority to. Also, what we hear at this table stays at this table, so long as it's not related to the murder that is. Even then, it won't be leaked to the media. You have my word of honor."

He stared at me a bit with hesitant eyes. I saw an opportunity in his silence and asked in a friendly voice, "Is Hacer Hanım really your first wife?"

I'd touched a sore spot again. I thought he would get up and go, but he pointed to his side pocket. "Mind if I smoke?"

"Makes no difference to me. It's the cafe owner who pays the fine."

He let out a small, strained laugh.

"Don't you worry about it, Chief. This is our turf."

From the pocket he'd indicated, he removed a silver cigarette case and a gold lighter. He took his own sweet time opening the lid of the case. As he pulled out a cigarette, a brand I couldn't distinguish, I read the inscription inside the lid. 'I'm yours till the angel of death takes me.' Underneath it was written 'Hacer'. Must be the fresh wife's wedding present. He nestled the cigarette between thin lips and lit it with the gold lighter. The smell of burnt tobacco all at once filled the air.

"My first wife was Kamer Hanım," he said, blowing smoke out of flattened nostrils. "She was my uncle's daughter, and the marriage was arranged while we were still in the cradle. We grew up in the same village. But we got married in Istanbul. I was nineteen when we got hitched, and she'd just turned sixteen." He took another puff on his cigarette. The marriage lasted three years, then there was an accident and Kamer died. He rocked heavily in his chair as if he still felt the pain. What can you say? It was God's will; things just worked out that way. I didn't marry anyone after that." He looked straight into my eyes. "If you don't want to give the angel of death ammunition, you have to limit the number of loved ones you have in this world. No woman, no child. And that's the way it's been till today. Then I met Hacer. Nothing was further from our minds but..." He smiled sheepishly. "It just happened."

"Why Hacer?" I asked immediately, so as not to give Ali a chance to rock the boat again. "How was she different

127

from the other women? Did she look like your first wife or something?"

He took another drag.

"No resemblance, actually. But for some reason, she does remind me of Kamer. I loved her... It isn't easy to forget. God gave me a second chance with Hacer."

The conversation had reached a delicate place. I had to choose my words carefully.

"So Ihsan..." I began to say.

"That bastard has no part in it," he said, getting angry. "Hacer comes from a poor family. Her father Ragip was working for them. Maybe you heard he was crippled after a fight? When the family got strapped for cash, well, a drowning man will clutch at a straw, and they went knocking on Dice Ihsan's door. How should they know the man had ill intentions?" He didn't go into more detail. "Anyhow, let's just say it was *kismet*. In the end we got what was ours."

He made it sound like the subject was closed, but remembering how Ihsan's face turned color every time Çilem was mentioned, I couldn't help thinking there was more to it.

"I understand," I said, appearing grateful. "So, when did Engin join you here?"

Before answering, he turned to his nephews.

"Medet, son, take this and throw it outside." He was showing the cigarette butt he'd been ashing on the floor. "We shouldn't dirty up the place." Medet snatched the butt with incredible agility. As Nizam watched his nephew move towards the door, he started to talk about Engin. "I met his uncle Durdu Abi before that. I won't lie to you. Durdu Abi was dealing in powder. Selling drugs, I mean. And not just on the side, he was doing big business... Very big. He was partners with an Italian mafia. The guys were from Sicily, although they were based in Milan."

"And you got wrapped up in that business. They even opened an investigation on you..." Ali slapped him in the face with the info he'd got from Zeynep. "You were smuggling drugs by ship."

"Lies, blatant lies... We were cheated in that business. We got our fingers burnt a bit, no thanks to Durdu Abi. But he's

128

done us plenty of favors, too. Anyhow, it's a long story. Luckily, justice won out and in the end we were acquitted." He turned his lentil eyes on me again. "I don't like drug users any more than I like pushers. I don't even condone marijuana, Chief. I've punched up a lot of young boys for smoking weed on these streets."

This ode to innocence would continue indefinitely if I didn't intervene.

"Was it Engin's uncle who got him into this business?"

"Sure. Durdu was the reason Engin was in Europe. Engin's mother died and his father remarried. Durdu had no sons so he took Engin in. He was about ten then. He rose through the ranks there, I mean. He was fluent in Italian, German and English. Durdu was a sharp cookie; he kept Engin aside. He didn't want to waste him, because he was going to con the foreigners and declare his own kingdom. But the Italians didn't bite. They weren't born yesterday either, and they were onto him straight away. They lost Durdu about three years back. Yes, Chief, one night Durdu disappeared. His body was never even found. After that they started polishing off the men one by one. Engin barely escaped with his life. He made for Turkey with no more than his jacket and a bag. He came to us afraid, and badly shaken. What could we do? Durdu was like a brother to us; there was a respect. And we don't turn away anyone in trouble, so we had to open our door."

The Italian mafia brought something else to mind.

"Couldn't these foreigners have killed Engin? I mean this drug mob?"

Nizam shook his head with certainty. "They wouldn't go to all that trouble for Engin. And anyhow, they'd sent their message loud and clear. Europe is out of bounds for you and you'll stay in your own country from now on."

"Who delivered that message?"

"Durdu's old team. Engin's relatives and whatnot... Some of them began to work for the Italians. Life is cruel, Chief. Bosses change, but the work never does."

I thought of the hitman in Engin's house.

"Do you know Tidy Tarık?" I asked. "He was waiting in Engin's house this morning with a gun in hand."

There wasn't the least sign of surprise on his face.

"I heard about it. Tarık is the quintessential hired dog. He worked for whoever paid him. But I doubt the Italians hired him. They wouldn't have touched Engin so long as he stayed in Turkey. Why should they stir up trouble for nothing?"

"What if Engin was thinking of leaving the country?" Ali said, voicing another possibility. "If Durdu has money somewhere, or a cache of drugs?"

He gently threw his head back.

"He hasn't got that kind of money, not drugs either... If he did I would know; Engin told me all about it. Whatever there was, the men took it. And anyhow, Engin was happy with life here. He wouldn't want to rock the boat, so why should he go abroad?"

"What was he doing with his life here?" I chided. "How was he helping you? In the construction business?"

"Construction..." He sized me up, not sure how much I knew. "Oh, you mean these new buildings that are going up in Tarlabaşı? It wasn't just that. Engin was our right-hand man. Our work is varied, Chief. We have two galleries, car rentals, there are three hamams and one sauna, even five kebab shops... One of which is in Ipek Street, in fact. You should stop by. Genuine Gaziantep chefs..."

My assistant, somehow managing to keep his mouth shut for a while, couldn't handle any more of this slackening investigation.

"Engin was up to something behind your back. He'd bought a bunch of buildings in Tarlabaşı."

"What?" He seemed genuinely surprised. "He bought some buildings?" His face fell as though he'd been betrayed but he couldn't speak ill of his dead friend. "Engin wouldn't do that. Is that what Ihsan told you?"

"We saw the title deeds."

He was listening in disbelief.

"Yes, they were all in Engin's name. Maybe he was putting the money Durdu left him to good use."

He looked confused. He started to recount bits of information he should have kept secret.

"He couldn't have accessed Durdu's money. He'd have to go to Switzerland for that. The Italians would've shot him down before he could step foot there. He tried before but he didn't succeed. He had to hightail it out of there. Without that money, he couldn't have bought a shanty in Şırnak, let alone a whole building in Tarlabaşı."

Ali grinned with the pleasure being right had given him.

"But he did buy them."

Nizam was desperately clinging to his belief in his friend; perhaps he couldn't handle being deceived.

"No, I doubt it. Those deeds are fakes. That crook Ihsan was up to something." His eyes were twitching in their dark sockets. "Yes, Ihsan is definitely up to no good." All at once, he enthusiastically put in, "That's it! First he had Engin killed. Then he forged those deeds and put them where you would see them intending to make it look like Engin had betrayed me, to create an atmosphere like there was some issue between us. That way there would be a motive for me to kill Engin. Or at least you would think so. You do see how these guys manipulated everything, don't you?"

He looked like he believed what he was saying. For a moment I wondered if it was true. Could Ihsan really have planned all this? There was no sense puzzling over it. It would be enough to just check the deeds.

"We'll see, Nizam," I said, as the chubby waiter brought our coffees. "If you're right, it'll make things easier, but don't leave town for a few days."

"I couldn't even if you ordered me to, Chief. They murdered my friend, don't forget. We have a funeral to go to, and we won't be able to get on with life till we see Engin laid to rest."

"Okay then. But Hacer shouldn't leave town either. We'll get her statement, too."

He screwed up his face but didn't object.

"What can I say, we get what we deserve."

"By the way," I said, congenially patting the tiny fingers of his hairy hand before taking a sip of my foamy coffee. "Where is this Neşe Pavyon where Azize works?"

"It's easy, Chief. It's on the main drag... In line with all the beer halls, just past where the old bus stop used to be. You go down a short stairway." He gave me a hopeless look. "But what use will the girl be to you?"

He'd put the question out there to pry some information from me, but I ignored it and took another sip of coffee. I still didn't know what to make of Black Nizam. It was hard to discern if he was one of those old hands with sharp intuition who was always on the make, or a just a friendly old tough guy trying to help us find his friend's murderer. At least one thing I knew he wasn't lying about anyhow, the coffee sure was good.

"Why are you pulling a gun if you haven't got the balls to fire it..."

✳

The snow kept unperturbedly coming down with its same lethargy and sluggishness. The light reflected from the beer halls, nightclubs, and dive bars outside the construction sites on the boulevard painted the snowflakes all different colors, but even this sight wasn't enough to allay the despondency that held sway over the street. In fact, the evening patrons had already filled the boulevard, irrespective of the white that blanketed the surroundings and the ever-increasing cold. When compared to Istiklal Avenue, the poor wretches in this place who suffered the blows of misfortune - the wan bodyguards, cunning waiters, women selling themselves and their hungry clientele, nimble drug pushers and sticky-fingered pickpockets, corner boys collecting money from pedestrians, lackadaisical drunkards and earlybird customers - were traipsing about every which way in front of watering holes and so-called entertainment venues as if trying to keep the snow from sticking. We suddenly found ourselves in the middle of a brawl. Just up the road in front of us three people had laid into each other, hooting and hollering, all profanity and pandemonium.

"Isn't that your old mobster?"

Ali was pointing at a burly man trying to land a punch on the two young boys circling round him like hungry wolves. The falling snow was blurring the scene and I couldn't quite

133

see. As we rushed ahead to pull them apart, I recognized him. Yes, it was Harem Süleyman. The boys he was fighting weren't exactly afraid and they were quite agile as well, but he was holding his own against them. Right up until the youth with the tattered silver anorak hoisted up a keg from where it sat at the door of a tavern and brought it down on Süleyman's back. Süleyman was in a bad way; he tottered on his feet. Seizing the opportunity, his opponent was about to bring the keg down a second time when the practiced old mobster dodged it with a dexterity not to be expected from his hefty frame. When the swung keg didn't find its target, his opponent stumbled forward. Our daredevil swung a hard blow, which I thought wouldn't stick, but it perfectly landed its mark. The boy toppled to the pavement with a thud as if his head had been struck by a sledgehammer. The keg rolled one way and he rolled the other. After witnessing the fate of his friend, the other youth went for him. Süleyman grabbed his attacker's fist in mid-air, with his left hand no less. He started to crush the fist in his palm like a toy. He was a head taller than the boy and at least three times his size. When faced with his enemy's massive bulk, the terrified youth tried in vain to liberate his hand. Then something else happened that we didn't see coming. The kid in the anorak quickly picked himself up and grabbed the keg again, bringing it down on Süleyman once more. It seemed the wind was knocked out of him and his fingers went slack. The constrained boy used the opportunity to free his fist from the titan's clutch and made a run for it. Süleyman turned to the one with the beer barrel now raised up in both hands, but he must not have fully recovered because he couldn't stop the kid from bringing it down again. Thankfully the boy's aim was off, and on impact the barrel, which he barely had a hold on anyhow, came out of his hands and rolled to the ground. Süleyman stared at him as if to say, *let's see what you're going to do now*. The defeat in his opponent's face was a sight to see. After a brief pause he did the smart thing and, like his friend, satisfied himself with spinning on his heels to hightail it out of there. Süleyman didn't have the energy to chase after him, but it didn't look like the hatred in his eyes was going to burn out any time soon either. With the skill of years of experience, he stuck his hand into his coat and pulled out a hunting knife equally quick.

"Don't!" I shouted, but he didn't hear me and he hurled the knife ambitiously at the youth. The child did hear me, thank heavens, and unwittingly threw himself to the ground. The knife flew past one handbreadth above him and stuck into a wooden sign on the curb. 'Our wigs are just like real hair' the sign read. The kid saw the sharp instrument quivering there and stayed motionless a moment as though his blood had frozen. Then he turned to Süleyman, the hate in his opponent's eyes now spread to his, and he reached a hand towards his waist. He tried a couple times, but whatever it was he wanted to take out was caught and he couldn't manage to free it from the garment. In the end, he succeeded, and turned a small pistol on Süleyman.

"Now you're fucked!"

Süleyman wasn't the least bit scared; who knew how many times he'd stared down the barrel of a gun in his nearly half a century of life.

"You'd better shoot, or you'll be the one who's fucked," he said, walking towards the gun. The anger in the boy's eyes gave way to uncertainty, then apprehension, and then fear. The gun he held began to tremble. Of course it didn't escape our old wolf's attention.

"Go on, shoot! Why are you pulling a gun if you haven't got the balls to fire it, you little shit?"

"Enough!" I shouted. "Stop it already!"

With my warning, my assistant also pulled his gun and aimed it at the boy. Süleyman paused and stared at us in surprise, wondering where the hell we'd come from. I took the opportunity to turn to the adolescent, shaking in his boots despite the gun in his hand.

"Drop your weapon. Now."

The boy was still wavering, uncertain who we were.

"Police!" Ali elucidated, gripping his pistol with both hands. "Throw the gun down."

Relief replaced the fear in the boy's face. With no more deliberation, he dropped the metal to the pavement.

"Good boy," my assistant said, picking up the gun. "You did the right thing. You were going to get yourself killed."

I turned towards the giant who was preparing to march on the kid again.

"Steady, Süleyman. You need to stop now."

The old tough guy swallowed his rage and put his right hand over his heart.

"Sure, Chief. Whatever you say." Despite his concession, he couldn't suppress the anger raging inside him. And as such, he couldn't help yelling at the fledgling taking cover behind my assistant.

"Thank your lucky stars for the Chief here, you little shit, or I would have shoved every last bullet in that gun down your throat."

I stood in front of him and shook my head with finality.

"All right, Süleyman. Don't drag this out."

He stopped and bowed his head.

"I won't, Chief. I'll stop now, but I'm not to blame here. It was this dirtbag that started it all. And this little hoodlum."

I turned to look where he was pointing. A few yards beyond in the crowd that had gathered stood the other young man who'd broken loose and got away.

"You're the dirtbag," he yelped, keeping in the crowd. "How many times did we tell you not to stand that woman there?" He pointed towards the cell phone shop at the top of the street. "He's hustling his woman in front of our store. All these shop owners are witnesses."

But nobody made a sound. He lost his hope in the crowd and realized he would have to fix his own problem.

"This place is our bread and butter, Chief. The woman is planted there from ten in the morning, every single morning... It tarnishes the street. We can't make any money. Our father opened up the shop." He pointed to his fighting partner, standing next to Ali. "My brother and me... My father is a *hadji*, so he can't come to the shop." His whole body was shaking, as was his voice. "We asked her to stand somewhere else. We got a mediator, sent a message... We pleaded but he wouldn't listen."

"That's right," Süleyman interrupted. "I didn't listen. I shrugged it off and didn't give a shit. This is my neighborhood, twit, you understand? I've been here a hundred years. You think you can chase me away over your meager thousand lira rent?"

It'd be wrong for me not to warn him.

"Careful what you say, Süleyman. The street doesn't belong to anyone."

"Okay, Chief. If that's what you say. Whatever the penalty is, I'll accept that, too. But these bastards' case is with me. What are they doing beating up on a defenseless woman?"

At the words 'defenseless woman', he turned to look towards the old bus stop. That's when I saw his wife Naciye, staring out blankly, with neither anger nor shame, just like the night before in the restaurant. One side of her black coat was muddy from top to bottom, but she herself just stood there under the falling snow as if outside of what she'd been through, outside time, outside of her entire life like a tree beginning to dry up.

"By the time I heard her voice they were kicking, Naciye, Chief." He sounded a bit sharper as he explained. I was in Sarı's meyhane and, sorry to be so blunt, but I'd gone to the WC. I mean I wasn't aware what was happening. Sarı's baby-faced waiter called out to me to come quick. That they were going to kill Naciye. And I came flying out. You should see how they were hitting her. If I hadn't got there, she would have been pummeled. That's how relentlessly, barbarically, they were hitting her, the sleazebags..."

Ali was the most affected by his words; he hated men who raised a hand against women.

"Were you going to kill her, huh?" he thundered, as though he was the one fighting the youth.

The kid taking refuge in the crowd averted his eyes. If he weren't so ashamed, he'd have melted into the crowd. Because he couldn't, he made do with hanging his head. My assistant turned his furious glare onto the big brother who stood next to me. "I'm talking to you. Were you planning to kill her?"

The flustered boy tried to recover.

"She swore at us, Chief..."

Süleyman exploded before my assistant, who thought it ingenious to act on his emotions rather than his rationale, could manage to.

"You lying little dog!" When he couldn't get past me, he wagged his finger in the air. "You're a big tough man, so go on and tell the truth. Naciye never even opens her mouth to talk but she's going to swear at you, is that right?"

"She may not open her mouth to *talk*, but for about fifty people a day she opens it..." said the little brother in the crowd, trying to interject.

"Shut it!" It was Ali berating him this time. "Still yapping away! Unbelievable!"

It wasn't good that my assistant was so obviously taking sides. There was no sense in making things more complicated.

"All right," I said, quieting everyone down again. "All right... I get it." I turned to the boy, who was being careful to keep his distance from Süleyman. "Look. If you have a complaint, there's a police station just up the road. You can't go around beating up women just to get your way. Submit your complaint and let our friends take care of it."

"We did, Chief," he explained with the distress his helplessness had given him. "But nothing worked. Everybody knows this guy. They took him in for questioning once or twice and that was it. Then it was business as usual."

"They're up to something there, too," said the older one, encouraged by the younger. "Not you, but there are some police..."

Ali was about to blow his lid. I couldn't let that happen.

"Then you open a legal case against him. There's no other way."

"But Chief..."

"Don't 'but Chief' us," our well-meaning rogue snapped. "Drop it, and just tell me if you've got a license for this thing?" He waved the gun he now held.

"Yes, of course. What were we supposed to do when the government didn't do its job? We got a gun... and a license."

His voice sounded gutsier now.

"All right then," I said, playing the role of authoritative cop. "You got a complaint, let's take it to the station."

The two boys' faces soured. The police station meant questioning, which meant a lot of trouble. Süleyman held his tongue, too. Naturally, no one had any intention of walking through the station doors. So now I could play paternalistic cop.

"Then we're good. What do you say we close the subject now? Ali, have our friends here show their gun's papers. If those are in order, there's no problem." I called to my assistant.

"Of course there's no problem, Chief. We never do anything unlawful. Come to the shop and we'll show you."

I called out after my assistant as he ushered the two brothers ahead of him and started off to the cell phone shop. "Get the knife out of that sign there, too. Don't just let it sit there."

"Yes sir, Chief," he answered, dragging the two young men over to the wig shop's sign.

"You aren't going to confiscate the knife, are you?"

Süleyman was practically begging, as if imploring us not to leave him weaponless in the middle of this war zone.

"Just be thankful we didn't haul you in," I rebuked. "You were about to kill the kid."

When he realized my intent was serious, he shut up and hung his head. I turned to the curious crowd around us.

"Yes, friends, go on... The show's over; you clear out too. Enough of the rubbernecking."

The crowd dispersed, grumbling. With the snow falling onto his dyed hair, Süleyman all at once became an old man. That's when I noticed the blood.

"Your eyebrow's cut."

He calmly reached up to his face. "Wow, I guess we took a punch, eh?" he abashedly put in, when he saw the dark liquid on his fingers. "It's slipping away from me, Chief. Used to be I could tussle with a dozen of these hamam boys and come out without so much as one fist landing on me. Look at me now. I got old."

"Azize is a good girl..."

Right up until we got to the Neşe Pavyon, my mind was on Harem Süleyman. I couldn't stop picturing the knife he'd hurled at the kid's back. He could very well have killed Engin in the same way. He had good enough reason to: Engin had taken away his capital, in the form of three women, at the gambling table. He sure hadn't bothered to hide his pleasure in the news of Engin's death, anyhow. But it would've been impossible for our tired old tough guy to do the job without some backing; he couldn't stand up to Black Nizam alone. Perhaps Dice Ihsan had put him up to it. Or even forced him. I really doubted Süleyman's passion for gambling had waned. It wasn't a habit that could be given up easily, this malady of his. Maybe there'd been a game turning over who would kill Engin, there on that green felt tablecloth. That would be just like Ihsan. Maybe Süleyman, with his big body and small brain, had been duped into becoming a killer whether he wanted to or not. So let's say Süleyman was the killer. What about Tidy Tarık then? What was his role in events? Did Dice just want to play it safe? Did he think Tidy would finish up the job if Süleyman failed? No, these men's minds didn't work that way. Even if they did, they wouldn't go to all that trouble for Engin. So maybe the Italians hired Tarık. They could ban Engin from Switzerland as much as they like, but he would find a way to get there eventually. In fact, as soon as he got on his feet again, he'd want revenge for Durdu.

140

One way or another, he posed a threat for the Italians. They might have wanted to kill Engin to get rid of the problem for good. In a globalizing world, what could be more natural than globalizing a crime?

"I finally caught you, Chief." Ali was out of breath. "The kids were telling the truth. The gun was licensed. But I'm still not sure. Shouldn't we have confiscated it for a while? I wouldn't want any harm to come to Süleyman."

"Don't worry. Those kids haven't got the heart to kill a man. They opened their shop up in the wrong place is all. The old *hadjis* will find them a shop in another neighborhood soon enough. Even if they raise an army they're not getting Süleyman off that street."

"You saw how Süleyman threw that knife, right?" he said, falling into pace beside me.

Well done, he hadn't skipped over that important detail. I gazed at him with pride, our smart cookie.

"Yeah, I saw it all right. Let's give the knife to Zeynep and have her look it over. Maybe it has Engin's blood or something on it..." As I finished my sentence, I saw the lights of the Neşe Pavyon's neon sign flash off and on among the snowflakes. "I guess we made it."

The Neşe Pavyon was just as Black Nizam had described it. The place under the garish sign was a big letdown. One of those dives, always in the basement floors, where the smell of mold permeating the stone couldn't be got rid of no matter how hard you tried. We went down the crooked stairs, stepped through the narrow doorway, and immediately tumbled into a mirrored room. Yes, the entire length of the walls and ceiling were covered in mirrors, which were lit with blue neon lights. Strange it was, but hardly a foolish idea, because this place was just as narrow as it was squat. It'd probably been the coal cellar of an apartment building constructed at the beginning of the last century. Shimmering balls hung from the ceiling. When the program started, all the different lights must really make it colorful. Eighties disco decor was still alive and kicking in this place. Only one of the tables was occupied. It was hard to tell the age of the three *konsomatris* thanks to the low lighting and their heavy make-up, but they wore dresses like the ones you usually see on the hosts of these women's morning shows that housewives so passionately watch. I looked to see if maybe one of them was Azize but none of them resembled the dewey-eyed girl. The mournful sound of a clarinet broke my concentration. We turned to look at a platform raised about ten inches off the floor in the middle of the room. No one was yet on the raised area that supposedly served as a stage, just five chairs waiting for the musicians. It was still early and the program hadn't started yet, so where was the clarinetist? We finally saw him, sitting on a chair in the dark a few feet to the left of the stage. He was dressed in black, his white shirt turned lilac under the effects of the blue lights. Ali was about to make his way over to him but I stopped him.

"Wait a sec, Ali. He's really good. Let's listen a bit."

And I wasn't exaggerating; he was playing beautifully. You know how they say music is the voice of God? Well it was that deep, that moving. A sound to cleanse and purify the soul. For a moment I forgot all about this dive, and Azize, and the corpse, and this investigation. I abandoned myself to the enchanting sound, its undulating melodies. Of course it didn't last long. Our clumsy Ali knocked a glass off a table and forced me to face my forgotten realities. The clarinetist also heard the breaking glass and stopped playing. He stared at us, puzzled.

"Good evening," I said admiringly. "The music is lovely."

The unfamiliarity lifted and he grinned, showing a broken front tooth.

"Good evening, sir. And thanks, but the *pavyon*'s not open yet. You should come back in an hour."

We ignored that and went over to his table.

"We're not customers," said Ali, flashing his ID. "We're looking for Azize Hanım."

"Azize Hanım?" the clarinetist repeated, his tone worried.

He'd come out of the shadows. He had a wide forehead that his fine strands of graying hair couldn't cover. His black eyes, like two olives, shone innocuously in his long face, and a pointy chin stretched beneath the thick lips that were pursed with misgiving.

"Yes," muttered my assistant in a monotone voice. "She works here."

His timid gaze scrutinized us.

"Why are you looking for her?"

"Why do you think?"

Ali was in his 'why are you giving us the runaround' mode.

"Is it this thing with Engin?"

"What else would it be?" Ali replied, in the same offhand manner.

The clarinetist stood there with the helplessness of someone witnessing a terrible fate play out little by little. As he plunked down into the empty chair in front of him, I changed the subject.

"Why are you playing in this place?"

He looked at me from the bottom of the pit he'd fallen into.

"I'm Chief Inspector Nevzat, by the way. I was just wondering why you don't play somewhere nicer?"

His big eyes got all moony.

"They'd scoff at us, Chief. I never went to school. I've had this same instrument since childhood. I learned the damn thing on my own, just blowing away on it. Why would anybody give a damn about us?"

His accent came out as he spoke.

"Where are you from?"

A sheepish smile spread on his swarthy face.

"Bulgaria, Chief. I came here in eighty-nine. We were being persecuted, seriously persecuted. So we abandoned our houses and came all the way here."

I was really warming up to this happy-go-lucky musician.

"What's your name?"

"Sadri. I got that name here. It was my dear departed grandpa's. In Bulgaria they changed our names. I was called Sergey. But my mother always called me Sadri... Sadri Klarnet."

Ali chuckled, but it didn't bother the musician.

"That's right, Chief. My last name's Klarnet. We're Romani, your dark-skinned compatriots... Gypsies, you call us. My grandpa was a master clarinetist, as was my father. Our line goes back like that all the way to the Ottoman Empire. So when I came to Turkey, I chose the name Klarnet for myself..."

I smiled amicably.

"What can I say, Sadri, you do the name justice."

"Thanks, Chief. I'm doing my best," he mumbled, with an expression resembling pride. Then he got pensive again. "She had no hand in that matter," he said suddenly. "Azize is a good girl... Clean and pure like her face. A saint, just like her name implies. She'd never hurt anyone. She couldn't if she wanted to."

My assistant looked Sadri over with suspicion.

"What is Azize to you?"

He looked away as though caught red-handed.

"What else, Inspector? She works here is all." He nodded towards the women's table. "Look, those girls are like that too. Şermin, Nükhet, Gülşen... We're all like family here. But Azize's place is different. She's not just a hostess here, she also sings. If you heard her, you'd know what I mean. Her voice is beautiful. Really beautiful... In truth, she's the one this place doesn't suit, not me. But someone will discover her soon enough. She's going to be a big star, like Sibel, like Kibariye. She'll have programs on TV, mark my words. As soon as she gets out of this place..."

Since we were on the subject of Azize, I cleared my throat and asked, "Did you know Engin very well? He must have come here a lot."

His thick lip sagged discontentedly.

"Yes. Lately he was here all the time." He pointed his clarinet at the next table over. The one right in front of the stage. It was set for two and in the middle was a white vase with a red rose. "That was his table. Even if he didn't come, no one could sit there. The table would just sit all empty till morning, like an orphaned child. Seeing Azize was important to him. 'If I don't see you, business goes bad,' he'd say to her. As if he was doing great business... Lately he wasn't allowing her to hostess. He was jealous."

"I'm guessing you didn't like him much?"

His prematurely wrinkled face scrunched up.

"He wasn't a likable man. He broke a lot of hearts, Chief, and hurt a lot of people. Especially women. Even worse, he was cruel. Black Nizam had his back, and he laid down the law on the streets. There was no consideration of feelings... But look what happened. Someone stronger came along and took his life."

"Who was this stronger person?" Ali stuck the question in straight away. "Do you know who killed him?"

The immigrant musician looked spooked.

"No Chief. How should I know? I'm just a clarinetist. What business would I have with these troubled men?"

I was worried if my assistant pressed him any harder he'd clam up and we wouldn't get another word out of him.

"What about Azize?" I said, dancing round the subject. "Did she love Engin?"

He sighed heavily.

"She did. A lot. She was crazy in love, Azize. But that man..." The word was there on his tongue but he swallowed it. "God rest his soul, but that man was using her. He had so many women around him. He didn't care about her."

"How's that?" For whatever reason, Ali was feeling the need to turn up the heat a bit. "Didn't you just say he wouldn't let her do the hostessing?"

"That was just for show." He lowered his voice as if there was someone that might overhear. "Would he let her work here at all if he was for real? No, he just had to be able to brag that he has a friend at the Neşe Pavyon. That she's the loveliest girl in the place and the best singer, too. But he also had to say she's no hostess. Where is the heart that loves Azize in a despicable man like that?" There was still something he wasn't coming out with.

"Why do you say that? Did he treat you badly?"

He bristled like a haggard rooster.

"How could he mistreat me, Chief? I don't give them the time of day, men like that. It was Azize he treated like dirt."

Naturally, this wasn't news to me. In this world love meant cruelty, it meant vulgarity and violence against women.

"Did he hit her?" I prodded. "Was he beating on the girl?"

He took a good look around.

"If the boss asks, you haven't heard it from me but yes, he was hitting her. In his own way, he was jealous of her. When

145

he got drunk he would tell her to quit. But how could Azize quit? It's not like they were married or anything. If he lost interest a day or two later then what? How would Azize feed herself? Excuse me but, would she turn to prostitution?" He gave me a look of despair. "That kind of job is tough, Chief. Even tougher for a girl like Azize."

"So what kept her from leaving him? Fear?"

He shook his head emphatically.

"Not fear. Love. Yes, she really did love the guy. All that swearing, all that humiliation... She just took it. Such is the heart; you can never know if it'll land somewhere good or bad. The silly girl was coming up with her own excuses. 'He's jealous and that means he must love me, Sadri Abi,' she'd say."

"Didn't anybody set her straight?" Ali barked. He must have started to feel sorry for Azize. "Didn't anybody tell her the man is no good for her?"

"Of course they did, Inspector. We all did. A lot. We got tired of repeating ourselves, but she wouldn't listen to anyone. That's love for you, Inspector. It's the usual madness. When it comes to love, that's it. The brain ceases to work. And Azize is young of course." His eyes got watery as if he were experiencing the girl's emotions. "She was so full of hope that she came up with excuses for even the most deplorable behavior on his part. It's not stupidity or naiveté, more like desperation. That's about as colorful as a young girl's dreams get in a swamp like this. Even a jackal like Engin can suddenly become a prince on a white horse."

"It's a good thing he's dead then." Was Ali testing Sadri or just saying what he felt? I couldn't be sure. "It's good," he repeated. "Go on and say it. The girl's free..."

Sadri shook his head mournfully.

"No, Inspector. I wish that were the case but it's not what happened. The poor thing's been crying her eyes out since she heard he died. I don't know how she'll ever get over the pain of it."

Ali looked over at the door as if he'd see her there.

"When does Azize get here?"

The clarinetist's long indigo lashes blinked nervously.

"What do you mean, Inspector? I'm telling you, the girl's taken to her bed from grief. How's she gonna get all gussied up and sing on a day like this? No, Azize won't be in tonight."

"I see," I said, trying to placate him. "But we do need to talk to her. I assume you have her address?"

He squirmed helplessly in his chair.

"She's on Kurtuldu Street, down there in Dolapdere. But she won't talk, poor thing. She swallowed a handful of Diazepam. She won't even understand what you're saying."

"We'll bring her round," my unsympathetic assistant insisted. "Come on, tell us what number she's at?"

Sadri stared at the insensitive officer. He understood there was no getting out of this.

"She's in the house at the top of the road, over Şık Market." He turned his black eyes imploringly on me. "But please, if you'll listen to me, don't go there tonight, Chief, don't. It'll be such a shame. Don't ruffle her any more; leave her alone. Let her grieve, let her rest a bit... I promise you, tomorrow I'll bring her down to the station myself."

I did pity her. And he was right. If Azize had taken that many sedatives, she wouldn't even understand who we were.

"Okay," I said. "But if anything goes wrong, I'm holding you responsible, accordingly. I'll be expecting you at the station tomorrow morning, all right?"

A bright smile spread across his tanned face.

"Bless your heart, Chief. Don't you worry; we'll be there."

"He may be police, but I am a citizen."

※

"They'll come back." The man with the white hair stood erect in front of me like a part of the darkness. "These deaths are just the beginning... A great fire will break out. Everyone, everything will be engulfed in flames, and then those who've gone will return. That's the only way the whispers will be silent."

I was waiting for our kids at the top of Kadın Çıkmazı. The snow had thinned and a harsh frost had begun to blast through the crooked streets. After leaving Neşe Pavyon, I'd sent Ali to the victim's house to fetch Zeynep. I was taking them to the dinner Evgenia couldn't make it to, at the Feraye Meyhane, as a kind of belated New Year celebration. And we'd assess the situation together at the same time. But suddenly this old man had popped out of the darkness.

"Who'll come back, sir?" I said to the man in the soiled clothes. "What whispers?"

With a trembling hand, he pointed to the dilapidated building at the top of the dead end street.

"The people who built these houses, who live on these streets." He turned around nervously as though he'd heard something and looked up the narrow road behind him. Whatever he saw gave him a fright. "Look, there they are! I told you they'd come back..." His eyes were fixed on some point. "They won't leave us be."

"Who won't?" I asked, turning to where he was looking.

148

There was no one, of course, neither human nor cat. But the old man must have been seeing someone, because he breathed, "Them!" His voice had begun to shake like his hands. "Don't you see them?"

It was an unnerving situation.

"What are you talking about, sir? There's no one there."

His black eyes gaped at me from beneath wide white eyebrows that drew two arcs towards his broad forehead.

"You really don't see them? Look, they're right there. There's the young woman holding the man's arm... the man with the navy blue coat and the same color fedora on his head. The woman's coat is cherry and her scarf is too, but with pink polka dots. And don't you see that little girl? Look, they've dressed her in a bright blue coat with a navy blue beret. She's holding a doll in a red dress..." He looked back at me; a flicker of suspicion appeared in his eyes. "Or are you trying to trick me?"

It was plain the old man had lost his mind.

"No, sir. Why would I do that? But I don't see any family there."

He was so convinced in his words that I took another look so he wouldn't feel bad. There was nobody there of course, but when I looked up I saw, under the dim light radiating from the windows of decaying buildings, the almost frozen laundry, abandoned to the wind, swinging gently from lines stretched taut between the houses. He must have thought the dresses were ghosts.

"What are you blabbering on about again, Diogenes?" said a voice ringing out in the night. "Look, don't push it or Chief Nevzat will lock you up."

When I turned to look, I came eye to eye with Keto, who seemed in high spirits despite his bandaged nose. Even more surprising was that Piranha was standing there next to him. Hadn't they just fought the night before?

"Who do you think you're fooling, you scoundrel," the old man said in greeting. "Who's going to lock me up?"

"Don't you understand, Dio? That's Chief Inspector Nevzat." He poked his bandaged nose my direction. "The man really is police. I'm telling the truth."

The old man didn't surrender right away.

"So what if he's police?" he bristled. "He may be police, but I am a citizen."

He had taken a few timid steps back, however.

"And anyhow, ghosts aren't afraid of the police." He stopped and leaned forward slightly. "The deaths will continue," he shakily repeated. His voice had taken on that mysterious tone again. "There will be a fire. It'll burn everything, all of us. There won't be a single person left. Just these peopleless buildings. If they don't burn down too..." His eyes were drawn to the street again. "Look. Look, they're coming!" His face was contorted and he started to back up nervously. "They're coming back for the stragglers. For you, for me... They're coming for all of us."

He turned round and hobbled off as if someone was chasing him, and before you knew it he'd suddenly vanished just as he'd appeared. It was sad actually, but Keto thought it was quite amusing and burst into laughter.

Piranha, shivering in his red leather jacket, went one step further. "Fucking freak," he swore at the man's back. "The smart ones never find us, and the crazy ones never leave us alone."

I felt like giving the two of them a good talking to, but I saw they were high so I didn't bother.

"Who's the old man?" I said, moving closer. My nasal burned with a smell that hit me like an invisible wall. Thinners. That magical substance that with a couple huffs rescued these kids from their suffering and led them to paradise. My gaze went down to Keto's right hand. There it was in his fist, the thinner-soaked piece of cotton wool. He clutched it in his palm like a precious gem. He couldn't have been completely wasted though, because he saw where I was looking.

"You asking about Diogenes, Chief?" he said, gently sliding his hand behind his back to hide his treasure. "Just some guy with no family. He lives in the churchyard back there. He's Armenian or Greek or something. He actually used to be rich." With his free hand he pointed towards the four-storey building beyond the small square. "Look, that was his house.

He had a bunch of shops, too. The church collected all the rents from them and in return, they looked after him. He never hurt anybody. But at some point, who knows what he took already, but he's always high as a kite. In the daytime he sings and dances. I don't mean just any old crappy singing though, that one's got a killer voice. Cultured too. Sings in all different languages. It'd blow your mind if you heard him. That coffee cook down there, Hunchback Şakir, loves the guy. He watches out for him. Diogenes gets his three watery teas every day there, free of charge. He loves that watery, lukewarm tea. If it's sunny out, he'll throw a chair outside the coffeehouse and sit there till evening. But the priest doesn't let him out at night. You saw what happens; the darkness gets to his head. He hears voices, talks to djinn, sees ghosts... His own fears pester him and he runs around the streets like a lunatic. Look, he's already started. Just one of the Tarlabaşı crazies, Chief. Just look at these godforsaken buildings. Would any normal human being ever come out of this place?"

It surprised me how much sense he was making. These kids were getting old before their time, just as they would die before their time. I pointed out the bandage sitting like a white dot in the middle of his dirty face.

"How's the nose?"

He grinned smugly.

"Good... Actually, we'll know when the gauze comes off. If it's bad, I'll get me some plastic surgery. I'll be like Kıvanç Tatlıtuğ. You know him, right? Our domestic Brad Pitt? Well, I'll be just like him. With all the ladies after me... Maybe the TV shows'll discover me and I'll get away from this shitty life."

Piranha made a fist with his right hand and with the other grabbed Keto's wrist and shook his friend.

"Like hell you will. People like us don't hit that kind of jackpot. Don't you get it, brickhead? Our fates are sealed, man, sealed. We get sentenced to a life of happiness today and tomorrow they'll pardon us. What cameraman? Who are you to them?"

Keto was not going to be outdone.

"So what? Maybe I won't pose for the TV cameras but the city surveillance cameras will recognize me."

In their own way they were being philosophical.

"Surveillance cameras won't make you famous," I said, joining the conversation. "If they catch you flubbing up, they'll show no mercy. You'll be a sitting duck. Straight to jail."

He shrugged off my words.

"That's all right, Chief. Musti's already in there."

It's true. The third kid wasn't with them.

"What happened?"

"What do you think?" he said happily, like it was some entertaining event. "You know that violin and darbuka you saw last night? He nicked them from some Dolapdere gypsy kids. He lied to us and told us he found them in the garbage. The kids squealed and the cops hauled him in. Nothing'll happen though. They'll let him out in the morning."

"Good thing they didn't also take you two in."

"So what if they did, Chief?" Piranha straightened the bandage over his right eye. "Inside, outside, it's all the same. It got cold out anyway. We struggle mornings, in these ruins."

"Where do you stay exactly?"

They exchanged a nervous look, wondering what was up and if I'd really haul them in.

"Don't worry. I'm not going to take the place out from under you. I'm asking out of curiosity."

They still had their doubts but they must have worried I'd land them in trouble so they had to explain. Keto pointed towards Tarlabaşı Boulevard.

"You know those buildings that are gonna be knocked down? Well, we sleep in one of those. The stairs collapsed and not everyone can get in. We climb up through the windows. There's furniture and stuff, too. It's no five-star hotel, but it'll do as your average apartment. A little cold, we're freezing our asses off actually, but we get by with blankets, quilts... It's a while before they're demolished yet. So let's just say that for this winter, it's home, Chief."

I felt a prick of pain from the state they were in, but they'd accepted this misery long ago.

"Isn't there anywhere better for you to stay around here?"

"There is." Piranha took a huff from the thinner-soaked cotton in his right palm before answering. His attitude was one of, *I'm not scared of you.* Keto glared at him, but he didn't pay him any attention. "There's this Ferhat Çerağ Culture Center up here. We stayed there for four months already."

"So why'd you leave?"

Without any reservations, he showed me the foul smelling cotton in his hand. "Thinner's not allowed there. Nazlı Abla doesn't let us."

"That's good. So just don't do it then. And you'd be rid of this shit."

He looked at me, then at the cotton in his hand.

"Why should I be rid of it? We wouldn't survive without it. Isn't that right man, Keto. Tell the Chief."

Keto tried to wheedle out of it. "He's talking shit, Chief. Thinner is not the problem. Nazlı Abla's a good woman, but she made us do things we didn't want to. First it was draw some pictures, then learn the computer, read a book... She was bringing in writers, and shrinks and whatnot. They kept yapping away and it really bugged me. After ten minutes I couldn't understand a damn thing they were saying. Which is all fine and good, but then they went overboard with this English shit. As if we speak Turkish great and all we're missing is a foreign language. Still, I would have gritted my teeth and put up with it." He nodded towards his friend. "But then this oaf here asked that freckled teacher 'Teacher, how do you say, "If you're gonna fuck a donkey you have to put up with its farts," in English?' And all hell broke loose."

They both snickered. When they saw I didn't approve, Keto tried to explain. "Aw, all right, Chief. The woman just wanted what was best for us, but everybody's got a different job they can do."

"And what job can you do?" I said, teasing him. "Acting in TV shows?"

It fell to Piranha to defend his friend.

"Don't kid around, Chief! Why couldn't he? It's not like the ones doing it now are so great. Like they aren't using. They're all potheads. And the ones with money snort coke. You know who they are too, but no one messes with them 'cause they're famous. So don't mess with them, but don't stick your nose in our business either. Yeah, we huff thinner and we drink wine too. If we still haven't got our fill, we pop pills. I'm not gonna lie. Makes no difference to me if you like it or not..."

I didn't mind Piranha's challenging me; I was thinking about the woman who owned the culture center. What were the photo and building diagram doing in Engin's safe?

"This Nazlı Abla... Is she the one they call Crazy Nazlı?"

"She's not crazy," Keto objected. "That woman's got balls, Nazlı Abla."

"Okay. Anyway, how do you know her?"

"From the park resistance..."

He was going to keep explaining but Piranha jabbed him with his elbow.

"Don't be a dumbass, man." With a fake smile, he turned his one eye on me. "We met her on the street. When she realized we were homeless, she invited us to the culture center."

He was lying through his teeth.

"What're you up to, Piranha?" I said, frowning. "What're you trying to hide?"

He pretended not to care.

"Nothing. I'm not hiding anything."

"Look here, son. Whatever it is, I'll find out about it. If you did something wrong..."

"I didn't do anything, Chief."

"He's just scared," Keto interrupted.

He really was giving me a begging look. Was it because I'd smacked him the night before?

"Why?"

He nodded towards Piranha.

"That you'll blind his other eye."

"What?"

I remembered the small black hole that appeared from under the patch as it slid off after I'd slapped him. What was it Keto was trying to say?

"How did Piranha lose his eye?"

"Your guys did it, Chief. The police..."

Piranha, putting his cotton wool to his nose, nodded gently to silently confirm what his friend said.

"Wha... What? When?" I stuttered. "When did that happen?"

154

"Last June... At the park..."

What on earth was the kid talking about?

"The park in Taksim..."

"Gezi Park... Last summer..."

Now I understood.

"During the Gezi Park resistance? What business did you have there?"

He grinned slyly, like he wasn't the one to lose an eye.

"There was free food. And they were handing out clothes: jeans, t-shirts, a bunch of stuff..."

"Son, is that any reason to go there? That park was hell."

"Not until your guys showed up." It was Keto who spoke. "Yep, the police played dirty, Chief." His voice had gone up an octave. "Go ahead and get angry; go ahead and shout! See if I care! Your guys were evil to those people. They were all educated types. And they were all really good people. They came there for the trees. They put on theater plays and gave concerts. They were making pictures. They had us painting pictures, too. They even made a film. And I acted in it. For the trees..."

"For the trees," agreed Piranha, with a momentary break from his thinner. "They were gonna cut down those trees and make a shopping mall. And all those nice ladies and gents kicked them the fuck out of there. You would never have expected it. There were girls with crazy-colored hair, boys with piercings and tattoos... But they were good people. They didn't even react to all that gas, all those water cannons... There were lots of police too, eh. They didn't give a shit about any of them, I swear."

I was about to tell him, *Son, what the hell are you still on about? You lost an eye,* but Keto didn't let me.

"Don't get us wrong, Chief. We weren't there for the protest. It was our place. We used to spend the night under a giant tree at the metro exit. You know, that big tree on the corner. Where we slept, I mean. We had a big sleeping bag. Piranha, Musti and me all slept curled up inside it. Then one morning... and by morning I mean the sun still wasn't up or anything... your police attacked like a surprise raid on the enemy. There were maybe thirty tents. They dragged them out and beat them, those girls and boys. They really were just kids, but they didn't lie down and take it."

"Didn't lie down and take it?" Piranha started in again. "They held them off, like lions... But there were so many cops."

I remembered only too well what they went through in Gezi Park. It was horrific. The government sent our men out to crush the demonstrators mercilessly. It was a humiliation for all of us. We saw once again that in a country with an authoritarian regime, the police force would be the first to lose.

"I know what happened, kids," I said, because I didn't want to hear any more. "But your eye. Tell me about that."

He suddenly stopped, throwing his empty hand up to the patch on his right eye as though it had just now gone blind.

"That bastard," he said, hatred in his voice. "That bastard shot me with a gas canister from three meters away. I was blindsided, otherwise I would have never let him near me. I turned my head and the man pulled the trigger. The canister stuck me in the eye. It felt like someone punched the living daylights out of me. Everything went dark, but I didn't realize my eye had exploded and I thought I'd get over it in a bit. I reached my hand up and my palm filled with blood. But I'm used to blood, and I just thought my eyebrow got cut. Then all of a sudden I got dizzy and fell over. When I opened my eyes I was in one of those makeshift first aid tents. Not in the hospital, 'cause the police weren't letting the ambulances into the square. In the park's first aid tent, there was a doctor called Şahap Abi. He was curly-haired like Keto, and chubby, and he helped me. And Nazlı Abla..."

"That's where we first saw Nazlı Abla," Keto cut in again. "She took Piranha to the eye hospital. The one there on the Italian Slope. They cleaned up the wound. And later Nazlı Abla had them put in a glass eye. It was prettier than his real one, eh? But the idiot dropped it."

My heart sank as I listened to them, but Piranha just started giggling.

"It was your fault, man," he said joyfully. He'd long since forgotten about the fate of his lost eye. "If you hadn't grabbed that apple off Rosy-cheeked Remzi's stall at the Fish Market, my eye never would have fallen. I stood in front of Remzi so the guy wouldn't catch him, Chief. You know these water cannon TOMA trucks of yours, Chief? Well, Remzi's built like one of those. Like a German lorry, I mean. As if I was gonna stop the man... He knocked me for a loop. I landed in the *kokoreç* stall next to his and my eye went flying. I searched all over, as if I had nothing better to do."

"Nazlı Abla was gonna make another one but we never went back to the culture center. It was all classes and paintings, a royal pain in the neck.

"So she's a good person, this Nazlı Abla..."

"Yeah, she is." He looked at Keto as if trying to understand. "Does anyone say otherwise?"

It would be helpful to learn a bit more about the woman.

"No, they don't. Just that her head's not screwed on right. Isn't she nicknamed Crazy Nazlı?"

Keto was angry.

"What, did Black Nizam say that?"

The conversation seemed to finally be going somewhere.

"Why?" I asked. "Is there some hostility between them?"

"Why wouldn't there be? Nazlı Abla was going to open a second culture center, only for women. There are these women who come here from Mardin and Siirt, Chief. They don't even speak Turkish, just Kurdish. And she was going to open classes for them. Nazlı Abla owns the building where the Genuine Tarlabaşists Club is. She inherited it from her dad. She's gonna open the new center there, but that scumbag Nizam won't get out of the building. They shot at the culture center and harassed them."

"But Nazlı Abla's no pushover," Piranha interjected. "She's got people behind her, tough boys with drooping moustaches and beards. They were at the park protests as well. You know, those revolutionist brothers who you call anarchists. But not only them. There's students, women, even transvestites. They all love Nazlı Abla. We love her too, of course. But anyhow, we all got together and hit Nizam's place."

Now that was interesting news.

157

"You mean you went on that attack too?"

"It wasn't an attack, Chief," Keto said, sniffling. "This idiot's exaggerating. We went to talk."

The one-eyed kid couldn't keep his mouth shut again. "It scared the shit out of Nizam's nephews, seeing us all there."

But it was another detail besides the nephew's fear that concerned me.

"Was Engin there?"

Piranha had hated the dead man, so he got the first word in.

"He was there all right. The twit couldn't even talk. He was scared shitless, that jackass."

"That's a sin, man, talking about a dead man behind his back," Keto complained.

"I'll talk about him if I want. He was filth, Engin. The guy was a pimp. More polished, is all. Harem Süleyman was like bathed in holy water beside him. Engin was luring the chicks in and handing them over to that monument to ugliness, Nizam. He cheats and lies, the son of a bitch..."

Worried a fight would break out like the night before, I wanted to change the subject.

"Anyhow, what happened at the club after that?"

"I'm getting there, Chief. If my friend here would give me a chance," Keto griped.

This time Piranha didn't interfere. He put his cotton wool to his nose and rested his head to one side like a young boy kissing his sweetheart. While his friend was buried in thinners, he took the opportunity to continue. "We went over to Nizam's. There were at least fifty of us. Some of us were inside the building and some outside the door. Transvestites, feminists, revolutionaries, huffers like us... The men were really surprised. And I'm not bullshitting, everyone inside was stood at attention. But we didn't make a sound. Anyhow, Nazlı Abla warned us, 'No one speaks but me.' And that's what happened. She walked up to Nizam and said, 'This building is mine. I'm not hurting for cash, but I need it. We're turning it into a culture center to help the people of Tarlabaşı. We have to evacuate all the tenants, and you also need to leave. If you don't, I will take you to court. And if you continue to resort to bullying me, I've got lawyers and will take this all the way.' Nizam's dark face went white as a sheet. But he saw the woman had sharp teeth and solid backing. So he lied through his grin. 'All right, Miss. We're also kids from this neighborhood, so seeing how you're trying to do something helpful for Tarlabaşı, we'll leave,' he said. He said his contract's not up for another ten months. 'Give us till then,' he said, 'and we'll hand over the building.' So things were smoothed over that way."

"Okay. Did Nazlı have any quarrel with Ihsan?"

Keto looked at me wondering where that had come from.

"They threw a Molotov through the window of Dice's place this morning."

"It was an accident," Piranha said, laughing. "They meant to chuck it into Nizam's club but they chucked it into Dice's instead. Nice work! That's not a bad thing. Did Ihsan also burn up?"

"Stop with the crazy talk, man," Keto shouted. "Nazlı Abla would never do that. She wouldn't hurt a fly. She's the nicest person I know on this planet."

"So who threw it then?"

Keto forgot about the cotton with thinners he was hiding behind his back and threw up his arms. "I don't know, Chief. Something's going down these days. I never could figure it out."

Piranha gave his friend a gentle shove. "And what's that, man? The Chief is taking care of them one at a time." He came a step closer and the smell of thinner rose in waves through the cold air. "Look, they took down Engin's killer." He looked at me with admiration. "It was you who bumped off Tidy Tarık, Chief?"

He was having a hard time standing. What had suddenly come over this kid? Maybe he'd dropped a pill before leaving his hovel and it was just taking effect. Keto hooked his friend's arm in his so he wouldn't fall.

"That's enough, man. Come on, we're going."

Piranha looked offended.

"Now what did I say?" He looked defiantly at his friend. When he got no response, he turned to me with the innocent look of a stray dog. "Did I say anything?"

"Oh, I see you've gathered the team, Chief." Ali's voice startled the children. He was standing a few steps behind us, Zeynep by his side. Our criminologist was staring sadly at the kids, but Ali was still making light. "The bandage suits you," he said, messing with Keto. "But don't run around the streets for too long. You'll get gangrene and your nose'll drop off."

Keto wasn't overly thrilled with the remark.

"It's nothing," he said, squinting at him with hostility. "Okay, we're going. Not because you're saying to but because my bonehead of a friend here is making the chief uncomfortable." He looked at me like he was saying goodbye to an old friend. "See ya, Chief." He took Piranha's arm and dragged him off. "Move it, man!" He took a few steps then turned around. "Hey Chief, don't be fooled into thinking this is the heart of the city. The place is crawling with jackals, so be careful."

Was the comment aimed at Ali? Or was he talking about Nizam and Ihsan? Maybe some pill was also taking its effects on him now.

"You be careful, too," I called after them. "I still need you."

This time Piranha turned round.

"Shame on you, Chief," he said, pulling away from his friend. "Even when you're driving us to our deaths, do we ever say 'sorry our petrol's run out'?"

"But it's still really nice that people love you."

✳

Müzeyyen Senar was singing. It was one of my favorite songs. We were sitting in Feraye Meyhane, in the oriel window that hung out over Istiklal Avenue. The snow had started up again and it didn't take long for the ground to be covered in white.

"Are these guys nuts?" Ali was referring to the Istanbulites; moving black dots on the white snow, stooping then straightening up, sticking to each other to keep from falling as they tried to walk. "What're they looking for out there in this freezing cold? They're going to fall and break something."

"Nothing's gonna happen, Ali," said Zeynep, moving so close to the window her head nearly touched the glass. "What are people supposed to do? They're here to have fun." She turned to look towards the sky, which was hard to make out between the buildings. "Look how beautifully it's snowing. The lights are so strange, too. People think they're in a fairytale world."

"A dreary fairytale world," I mumbled, after which I half-jokingly scolded, "Aren't you listening to the song, kids?"

They really hadn't been hearing it, but they sat up straight away and started listening so as not to be disrespectful to their Chief Inspector. Müzeyyen continued to sing in that most intimate way of hers.

Zeynep's eyes grew intense, as if she were revisiting a beautiful memory.

"Yes, I know this song. Nihal Abla used to sing it. She was our next-door neighbor. We'd hear it every evening while making dinner. She had a lovely voice. She always sang songs like this."

"But some people take it to extremes," Ali lamented. "In our school dormitory there was a literature teacher, Şinasi Bey. He was really into these songs. He made us listen so that we'd get an ear for them. Dede Efendi, Itri and such... It'd bore us to tears."

I didn't want to lecture, but it didn't sit well with me that he had the wrong idea about the great composers he was talking about.

"Maybe your teacher didn't choose the right songs. I'm sure you wouldn't have got bored if he'd played Dede Efendi's 'A Rose has sprouted in this Heart again', for example.

"I don't know it, Chief," he said, uneasy with not having understood. "But this song is nice." He wagged his head in time with the melody and muttered. "Take a look at days gone by, the things we left behind... Nice words." He must have been feeling trapped; he looked over at his friend to get off the hook. "Really, though, why don't we listen to this music?"

Zeynep didn't know what to say.

"Maybe there's no time left after all the ridiculous pop songs," I needled. "You know, those songs that try to get your attention with a singer's body rather than her voice?"

They laughed quietly like children accepting their guilt.

"That's true, Chief," said Zeynep, still in high spirits. "This morning there was a song on the radio. 'You held my hand, wrapped your arms round my back, do you really like me, did you really come back...' I swear I'm not exaggerating; it just kept going on and on like that."

"There are some good ones though, too. They're not all bad."

When I looked up, I was facing Erdinç. He was standing at the head of the table, watching us with a warm smile.

"Hi there, Chief!" He shook our hands in turn. "Isn't that true, though?" he added, looking at Zeynep. "Barış Manço, Cem Karaca, Sezen Aksu... They have some lovely songs."

Ali wasn't too thrilled about his chatting with Zeynep out of the blue like this.

"That's not who we're talking about. We're talking about these ludicrous pop singer types."

"This is Erdinç," I interrupted. "One of this *meyhane's* partners. And Zeynep and Ali here are my assistants."

Erdinç looked us all over fondly.

"I know, Chief. Everybody knows your team."

I have to say, I was surprised. Erdinç knew me, but how did he know Zeynep and Ali? As if reading my mind, he explained.

"From what's been written about you."

He must have been talking about the news in the papers. We were actually quite careful to keep our names out of them; this meant we'd have to be even more careful.

"Isn't Evgenia Hanım here?"

"No," I said, trying to look like I didn't care. "Her relatives from Greece showed up so she won't be here tonight."

"In that case, I'll tell them to fix the place settings." Before he left, he gave the table a onceover. "Is everyone having raki?"

Zeynep gently raised a hand. "I'd like wine. White, please."

"And I'll have a beer," Ali muttered frostily. "Make it a draft, though. You have draft, right?"

"Of course!" Erdinç said, with the easy-going nature of a competent venue owner. "The drinks are on their way." He turned his almond-shaped eyes on me. "And you'll be having raki, won't you, Chief? As usual?"

"That's right, Erdinç. But we're famished. So the sooner we're fed, the better."

Before heading to the kitchen, he didn't neglect to reassure us.

"Sure thing. I'll rush straight back to Cengiz now."

As I watched Erdinç make his way back, I noticed the *meyhane* was bigger than I'd remembered it, and was lit in a warm yellow light that was easy on the eyes. Even though there was no one but us, they'd lit a fire in the fireplace off to our right so that we could go back in if we got cold at the window. This was one of the few places in Beyoğlu that kept up the old *meyhane* traditions. And on either side of its hanging bay window were two tiny balconies with one table each that also overlooked the avenue. In summer, you could never tire of sitting there, watching the waves of colorful people below as you sipped your beer.

"You didn't forget, did you, Chief?" I turned back to the table at the sound of Zeynep's voice. "You're coming to our place this week. Last night my mother asked three times to be exact. And my father also reminded me as I was leaving this morning. He said to tell you hello and that they're definitely expecting you. You were supposed to choose the day. That's what they said."

It was shameful. People had been inviting me round for ages. And I really liked Zeynep's father, Veli. An honest man making an honest living. The same went for her mother. It couldn't have been easy raising three children on her husband's meager salary. Then again, Zeynep also contributed to the family budget now.

"They invited you too, of course, Ali," she continued. "There's never been a wedding without a groom, so my dad says."

Our little scamp went red as a beet at the wedding comment, though he tried hard not to show it.

"Thanks. I'll be there, of course," he said solemnly. "He's great, Veli Amca. And I love Sakine Teyze's cooking."

You're a lucky man; the woman's going to be your mother-in-law, is what passed through my mind. I worried about upsetting the balance though, so I didn't say it.

"Let's do it this week," I said, agreeing with our shy lovebird and leaving it at that. "It'd be rude to put it off any longer. Today is Wednesday. What do you say we go this Sunday?"

Ali nodded to answer that it suited him.

"Okay then. Sunday it is, Zeynep."

She seemed worried she was rushing us.

"If it were up to me, I wouldn't be in such a hurry but..."

"Don't be silly, Zeynep. How many times have they invited us now? We'll do it this week."

"Thanks, Chief. Evgenia Hanım will be there too, won't she?"

Evgenia loved this kind of invite.

"Of course she will. The last time I saw her, she reproached me for not rounding you both up and bringing you to Tatavla. She really misses you."

A sweet smile appeared on both their faces.

"We miss her too, Chief," Ali said warmly. "I love her as much as I would a sister, if I had one. She's a wonderful person." He gave me a curious look. Could he be pondering the issue of marriage for me at the same time I was doing it for him?

"That man," said Zeynep, scattering my thoughts. She was staring at the door. "Isn't that what's his name?"

I looked over and saw that oddball detective novelist; he'd taken off his beret and was shaking the snow from his coat. Next to him was a thin man with a tangle of hair and a beard. Him I'd never seen before. But wasn't it just that morning that I'd run into the writer? What, was he following me? He didn't look around the moment he came in as you would if you were searching for someone. And Erdinç must have known him because they immediately embraced. After the hugs and the back pats, the *meyhane* owner pointed over to our table. So then he knew the writer was interested in me, and may even be aware we were neighbors. Or had he been the one to whisper in his ear that I'd be coming to Feraye tonight? No, Erdinç was no blabbermouth; he wouldn't do that. It was obviously coincidence. Just look how surprised he was to see me. It made no difference; he immediately overcame his bewilderment. And yes, he smilingly made his way over, just as I suspected he would. Man, was he a strange one, the way he sidled over to us all nonchalantly, as though we were best buddies.

"Who the hell is that guy?"

Ali had noticed the overly bold writer as well.

"Isn't it, uh..." Zeynep faltered. "It's on the tip of my tongue. You know that writer... who does those crime novels? He has that book called Beyoğlu Rhapsody. Strange book, that. I'm not sure whether I liked it or not. He supposedly wrote it in response to Agatha Christie. But it's not like the crime novels we're used to. He hid the killer well enough, but it seemed to me like he was playing his readers for fools. Still, I'll give him his due; he sure did a great job explaining Beyoğlu's history."

"Is he coming over here?" Ali muttered nervously, his eyes still on the writer. When he got no response, he continued, "Yes, he's smiling at us. I think he knows you, Chief."

"He's my neighbor."

"Your neighbor?" my two young friends asked in unison.

"Yes, Nevzat Bey and I are neighbors," said the writer.

Would you look at the nerve of this guy? Jumping into the conversation without even feeling the need to be introduced.

"Good evening." He'd already held out a hand; it'd be rude not to shake it so I did, albeit unwillingly. He didn't take it to heart. He just turned to my assistant, who was still eyeing him over. "Hi, Zeynep Hanım. Inspector Ali. It's nice to see you here." My friends, unable to solve the mystery behind this air of familiarity, watched him with bewilderment. "How's the Tarlabaşı murder investigation going?"

I was worried Ali would snap at him, but go figure, he didn't even take issue, and it was Zeynep who surprised me.

"Still in its initial stages," she said, jumping to particulars. "It's more complicated than we first supposed." She smiled almost flirtatiously. "Maybe you can get a book out of it."

Pleased with the attention he was getting, he bantered on jovially.

"I'll write it if I can get your help, of course."

She must have had some small shred of common sense left because she responded by laying down a condition. "After we've solved the case and apprehended our murderer," she said.

"Of course. I wouldn't want to go sticking my nose in your business."

He was supposedly trying to be respectful, but that self-confident look on his face... It was driving me crazy. The gentle nod, as though he knew what all was up, those introspective eyes that seemed to say everything was under his control... Yet Zeynep's interest had gone to the tall bearded man who stood behind the author.

"Is your friend a writer too?"

"Yes," the detective novelist answered. His dark face looked amused. "Ayhan is also a writer, as well as a poet and an actor."

166

An urbane smile appeared on the multi-faceted artist's face; he gave a small bow and politely greeted the table.

"Good evening. It really is a great pleasure to see you here."

"So, do you write detective poems then?" I needled, unable to stop myself.

He shrugged it off and responded with the same humility.

"No, Chief. I wouldn't dare. But Attila Ilhan's written one: The Murder Hour."

"Seriously? There's a detective poem?" asked Zeynep incredulously. "I've never heard of such a thing. Did you know that, Chief?"

Frankly, I didn't want to get into the subject, but I was afraid to leave the floor to these two hacks. They'd already succeeded in affecting my kids; if I didn't intervene they might suddenly pull up some chairs.

"I do, of course. It's a lovely poem."

"Can you remember it, Chief? Tell us."

What in the devil was up with Zeynep? Why was she insisting like this?

"This is not the place. I'll tell you some other time."

Almost like a spoiled little girl, she persisted.

"Come on, Chief. I'm so curious what a detective poem is like."

The poet stood beside the smug author, eagerly waiting for me to recite the poem. "Fine," I said, when I noticed him. "I'll recite a couple lines then." Not because I was so keen on reciting poetry, but because I wanted to send these inopportune visitors packing as quickly as possible. "I think it started like this:

'On the Golden Horn, four men stabbed a ferryboat
Which sat anchored, bound hand and foot, and crying
Four knives were drawn, and four men stabbed it
An emerald green moon splintered in the sky.' "

I looked over at the poet, who listened with admiration. "That's how it went, isn't it, Ayhan Bey?"

"Sure is, Chief. Why did you stop?"

Leaning back, I grumbled soberly, "We were just discussing a rather serious subject. We don't have much time for poetry at the moment."

It wasn't just the two literary hacks but those at the table who also sensed my discontent.

"We'll let you get back to it, then," the detective novelist said, collecting himself. "Enjoy your meals."

"Good evening," his friend said, mimicking him. "A real pleasure to meet you."

They parted without any resentment and went to sit at a table where they couldn't see us.

"Weird," Ali muttered. "I feel like I've met that detective novelist before."

But what was really weird was that our wild boy, who never took a shine to people when he first met them, had taken a liking to the writer.

"You saw him on TV. He does the interview circuit on all the channels whenever a book is released."

He squinted and shook his head.

"No, Chief. Not like that. It's like I know him from a long time ago. I wonder if he ever taught in the orphanage. If we met somewhere around there. He seems so familiar."

"Can I tell you something?" said Zeynep, lowering her voice as though afraid of being overheard. "I feel the same way. I mean, I've heard him talk on TV before and I've read interviews in the papers, but seeing him face to face, I also feel like I know the man. Like he's family..."

They were really starting to talk nonsense.

"What family? I'm telling you, you saw him on TV or in the papers and that is the only way you know him. They've invited him to talk on TV about certain murder cases, too. Asking him how he would solve them and that sort of thing. That's how you remember him. His being an author has affected you, and you're throwing in the mystery for good measure."

They gave me a strange look. Our girl proved bolder than our boy.

"Do you not like him, Chief?" she said.

Of course I didn't like him. He lived right under my nose and was always just popping up, poking around in my investigations... He was extremely irritating. Why should I like him? But if I were to admit that, they would ask why, and I would have to come up with a more concrete explanation.

"Don't be silly. Where did you get that idea, Zeynep?" I said. "He's just too nosy. Whenever I bump into him, he asks me about whatever case we're on."

Yes, I finally succeeded. The clouds of doubt in their eyes began to dissipate.

"That's true. Look how he just asked about the murder in Tarlabaşı. Seriously, how does he know all this?"

Finally Ali was supporting me, though Zeynep was of another mind.

"From the papers, television... Where else?" she said, attempting to answer. "The man writes about murder. He probably reads about them every day in the newspaper and takes notes."

Why was it women always saw artists in a good light? Always with a positive bias? Thankfully, my stubborn Ali wasn't so easily convinced.

"We got that, Zeynep. But how does he know it's us dealing with this case?"

Our pretty criminologist's smooth brow wrinkled up. She was puzzling over it, but I was sure she'd come up with some logical explanation in the end. Then when she saw our charming waiter Cengiz with his tray full of *mezes*, the subject spontaneously petered out.

With a broad smile on his long thin face, he put the tray onto the table, saying, "Hello, Chief! Glad to have you!"

"Happy to be here, Cengiz. Where have you been?"

"I was in the kitchen, Chief. The kitchen boy is late so I'm helping out."

As he competently lined the *mezes* up on the white tablecloth, I asked half-teasingly, "What's happening with this engagement thing of yours, Cengiz?"

He put down a plate of sardines rolled in vine leaves and then stopped. With shy eyes, he looked from Zeynep to Ali. Apparently, I'd stuck my foot in my mouth. But I couldn't leave him in this state; I had to encourage him.

"You know, you were saying you were going to go talk to the girl's parents?"

With an innocent smile, he squirmed out of his embarrassment.

"We will, Chief. My girlfriend is ready. We spoke and we're on the same page. We'll go this summer, god willing. Remember, you gave me your word you'd come too."

"Sure, Cengiz. Whatever my part is, I'll play it."

"Thanks, Chief. Anyhow, you've never let us down."

As the charming waiter lined up the dishes of marinated sea bass, glasswort and octopus, Ali opened another completely unnecessary subject.

"Chief, you know all this talk about Beyoğlu's Finest Big Brother? Dice Ihsan was telling me about it today before you arrived…"

Again this menacing subject. I had to keep a lid on it.

"Don't believe everything you hear," I said, trying to circumvent the subject. But Cengiz had overcome his shyness to suddenly turn into a busybody.

"No. No, it's true," he agreed with my assistant. "They call the Chief 'Beyoğlu's Finest Big Brother' here. I first heard it when I moved here from my village. I was really curious who it was, actually." A blush spread through his bony cheeks again. "I'm sorry, Chief, but I was thinking Beyoğlu's Finest Big Brother was a film star, like Cüneyt Arkın or something." He turned to Ali and kept explaining. "Then one day I was picked up by police. Some woman's wallet was stolen, a tourist, and they accused me. Three huge officers had me surrounded in a holding cell with pieces of hoses in their hands. It was serious, I mean. I owe a huge thanks to the Chief. He came in the nick of time. And that's the day I understood who Beyoğlu's Finest Big Brother was. You can ask any shopkeeper on Istiklal Avenue. They all know the Chief. The old ones, that is."

I didn't deserve this praise at all.

"Come on, Cengiz," I said, interrupting his commentary. "Stop blathering and bring us some bread. We're dying of starvation here. And look, still no raki…"

"Right away, Chief."

I watched the waiter make his way to the kitchen with the empty tray and grumbled, "People love to exaggerate."

"And you are too humble."

Apparently these guys were ganging up to push my buttons tonight.

"Knock that off, Zeynep," I grumbled. "What has humbleness got to do with anything?"

Her friend immediately came to her aid.

"So you didn't rescue Cengiz then?"

"There was nothing to rescue, Ali. The woman who claimed her wallet was stolen had Alzheimer's. It hadn't progressed much yet, but with a careful eye you could discern it. She thought she'd brought the wallet with her but she'd left it in her hotel. Anyhow, the truth came out in the end and they let Cengiz go. That's it."

"I doubt that's all it is." Yes, it was Zeynep again. They had their boss in the middle and were putting the squeeze on him. "If it weren't for you, no one would have noticed the woman was sick. Poor Cengiz would have got a beating. He may even have gone to jail. The kid is right to shower you with praise."

Yes, once upon a time someone else had also showered me with praise, and had faith in me, but in the end they'd paid a heavy price for that. No, now was not the time or place to broach the subject.

"I didn't do Cengiz any special favors, friends," I said, staying loyal to the current talk at the table. "I just fulfilled my duties as an officer. Repaying him for the tax money he pays my salary with. Don't look at me like that, Zeynep. It's a messed up situation I'm talking about. If the state carried out its duties to its citizens like it's supposed to, there'd be no 'Beyoğlu's Finest Big Brothers' or 'Fantastic Fathers' or whatever... So now, because the government doesn't do its job, any civil servant who fulfills their duties is treated as a hero. There's really no such thing. I did what I was supposed to do. What every police in my position should have done. You understand?"

"Yes, we understand," said Ali, nodding slowly. His excitement had passed but the look of admiration on Zeynep's face was still in place.

"Maybe so, but it's still really nice that people love you, Chief."

"A world where nobody kills anybody..."

✳

"What a coincidence, two people planning to kill Engin on the same night." After her first glass of wine, Zeynep's eyes glossed over. She was starting to very charmingly talk in circles, yet persisting in her commentary on the investigation nonetheless. "The man had so many enemies that two separate killers could make a move on the same night... unbeknownst to each other."

The snow had completely stopped, but a blustery wind was pushing at the panes of our bay window with its invisible hand. An Aegean folk song I didn't recognize was mingling with the sound of the wind on the avenue, creating a strange howl.

"Isn't this one too many coincidences?" Ali held his glass of golden liquid between his palms. "Two attempted murders within only a few hours, I mean..."

His eyes were also foggy, and his face had fallen. The fatigue from what he'd been through the night before was setting in. Not to underestimate the effects of his beer, of course.

"But let's not forget this happened on New Year's." Zeynep raised a forefinger into the air, a clever expression on her face. "Celebrations and pandemonium all over the place. Taksim, Beyoğlu, Tarlabaşı... The streets swarming with people, everyone drunk. Everyone's gone berserk. It's a great time for a murder, isn't it?"

"All speculation, Zeynep," Ali insisted. He took his right hand off his frosty glass and put it to his burning forehead. "It's true that Engin had a lot of rivals. Okay, it's possible there were two attempts in the same night, but if we don't find out who gave Tidy Tarık those keys, we'll never figure this thing out."

We'd supposedly come here to enjoy ourselves, to let our hair down, but the subject had come back round to the murder again. The bad thing was I didn't even mind. After savoring a sip of the chilled raki in my glass, I also joined the conversation.

"It's not enough just to find out who hired Tidy. His was a failed attempt. There's a real killer out there who succeeded."

Ali held up the four fingers of his right hand.

"And at least four suspects." He kept talking as he closed up his fingers one by one. "Dice Ihsan, Black Nizam, the Italian mob, and Harem Süleyman."

Zeynep frowned.

"I undersand the first three, but who's Harem Süleyman?"

Our brat gave a cheeky smile.

"A flesh-peddler..." He'd got quite daring after the little bit of comfort he'd gained from his drink. "Just your usual pimp, though there's a funny story to it. Engin took Süleyman to the cleaners at the gambling table. Relieved him of his assets, his three women that is. We don't know when this happened, but we did witness a fight before we came to get you. Süleyman uses a knife like nobody's business. He almost skewered someone right before our eyes." He smacked his palm on his forehead. "That's right! I forgot to give it to you." He reached into the inner pocket of the navy blue coat he'd laid next to him. "Yes, here it is." He held the sharp pointy tool out to his friend. "And here you are..."

Our criminologist gave the extended knife a funny look.

"Is that any way to carry evidence, Ali?"

A colder wind than the gales outside the window blew across the table. My assistant was caught so off guard by Zeynep's reaction that for a moment he didn't know what to say.

"It wasn't Ali's fault," I tried to explain. "Things happened so quickly, we had to just take the knife as it was."

No, our meticulous girl wasn't going to leave it at that. The left side of her face was covered by the hair that had fallen over it, so her right eye glared.

"If nothing else he could've wrapped it in paper. Now there won't be any prints left on it."

"What am I supposed to do about it?" Yes, Ali had recovered and was wasting no time going on the attack. "People were all piled on top of us. Someone had a gun, another person a knife... Where am I gonna find paper at a time like that? It took me ages to get the knife unstuck from the sign as it is."

I was used to them bickering like this. Still, I wanted to nip it in the bud.

"Well, let's not dwell on it, Zeynep. Take a look at the knife. You can spray it with luminol solution or something. If you found some of the victim's blood, it would make our jobs much easier."

Our criminologist gave up, but our pugnacious friend rekindled the fire from the ashes, saying, "It's a waste of energy, Chief. Süleyman didn't do it."

Without even feeling the need to answer, she put the knife in an evidence bag she'd removed from her purse. I reached for my raki glass as if I hadn't heard him either. But our silent strategy failed.

"Süleyman, I'm saying, Chief," he pestered, a chip on his shoulder now. "In my opinion, he didn't do it. He's not the type to do something so devious. You saw that today too. If he were going to kill someone he'd do it out in the open..."

He wasn't interested in proving Süleyman's innocence; he just wanted to squabble with Zeynep. But the girl didn't comply, maybe because she realized she'd been unnecessarily hard on him. As she tossed the knife in the evidence bag back into her purse, "It's possible, Ali," she said calmly. "Still, I'd better give it a look."

"Wasted effort." He was so angry he wouldn't even look her in the face. "You won't find anything. And that's why I didn't make too much of your knife."

Zeynep shot him an icy look.

"*My* knife?"

Here we go. The storm was about to break.

"Frankly, I suspect Dice Ihsan." The words poured from my mouth without me thinking about them. "And I don't believe Engin's murder was planned either. What I think is that the dead man is a victim of recklessness. He shouldn't have been walking past Dice's place at that time of night." This scenerio I'd created, I wasn't sure how much help it would be in finding the killer, but it succeeded in getting the attention of these two fools in love. "Yes, friends, here's how I see it. Engin was passing by the Tarlabaşists Club. He'd probably been out having a good time and was most likely drunk. As he passed the gambling den, he ran into some people from Dice's team." I looked at Ali. "One of the guys from the gambling den today."

"Are you talking about that pocket Hercules?"

Our eager police officer was getting his groove back.

"Why not?"

He straightened up in his seat.

"I suppose it's possible, Chief." His voice took on a mysterious air. "The guy didn't seem that trustworthy to me. And those two jackasses sat at the bar for decoration didn't have the faces of killers. But the look in that little runty guy's eyes wasn't right. What was his name?"

"Necmi. Flea Necmi... He and Engin met outside the Tarlabaşists Club. They puffed up like angry tomcats when they saw each other... They shot each other looks, tried to intimidate each other, swore and whatnot, and Engin's hand went for his gun. But Flea Necmi acted faster; he'd already drawn his knife and he swung first. Engin was gone for good. There was no time to get rid of the body. They closed up the gambling den and hightailed it out of there..."

"Possibly." Zeynep, her elbows leaning on the table, studied my face with questioning eyes. "So, how do we explain Tidy Tarık's presence at the victim's house?"

Our fickle police jumped in eagerly, as if he weren't the one squabbling with Zeynep just now.

"I just had an amusing thought..." He laughed quietly, unable to hold back. "Now, let's say Dice Ihsan decides to finish this business. Doing away with Engin, I mean. He hires Tidy Tarık. Isn't that right, Chief, that Tarık was in and out of his gambling den? Maybe he had a debt he owed Dice. So the gunman gets down to business; he does the math and decides to take out Engin on New Year's Eve, in the man's own house no less. But by a strange twist of fate, Engin is walking past the Tarlabaşists Club that night. Like you said, he runs into Ihsan's jackals on the street, what happens happens, and Engin's off to the happy hunting grounds... Odd circumstances. But stranger things have happened. Let's consider it from Dice Ihsan's perspective. The man planned it to the finest detail, getting himself a hired killer, sorting out his enemy and no one will blame him. However, something unforeseeable happens. Just when his foe's in front of his venue's door, he is murdered by his own men. Imagine the shock."

What had started off as a lighthearted conversation was giving way to an interesting line of reasoning. And Ali's assessments weren't to be taken lightly. Swank Cemal's calling me at the break of dawn was testament to just how nervous Dice had become. Having a man murdered in front of his place, an enemy no less, would of course be cause for worry, but so much panic from an innocent man also raised flags. Still, it was hard to be certain. The good news was our stubborn lovebirds had stopped bickering and put their heads together to concentrate on the murder.

"What about the key? Engin's house key." Zeynep's question created a new wave of silence over the table. "Tidy Tarık, I'm saying. Did he get the key from Dice Ihsan? And in that case, who did Dice get it from?"

She wasn't asking to stir up trouble; she was just trying to complete the missing chapters of the story, as were we. But somebody had to play devil's advocate, so I took on that task.

"What if we're wrong? What if it isn't Dice, but Black Nizam that we're looking for?"

They looked at me in amazement; why the sudden flip? Wasn't I the one who just said I suspected Dice? What changed that I'd suddenly abandoned that theory?

"Stop giving me the strange looks. I'm not waffling. I'm just conjecturing. I'm not giving up on the possibility that it was Dice's men who murdered Engin. I'm trying to say if that's what happened, it was the result of a coincidence, and in fact Black Nizam's plan to have Engin killed could have already been set in motion. I mean, if Engin hadn't been murdered by Dice's men outside the Tarlabaşists Club, he would have been killed in his house by a bullet from Tidy Tarık's Glock after his own boss hired him. Isn't that right? It would be much easier for Nizam to get his hands on the house keys than Dice. What's more, we know Nizam had every bit as much reason to kill him as Ihsan did. Don't forget, Ali, just how upset Nizam was to find out about those house deeds."

"Nizam didn't know about the deeds?" Zeynep muttered, surprised.

"No. In fact, he even suggested the deeds were fakes. 'It's all just Dice's game; he set me up to look like the murderer,' is what he said. But what if he himself was the one to set it up? If what Dice said is true? 'Engin wants to be head honcho, and that's why Nizam killed him,' were Dice's words, if I'm not wrong, Ali?"

The drinks we'd been tossing back since we sat down had lost their effectiveness. We were all alert.

"No, you remember correctly, Chief. That's exactly what he said. And let's not forget about Çilem. If what Dice says is true, I mean that Engin used the girl in this business, Nizam could be really upset. His nephews weren't so thrilled with this Çilem thing either."

"Are you suggesting a crime of passion?" said Zeynep, straightening her hair. "That it may turn out to be a woman behind these mobsters settling their accounts?"

I doubted it, but the idea didn't seem so far-fetched to Ali.

"Why not? Most murders in the world are over love. Folks slaughtering each other over honor, morality, jealousy and such."

"It's women that are murdered more," our criminologist muttered with an anger that came from deep within, as she reached out her hand to take the glass of wine in front of her.

"But not in this particular case..." Ali objected. "In fact, in this case the killer, or instigator, may even be a woman. If it was Nizam that killed Engin, it may be Çilem who provoked it."

He was getting ahead of himself. This explanation didn't make any sense, and Zeynep didn't hesitate to respond.

"I don't think so, Ali. We haven't questioned these three women in the photos, I'll give you that. But we have no evidence to suggest that's the case."

Her wine glass hung there in her hand. Was a new tension brewing between them? Maybe I was to blame; I should never go out drinking with people I work with. But they weren't just colleagues, this was Zeynep and Ali. They were my family. Well, what's done was done. It was time to put an end to the brainstorming.

"We'll get to the bottom of it, friends," I said, as I also reached for my glass. "Come on. Let's drink to a world where no one is murdered, neither men nor women."

Naturally they both understood my intentions. They didn't object, conforming to my wishes and raising their glasses. They'd probably got tired of bickering, too. Zeynep's face lit up with a hopeful smile and she repeated, "Yes, a world where nobody kills anybody."

Just as our glasses were clinking, I heard my phone was ringing. I ignored it. The caller could wait. I took a long pull off my raki, which was getting tastier by the minute. Zeynep also heard the ringtone and alerted me as we placed our glasses on the table.

"Your mobile's ringing, Chief."

"I know."

I took my time removing the phone from my pocket. I didn't know the number.

"Hello?"

"Hi, Chief... It's officer Sami... We met at that murder site yesterday?"

It was the wimpier of the two we'd seen at the crime scene.

"Yes, Sami. Hope everything's okay?"

"Not really, no, Chief," he said, though his voice didn't sound at all distraught. "There was another murder... outside the Genuine Tarlabaşists Club this time."

"Don't you see the killers are there?"

※

The Genuine Tarlabaşists Club was located on the parallel street below the Tarlabaşists Club. That twisted street with the stone buildings gone ramshackle and decayed in the hands of the neighborhood residents who didn't know their value. Nizam, like his adversary Dice Ihsan, had outstayed his welcome in one of those century-old buildings. Admittedly, this building was grander and more beautiful, and even if it wasn't completely visible in the dusk, its facade had been overhauled. Still, the lighted orange letters of the Genuine Tarlabaşists Club sign could be seen even from the head of the street, and they clashed severely with the architecture of the historical building. There were many more police in the street than the night before, and the red and blue lights of the two squad cars at either end of the street flashed on and off on the snow. Sami was waiting in front of the one at our end. He recognized our silhouettes in the dark. He took a step forward and stood at attention.

"Hi, Chief." He turned towards the Genuine Tarlabaşists Club. "This way, please."

I immediately asked about the thing that had been bothering me since the news of the murder. "Was the victim killed with a knife?"

His skinny frame shook along with his head.

"No, Chief. A gun... There were seven shots fired."

"Seven shots?" I asked in amazement. "Did the victim also have a gun?"

He averted his eyes.

"The victim's friends did." He couldn't stand behind his words. "Or so the suspects say. We didn't find any other guns at the scene. But there were no bullets, or casings either for that matter."

"Was the murder weapon recovered?"

His taut face relaxed.

"Of course, Chief. A 9mm Browning. One of those custom-made jobs, silver-plated... It's licensed, too. It was fired from inside the building." He pointed towards the first floor window. "From right there."

When he noticed my surprise, he let the cat out of the bag.

"The suspect was waiting at the club for us. He told us everything."

Ali couldn't take the nonchalant attitude anymore and lost his patience.

"Tell us who the suspect is."

"Kudret." He couldn't figure out why we were angry. "Black Nizam's nephew Kudret," he whined, as if we were being too hard on him.

He must have been one of the dark-eyed twins sitting at the next table as we spoke to his uncle. I wondered which one. Did it matter? And what about yesterday's murder? Was it Kudret who'd murdered Engin? The questions leapt to mind one after the next but Ali acted faster, as usual.

"Did he confess? Why did he kill him?"

"Because they are terrorists..." he answered with that same infuriatingly casual attitude. "Because they threw a Molotov cocktail into their venue..."

"Wait, wait," I said sternly, trying to see the relevance. "Start from the beginning. But from the very beginning, without skipping anything."

He misunderstood and froze in his tracks.

"No, don't stop. Keep walking while you explain."

His eyes rolled uncomfortably, but he complied.

"Sure, Chief. An eight or ten-member terrorist group, we couldn't determine exact numbers, came to the Genuine Tarlabaşists Club round about eleven o'clock. Actually, the club was closed because of what happened to Engin, but

Kudret and Medet and their two cousins were inside boozing it up. One of the people in the group lit a Molotov and threw it at the window. The burning bottle broke the glass and fell in front of the table where they were sitting. Everything caught fire of course, and while Medet and his two cousins were attempting to put it out, Kudret went into the adjoining room, opened the window and shouted, 'What are you doing? Stop that!' But the activists on the street ignored him, shouting back at the top of their lungs to get the hell out of there, and then flung another bottle of gasoline at Kudret. The bottle didn't hit Kudret though. It bounced off the wall and fell to the floor. They had guns, too. Kudret mentioned two Kalashnikovs. When he saw the Kalashnikovs, he pulled his own gun on impulse. He's saying he didn't shoot with intent to kill and was just trying to protect himself but the activist died." He nodded to some place behind two uniformed officers. "The body is over there. You'll understand me better after you examine it."

"Is that what the suspect told you?"

He must have thought I didn't believe him because his face fell.

"Not just Kudret, Chief. The others said the same thing."

He was mealy-mouthing.

"By others you mean Kudret's twin Medet and their cousins?"

His dark eyes opened wide.

"There weren't any other witnesses. Anyhow, I know them. Kudret wouldn't lie."

"How do you know them?" Ali needled him. "You friends or something?"

"No, sir. That's absurd. Why would I be friends with punks like them? These guys have been in and out of the station a lot and that's how I know them all. What I'm saying is, Kudret may have got up to every kind of dirty business but I've yet to catch him in a lie."

"So last night, why did you claim you didn't know Engin?"

Ali's question was like a slap in the frail cop's face.

"Wha... What do you mean, sir?"

"And now you're playing stupid?" my assistant bellowed. "Didn't you say you didn't know Engin? Now you say you know all of them. If you know all of them, how is it you don't know Engin? Isn't Engin one of their men?"

"No, I mean, you misunderstood me. Yeah... Yes, of course Engin's one of their guys..."

He was digging himself in deeper every time he opened his mouth.

"All right, Sami. All right," I said, so as not to drag it out. "We'll discuss this Engin thing later. For now just tell me straight. Did you talk to these activists? What did they say?"

Our skinny colleague swallowed a couple of times.

"We were gonna talk to them of course, but they weren't here. They ran away after the gun fight... That's why we couldn't put a number on how many terrorists there were. I guess they panicked when their friends were shot at."

"What kind of terrorists are these?" Ali said sarcastically. "They have two Kalashnikovs but when they see a handgun they run for the hills?"

Sami went completely quiet. He wasn't worth the hassle.

"It must've been the same ones who threw the Molotov at Dice's place this morning," Zeynep muttered. "I doubt those guys had any guns. When Kudret opened fire, the foolish kids probably just panicked and ran away."

That was it most likely. Right now though, the suspect we had was of more importance than these anonymous activists.

"Where is Kudret now?"

"At the central station, Chief. We thought it would be ill-advised for him to stay here. We were worried the victim's friends would get together and attack the club. It's obvious the slain activist was a member of a political group. So we sent the suspect out just in case. Kudret's at the station, waiting for you to interrogate him. I mean, it's late but if you want to question him... You could leave it till tomorrow of course."

When I failed to respond to his blathering, he pointed towards the crime scene.

"So the victim is over there Chief. And don't worry, I didn't let anyone touch anything."

We looked over towards the Genuine Tarlabaşists Club. The victim was lying in an island formed from the blood in the white snow. The smell of petrol wafted out into the chilly air from the bottle he still clutched between stiffened fingers. He wore a green anorak, blue jeans on his legs and surprisingly, sneakers on his feet. I couldn't see the head at first because one of the uniformed cop's legs was in the way. He'd fallen face up, just like Engin. But it wasn't just the left side of his chest, his entire anorak seemed drenched in blood. Blood and snow... When the police between us took two steps to the right, I saw the head and the thin face. Hair the color of night spread out like a veil of mourning on the white snow...

"It's a girl!" Zeynep exclaimed in astonishment. "They killed a girl..."

It was indeed a girl lying there, her green beret just beyond her head. Her eyes, their color indiscernible, were stuck on some indeterminate object in the sky just like Engin's had been. All at once, a vision from seven years earlier settled over the young girl's corpse. The image of another young girl, probably about the same age. Petite, curly-haired and dainty-faced, with eyes like grapes... A girl killed not by a bullet but by a knife, by her biological father's hand just a few streets away. No, it hadn't been snowing and it wasn't winter. It was hot and humid, a muggy July night. That cursed summer evening that evoked the last day on earth. On her back, just like this poor girl... Lying in a pool of her own blood. The only difference was there was nobody around that corpse. Despite it being a summer night, we couldn't find a soul on the streets. It was as if all the people in this huge neighborhood had dug a hole in the ground and crawled in. There was only the girl, murdered by her own family, her body growing cold on the warm stones of that steamy evening.

"Murderers!"

No, it wasn't my voice. Nobody, including me, would have the guts to shout that out on the street.

"Murderers!"

No, it was not the forgotten memories in the hazy rooms of my mind either; the voice was coming from the top of this Tarlabaşı street dominated by the cold winter night. An agonizing female voice.

"How could they do this to my Fidan? Animals... Murderers..."

"Was this the girl's mother? I was pleased that, if nothing else, she had a mother who grieved for her. On that summer night when that other poor girl's body was slashed to bits, the mother never shed a tear. I looked intently in the direction of the woman's voice. As she grew closer I recognized it. It was that woman Nazlı, the demonstrator at the head of the protest we'd seen that evening. The woman who owned the culture center. It seemed two officers were trying to stop her, but who would listen? With a frame that was quite large for a woman, she had already pushed through the police, crying, "Let me go! Let me go in..." It really was a sight to see. She reminded me of the goddess statues I'd seen in museums. Profound grief in her eyes, ignoring the wind that blew her hair about, she had thrown back her head just like those statues and walked straight towards the young girl's corpse. We watched her in silence. They saw it was impossible, so our wimpy Sami and another officer joined the team of those trying to restrain her, and when she was five or six meters from the corpse the four men barely managed to hold her back.

"Let me go!" she howled again. "Why are you trying to stop me when it's the dirtbags who shot Fidan you should have stopped?"

She saw the futility in her shouting and struggling and began to cry. It wasn't long before she regained her air of dignity though.

"All right, all right. Take your hands off me. I'll stay calm. But let me see Fidan. Just once."

"That's not possible, Nazlı Hanım," said Sami. So then he knew her. "It's a crime scene and you'll disturb the evidence. You'll get us in trouble."

A pleading look appeared in Nazlı's eyes for the first time.

"I won't. I just want to see her one last time."

"Let her go," I called out. "Let her come over."

Sami gawked at me, unable to believe his ears.

184

"Go on. Let her through, kid."

"But Chief..."

I had to raise my voice in order to get through to him.

"I said it's all right, Sami. Let the woman go."

It wasn't just the officer, Nazlı's face also took on an odd expression. But the look didn't last long and her gaze slid back to the young girl's lifeless body. She walked slowly through the police, who stepped out of her way. When she saw the girl's corpse, she stopped. I noticed her large frame shake. She was crying silently. No shouting, no wailing, her tears just spilled out like that from despair. Signaling to Ali and Zeynep to stay where they were, I walked over. As I reached her, I realized she was mumbling something. Was she praying? No, it was more like a confession. A couple more steps and I could make out the words.

"I couldn't save her," she was saying, gently shaking her head. "I couldn't save her..."

My curiosity defeated me and I asked, "Couldn't save her from who?"

She turned her head, startled.

"What?"

I put a measured smile on my face.

"The victim, I'm saying. Was she being threatened?"

"Who are you? I've never seen you around here before."

"Chief Inspector Nevzat," I said amicably. "From homicide. I'm heading this investigation. Was the victim a relative?"

That deep sadness settled into her eyes again.

"Fidan? She was like a daughter..." She was biting her bottom lip so as not to cry. When the wave of grief pressing her heart had passed, she continued. "Or at least I thought she was, but then she left me. I couldn't take care of her. I couldn't protect her."

"Who couldn't you protect her from?" I asked one more time.

She looked me over as though seeing me for the first time, trying to decide whether I was a friend or foe.

"From who? From these guys of course." She pointed at the Genuine Tarlabaşists Club. "The filth in this building, this neighborhood, this city... These monsters who appear human, these money-worshipping cannibals." She looked back over at the young corpse. "I said it so many times. I explained it over and over, how you can't beat them like this. But she didn't listen..." She'd started to cry again, continuing to talk all the same. "She wouldn't listen to me. She accused me of being scared. 'I'm going to get revenge for my sister, and for my mother,' she said. But look what happened. I shouldn't have let her go. I had no right to be angry with her, no right to let her go alone..."

Her speech was wandering and so fragmented it was difficult to understand what she was talking about. I continued to pry at the subject so she might go into detail.

"What happened to her sister and mother?"

"They destroyed them," she said, shaking her head in despair. "They destroyed them."

"Who?"

"These guys, this gambling mob... There's that dirtbag, Dice Ihsan. Him. And then Black Nizam, the crook in this building. His nephews... Engin, who was killed yesterday. Where should I start?" She threw her hands up. "This abandoned neighborhood, this cruel city, you, me, all of us... We all destroyed them."

Her voice slammed against the dilapidated walls of the century-old buildings and echoed into the night. Everyone in the street had turned to watch us, but she didn't care one bit. Maybe the real reason behind these murders was hidden in what this quirky woman was saying.

"They killed Fidan's mother? They hurt her sister? I don't understand. Can you be clearer?"

Her moist eyes landed on my face.

"How can I be any more clear? They destroyed them. They murdered them both at the same time. They took everything from them. Their house, their possessions, their bodies, their lives..." She gestured towards Fidan once more. "She's all that was left, and in the end they took her too."

Her eyes had welled with tears again.

"Nazlı Hanım," I said, trying to be as respectful as possible. "Let's go some place more suitable, if you want. It's really important, what you're saying. It would help me to pinpoint the murderers and those behind them."

186

There was fire in her wet eyes.

"The murderers?" she said. She seemed to have lost all reasoning and was giving me a crazed look. "It's plain who the murderers are, Nevzat Bey. Can't you see the obvious? They've ruined this neighborhood, ruined this city, this country... they've ruined us all. Don't you see the killers are there?"

"I understand, but the situation is more complicated than you think. If we could sit and talk it over..."

She shook her head and looked away.

"Why? What difference would it make?" She turned to look at me again. "Instead of talking to me, talk to that crook Black Nizam..."

She must have uttered her final word because she turned round the direction she'd come from. It was no use insisting, but we needed her statement and I was afraid we'd have to bring her in with a court order. How much help it would be to us under such forced circumstances, that was another story. Then she suddenly stopped. Whatever it was she was thinking, she turned around.

"What is it you want?" she said, her tone challenging. "Are you just trying to close a file, or do you want to learn the truth?"

Her eyes never left mine for a second as she asked the question. She wasn't threatening me, just trying to understand.

"Of course I want to learn the truth. If those who know it would only explain it to me."

I guess my answer wasn't sufficient, as she threw her head back softly and looked me over a while longer.

"Well then, let's go," she finally said, hugging her ash-colored coat. "It's cold out. Let me make you a cup of tea and we'll talk."

"In this country a woman's flesh, her life, are cheaper than water."

※

On the corner where the Sakız Ağacı slope meets Tavla Street was a tall building, the Ferhat Çerağ Culture Center, which despite its age was well looked after. A dark-skinned child with a pockmarked face opened its huge wooden door. He must have been Keto's age, or maybe a couple years older. He was staring out with a curiosity that could turn to grief at any moment.

"What happened? Is it true? Is Fidan Abla dead?"

Nazlı swallowed. She said not a word but just held the child close, hugging him like a mother would hug her son after losing her daughter. She stayed that way a while, then planted a kiss on the dark hair of the child who barely reached her shoulders.

"Go on, Bahri. Go on now and get to bed. We'll talk in the morning."

For a moment the child didn't know what to do, but faced with Nazlı's decisiveness, he couldn't object.

"All right, abla. We'll talk in the morning," he said before heading for the stairs. "Good night."

"Good night, Bahricim."

"Fidan was like that," she whispered sadly as the boy climbed the stairs. "But she wasn't as brave as Bahri. She was afraid to sleep alone."

I thought she was going to start crying again but no, she didn't let herself. She contented herself with a sigh.

"Come on in, Nevzat Bey. I'll put on the tea and be right back." She paused. "Or would you prefer coffee?"

Was she implying she'd sussed out I was a little drunk? I gave nothing away.

"I'd prefer tea if it's no bother..."

I was wrong; her offer wasn't hinting at anything.

"It's no bother. I'll use tea bags, in any case," she murmured with the familiarity of an old friend.

"Of course. So long as there's something hot in our throats."

I took a look around before going into the room Nazlı had shown me. Four rooms faced each other. Although the steel beams used to retrofit the building were painted the color of paper bags, they stuck out like sore thumbs. Apart from that it was fairly charming for a culture center. They'd maintained the integrity of the original building: the wooden floors, the window frames, the stairs and railings, the doors to the rooms...

On the walls hung delightful nature paintings which must all have been painted by the same person's brush. Getting a bit closer, I could read the artist's name: Claude Monet... There were vast stretches of countryside, poppies, violets and water-lillies...

If we didn't count the kitchen Nazlı had gone into, it was difficult to discern what the other two rooms with closed doors were used for. My gaze went to the stairs Bahri had gone up; I supposed there were three or four more floors above.

I headed into Nazlı's office. The room was quite a large, airy place, and very nicely decorated. A woven Bünyan carpet in vibrant colors on the floor, a rather large handcrafted wooden table with milky-brown velvet chairs... a pale green divan that could easily seat four people and brocaded scatter cushions in the corners. The room's walls resembled a primary school exhibition. There were pictures stuck everywhere, a few more Monet prints, but mostly the enthusiastic sketches of amateur hands. Naive, like my Aysun used to draw, though perhaps darker... So what Keto said was true. Nazlı must have been bringing in artists and authors to educate the children. These pictures would be the products of that endeavor. The only wall without pictures was the massive one behind the table. Just an old wooden clock hung there, slightly smaller than the one in my house, and from a frame directly under the clock the bright eyes of an eagle-nosed man with brown hair and a lush red moustache watched me.

"The tea's almost ready."

She'd caught me looking at the picture and hesitated a moment but then ignored it. She hurriedly got to the subject as if afraid I'd ask who the man in the photo was.

"Yes, Fidan stayed with us. For two years..."

I was still standing, my coat still on, but what could I do? Once the woman started to explain, I was all ears.

"She knocked on our door the day she turned eighteen. She'd actually wanted to come much earlier but was afraid the courts would give her back to her father. He was a real lowlife, Yakup. A gambler and a vile man. I'm talking about Fidan's father. He was unreliable, a real bastard..."

She wasn't holding back, Nazlı. In a strange way it suited her, speaking like this without censoring herself. She suddenly went quiet, finally noticing I was still standing. She laughed sheepishly.

"I'm a terrible host, aren't I? I didn't show you to a seat or take your coat." She paused. "You aren't cold, are you? I can turn the heating up."

"No. No it's really cozy inside," I said, taking off my coat. "I was distracted by the pictures."

She politely took my coat to make up for her gaffe.

"Over here, please."

As I sat in the chair she indicated, she went over to the hooks behind the door.

"Have you ever met this Yakup?" I asked at her back.

"Of course," she answered as she hung my coat. "That sleazeball darkened our doorstep the moment he heard she'd come here."

She turned and looked at me as she continued.

190

"I was straight to the point with him. 'Your daughter is eighteen years old,' I said. 'She has the right to stay wherever she wants.' I told him if he tried to force her or started harrassing us I'd have him locked up. He balked a bit but when I told him I was calling my lawyer right then and there he gave in and went off with his tail between his legs. And he never came back, though he did approach Fidan. 'I'm in a bad way, float me some cash,' he told her. Fidan swore she didn't give him any; I don't know..."

As she took off her coat, her large frame in its black turtleneck emerged. She hung her coat and turned back round, continuing to explain as she walked over.

"They didn't have such a bad life, in fact. At some point he ran a tea stall in Narmanlı Han. His wife Rümeysa cleaned houses, despite her poor health. Her cleaning job wasn't to be taken lightly; she probably earned more than her husband..." She'd stopped opposite me and was giving me a curious once-over. "You're comfortable there, aren't you?"

"I'm fine. Please don't worry about me."

As she sank into a chair, she went back to the subject.

"But that wimp gambled away all his and his wife's earnings. You know that fools' trap the Tarlabaşists Club? Dice Ihsan's den of cheats? Well, that's the one Yakup frequented. He'd win once then have a losing streak of course, and his appetite grew as he lost so first he bet his tea stall, after which he bet the things in his house. And I'm not embellishing. Fidan would be in tears as she explained it. Not only the fridge and TV but everything, right up to the pots and pans. And when those were finished, the girls were next in line. Kumru was only a year older than Fidan. He bet her away..."

"What on earth?" I protested. "What century are we living in? Kumru should have gone to the police."

"She did, but it had all been plotted out. The man who won Kumru told him he'd marry the girl. And that's how that disgraceful man Yakup put it to his wife Rümeysa. 'The man's rich,' he said. 'He has a petrol station in Dolapdere. He'll give Kumru a better life.' And this man who proposed to marry her was ten years older than Yakup himself. Even worse, he was already married with three children. He never even had an official marriage with his first wife, just a religious ceremony."

She sighed a deep sigh.

"It's the same old scandal... Yes, in this country a woman's flesh, her life, are cheaper than water. In this country women are offered up as sacrifices to men to amuse them, to serve them, even to be killed by them..."

At that moment I understood what it was about this woman that had drawn me to her from the moment I saw her. Heartbreak, that's what I saw when I looked at her. A boundless, toughened heartbreak. It wasn't just the lines on her brow, the unforgiving wrinkles collected around her violet eyes, or her auburn hair beginning to go grey. The cheeks that had grown chubby, the prematurely collapsed shoulders she tried to keep straight and the hoarse voice all roused the same emotion in me: pure heartbreak.

"They gave Kumru to the man, and of course nobody asked the poor girl her opinion. Maybe she loved someone else, but who gave a damn? In the end Kumru became a second wife to a woman older than her own mother. Only three months later... Three months later she left the house in a body bag, that same one she'd entered in a bridal gown. They called it suicide and said she couldn't take any more, swallowed pills, poisoned herself... Is it true? Who knows? In this country everything animal and mineral is for sale, Nevzat Bey. You can buy anything if you have the money, not least of all people. Doctors, judges prosecutors, policemen... everyone. This country's problem, is its immorality, lack of honor, loss of dignity..."

In her violet eyes, electric blue sparks burned. It seems the only time that chronic heartbreak dispersed was when she got angry.

"Yes, Nevzat Bey, the death of that unfortunate girl should be one of your murder investigations. Maybe you should reopen that file... It's not a situation the human conscience can accept, nineteen-year-old Kumru's entering a house in a veil and leaving it in a shroud. And Rümeysa, already ill, couldn't take the pain. She died within a year. Fidan was left alone with her irresponsible, gambling-obsessed father. The

192

poor girl spent every night in fear, wondering if her father would bet her away too. And that is why the day she turned eighteen, she ran away and took shelter with us. I gladly took her in. I put her to work with a dentist friend. She continued to stay nights here, but said she'd move in with friends when she earned a bit of money. I approved, happy that she'd be standing on her own two feet. But then she joined a political organization. Don't go picturing a terrorist group or anything. It was for disgruntled youth like herself to gather. Yes, they were all full of rage. And yes, they were all rebelling against the injustices they'd been through..." For a moment she stared into space. "And maybe..." Whatever was going through her mind prevented her from finishing her thought. She couldn't go on any longer; her eyes grew moist again and her lower lip sagged. She started to cry, tears streaming silently from her eyes. She covered her face with her right hand and stayed that way a while. Before long she pulled herself together, continuing, red-faced, from where she'd left off. "Maybe," she said sniffling, "she was trying to help me. Fidan loved me. We went to court over the building this... this dog Black Nizam inhabits. I own the building where his horrible club is. They are my tenants, I mean. They stayed there dirt cheap for years. I wanted to throw them out, not because of the money but because I needed the building for another culture center. Nizam thwarted that plan. Threats, swearing, firing guns outside our door... But he couldn't break our will. And finally Nizam gave up. He submitted a formal document saying he'd vacate the building. I guess that means Fidan didn't trust them; she got it into her mind to try and scare Nizam off herself. She didn't know how ruthless these men were. It may be my fault the girl's dead..."

I couldn't take her beating herself up anymore.

"You're wrong. It had nothing to do with you."

She didn't understand. I enunciated the words again.

"It is not your fault. It wasn't only Nizam's venue; the Tarlabaşists Club also had a Molotov thrown at it. Dice Ihsan's place... Their intentions were not to help you. In their minds they were trying to punish all the bad guys in Tarlabaşı. Of course Fidan had a much better reason, trying to avenge what

193

happened to her mother and big sister. They must have made a decision to burn down the gambling dens, so don't blame yourself." I threw her a pointed glance and lowered my voice. "That is if there's not some other issue I don't know about..."

The sadness in her face disappeared immediately and the quarrelsome woman appeared once more.

"Don't you criticize those kids. They were doing what you should have."

I laughed calmly.

"What, we should have burned down the gambling joints?"

I thought that would make her angrier, but surprisingly her voice softened.

"I'm not condoning what they did. When I say 'you' please don't take it personally. I don't know you, but you seem like a nice person and you aren't trying to pull any police tricks over on me. You're different from other police I've encountered. I'm talking about the ones who turn a blind eye to gambling even though it's illegal. Those police who are in thick with the mafia." She nodded towards something outside. "You know that officer who tried to stop me? The one called Sami? How many times have I seen him with Nizam. And he has a buddy, an officer with a huge head named Zeynel."

She was talking about our two colleagues from the night before.

"Yes, those two divided up tasks. He's always in Dice's place. They both back the mafia bosses. Of course, these are the two we see. Then there are the ones behind the curtain. The ones who probably share out the money that's collected... You are going to say their salaries aren't enough, so what can they do?"

I wasn't sounding off about her accusations, though it bothered me that she was putting words in my mouth.

"I wouldn't say that," I cut in. "It'd be nonsense. Police who think their salaries insufficient should find another career. There is no excuse for an officer turning a blind eye for his or her own gain. You're right. These things happen because we aren't fully doing our job, but it's not just police that are broken, it's the whole system. The one that allowed a ghetto to form in the heart of the city to begin with..."

194

Beneath wet lashes, her blinking eyes scrutinized me as if to understand whether I was sincere or just saying what she wanted to hear in order to trick her.

"Then we'd have to take a look at the past. At those days when the wealth tax was being announced, and the events of six and seven September. Those cruel, shameful days when we drove out the true owners of these buildings..."

"You're right," I said, surprising her once more. "This country's past is full of plunder, exile, and death. Just like all other countries' histories. We could discuss it all night and still not finish, nor find a solution. We do have two murders which can be solved, however. If you'll help me, at the very least we can catch these murderers."

She didn't know what to say, so I thought she was done objecting.

"So what if you do catch them?" she finally grumbled. "It's obvious who killed Fidan anyhow. But you'll see, they'll plead self-defense and her killer will be out in six months. As for Engin, don't think I've got a heart of stone, but he was beneath contempt. If he hadn't died, I'm sure he would have killed others."

"We also had our doubts in that respect. And it involved you."

There was no fear or anger in her eyes now, only curiosity.

"That's right. We found a diagram of this building in a hidden safe in Engin's house."

Her brown eyebrows furled.

"A diagram?"

"Sketches, detailed ones... Of where you could enter the building, exit it, the back service door, the windows, which ones had metal bars on them and which didn't, the fire escape stairs..."

There was not the least sign of concern on her face.

"I guessed as much." She smiled bitterly. "I'll be honest with you. At one time I was ready to believe Nizam. That humble attitude, the broken Turkish, maybe his ugliness... I thought he was a victim, too. Someone with no other choice."

I nodded.

"Yes, today I spoke with Black Nizam. He comes off as compassionate and understanding. Ugly, but with a conscience. Maybe he considers himself compassionate. But then a few hours later one of his nephews mercilessly guns down a young girl. And I'm sure it's not the first person he's killed." I leaned back with a dismal sigh. "This is nothing to do with a person being good or bad. The underground world has its own rules. They experience cruelty too. And they don't respect a man who doesn't spread fear. For them, cruelty is the greatest of virtues. For that reason alone they may not want to give you the building. And if they do give up the building, they may plan to make you pay in some form. So they don't lose the effect of the wave of terror they spread around. It wasn't for nothing they made that diagram, I suppose..."

She was puzzled; the time was ripe to bring up a subject I wondered about.

"So, did Engin have a personal issue with you?"

"A personal issue?" She seemed to find the question nonsensical. "No. Why would he? He came here from Germany, or Switzerland. Sure, he was really different from Black Nizam's nephews, but not in a good way. He was more uncompromising, colder, nastier... Yes, he was a good-looking guy. You know those arrogant handsome types? One of those... Some women are a sucker for that type. He was quite the lady-killer. Still, his women were not the be-all and end-all for him. He had loftier goals. It seemed to me he was manipulating Black Nizam. Maybe he was planning to take Nizam's place."

It was worth noting that Nazlı was framing it as Dice Ihsan had.

"You're saying Engin's boss killed him?"

"No. That's not what I meant." She gave me a funny look. "You police have such an interesting train of thought. I don't know who killed Engin. Could it have been Black Nizam? Maybe, but he had so many enemies. I really have no idea."

"Had Engin arrived by the time the situation with this building was being discussed?"

"Of course. He was in this from the beginning. He was the first one to talk to us, in fact. He phoned me. His demeanor was cold, albeit polite. 'Drop the subject and we'll find you another building,' he said. And I told them to go find another building themselves. He said, and I quote, 'It's not in your best interest to talk this way.' I asked him if he was threatening me. When he said 'I'm just cautioning you. You are a woman, and you're alone.' I lost my temper. I screamed and shouted and then hung up in his face. That evening there was gunfire outside the door and the following day the ground floor windows were smashed. In the morning when we got up, we found a dead cat outside the door. That poor cat, they'd shot it in the head... They thought they could frighten us. It was unbelievable. I gathered the kids together and we stormed the Genuine Tarlabaşists Club." She giggled like a naughty child. "Nizam was taken so off guard he nearly swallowed that enormous tongue of his. I talked straight to him, anyhow. 'Don't mess with us,' I said. At first he told us he respected the work we did and other such lies, and then he tried to bargain. He implied that if we gave up on the building he'd make us a donation. Naturally, I didn't accept. In the end, he presented us with an affidavit claiming he'd vacate the building within ten months. But I guess that means he hadn't really given up." She went quiet again and turned her questioning eyes on me. "So if we're mistaken... What if the diagram was old, from the days they were trying to intimidate us. Isn't that possible?"

It was possible, but we needed to be sure.

"I don't know," I said, looking away. "It could be, though Fidan's murder just goes to show how sensitive the men are about this building. You should tread lightly."

At that moment, the door opened and a petite woman in a pink tracksuit entered. Even without makeup she was pretty. Her black eyes were misty; she must have just woken up. When she saw me, she collected herself as though with disappointment.

"Excuse me," she said, in a voice too thick for a woman. "You have a guest."

It turns out it was a transvestite standing at the door. Her face was so slim, its lines so agreeable, if she hadn't spoken it would be very hard to discern.

197

"It's okay, Ayşen. Were you going to say something?"

The young transvestite was flustered.

"The kids in the room across from mine were talking. I guess someone's been killed? I got curious."

"Thank you for asking, Ayşen. It was a girl called Fidan..." Nazlı explained stoically. "She used to stay here. She was one of our kids..."

"I'm so sorry, Nazlı Abla." She looked back over at me again. She wasn't flustered anymore; there was just a vague look of doubt in her black eyes. "Everything's okay, isn't it?"

Nazlı knew what she was thinking.

"Yes, it's fine. But seeing as you're down here... I put some water on for tea. It's boiled, so if it's not much bother would you mind serving it?"

"Of course, right away," she said, diligently setting about to do so.

Nazlı tenderly called after her. "The tea bags are on the second shelf. And we'd really appreciate if you could bring some of those biscuits, too..."

"Our New Religion and Worshipping Rituals"

※

The tea's bitter heat spread through my whole body, leaving a familiar taste in my mouth. I didn't admit it to Nazlı, but it was the first time I'd felt warm since coming into the building.

"Help yourself to these too, Nevzat Bey." She pointed at the biscuits in the yellow dish on the coffee table. "They're really delicious, all organic..."

I was full, but I set my cup down on the table and took one to please her. It was tasty, all right.

"Did you make these?"

Her eyes shifted to the door the pretty transvestite had just left through.

"Oh, no. Ayşen made them," she said, in a voice filled with pride. "Everyone here is so talented. I'm the only one here who has no skill for things like this. Strange, considering my mother was so competent. Even with all the cooks and servants in the kitchen, she wasn't too lazy to make pastries and biscuits with her own hands..."

While she was talking about her family, I took the opportunity to learn more about her.

"Is your mother alive?"

A tender despondency licked her face.

"Unfortunately not. I lost her ten years ago, and my father four years after that... I have no siblings." In her voice could be heard the humbleness of a person who'd come to grips with their pain. "I do have plenty of cousins. Dozens, both boys and girls... That's what happens when a person has three aunts and five uncles. Lots of children... But we're not so close. They all think I'm crazy. They call when they are in trouble, when they need money..."

"Seriously," I asked, glancing around. "How do you get by? The expenses for this place must be phenomenal, and you are thinking of opening yet another one?"

She took a sip of her tea then gave me a long hard look. It wasn't suspicion in her eyes. On the contrary, her expression was more one of amusement.

"Go on, admit it," she said, before leaning forward. "You are looking for some illegal political organization behind this, aren't you?"

"Of course not. Where did you get that idea?" I said, trying to recover. "I'm just asking out of curiosity."

Naturally, she didn't believe me. She took another sip of her tea, or a big gulp rather. She must be a big tea drinker.

"It's not important, Nevzat Bey. I have nothing to hide. Real estate. The apartments left to me by my father, land in Silivri and Çatalca... If you'd like I can introduce you to Fırat Bey and he can explain the details. He looks after my finances. He's an honest man, and more fastidious than I am. We haven't got a penny's tax debt. The government probably owes us. To that extent, I mean..."

She'd keep going if I didn't stop her.

"Please, you misunderstood me. I wasn't thinking you would do anything illegal in a business sense..."

"In a business sense..." she jibed. "But when there are protests it's another story, you mean." She wouldn't let me get a word in edgewise. "No, Nevzat Bey, whatever doubts have been chewing at you since you first saw me, go on and say them. You think I have some connection with the organization Fidan was a member of. That maybe I formed the organization myself. Isn't that so? Why would a woman run a business like this on her own? And in such a dodgy place as Tarlabaşı, no less."

It's not like the thought hadn't crossed my mind, but I denied it.

"I don't know. I'm sure you had your reasons."

"It makes me feel good," she said, shrugging her broad shoulders. "Yes, helping others gives me pleasure. And I suppose I love these people..."

I thought it wouldn't hurt to be a bit contrary, now that we'd got used to each other.

"But you're not one of these people. You had an affluent upbringing. And probably got a stellar education..."

"What exactly is a 'stellar education'?" she said dismissively. "Is it your time in school that makes you successful? It's okay, but if that success breeds unhappiness, what good is it to anyone? No, I don't believe in that kind of education. If it's studying in a private school you're referring to, then yes I did, and I finished university too. But what the last four years in Tarlabaşı have taught me, I couldn't have learned in any school."

I thought about what she'd been through before she came here. She may have been a woman of means, but I don't suppose she'd had an easy life. She could have been an alcoholic or got into drugs for a while... I suddenly noticed she didn't smoke and was quite surprised, for some reason. Why had I thought she was a smoker? Because women like Nazlı all smoked, that's why. But was that true or was this just occupational bias?

"This place is the real school, Nevzat Bey," Nazlı continued to explain, unaware of what was going through my mind. "A school risen from poverty, disgrace, and misery. It's not so much real people, but people's reality that you see here. Not just other people's, but your own reality. And yes, I'm happier here than anywhere."

My eyes shifted to the photo of the young man with the copper moustache hung on the wall behind the table. Nazlı caught it straight away.

"Never mind the photo," she said, giving my curiosity a thorough whipping. "Come on, say it. Ask me about that political organization."

I decided it might be in my interest to play by her rules a bit.

"All right," I said, reaching for my teacup again. "What kind of setup is this organization Fidan belonged to?"

Before answering my question, she also picked up her cup.

"You couldn't even call it a political organization, really. It's more an association. Even the name is unconventional. Tuesday..."

I kept hold of my tea glass.

"Tuesday?"

"That's right, the Tuesday Group. You remember the resistance? I mean in Gezi Park... That demonstration started the morning of Tuesday, 28 May. So the association takes its name from that day. It's meaningful, yet very innocent if you ask me. And the meetings are always held on Tuesdays."

"What do they do at these meetings?"

She took her time answering, sipping her tea, so I raised my glass to my lips, too.

"What do you think? They just talk. Discuss what's going on in the world, the country's problems, what's happened in the city... It's true they're mostly leftists. Environmentalists and leftists, actually. There are some Kurds among them, and anarchists. By anarchist, I don't mean kids with weapons or anything. They're all opposed to violence..."

"So you say, but throwing a Molotov cocktail is violence." I put my glass down on the table. "It can kill someone, burn them no less."

She averted her eyes and placed her glass on the coffee table. "You're right," she anxiously backpedaled. "I don't know how they could do such a thing. Even with the police's brutal crackdown during the Gezi Resistance these kids didn't use Molotov cocktails." She paused again; her eyes stayed on my face. "Are you sure it was the Tuesday Group that did this?"

I spread my hands open.

"Who else would it be?" After a brief silence, I asked, "Are you saying there's another political organization?"

She didn't like the question; she folded her arms and leaned back in her chair.

"I doubt it. Like what?"

There was no sense to her obstinacy.

"How did Fidan meet this Tuesday Group?"

"I don't know," she answered without hesitation. "But I was a bit worried when I first heard of them."

Was this some kind of confession?

"A bit worried," I repeated emphatically. "What was it that worried you?"

"No, no it's not like you think." Her gaze went to the half empty tea glass on the table, but she didn't reach for it. Instead she turned to me. "I'm not one of these fools who has a phobia about political groups. On the contrary, everyone should be a part of several of them. In a country where the state is this strong, individuals have no other chance of defending themselves. Believe me, whatever bad things happen to us happen because people are unorganized. What I am against is people devoting themselves to a political organization without having read, understood or listened enough. That's why I was worried. I didn't know the Tuesday Group. And Fidan was so young. In the craziest times of youth, that age where she'd throw herself into the fire without a second thought."

"Didn't you discuss it with Fidan?"

"I did. In detail, actually. She swore she wasn't joining any protests. 'I'm just reading books, going to seminars,' she said. But I still wasn't convinced. I sat in on one of those seminars once. Even now I remember it well. 'Our New Religion and Worshipping Rituals'. Funny subject."

Now where did religion come from all of a sudden?

"They were talking about capitalism," she clarified. "It was a naive commentary of course. The new religion they spoke of was money, worshipping was trade, and the temples they referred to were shopping malls. They were talking about the Demirören Mall on Istiklal Avenue and this hideous building they'd planned for Gezi Park that they didn't manage to build due to the backlash against it. Of course they were absolutely right in every respect. You know we have the distinction of being the city with the highest number of shopping malls in Europe? Well, how many parks are left where our children can get a breath of air? How many new museums have opened? How many new culture centers? This is not just a building being constructed, Nevzat Bey, it's imposing a lifestyle on people. In the same way that when the Ottomans took this city they built these Islamic social complexes, transnational companies are opening these kinds of centers with their own agendas. Those Ottoman social complexes with the mosques, madrasahs, libraries, hospitals, guest houses and soup kitchens were some kind of cultural service institution, whereas the only issue for the brands and shopping centers is money and more profit. Nobody gives a damn about Istanbul's history, its beauty and its culture. They just keep piling on the touristic hotels, the ugly bridges and hideous skyscrapers... All they care about is land grabbing, profiteering, and getting rich off rents. Well, the Tuesday Group's kids were opposed to all that. But no one at that meeting said 'let's go throw a Molotov cocktail into those buildings'. That's why I can't understand why these kids would attempt such an act. And that's why I thought Fidan may have been doing it for my sake." She went quiet and shook her head in pain. "Whatever the reason, she is gone..."

I was afraid she'd stop talking and be overcome with grief again so I didn't allow the tension to slacken.

"Maybe there's a faction of the Tuesday Group that advocates violence. I don't know, members who are more radical, who find what the association does insufficient. Extremist types... Was there anyone like that?"

Her reaction caught me off guard.

"Don't you dare ask me to name names!" Her voice and expression were uncompromising. She wagged her index finger angrily at my face. "Don't you dare, Nevzat Bey! Don't ask me questions like that. I'm no informant. We're just talking about Fidan here. Who threw that Molotov? That I don't know. And I'm not going to make guesses and get innocent young people in trouble. It's your job to find who's responsible."

I'd never met someone whose mood changed so quickly before. I'd have to be more careful speaking with Nazlı.

"You misunderstood me," I told her. "As a matter of fact, figuring out who threw a Molotov is not my job either. We're not political police; we're homicide. But in order to find out the truth of Fidan's death, we'll need to take statements from her friends. So..."

I was on the wrong path; her temper flared again.

"That's good. Then find Fidan's friends in that case."

No, she'd never cave.

"All right, stay calm." I smiled. "I wasn't asking you for names or anything. I'm just trying to get a grasp on the situation."

She didn't even stoop to answer. She just sulkily reached for her glass. I followed her lead but the tea was still hot and I could only take a tiny sip. I smiled again but she didn't make a sound. She wasn't looking at me anymore. After I'd put my glass back down I pointed a finger up.

"Is there a dorm on the upper floors?"

"What?"

Refreshing my stale smile, I repeated, "Upstairs. Is there a dormitory?"

Now why did I ask that? I thought she'd snap at me again but she didn't.

"Not a dormitory. Rooms," she reluctantly answered. She went quiet, but not for long. She raised her head and looked at the ceiling as though she'd see them. "A separate room for women, for children, and for trans... The classrooms, workshops, and a library are also up there. This is not a shelter, of course. We want to educate those in need and if possible find them jobs. If this miserable society will allow it, that is."

She'd started to talk tough again. I guessed she'd throw me out on my ear in the end.

"Yep, it's a society full of miserable, contemptible people," she continued, her voice came out hard like a scolding. I ignored it and kept listening with the meek eyes of a sensitive man.

"You know that friend of mine who was just in here, Ayşen. She's done everything in her power to keep from turning to prostitution. There's no job she hasn't tried, from selling stuffed mussels on the street to cutting fabrics in a sweatshop. But people won't leave her be. She's not like them so they assume she's immoral, when in fact she has far more integrity than they do. And she's braver than all of them as well. It's just her sexual preferences are different. She wants to lead a different life and they don't let her. They don't recognize her right to a life as anything other than a sex worker. And then they try to lynch her because some transvestites prostitute themselves..."

She looked at me as though ready to fight.

"Unfortunately, your officers treat them pretty badly, too. They approach them like they're dirt, like potential criminals capable of committing a crime at any moment. So we... We open our arms to them so that they can move on to a new life. Not just them of course but anyone who needs help, although our priority is women and children. Sex workers who've been tossed onto the street because they've grown old, kids who use drugs, homeless people... We never think of helping reckless men like Fidan's father Yakup though, for example. Let the government who allows them to gamble in the first place look after them if it's not too much trouble... Yes, we do discriminate like that. What's important for us is the women and children. The situation for women in Tarlabaşı is dire."

I calmly agreed, tolerating her accusatory manner.

"I know. I was stationed here for five years."

I'd kept my cool in the face of her shouting and screaming as if I was the guilty party in all these wicked deeds, and it was having an effect on her.

"Really? When?" she asked, not out of curiosity but because continuing to be insensitive would be rude.

"Seven years ago. You weren't here then, were you?"

She winced, her expression contrived.

"No, we weren't. I've been here four years." She'd completely shaken off her anger. "So in that case, you know these people here. For example, there's that guy Cemal. One of the old mobsters..."

"If it's Swank Cemal you're talking about then I know him. Did you have a problem with him too?"

"Oh, no. Cemal Bey is a good guy. He supported us against Black Nizam in this issue with the building."

I was happy to hear it.

"Swank Cemal is different..."

Another possibility came to mind. Could there be some hostility I didn't know about between our Swank and Nizam? He was defending Dice against Nizam, giving his support to a woman he didn't know. If I didn't know Cemal, I'd smell a rat.

"Yes, I think you were going to say something else about Cemal Bey?"

"He's a good guy," I said, pulling myself together. "Always helpful to everyone. How did you meet him?"

"Through an acquaintance. Kâzım Abi. They were in prison together during the period of martial law."

She noticed me trying to make sense of this and saw no harm in going into the details.

"Kâzım Abi was a trade unionist, one of the administrators at DISK, the Turkish Revolutionary Workers Syndicate. He and Cemal stayed in the same ward. After I said I was going to open a culture center in Tarlabaşı, he called Cemal to tell him, 'Look after our girl.' And whenever we have some trouble, big thanks to him, he rushes in and saves the day."

As to the situation with Cemal, there was no sense in raking it over the coals. I took the last sip from my glass and stood up.

"Thanks so much for the tea, Nazlı Hanım. It was good to meet you."

Her violet eyes narrowed with suspicion again.

"Same here," she said, standing up. "If I'm right about you, that is." She put her hand out. "You won't let Fidan's murderers go free will you?"

"Don't worry. I'll do whatever it takes to see justice served," I answered, shaking her hand. "I'd do the same even if I hadn't met you."

"They shot her seven times."

✵

Where Fidan's slim body had been was now an empty spot in the shape of a silhouette. A space in the form of a human body with white dots where the wind-blown snow had occasionally settled. The street had emptied; the squad cars at the street's entrance and exit, the crowd of police, were gone. There was only the three-man CSI team in getups I've never been able to get used to. They had already started packing up. Şefik was smoking a cigarette a few steps back from the men, and my team was planted in front of the Genuine Tarlabaşists Club, Zeynep calmly showing Ali the bag in her hand as she explained something. None of them had noticed me, yet I felt the weight of someone's stare. A shadow stirred at the far end of the street and I squinted at it. I fancied it was that strange author's smile I was seeing, that supposedly friendly grin spread across his face, the white teeth shining in the darkness. What the hell was he doing? Had he gone so far as to follow us? I was about to march over in a huff when the vision disappeared. Yes, like the smoke rising off Şefik's cigarette, he'd wafted into the night. I looked around, but neither the author nor his nasty grin were anywhere in the street. Where could the man have got to in the blink of an eye like that? Was I seeing things? It was possible, maybe the effects of exhaustion or alcohol. I'd felt sober enough since leaving Feraye though, so I doubted it was that. What was he doing when we left the *meyhane*, anyhow? Boozing it up with that poet friend of his, I suppose. He'd given us a wave as we walked out. He couldn't have fallen in behind us so quickly. And anyhow, we would have noticed. So then had I imagined it? There was no other explanation. I'd already felt like I was being followed, ever since leaving the Ferhat Çerağ Culture Center. "Police turn into paranoiacs," was what my father used to say.

"Nevzat. Nevzat..."

And now I was hearing voices from out of nowhere. As I turned, expecting to see the empty snow-filled street again, I was met with Swank Cemal's sparkling eyes, watching me from beneath a black hat.

"Cemal. It's you."

"Yes, it's me," he said with a huge smile. "I've been calling out to you since way back there but you couldn't hear me."

"Sorry. I was lost in thought."

He didn't mind. He opened his arms and came over.

"I finally caught up with you."

"Yes, finally..."

We had a friendly embrace. His black cashmere coat and cashmere scarf smelled like nicotine. So he still hadn't given up smoking, despite claiming every six months or so that he was going to 'quit the damn things'.

"What are you doing here this time of night?"

I hadn't even finished my question when my voice bounced back off the dark walls of the snowy street. This meeting was not by chance.

"Really, what are you doing here?" I couldn't keep my voice from rising. "Were you following me?"

He froze; his acute disappointment could be felt even in the darkness.

"What are you talking about, Nevzat?"

"I don't know," I said. "You say you've been calling out to me since way back there..."

He was hurt, but he remained a gentleman.

"You've got it all wrong." His hand in its black leather glove, he pointed. "Following you? I was standing back here."

"Yes, but why were you standing here? Who were you waiting for at this ungodly hour of the night?"

He slowly lowered his hand.

"For you, who else? I came when I heard there was a murder."

He was speaking so calmly, so nonchalantly, that it really got my goat.

"Who told you about the murder?"

Despite my accusative tone, he chose a conciliatory route.

"This is my neighborhood, Nevzat," he said, his voice sincere. "If a cat gets run over on the street or a window breaks, we hear about it."

"What the hell?" I grumbled. "Everyone in Tarlabaşı keeps using that same line..."

His sparkling eyes opened wide.

"Somebody else said that?"

"Not just anybody. Your Beyoğlu friends... Dice Ihsan, then Black Nizam."

He guffawed.

"Those tramps! So they've been parroting too, huh... When the smile disappeared from his lips, he explained. "Âgâh used to say that. The words are not mine or theirs. They're Lazy Âgâh's. You knew him, right?"

I pictured the doughy man with no eyebrows or lashes, a tiny chin, chubby red cheeks and puckish black eyes. He'd been killed in a hamam, strangled with a plastic bag over his head. Even though it was being called a 'homosexual' murder, there was no evidence pointing that direction. Perhaps Âgâh's opponents had spread the rumors to discredit him. The murder suspect was young and handsome. He said Âgâh had made a pass at him and he'd flown into a rage and suffocated him but that wasn't true. That boy's delicate wrists weren't capable of getting a bag over Âgâh's head. Âgâh was a sluggish man whose nickname suited him; he didn't like to move and never wanted to leave his seat. But he was strong as an ox. His first incident was when he was young and he killed an elderly lawyer with one punch. It would take at least three men to overpower a guy like that. Strong ones, no less. But the crime scene had been cleaned well, with no traces or clues left behind. And the only one who witnessed the event was that handsome boy whose name I can't remember, that had claimed he was the murderer. They skewered that boy in prison before long. But Âgâh's killers were never found. During those days, Swank Cemal had talked about a drug gang that hung out at Galata... Âgâh was in the ecstasy business. I was worried there was more to follow and it looked like the reciprocated killing would continue, but it didn't. In every world, at all times, money is always more valuable. Âgâh's men had struck a deal with the drug ring. Most likely they split the area up between them. And just like his victims, Âgâh's life concluded in an untimely death.

"I knew him, of course," I said, though I was fixated on this tough guy, one of Beyoğlu's oldest, who stood planted here in his fancy coat. "The man was no prize. Wasn't he in the drug business?"

His face clouded over.

"That's right. I warned him a lot, but he didn't listen. And that's how he died. It was fate; what are you going to do? We'll all end up there one way or the other."

"Some of us get there earlier, though," I said sarcastically. "A lot earlier."

He thought I meant his friend.

"Unfortunately so..."

"I wasn't talking about Âgâh," I chided. "I meant the girl who was gunned down two hours ago. Fidan. A girl who lost her mother, her sister... everything to Dice Ihsan's place. A young girl who then took a bullet from Black Nizam's bastard nephew. That girl wasn't half Âgâh's age."

Cemal's shoulders dropped.

"What fault is that of mine, Nevzat?" His hand went to his graying moustache just like it always did when he got nervous. "I have nothing to do with this vileness."

If he didn't act pure as driven snow... It made me crazy.

"Why are you here then, Cemal? Why did you call me this morning? Why are you trying to help Dice Ihsan?" He gave me a stunned look, like a boxer still reeling from a triple hook. "And what about now?" I continued to scold. "Are you here for Black Nizam this time? To say his nephew acted in self-defense?"

"Don't, Nevzat." His voice had begun to quiver. "Don't you know me at all?"

For a moment I wondered if I'd laid it on too heavy, but only for a moment and then I shook off the burden of that emotion.

"I thought I did. But what I've been through in the last twenty-four hours has got me confused. Three people dead in Tarlabaşı in the past twenty-four hours. We have two important suspects: Ihsan and Nizam. And you are connected to both of them. Isn't there something fishy about that? What's going on, Cemal? What is it you aren't telling me?"

He seemed to tremble slightly.

"I'm not hiding anything from you, Nevzat. You're right. From the outside, it might look suspicious. But I swear on my mother's grave I have nothing to do with these murders. I'm done with that kind of thing."

"Yet you keep helping men who aren't," I said, with no intention of letting up.

"You've got it all wrong." He looked me straight in the eye as he spoke. "Dice Ihsan wants out of that world, too. I believe he's sincere, and that's why I called you. But Black Nizam isn't like that. Don't fall for the docile front; he knows very well how to talk to police. But he's got the devil in him, Nevzat. He's capable of every kind of evil. He's ruthless."

Could what Cemal said be true? Was Nizam behind all this? Or was Cemal in cahoots with Dice and trying to pull the wool over my eyes?"

"I'm telling the truth. Nizam is far more devious, far crueler than he appears. And his sights are set high. I don't know what he told you but his real money came from drugs. It's a family business. There are eight brothers, of which Nizam is the oldest as well as being the gang leader. He has twenty-one nephews. Every one of them is in on it. That Kudret who shot the girl is one of them. Look how he killed the poor girl without batting an eye. They'll kill all right, and none of them gives a damn. They're vicious, and they take out anyone who gets in their way. I'm not joking. Believe me, Nevzat, they'll kill you too if you cross their path..."

Was there a veiled threat in his words? No, he was just trying to inform me. In fact, it could even be said he was worried about me.

"All right, I came here to talk to you. Dice gave me the news. They heard the gunfire. The Tarlabaşists Club is just one street away, you know. Dice immediately rang me from his house and I came rushing down here..."

Ali's assertive voice interrupted him.

"What's going on, Chief?"

They'd also noticed we were arguing, and it looked like they'd quietly sidled over to us. I gently grasped my assistant's elbow.

"Okay, Ali. There's no problem..." I turned to Zeynep, who eyed me apprehensively. "What did you two do? Are you all finished?"

Her anxious face relaxed.

"Yes, Chief. We were waiting for you. We can go back to headquarters whenever you want."

My gaze went to Cemal. I couldn't leave this account half settled.

"You two go on, Zeynep. I'll be along in no time."

Ali objected, of course.

"No way, Chief. I'm staying here with you."

"I said it's all right, Ali." I raised my voice, half serious, half joking. "Go on. Stop dawdling. Pull the file on this suspect Kudret. When I get there I want to see it, what stunts this guy has pulled..."

My assistant didn't persist but as he left he turned round and gave me a concerned look.

"Your men love you," Cemal murmured. "I know that feeling. It's a nice thing."

I combed the street with my eyes again.

"Isn't Mizgin here? He never leaves your side."

With his confident smile, his grizzled moustache grew wider.

"No, he doesn't. And he didn't this time either. He stayed in the car because he knew I'd be with you. If you want, we can go to my car too. We can talk and I can drop you at the station."

That wouldn't be so bad except I didn't want Cemal to get too comfortable.

"There's no need. Let's take a little walk. I'll make my own way back to the station. Yes, you were telling me you came here to talk to me. Why is Dice Ihsan so concerned with Fidan's death?"

Cemal's face took on an insulted expression.

"I'll explain, Nevzat, but you can drop your guard now. I'm not the enemy."

Of course he wasn't my enemy, but whether he was someone I could entirely trust, I wasn't so sure of any more.

"Of course not," I said flatly. "I'm just trying to understand what happened. Come on, let's walk..."

Powerless, he fell in step beside me.

"It's not just Dice who's concerned; these murders concern me, too."

I stopped.

"And that's what I don't understand. Didn't you just say you were done with this business? What do you care about these incidents?"

"See, it's not like that." It was the first time he'd raised his voice. "You forget what our world's like, Nevzat. You can't just walk away from here, arms swinging. You can't just say, 'Well, I'm retired now, so wish me luck.'" Steam rose from his mouth as he spoke. "Even your breathing is a threat for some people."

He went quiet as if he couldn't find the words to explain, then huffed and continued walking as if maybe they'd come to him if he moved. "I hurt a lot of people," he said, watching his stylish boots stomp the snow. "Somebody's father, somebody's brother, somebody's son... I have a lot of blood on my hands. I wouldn't have done it with the head I have now." He looked at me from the corner of his eye. "I really wouldn't have, Nevzat. I'd make it up to all of them if it were in my power. I have so many enemies. They'd kill me in a heartbeat if they could. That's why I didn't sever all my ties with these men. It wouldn't be six months before they shot me. And you'd never know who did it. So be it, I'm not afraid of death. I never was. But I've got Sezgin and Tahir.

214

I don't want anything to happen to my sons. That's why I backed away to a place where I could keep an eye on what's happening. And also, I owe the people in this world. I was given a duty..."

"To make the rules," I jeered. "As if they follow your rules..."

"They do," he said, turning to me. The light in his eyes had gone out and he looked like an innocent child. "This world has its laws too. It wouldn't turn otherwise."

I didn't care how sincere he seemed.

"Don't give me that, Cemal. There's only one law in your world, and that's money. There's nothing your glorified tough guys won't do for it."

He shook his head despairingly.

"Not all of them... You're right, Nevzat. Sometimes our code is more important to us than the law of the land. Ever heard of Judge Halil?"

"The guy in that hookah cafe in Salı Pazarı?"

"That's the one. He was a legend. The biggest provider of justice in this underworld. That's how he got the nickname Judge Halil in the first place. His scale was spot on; he never misweighed. He was afraid of no one and he told it like it was, without holding back. He was ruthless and he never went back on a decision. That's why his words were law. Even the most notorious hoodlums had to heed whatever left his lips. How many self-proclaimed wise guys did he give a death sentence? Interestingly, nobody ever got angry with him. Or if they did, they never showed it. Because everybody knew he'd never be unfair."

"But look what happened. He killed himself in the end," I interrupted.

"That's what I was telling you, Nevzat. Why he killed himself. The day came when fate wanted to test Judge Halil's impartiality. He had a son named Yasin, his only child and the apple of his eye. Because of that he grew up spoiled. He never went to school. When he grew up, he didn't just pussyfoot around the edges but dove straight into our world because of his father. Maybe that's why he stayed so raw and never learned any manners. Because he'd never got a beating, never

slept in jail. Judge Halil had a man, Mihri. Whatever Mizgin is
to me, Mihri was to Halil Abi. He was tall and lean, a strong,
fearless man. If Halil said kill, he'd kill, and if he said die,
he'd die, without question. He was that loyal, that brave, that
unspoiled. His only offense was to fall in love when he was
forty. With a woman from the Çorlu brothel, no less. But such
is the heart, there's nothing to be done. Anyhow, when I say
he fell in love, it wasn't the fickle sort young people have these
days. It was to the extent he took her out of the brothel and
married her. I mean, the man had such a big heart, this Mihri.
A rare breed, an angel... Once they were married, he had
two children with the woman, one girl, one boy. But Halil's
son, that filthy piece of work, got his eye set on the woman.
Mihri didn't know about this nasty business. The thought
never crossed his mind that Yasin, who he loved like a son,
would make a move on his wife. But Yasin lost his mind, and
I guess he trusted his father. Maybe he was encouraged by
the woman's stained history. At any rate, that sleazeball came
on to her every chance he got. All the same, the woman had
principles and she wouldn't give him the time of day. When
he failed to get a response, it turned him on even more, the
bastard. One evening when Mihri was at his father's, Yasin
knocked on their door. The woman didn't want to let him in,
but he pushed his way in. He forced himself on her and then
after he'd had his fill, he relaxed and let his guard down, the
animal. The woman took the opportunity to attack her rapist
with a knife she'd grabbed from the kitchen. The bastard
got off with a slightly wounded leg, but the pain from the
knife made this half-wit lose what little sanity he had. Yasin
pulled a gun and emptied all his bullets into her. The children
sleeping in the next room were woken by the gunfire. The
boy was two, the girl five... As Yasin was about to make a run
for it, the devil whispered in his ear that the children had
seen what happened and they'd be witnesses. He turns and
puts two bullets into each of them. Then he makes it look like
a robbery so they won't figure out it was him. The five-year-
old girl was injured, but survived by some small mercy. As
they were getting round to the inquiries, the interrogations,
the blood types and the fingerprints, the girl identified the

killer. Now what is Judge Halil supposed to do? He summoned Mihri and told him, 'All right, Yasin is guilty. My son deserves to die. But I want you to let me do it. I know you're in a lot of pain, but that won't go away no matter what you do. I'm also seriously at fault and I should be punished too, not just Yasin. Let me be the one to take his life.' Mihri starts shaking like a leaf. On the one hand he's sobbing, on the other, trying to kiss Halil Abi's hand. The huge tough guy pulled the man to his feet. 'Don't cry, son,' he says. 'There's nothing to cry about. According to the rules, whoever is at fault pays. Yasin will pay like everyone else, and so will I.' He paid all right, but first he put a bullet in his son's head, then in his own..."

I'd heard that story but thought it was just an urban legend.

"Did that really happen?"

"Of course it did. I'll call Mihri if you like and you can hear it straight from the horse's mouth. I took over the post from Judge Halil. He called me six hours before he shot his son. I went to his hookah cafe. He sat me down opposite him and said, 'My time's up, Cemal. Our fate's been determined. You are the one who will take my place.' He took out his prayer beads, amber stones that swung like huge drops of honey. 'Ten years ago, the now-deceased Moustache Şevki gave me these. And I want to pass them on to you, if you'll accept. Still, if your heart's not in it, there's nothing to be done...' I looked at the delightfully sparkling prayer beads on the table. 'I'm sorry, Halil Abi,' I said. 'This job's not for me.' He smiled absentmindedly. 'Fair enough, Cemal. Whatever you say, I'll accept. But if you change your mind, the beads will be hanging on that sword handle on the wall there. Rumor has it the old sword belonged to the prophet Ali. The bearer of these beads has to be as fair and just as the prophet was. Don't worry, the kids will be warned. You can come get them if you want.' I didn't think I would ever take the beads. Frankly, I didn't believe Ali would shoot himself or his son. But he did, on the very night we spoke. I heard about it the following day. Around noon I went to take the prayer beads off the sword handle without giving it a second thought. I don't know how word got out, but the next day at the funeral everyone approached me with a respect I'd never anticipated. Even those with bad blood now kowtowed..."

He sized me up with his eyes, Cemal.

"I mean, money isn't the only thing in the world, Chief. At least in this world there are still people who care about honor and morality."

Maybe, but right now it wasn't the meaningfulness of the tough guys' world I was interested in, but why Cemal, despite the long speech, still hadn't said why he was interested in these murders.

"Which is all fine, but what has that got to do with our case?"

"A lot. Black Nizam is one of those men you talk about who has no code. 'Whoever has the power, that's who makes the rules', he says. That's probably why he had Engin killed. Because he had his eye on his spot. And it wasn't Kudret's being a maniac that got the young girl shot, but Nizam's keenness to intimidate everyone, particularly Dice."

I couldn't make the connection.

"They wanted to intimidate Dice by killing Fidan?"

"Not just Dice," he explained with utmost conviction. "But me, or anybody else in Tarlabaşı who got in his way. Think about it, Nevzat. These kids who threw the Molotovs also threw two into Dice's place that morning. A small fire even broke out in the club. But anyhow, you saw that. Dice knows who these kids are, the Tuesday Group or whatever, but he doesn't care. At most he'd just pull them aside and have a talk with them. But Black Nizam isn't like that. Like I said, his sights are set higher. He wants to show everyone just how cruel he can be. So they'll be scared of him and bow down to him. They shot her seven times. Seven times, Chief. You wouldn't do that to your worst enemy. His goal was something else. To scare everyone into submission... That's what I'm trying to explain to you. Not so you'll help Ihsan or me, but for you to understand what's going on..."

He'd got carried away and was heatedly spilling it out, Cemal. I'd never seen him worked up like this. He genuinely hated Black Nizam, but whether his enemy was truly evil or they just had a conflict of interest, I couldn't be sure.

"He committed his first murder at sixteen."

✠

The interrogation room always reminds me of a chamber theater. A suspenseful theater play performed on a small, confined, bleak stage, usually by a three-actor group made up of two interrogators and one suspect. You may not see a script in their hands but they each have the scenario in their head. We may not stay true to it, but it's this scenario in our minds that mostly determines our dialogue, facial expressions and actions. I should also add that there's a greater possibility the script in the suspect's mind will change because it is shaped according to our questions. The fate of the interrogation is determined more by how we play our roles than by what we say. Whoever is the most clever and cold-blooded carries the tense play along.

When I saw Kudret in the interrogation room, its props consisting of a long table, three chairs and a huge mirror, I remembered that he was the twin with his back turned to us in the coffeehouse the day before. He was wearing the dark green anorak with the fur collar, and beads of sweat had collected on his forehead and at the roots of his short spiky hair. He was blinking at the bright light overhead, but the heavy drowsiness in his dark eyes hadn't yet dissipated. His hands were on the table; his fingers were short and his palms small, just like his uncle Nizam's, though not one tiny hair could be seen on his smooth skin. His face was like that too,

219

and actually, if we didn't count his sparse stubble, his healthy skin was ablaze under the light.

"How many Kalashnikovs were there?"

"Ha..." is how he answered Ali's question.

My assistant landed a hard flick on his head.

"Ha? What the hell does that mean? And you'll say 'sir'."

He was caught off guard. His head had bobbed forward.

"Hey!" he squealed. "Stop that..."

His words stuck to his tongue.

I noisily pulled up the chair opposite his and sat in it.

"Are you high, Kudret?"

He gave me a strange look as though I was talking a language he couldn't understand.

"Tell me. Are you on pills or something?"

His sleepy eyes parted a bit.

"Ha..."

He got another slap from Ali.

"Quit saying 'ha'. Didn't you understand me? You'll call me sir, you jackass... Sir."

This time Kudret was on the ball. He held his head upright against the blow.

"Ah... Stop hitting me... I didn't hear you is all."

My assistant put his face right up into Kudret's.

"Why not? Your ears broken?"

Kudret was getting angry and saw no need to hide it.

"They're in working order, but your voice doesn't carry."

Ali gave a calm smile.

"All right, so I'll talk a bit louder then." He put his lips up to the suspect's ear and shouted, "How many Kalashnikovs were there?"

Kudret hurriedly attempted to cover his ear but my assistant caught his wrist. He stuck his hand to the table and shouted again.

"I'm asking you how many Kalashnikovs. Did you hear me now?"

"I heard. I heard." He'd lost it and was also yelling. "Three... There were three."

Ali dropped the suspect's hands and stood up straight. Kudret quickly brought his fingers to his ears. He kept massaging them, as if by doing so the ringing would stop.

"Why are you lying?" I calmly leaned back in my chair. I looked him up and down, not missing a single move. "You think you can pull one over on us?"

"I would never, Chief... How could I ever pull anything over on you?" His hands were still on his ears but he seemed to have shaken off the stupor he'd been in. "Everything is obvious. What reason could I possibly have to lie?"

"To save your ass..." Ali spoke from where he stood. "To present the incident as self-defense and beat a murder rap."

The suspect had the innocent stare of someone newly woken from sleep.

"Don't give us that look, son," Ali snapped. "We didn't drag you here from the mosque courtyard. You killed someone. A young girl in her prime..."

His eyes opened wide and his damp face grew tense.

"They attacked first."

"Yeah, yeah," my assistant responded, swaying gently in his place. "And they had guns..."

Kudret nodded his round head emphatically.

"Yes, they had guns. Three Kalashnikovs."

My assistant bent down and grabbed Kudret by the shoulders.

"You think we are stupid?" He shook him with all his might. "There was no Kalashnikov... Not one shot was fired from that crowd. If we don't count the magazine you emptied, that is..."

Kudret blinked twice; he must have been having difficulty collecting his thoughts. Maybe he really had dropped some pills.

"There were. I swear it. They attacked the club. They were going to burn us all alive. They had Molotovs, Kalashnikovs..." He seemed confused. "There was even a girl with one."

An image of Fidan with a Molotov cocktail appeared before my eyes, though I couldn't manage to conjure up an image of that giant rifle between her slender fingers. The suspect had collected himself and carried on reading the scenario in his mind.

"There were about fifty of them. With handguns, rifles, meat cleavers..."

"Any rocket launchers?"

He didn't even realize my assistant was mocking him.

"No. No rocket launchers," he explained candidly. "There may have been hand grenades..." He paused as he caught on and gave a hurt look. "You don't believe me, but they'd all gone crazy. They were going to kill us. They had Molotovs..."

"There's no issue with the Molotovs..." I interrupted. "But you told our colleagues two Kalashnikovs, not three."

"Two?" His tiny pupils spun like balls of mercury in their sockets. "No, three... There were three."

I gave him a look like someone genuinely interested.

"You told Sami there were two. You know Sami, right?"

He seemed to relax.

"Of course I know Sami Abi. Sami Abi is like a brother. He's a great cop." A crafty smile spread across his semi-wet face. "All the cops are our pride and joy, really. We love our police brothers."

As a police brother, I gave him a bit of friendly advice.

"So then you should tell us the truth, Kudret."

His beady eyes looked more trusting now.

"I am telling the truth, Chief."

"You mean Sami is lying?"

He swallowed uneasily.

"No, of course not! Why would Sami Abi lie?" He swallowed again. "He must have misunderstood..." He was really stuck. He'd either admit everything or take responsibility for the mistake. "Um... and maybe I said two instead of three. In all that chaos..."

"How do you know Sami?"

Supporting himself with hands on the table, Ali had swooped down like an eagle over Kudret. The suspect didn't know how to answer and just gave a blank stare.

"Tell us, how do you know him?"

He leaned back with dread.

"From, um..."

Ali didn't give him a chance, of course.

"From where? From gambling? Did he come to your club that often? Haa..." With his right hand, he landed another small slap to the side of his neck, and the dingy room echoed with a 'shlapp' sound. Ali's hand was wet with sweat. "God damn you," he said, grimacing. "You're sweating like a pig." He reached out and wiped his hand on the sweater under Kudret's anorak. "That's vile!" He stared into Kudret's face again. "Why aren't you talking? Was Sami your man? What are you hiding? Was he helping you with your dirty work?"

Kudret's reaction came unexpected.

"There is no dirty work," he said, raising his voice. "It was us helping Sami Abi, actually."

It was clear another lie was on its way, but this time Ali lost his temper.

"So then *you* helped *him*? You mean you gave him money?"

"Money? No, we saved his life." He saw an opportunity in our surprise and took it. "Not just Sami Abi's, but the two officers with him, too..."

He'd taken control of the interrogation, if only for a split second.

"You're full of shit," Ali said, though his threat didn't change the situation.

"I swear on my mother's name, I'm telling the truth..."

"Shut your trap, you piece of shit," my assistant said, abasing him. "If nothing else, don't drag your mother into this."

The suspect's sweaty face turned the pink of a lightly roasted onion, but his will to talk was gone.

"Would I insult my own mother? It's a figure of speech."

"You're wasting time, Kudret," I said, my tone bittersweet. "Come on, tell us already, whatever it is you have to say."

He sat up in his seat.

"All right, Chief. I'll explain but..." He looked over at Ali then changed his mind, understanding nothing good would come out of complaining about this inspector whose moves were so unpredictable. "We rescued Sami Abi from terrorists."

His explanation was interrupted by Ali's exaggerated laughter.

"Terrorists? Where did you do that, pray tell? Şırnak?"

Kudret didn't get upset. On the contrary, he calmly, confidently, explained, "Not Şırnak, Beyoğlu... And hundreds of terrorists, at that." His voice gradually grew louder; he'd got over his diffidence and was singing away like a hero waiting for praise. "Last summer. During the Gezi Park incidents... Near Istiklal Avenue on Mis Street..."

His confident talk had started to annoy me.

"Just explain the situation, rather than testing our knowledge of the city," I warned him. "How did this thing come about?"

"I'm telling you, Chief... There were hundreds of terrorists. I swear it's no exaggeration. Maybe thousands... You know there's that exam prep school on the corner? Well right at that spot, they had Sami Abi cornered. There were two other officers there, too. There was some confusion and it was evident that he'd got stuck in among the terrorists. Some of the people who threw a Molotov into our club tonight were in with those demonstrators. I know the little slimeballs. Kurds, communists, queers... Every kind of miscreant. If we'd been a minute later, they would have lynched Sami Abi. Luckily, we reached him in time. There were close to thirty of us. We had sticks and whatnot; we shouted 'Bismillah' and attacked. They were all a bunch of momma's boys anyhow... Little bastards with long hair or piercing... Girls with mini skirts and cropped hair..."

Ali couldn't stop himself interrupting again.

"I thought you said they were terrorists. How can a 'momma's boy' be a terrorist?"

Kudret wasn't backing down.

"Remember how they tore the place apart? They fought against our government and our police. Doesn't that make them terrorists?"

There was no use in continuing this idiotic argument.

"Demonstrators. We call them demonstrators," I intervened. "Anyway, go on."

"All right, Chief. So we had them in front of us and were chasing them. Thirty of us ran three thousand of them off in every direction, I swear."

Ali couldn't stay still again.

"You're laying it on too thick."

"I swear it, Chief... Sure, the police teams caught up behind us. When they came, the group really fell to pieces, the little pricks." A saucy look of complicity shone in his eyes. "That tear gas is bad, though. It knocks the hell out of a man. And you know we didn't have masks or anything. I thought I was gonna die. Don't get me wrong, they didn't fire at us, but the wind brought it in. It wouldn't be an exaggeration to say half my cousins dropped like flies."

I remembered how some people with *döner* knives and sticks had gone out to hunt demonstrators during the Gezi Park incidents. Looks like Black Nizam's nephews had been among them.

"You took matters into your own hands, you mean," I goaded. He didn't know what I meant.

"Sorry, Chief?"

"I mean, did you go there of your own volition? To help the police?"

He smiled graciously.

"We wouldn't dare, Chief. Uncle Nizam sent us. Anyhow, we'd had enough of those louts occupying Gezi Park for days on end. All our shops were closed up. No one coming in or out of the parkades, the kebab stands were chasing away flies... I guess there was a phone call from higher up."

Ali jumped on it.

"Higher up?"

Kudret shrugged.

"I don't know who from. Could have been ruling party supporters, or the police station... What does it matter, Chief? The goal is to serve the state and the nation. When the order for action came, we took to the streets. To put these little bastards in their place." With the anticipation of a child hoping for an award, he continued to explain his accomplishments. "We beat up a lot of demonstrators, Chief. We fucked them up, the queers..."

"Was Fidan one of those demonstrators?"

"Who? Who's that, Chief?"

"Fidan. That girl you just killed a few hours ago."

His cheeriness deflated like a balloon.

"The dead girl's name is Fidan?"

"Not the dead girl, the girl murdered by you," Ali corrected him. "That petite young girl you put seven bullets in."

He didn't avert his eyes, nor bow his head like someone crushed by guilt.

"I didn't want it to be like that," he said coldly. "When I saw the gun she held aimed at our window, I defended myself. Otherwise, it's not good to take a life."

"Is that why you've killed four people?"

Kudret gently raised his head and looked out from under his eyebrows with hatred at my assistant. His beady eyes grew sharp and took on a wild gleam. This was the face Kudret had tried to hide from us since sitting down at the table. The face of someone who could become a ruthless killer when required. But it didn't last long; his face muscles relaxed and the killer hid behind a different expression.

"I... I didn't kill four people."

My assistant understood he was on the right track and kept up the pressure.

"How many did you kill?"

He gave what was supposed to be a frank confession.

"One, and that was because he insulted my uncle. Uncle Nizam's like a father to us. He's the head of the family. And family is important for us. First God, then country, then family. Anyone talks shit about those, we cut their tongue out."

Ali got a sly look.

"The man didn't talk shit, he just smacked your uncle up."

The veins in his neck swelled up as though he was reliving the moment. Kudret's nostrils were flaring.

"Slander! An out-and-out lie; that didn't happen."

My assistant was enjoying seeing the suspect squirm.

"The man went up against the lot of you; don't deny it. You turned into a bunch of scaredy cats," said Ali, turning his fiery gaze on me. "A man called Sailor Abbas, Chief. He ran a car park in Tophane. You know how these guys are buying up Beyoğlu lot by lot? Well Black Nizam gathered all his relatives together and attacked the man's place. But Abbas is no sucker. He'd already been tipped off. He made his preparations and met them as he should. It put them in their place, being faced with this scene they'd never expected. Add to that, Abbas slapped Nizam silly. Right there in front of their eyes, no less..."

226

"That's a lie!" Kudret shouted. "It's not how it happened. Abbas was squatting in the car park. Its real owner was an old Jewish man, a friend of my uncle's. He asked us to get the guy out. That's why we went there. Actually, Uncle Nizam called him first to talk the situation over and Abbas told him, 'Be my guest. I'm waiting'. But when we went to the car park, he pulled a dirty move. He set all the people from his town on us. And the 'slapping up' incident is also a lie. That never happened."

"So then why did you kill Abbas?" Ali vacillated as though stuck on some other thought. "Wait. Wait, maybe you didn't do it." He snapped his fingers in the air. "Of course, it wasn't you. It was Black Nizam who shot him. You took the blame because you're underage. Yes, that's exactly what happened. Sailor took Black Nizam down a notch and he lost his reputation in Beyoğlu. He didn't come out in the open for days. To get his credibility back, he'd have to kill Sailor himself. And that's what he did. But according to the plan, you'd take the fall..." He poked a finger into Kudret's shoulder. "Tell me, boy, if that isn't what happened?"

Once again, not a word left Kudret's mouth. He swallowed his rancour and continued to listen to this damned police officer's words.

"Of course that's what happened. Abbas wasn't your first murder. Not counting the poor girl from tonight, you killed three people in between. After leaving prison. But your other underaged cousins claimed responsibility for those murders. So that's how things work with you. The adults do the murdering and the minors take the blame. And learn to be hardened criminals in prison."

My assistant must have given Kudret's file a once-over when he'd come to the station. He didn't have much time, so it's the best he could do. But as he spoke, the stones began to fall into place in his mind.

"This dimwit committed his first murder at sixteen," he said, starting to explain to me. "Or more accurately, he took responsibility for his uncle's crime just as you thought. He went to the station and turned over Sailor Abbas' two severed ears along with the gun. In that way, he protected his uncle while gaining false notoriety as a killer. And five years later he was out on amnesty, of course. After getting out, he was thought responsible for three more deaths within two years but, as I just explained, his underage nephews took the fall for all three of them. I mean, it's possible this dirty bastard could have murdered roughly four people..." He took a sideways glance at the man who sat melting away in his chair from sweat. "Isn't that right? Did I leave anything out?"

Kudret didn't answer; he just stared without fear or hesitation, with eyes that shone like honed blades. As if to say he knew what he'd do to us if we should ever fall into his clutches.

"What's with the pose, boy?" our fearless police growled. "Are we making a film here? Or are you trying to scare me?" He was starting to get genuinely angry. I was worried he was going to slap him.

"All right Ali, all right. Sit down a bit."

He didn't sit; he kept standing where he was though he got off the suspect's back, at least for now.

"How were things between you and Engin, Kudret?" His mind was still on Ali, so he couldn't understand what I was saying.

"What... Engin?"

"Yes, I'm talking about your friend who was killed the other night. Did you like him?"

He'd started to calm down and took a deep breath.

"Yes, I did," he said, trying to wipe the sweat from his brow with his anorak sleeve. "Why shouldn't I like him? He never did me any harm, God rest his soul."

His anorak sleeve wasn't soaking up the sweat. I took out my handkerchief.

"Take it. Use this."

He looked at the kerchief and then at me, like he found the gesture odd.

"No, thanks..."

"Go on, take it. And take off your coat and cool down a bit."

He weighed me up, then looked with suspicion at Ali and shook his head.

228

"No, I'm fine like this." He grinned slyly. "The doctor told me sweating is a good thing."

Who knew how many of these interrogations he'd been through before. I was sure he'd had his own share of beatings, too. He must know all our good cop, bad cop routines. By refusing my help, he was saying he would by no means compromise.

"Suit yourself," I said, putting my kerchief back in my pocket. "Recently things weren't so great between him and Nizam."

He was all ears, trying to figure out what we wanted.

"Engin, I'm saying. There was some issue over a woman between them. A woman named Çilem..."

He moved his head as though he was uncomfortable.

"Not Çilem, Hacer... Aunt Hacer... Uncle Nizam married the woman."

Interesting that he called her 'the woman'. What Harem Süleyman had said turned out to be true. Black Nizam's nephews didn't approve of the marriage.

"Your uncle told us," I said politely. "I wish them happiness. But Hacer Hanım was seeing the now-deceased Engin, too."

Kudret objected at once.

"There was nothing like that. And anyhow I can't talk about Aunt Hacer. She's joined our family. It's on our honor too, now."

With great pleasure, my assistant continued to push the suspect's buttons.

"Your honor? Wasn't the woman Dice Ihsan's mistress? And if it were just Dice it'd be great, but then Engin? Or was it Engin first and then Dice?"

Kudret's face turned three shades of red, but he didn't protest.

"It seems a bit of a mistake, someone with Nizam's good name marrying Çilem," I said, to vent what was going through Kudret's mind. "He could have found someone who wouldn't cast a shadow over the family name."

"It was my uncle's choice. We have to respect it," he muttered in a barely audible voice, without looking at our faces.

"As a nephew, you're right. Are you going to argue with big Black Nizam? But you can't stop people talking. Anyhow, what people say doesn't concern us. Okay. Is it true that Hacer was in a relationship with Engin? I mean, before she met your uncle... Because some people are claiming it never stopped."

"That's slander!" he said again, looking up angrily. "There's no such thing. Who told you that?"

"Cool down, Kudret. We didn't hear it from just one person. Whoever we spoke to in the last two days, everybody in Beyoğlu is talking about it. Anyhow, it was Engin who introduced the girl to your uncle. Isn't that right?"

Logic was telling him not to answer but his heart, and the culture he'd been exposed to all these years, wouldn't let him accept this mistake his uncle had made.

"Yes, but Engin never had a relationship with Aunt Hacer. Not before and not after. Look, Engin may be a sneaky one, but he's no idiot. He knew what would happen if he looked sideways at our women. Not to mention he was in love with someone else..." He saw we were curious. "He's a fool. He fell for a girl in a *pavyon*."

"Azize?"

"Look, you know about it already, Chief. Yes, he fell head over heels for that skinny little girl. And you can't imagine the women he had around him. He was a good-looking guy, Engin. Well-proportioned, blue eyes... There was this rich woman, for example. Jale. She was a bit past her prime, but still beautiful..."

He was talking about the woman in the photographs in Engin's house.

"Jale was madly in love with him. And the woman is loaded. Her husband has factories, property... The man had a stroke; he'll die soon if he hasn't already. But the fool went and fell in love with that *pavyon* tramp instead."

"So, was Azize in love with Engin?"

A snide expression spread on his face.

"So what if she was? Could that girl be any kind of wife to the man? Everyone who came by took a bite out of her. Engin wouldn't have married her anyhow. He could never bring himself to do it."

"But your uncle did." It was Ali who hit the nail on the head of course. "Look what a nice lady of the house he's made of Hacer, or should I say Çilem?"

He looked away again, but he couldn't resist commenting.

"He did it out of the goodness of his heart. To rescue Hacer... And Aunt Hacer became an honest woman. They went to the imam at the Eyüp Mosque. He prayed for them. Then they went to the hamam and washed away their sins; it was like she was reborn." With a sarcastic grin on his lips, he looked at Ali and reiterated, "Yes, she became an honorable woman. Anyhow, she wasn't a bad person to begin with. She was young, and happened to meet some weasels like Dice. But she was never with Engin."

He drew out the subject so much he must not have believed it himself. But this story revolving around this poor woman falling into a den of wolves was of no use to this interrogation.

"Actually, it seems that way to me too," I said, leaning back again. "I seriously doubt Hacer Hanım was having an illicit affair. But couldn't Engin have been trying to use your aunt?"

His face fell again.

"No, not like that. You know Engin came here from Europe. His uncle, Durdu, was a drug smuggler known the world over. And Engin was his right-hand man. If the Italians hadn't killed Durdu and broken up their gang, he may have taken over for his uncle. I mean Engin had prepared himself for bigger things. But look at the irony of fate; he was forced to come here and take refuge under Black Nizam's wing. Sure, anything can happen to anybody, but as I understand it Engin was ambitious. I mean he was greedy enough that he could never accept the role fate dealt him. He got really close to his uncle. Maybe he introduced his uncle to Hacer Hanım to earn his trust. But from what we heard, lately he was trying to get the men scattered around Italy back together again. He was getting ready to bring them back to Istanbul."

He wasn't going to let his guard down, but at least my lies were beginning to have an affect.

"Where did you hear that?"

"Well, presumably not from Dice Ihsan. It was from Interpol reports. Because ever since he came to Istanbul,

231

Engin was being monitored." Seeing the fear in his eyes, I continued my scenario. "Our friends at the Italian Interpol surmised that Engin was gathering his strength in Istanbul on his way to proclaiming his kingdom again. He was using your family as a lever."

His chin dropped ever so slightly. He was dumbfounded.

"Did your uncle ever talk about the property deeds with you?"

His beady little eyes opened wide.

"What property deeds?"

"The deeds for nine buildings in Tarlabaşı... Engin was collecting houses of his own. With the upcoming urban renewal project, the value of the buildings is going to skyrocket. But he hid them from your uncle."

"That dirty crook!" he growled. "And he told us he was buying houses for us." Kudret had finally caught on. "I told Uncle Nizam to be careful with Engin. The guy turns up out of nowhere and slinks into our midst. Finding skirt was also part of his plan, of course. He knows my uncle's weakness." He paused. "So who killed Engin? The Italians?"

This time I eyed up the young man sitting at the table more carefully. Was he playing us the same way we were trying to mislead him? Was he planning to sneak out of this business by leaning on the scenario we'd written while really having killed Engin himself? No, he seemed sincere. This killer, who only a few hours ago shot seven bullets into a young girl without blinking an eye, most likely had nothing to do with Engin's murder. But that didn't necessarily mean Black Nizam had nothing to do with it.

"It could've been the Italians, sure," I said, intertwining my fingers. "But I suspect this woman Nazlı. We found a diagram of the Ferhat Çerağ Culture Center in Engin's safe."

Yes, he looked away, because I was talking about a crime he was involved in.

"Apparently he was planning an attack on the building."

"Was he?" he said in a measured tone. He was on guard again, wondering what I was trying to get at.

"That's right," I said, doing my best to appear calm. "And Fidan, I mean the girl you shot, was also coming and going from the culture center."

I'd emphasized the words 'you shot' but there was still no humility, no shame. On the contrary, he raised his voice.

"All of this is that crazy woman Nazlı's fault, anyhow. That place she calls a culture center is a nest for separatists. The fags are there, the Kurds are there, the leftists, the feminists... As if that weren't enough, she was going to open another one in our building. We've had that contract for donkey's years, and the woman's not listening. She got it into her head that we're on our way out."

"Is that why you fired a gun in front of the culture center? To frighten Nazlı into submission?"

Ali's words had drowned out the young killer's prattle. As if he'd just caught on to the trap he'd fallen into, he first looked all spooked at me, then at my assistant, but it was too late.

"Tell us!" said Ali, moving in closer. "How many times did you break that building's windows? How many times did you harrass those people?"

Kudret didn't make a sound.

"What was that diagram for? Were you going to plant a bomb there? Open fire on the people? Tell me! What were you gonna do?"

"I don't know," he said, throwing his head back angrily. "I never heard of any diagram."

That's when Ali's heaviest slap landed on the nape of Kudret's neck.

The suspect fell forward so far he nearly hit his nose on the table. As he sat back up again, the profanities spilled from his lips.

"Son of a bitch! What the fuck are you hitting me for?"

Ali reached over with one brisk movement and grabbed him by his anorak's collar. He lifted him to his feet without giving him a chance to open his mouth again. I should have been stopping him, but the slender, bullet-torn body of the young girl lying in a pool of blood that gradually spread throughout the snow prevented me from doing so.

"Swear one more time, you little shit!" he shouted. "Go on, swear one more time!"

Kudret's face went chalk white, his feet kicking the air. He wanted to turn his bulging eyes on me but couldn't, as Ali was shaking him. "Open your mouth, you shit!" Ali ordered him just as I was starting to worry Kudret was going to get headed in the nose. "Open up or I'll pick you up and toss you off the fifth floor."

Kudret balked.

"Open up, man. Open that mouth!"

Realizing he somehow wasn't going to get the help from me he wanted, the suspect dropped his jaw in fear. Ali noisily collected all the liquid in his mouth and spit it in through Kudret's half-opened lips. Then with both hands, he closed Kudret's jaw.

"Now swallow. Swallow, you bastard!"

At that moment, there was a knock on the interrogation room door. I was sitting in my chair, and Kudret's jaw was still between Ali's paws. We turned to look and Zeynep's troubled face appeared from behind the open metal door.

"The suspect's lawyer is here, Chief. He wants to sit in on the questioning."

"It's our ancestral heritage, for heaven's sake; doesn't it weigh on their conscience at all?"

※

Under snow that had begun to fall again, over asphalt with patches of ice, the taxi was slowly making its way down from Tepebaşı. I'd left my car in the police station's parking lot, but no, it wasn't the car that had broken down this time, it was me. My head was spinning which, whether from exhaustion, nervous tension, or the old age that was sneaking up on me, it did from time to time now.

My mind was still preoccupied with Kudret's lawyer Sacit as I looked out at the darkness through half-parted eyes. Sacit Kasımoğlu, once one of the most sought-after lawyers around. 'Groom' Sacit, as he was known, had studied at the Istanbul Law Faculty and got his master's at the Sorbonne. I'd known him for quite some years. Not just from his time as a dazzling lawyer, but from the days he was at the height of his political power. The nickname 'Groom' came from the era during which he married the daughter of a minister. Don't take my word for it, but they say he made a killing in the early 80s, back when Tarlabaşı Boulevard was opened. You know these degenerates who say Istanbul's streets are paved with gold, and if they don't benefit from it someone else will? Well, he was one of the most adept at that. From that shrewd business team with close ties to Ankara, one of those tightrope walkers of the law that think it a special talent to be able to take advantage of loopholes. Call it divine justice, or the curse of the city, his luck turned on him when his wife was flagrantly caught at a cocaine party. Of course he didn't divorce his wife. Calling it defamation, he first filed a lawsuit against the woman who'd reported the news, and when that didn't stick, he had her shot in the foot. But the journalist proved unshakeable, and she kept going after him; with the help of her colleagues, the dirty files began to open one by one. You know they say when it rains it pours, well that's what happened; his father-in-law's party lost its grip on power in the elections. In the newly formed parliament, his father-in-law was accused of corruption, and through the subtle tunings of politics, made a narrow escape, taking refuge in Canada. After that, Sacit's already shaky marriage really began to crumble. Before long his wife, a constant tabloid heroine, went straight over to her father. If it weren't for the seizure of his property, our well-known lawyer would have had no objections. But our defender of justice was thought to be a secret partner of his father-in-law's, so he brought on the new government's wrath and lost everything he had. Even worse, his reputation was being destroyed as his fortunes melted away. Sacit's respected and of course wealthy customers dropped him one by one. That's how this bright lawyer fell to representing second-rate mobsters like Black Nizam. Though it must be said, he never compromised his civility. Through the evil and the disgrace, he maintained a certain elegance. He never acted defeated.

And on this night, he entered the interrogation room with the same aplomb. He'd messed up, though. He was late, and he'd left his client in the lurch. He smiled at us all in greeting like he didn't give a damn. To be honest, his window dressing was spot on. His new teeth may have been slightly too big for his mouth, but he stood in front of us a dashing warrior of justice, with his carefully combed hair transplants, his classy black coat and dark blue suit, burgundy tie and a patent leather bag. After wishing everyone a good evening, he folded his coat and hung it over the back of the chair he would sit in. He looked over at his client as if noticing him for the first time, his hazel eyes widening in feigned surprise.

"Kudret, son, why are you sitting there in your coat? Aren't you hot?"

I thought the suspect was going to complain about us and tell the lawyer he'd been tortured but he didn't.

"I'm good like this, Sacit Bey," he said, trying once more to wipe the sweat from his brow with the sleeve of his anorak. "I like the heat."

He'd experienced so much indignity before, that he no longer cared. Maybe he thought since he was claiming self-defence, he had nothing to gain from more squabbling with us. His clever lawyer understood what had happened of course, but he kept the lid on it too. He knew very well that quarreling with us would be of no benefit to his case.

"You like it, huh?" he said gloomily, looking over at his client. Then he turned his tired hazel eyes on me as though unburdening his troubles, with the helplessness of a father who can't get a handle on his naughty son. "Strange kid this Kudret, Chief. How can anyone like this heat?"

I hid my displeasure.

"Well, there's nothing to do about that, Sacit Bey. You can't argue over a person's preferences."

"Right you are," he said, with no change in his expression. "There's no arguing preference." Then, as if he'd just noticed, he suddenly proclaimed, "You started without me."

"We were just chatting," I answered. "Kudret and I have met before."

He didn't want to dig.

"All right then, I'm ready. You can start questioning whenever you'd like."

He was completely unruffled, as if we were questioning his client not about his killing someone, but about some minor traffic accident.

Kudret had stuck with his story till now; only the number of Kalashnikovs had changed. Ali was about to intervene but then caught my harsh look and didn't bring it up. When the questioning was over, we sent Kudret to a holding cell. Only then did Sacit ask, "Wasn't it self-defense, Chief?"

He wanted us to tell him what we were thinking; his real problem was how we would write up our statement.

"There's no evidence that the people attacking the club had any rifles or handguns," I said, as though faced with a hopeless situation. "The demonstrators didn't fire a single bullet. Moreover, we weren't able to detect any attempt to enter the building..."

Without getting demoralized, he just nodded gently as he reached for his coat.

"Yes, that's important of course. But aren't Molotov cocktails also firearms?"

He was right, and Kudret would probably get off scot-free. Maybe he'd be convicted if he came before a high court jury that was especially sensitive to the death of a young girl, but that wouldn't carry a stiff penalty either. Kudret must have taken the rap because he knew the outcome. Otherwise one of his underage cousins would have stepped up and saved him. Killers like Kudret who tried to survive in the labyrinth of this crime world usually knew the legislation better than we police, especially those criminals who stood to gain from it.

Maybe we should meet with Nizam again. Yes, we still didn't understand the ugly man's true feelings on the subject of Engin. From what Kudret said, it was emerging that his uncle had been protecting Engin. And it was clear that his gunman nephew was upset by this attitude of Nizam's. But perhaps Nizam wasn't being completely open with his nephew. Maybe he also hated Engin and wanted him out of the picture, intending to solve the problem without letting on to his nephews. Possibly, when he found out Engin was using the woman he loved for his own interests, that's when he hired Tidy Tarık to put an end to the matter. One might wonder why he would hire a hitman from outside when he has nephews so skilled at killing a man, like Kudret. The answer is simple. To cover up what his new wife, Hacer, had been through. And maybe Hacer was still seeing Engin, or at least Black Nizam thought so. Any ugly old man with a beautiful young wife could easily get carried away by such a delusion. But then why marry Hacer? Maybe his young wife had come clean with him. Maybe the woman hated Engin, or was jealous of him. Wasn't that possible? Hacer might have heard that Engin had taken a shine to the *konsomatris* Azize, wanted to take revenge on her ex-lover, and provoked her old yet powerful husband. But then wouldn't Black Nizam have killed the disloyal man with his own hands? Yes, that would be the appropriate response according to their code. But it would have brought his wife's relationship with Engin out into the open... Not only that, everything Hacer had been through would come to light, starting with Dice Ihsan. Whereas when a professional like Tidy Tarık with a hitman's proficiency got rid of Engin, nobody would be the wiser about the unsavory incidents of his wife's history. In that case, Zeynep's assumptions seemed logical. Two murder attempts on Engin had been planned for the same night, and of course the killers or the instigators were not aware of each other. While the first attempt was successful, Tidy Tarık waited unaware and ready to carry out the second attempt, and misfortune fell when he ran into us. It made sense, but then who had carried out the first attempt to kill or have Engin killed in front of the Tarlabaşists Club? Probably Dice Ihsan. He was the one to top the list of suspects. But why would someone as sharp as Dice do that outside his own venue? On that point, it was my theory that gained validity: If events unfolded spontaneously, that is, if Engin ran into Dice's men outside the club... If they went for their guns... If Engin was too slow... Yes, these two scenarios both seemed plausible. But if there was some other unknown dimension to it, that'd be a different story.

Yes, it'd be good to meet with Nizam. This problem of the title deeds could be cleared up as well. I wondered what kind of cut he was taking from the urban renewal of Tarlabaşı. We never got into the details when we spoke today.

"Isn't it ugly, sir?"

My thoughts were interrupted by the driver's words. The wipers worked diligently on the windshield to clear the snowflakes away. He was pointing at the concrete overpass running parallel to the Unkapanı Bridge.

"The metro bridge, I mean. Look, it blocks the view of the mosque."

He was right; the slender body of my darling Süleymaniye Mosque which gave Istanbul its silhouette was obscured by the unsightly appearance of the bridge that was a sign of these times. I suddenly remembered Nazlı. The woman's brave voice rang in my ears: "They don't give a damn about Istanbul's history, her culture, her beauty. They just keep piling on the touristic hotels, the ugly bridges and hideous skyscrapers... All they care about is land grabbing, profiteering, and getting rich off rents." How angry she'd been, how full of venom when she spoke. Could it be that Nazlı had killed Engin? Had she pretended not to condone this type of violent protest while all the while setting her kids loose on the mafia gang? This attack organized on the gambling dens after Engin's death... was it all part of a bigger plan of action? Maybe there was no Tuesday Group. This Ferhat Çerağ Culture Center could be a front to execute acts of terrorism... Bravo Nevzat, you've started to think like those biased police. Didn't you see that woman, and how broken up she was over Fidan's death? How could she willfully send that girl to her grave? Save her from a mire, help her to start a new life, and then throw her in front of a bullet? Maybe she didn't think she'd die, or that no one would be at the club at that time of night. Maybe she'd just meant to harass them a bit. Would she do that? Why not? There was a deep animosity between them. How many times had Black Nizam's minions harassed them? The woman's explanation had sounded sincere enough, but that darkness in her violet eyes, that reticence...

"Don't get me wrong, sir..." Again the taxi driver's voice sent my thoughts scattering. When I didn't answer, he must have concluded that I disagreed. "I'm not saying it because business will suffer. The metro's customers are one thing, ours are another. And also, I'm not against public transport. It's a big convenience for the poor, but still, they're destroying the beauty of Istanbul. Tourists get into my cab, for instance." He pointed out the left-hand pavement of the Unkapanı Bridge we were now on. "So many of them ask me to stop as we're crossing here. To take photos. Day or night, it makes no difference; they always gawk when they see the view. Especially at night. Would you just look at this view? Under the snow, it's wrapped in some otherworldly atmosphere... Isn't it a shame, a sin, to block this magnificent view? It's our ancestral heritage, for heaven's sake. Doesn't it weigh on their conscience at all? How could anyone do this?"

240

In the rearview mirror, I smiled at the driver in acknowledgement. That's when I noticed how old he was. His still voluminous curly hair and the pencil moustache were as white as the snow beginning to blanket the street again.

"You're right," I said respectfully. "It's a shame we don't appreciate this legacy."

It seemed the old man was heartsick.

"No, we don't," he lamented. "We have a house in Arnavutköy left to us by our grandfather. Just a bit up from the waterfront. A two-storey wooden house with a garden. And I swear, so many building contractors knocked on our door. Give it to us and let's build an apartment, and three of the flats will be yours, they say. I ran them all off. There are two apricot trees in the garden that I planted with my own hands. How could I ever allow them to be chopped down? They are living beings, too. I have two grandkids who wouldn't know what grass, trees, or sparrows were if it weren't for that garden. Where will those sparrows go if there are no trees? Is that any kind of city? No sir, I won't give it to them. I'll drive every night till midnight, but I won't violate my father's last wishes. What the kids will do after I'm gone, that I can't say."

I looked lovingly at the old Istanbulite.

"Don't worry," I said to console him. "Your children won't give it up either."

His eyes grew sad in the rearview mirror.

"No, sir. No..." He put his hand to the dashboard as if holding a pen. "I'm writing it here, that house will be on the market not three days after they've dug my grave. They won't even hesitate. You think I don't know my children? They won't wait a week. They'd sell it now if they could, but they still can't take on their old man..."

"You're exaggerating," I said, to snap him out of it. "Your children can't be that bad."

He sighed deeply and his hunched back trembled slightly.

"They'll do it, sir. You mark my words. Humanity is a thing of the past and this city is finished..."

He was right. Contrary to my unnecessarily kind, hollow optimism, I could see all the reality in the bitter truth of this old man driving a cab in the middle of the night in the wind and snow to earn his bread and butter. Istanbul really was finished. Not just because of the dregs of society like Groom Sacit and Black Nizam. We were all complicit in our passivity towards the ignorance and cruelty that finished this city off. Yet we all just kept feeding on the remains, like vultures picking over the giant carcass of an elephant killed for its tusks...

"Kindness is one thing, what people feel is another."

※

From the time it took me to get out of the cab and get to the hanging bay window, I'd turned into a snowman. The snow had suddenly dumped down. If the car had no chains I might have been worried for the old driver, as it took no time at all for the asphalt to go white. Nervously, I checked in front of the door. Still no Bahtiyar on the rug. But of course he wouldn't be there. Honestly, this was the first time I'd felt grateful to the author. The winter before I'd left Istanbul for a murder investigation and when I'd got back, Bahtiyar was urinating blood. Nobody in the neighborhood had taken him in. But this man had a conscience. Either that or he was faking an interest in Bahtiyar because he wanted to build a relationship with me. Was it really him I'd seen at the crime scene tonight? No, it had to be a hallucination. Nothing good comes of a cop who can't overcome his paranoia. I guess I was obsessing on the man too much. Not even Zeynep and Ali were bothered as much as me. They weren't bothered at all. In fact, they liked him. I might have liked him too, if it weren't for those know-it-all looks of his. I'll admit that expression had some fondness, even tenderness in it. As though we were family. Zeynep had said just that. Maybe we resembled the characters in his books. Maybe we inspired them. I really needed to read one of them. I'd find out just what kind of writer he was.

I shook the snow off my hat and coat and, shivering from my wet hands, unlocked the door and went in. The door opened and I noticed a light at the top of the stairs. Strange, hadn't I turned it off when I left that morning? As I took off my hat and coat, I noticed the smell. Was I mistaken? No, the house smelled sweetly of lavender. Or else...? Had Evgenia come round? At first I felt uneasy, as though my privacy had been violated. I thought I'd got over that feeling. Evgenia and I'd had a long talk about it. And after that talk, I'd directly handed the house keys over to her. I didn't allow her time to think it over, but said, "Please, take them. It's the only way I'll ever beat this thing." Evgenia had been here several times since then, but this was the first time she'd done it this way. Marching in before giving me a heads up, and while I was out no less. But so what if she did? Evgenia was everything to me. This house was as much hers as mine. So why was my heart twisting up? Why was I hesitant? It suddenly struck me that Evgenia may have heard me open the door. I immediately pulled myself together.

I gently closed the door and walked silently towards the stairs. Taking care not to make a sound, I began to climb the steps. Still, I was breathless by the time I got to the second floor, though I didn't worry about it. My eyes went to the bedroom. The door was ajar and it was dark inside. Maybe Evgenia wasn't here after all. My uneasiness and excitement quickly passed. Why would Evgenia be here? And if she was going to come round, she definitely would have let me know. Even though she tried not to show it, she also still walked on eggshells when she came to this house. I was the reason for that of course, my discomfort when she was in this house. She may not say so but she felt the tension, Evgenia. Whenever she wanted to drop by, she made sure to call me and never showed up earlier than we'd agreed on. She even came late so I'd be sure to be home. That's why it seemed a pretty big stretch that she'd be here now. I'd fallen prey to another delusion, just as I thought I'd seen the author in Tarlabaşı. I had left on this light illuminating the second floor landing, and the smell of lavender wafting through the house was just a memory from when Evgenia had last visited. Maybe there wasn't even any smell at all, but the effects of exhaustion and solitude were playing pleasant tricks on my mind.

But now a bitterness settled into my heart. I felt like a child all alone in my father's house. The image of that lonely child made me smile. "What next? Why not shrink down and climb into my pocket?" is what Evgenia would say if she heard this. No, it was Güzide who'd say that. Evgenia would smile with sympathy and say, "Yes, you are a small child all right," and perhaps even plant an exaggerated kiss on my cheek. At that moment I felt how much I missed both of them. "One heart cannot have two longings, it would be a lie," a poet once said. I don't want to disappoint that poet, but truth or lie, I was missing two women at the same time right now. How hopelessness pains the human heart! I dragged my tired body, which struggled to carry my still slightly dizzy head, towards my room. When I pushed open the door, the corridor light broke through to inside. It seemed there was a movement in the bed which I couldn't quite make out.

"Nevzat," a woman's voice said. "Nevzat, is that you?"

It sounded like Güzide's voice, a hopeful voice, gruff from sleep. After my neverending duties, these are the words my wife would say to me when I came into the room in the middle of the night.

"Nevzat... Is that you?"

I was neither startled nor afraid, but confused. Even if it was a delusion, it was nice to hear her voice. I answered as I always did.

"Yes, it's me. I'm sorry, work took a long time again..."

"I should be apologizing to you," she said, sitting up a bit. "I came unannounced this time."

Her face entered the scope of the light reflected from the landing. It wasn't Güzide, but Evgenia addressing me. Could a person feel grief and joy at the same time? Apparently they could, because something knotted in my throat and I didn't know what to say. I went quietly over to her, settled on the edge of the bed and gave her a big squeeze.

"Whoa! Nevzat, you're hurting me!" she complained in a cheerful voice. "Let me breathe."

I took in her smell and slackened my hold on her. As I pulled away, she looked carefully into my face.

"Are you all right?"

In place of an answer, I leaned in and kissed her. Her breath smelled of anise, as she'd come here from the *meyhane*, but I couldn't understand the taste of strawberries on her lips. She didn't kiss back but gently pushed me, giggling.

"I'm serious. Are you okay?"

As I drew back, she made a sudden move to grab my hand again, like she'd regretted it.

"I'm fine," I said, watching her face, which maintained its beauty even in the nightfall. "I'm so happy you came. It couldn't get any better."

I really had started to feel fine, as if the dizziness had passed and my body was suddenly rejuvinated.

"Thank you." Her green eyes were drowsy. "To be honest, I wasn't sure. In fact, when you came through that door, I had second thoughts. I wondered what on earth I was doing here..."

I understood exactly how she felt, though I pretended not to.

"Why, sweetheart? What made you think that?"

She stroked my hand affectionately.

"I don't know, I just did. I wasn't going to come here, actually. I went to Asmalı Mescit with Fofo and the others. To Cross-eyed Vasili's meyhane. Vasili Amca's wife, Lena, is a very old friend of Fofo's. From Tarlabaşı. Their houses were next door on Kalyoncukulluğu Street... Fofo and her family went to Greece, but they stayed."

How strange that she was talking about the street I'd been on all day and night.

"Lena Hanım still lives on Kalyoncukulluğu?"

She looked at me in amazement.

"Of course not. How could she? You know what that area's like now. They moved a long time ago. My beautiful Tarlabaşı is an entirely different place... They live in Tomtom now, above Tophane, near their *meyhane*... That's why they took Fofo back to their house. Anyhow, that's what I was saying. It was a wonderful evening. Only when she got drunk she started to recall the past. Her mother and father and friends who'd died... Those memories she somehow could never forget. Forced exile is hard work, Nevzat. To be snatched away from the neighborhood you're born into, from the city, the soil... She got so emotional, Fofo. She hugged Lena for a long time and cried. I've never seen her so sad before. That happy-go-lucky woman was gone and in her place was something like a grandmother mourning the loss of offspring. Lena was affected too, of course. She didn't want to let her go. Imagine, Nevzat, the two have been friends since childhood. They suffered the same pain, went through the same ordeals... Angeliki was also worried about her mother. When she said she'd go with her too, I was left on my own, and I have to admit I felt incredibly lonely. The idea of going home seemed difficult. I thought maybe we could salvage the evening and I wanted to surprise you. I went to Feraye but you'd gone, so I got even more disheartened. I walked down Istiklal intending to go home, but then I saw all those elated people on the snowy avenue. Everyone had turned into children. People had thrown off their heavy, boring masks and were playing with the snow and having a ball. An unexpected delight swept over me. Like my broken enthusiasm was suddenly mended. I came to your house hoping to find you."

"Why didn't you call," I asked, as if I was in any state to see her. "I was also around Beyoğlu."

She pulled my right hand up and pressed it gently to her lips.

"It wouldn't have been a surprise. And I must admit, I was a bit afraid. Not of not finding you at home, but of how you would react."

I pulled my hand away as though offended.

"Don't be silly, Evgenia. When have I ever reacted badly to seeing you?"

She looked into my eyes, afraid she'd hurt me.

"Never... You would never react badly to anybody, Nevzat. But people have feelings they can't put into words, thoughts they can't prevent. Kindness is one thing, what people feel is another. But anyhow, I came here to your house. I knocked, then got my second disappointment. You weren't here. I was about to turn and go when a taxi stopped up ahead. That author got out, your neighbor. He'd been at Feraye too. In fact, he'd seen me poke my head in. He even knew where you were. That there had been a murder in Tarlabaşı and you'd gone there."

How could he know that? Was it really him I'd seen in the dark there? But if he was at the crime scene, how would he know Evgenia had come to Feraye? Maybe his friends had told him. The bearded poet, or Erdinç... Yes, Feraye's owner and he were good buddies. What was the guy trying to do? Why was he so interested in me?

"He meant well," Evgenia continued, as if reading my thoughts. "He even asked me in. 'My wife would love to meet you, too' he said. I guess you've talked about me? He was very warm, like we were old neighbors ourselves."

I couldn't take any more.

"No, Evgenia. Why would I talk about you with a man you don't know? The guy's a writer. He writes crime novels and such, and is probably trying to forge a relationship to get information out of me. With everything I have on my plate, I can't deal with him now too."

Her eyes said she disagreed.

"You're right of course, although I got a good enough impression of him. He seemed very sincere when he invited me in. A little too friendly, if anything..."

All the blood rushed to my head.

"What do you mean? He didn't hit on you?"

She gave my hand a light smack.

"Give me a break. I'm telling you he's not that kind of guy. He was treating me like family. The strange thing was I also felt a familiarity with the man."

She realized I was pouting.

"What, are you jealous?" she chirped. "Come on, Nevzat, it's not like that. He treats me like a relative. Like a big brother would."

It looked like he had the same effect on everyone, that man. Was it because he knew how to empathize? My father used to say writers had keen observational skills, that they easily understood the people they came across and could even figure out what they're made of. But he'd been talking about great authors, not your run-of-the-mill detective novelist like this one.

"Have you ever read anything by him?"

Did Evgenia know what was going through my mind?

"No, I haven't," I stated flatly. "And I'm not planning to. What could he possibly have written? He just churns out a bunch of words on murders he's embellished."

"Maybe it's not like that. If I were in your position, I'd read him." A sarcastic smile spread on her lips. "In fact, I think I will read him. There's a book, Love is for the Dogs... However much I may not like the name... What do you think? Is love for the dogs, really?"

I was tired of all the talk about this author so I reached gently down to my lover.

"Forget about the author," I said, moving closer. "However you define it, love is a marvelous thing..."

This time she didn't push me. On the contrary, she snuggled up to me like a pampered cat. Her warm breath still smelled of alcohol, her moist lips of strawberries.

"Some people are so evil, your curiosity pales in comparison to their savagery."

※

As I stepped out of the bathroom, I was met with the enticing aroma of tea. An elaborately laid table stood in front of me and a cheery Istanbul folk song played on the radio. Evgenia danced around with plates in her hands. You may say it's old-fashioned, but a house without a woman could never be a nest. As she placed a dish of olives on the table, she realized she was being watched.

"Nice shower, Nevzat?"

"It was, thank you." I looked over the plates of cheeses, jams, and omelet. "You've already fixed breakfast. That was fast."

"Well, yeah, it better be," she murmured with a sweet smugness. "I do serve food to a hundred people every night, after all." She suddenly got flustered. "Oh no, the toast is going to burn."

As she ran to the kitchen, I sat down at the table in my usual place, the chair that faced the window. Nobody else sat there when my wife and child were still alive either. Like there was some kind of unspoken agreement. It was my place, every breakfast, every dinner. Güzide would sit opposite me, Aysun by my side. I always had to butter her bread at breakfast. A father should show his daughter love at every opportunity, right? Güzide was efficient, like Evgenia. One foot at the table and one in the kitchen, she'd run back and forth during the meal. Whether the radio was always on, whether it always played Istanbul folk music, that I didn't know. But there would be at least as much happiness at our table as there was this morning. Not always, for certain, but that's how I remembered it.

"Who is Beyoğlu's Finest Big Brother?"

Evgenia's question caught me off guard. My lover approached the table, a blue teapot in one hand, a basket in the other, and eyes full of questions.

"Where did that come from?"

"The phone rang while you were in the bath and I answered it, in case it was important. Some man said, 'Good morning, Beyoğlu's Finest Big Brother!' And when I said, 'Yes?' he got flustered, said he must have a wrong number, and hurriedly hung up."

It must have been Swank Cemal. He probably realized our unpleasant conversation from the night before had got to me and was calling to make amends.

"Was it for you?" Evgenia's eyes sparkled in the light of the snow reflected off the window. "The poor guy got a surprise when he heard my voice, of course."

I didn't want to get into the subject at this time of the morning but the landline started to ring again. I was sure it was Swank. My curious lover looked from me to the phone.

"Aren't you going to answer it?"

There was no escaping anymore.

I reached over to the small side table and picked up.

"Hello?"

Cemal launched into conversation as if we'd never argued the night before.

"Hi, Nevzat. I found you. I dialed your number just now and got a woman..." He stayed quiet, as though waiting for an explanation from me, but when I didn't give him one he kept talking. "Dice just called me. He's heard something interesting about Engin's murder..."

The words poured out of my mouth almost spontaneously.

"Cemal, you're wasting my time again."

"Come on, Nevzat." He sounded hurt. "When have I ever wasted your time?" There was a brief pause. "All right, whatever you say. I'll see you later, then."

"Hold on. Don't hang up," I said, finally coming to my senses. "What did Ihsan say?"

He didn't answer straight away.

"I think you'd better talk to him. You have his number."

I wasn't going to insist.

"All right, Cemal. Thanks."

"See you, then..."

And that was it. He hung up without another word. I suppose I'd really upset him this time...

"I take it it's someone you don't like?" Evgenia asked, while I still held the receiver.

"No. He's a good guy, actually. At least I think he is." I put the phone back. "The same person who called before." When I realised I wasn't going to be able to escape Evgenia's curious eyes, I explained. "An old tough guy... But not of those dirty bullying types. He gave all that up."

She still looked curious.

"Why did he call you 'Beyoğlu's Finest Big Brother'?"

"It's nothing to take seriously," I said, reaching for the teapot. "I can't stand that title, anyhow."

I poured the dark red liquid from the teapot into Evgenia's glass then topped it off with hot water. To get off the subject, I began to praise her.

"The tea looks perfectly brewed... Nicely done!"

"Thank you," she answered, pulling her cup in front of her. But she hadn't forgotten the real subject. "Why don't you like it?"

As she added a sugar cube and began to stir her tea, she stared up at me again. I filled my own cup then put the pot back on the trivet.

"Never mind, Evgenia. Come on, your tea's going to get cold."

I tore off a piece of toast and popped it into my mouth as if I was starving. As my fork reached towards the cheese, my lover persisted. "Now you've really got my curiosity up. Who gave you the name?"

"What do you say we talk about something else. Can we, Evgenia?" I threw in, before bringing the small piece cheese I'd skewered to my mouth.

252

She acted like she didn't hear me.

"Why? You're being humble again, aren't you? I think it describes you to a tee. What's more, it's classy... Beyoğlu's Finest Big Brother... Like the title of a film..."

The morsels were starting to swell in my mouth, but I didn't swallow. My silence immediately engulfed the table. Evgenia noticed it, too. She suddenly stopped talking, looked away and dipped her fork into the dish of olives. The breakfast's mood was broken and even the song on the radio didn't sound so cheerful anymore. I got up and turned it off. As I sat back down, I mumbled, "It's not a nice story. Not nice at all."

Her eyes, like two crystal clear water droplets, turned to look at me tenderly.

"Don't tell me if you don't want to, Nevzat..." she said, her tone apologetic. "I'm just babbling..."

I tried my best to return the same tender look.

"No, I want to. I've never talked to anyone about it till now."

She watched me as if trying to understand.

"No, don't think I'm angry. It was an incident I kept to myself. A moment I wanted to forget. But it doesn't work; little by little, the past catches up with a person. Time creeps up on you without asking whether or not you're ready for the hour to arrive. Yes, the last two days I keep hearing these words. Beyoğlu's Finest Big Brother. It's because I've returned to the crime scene. Like some foolish murderer aching to see his victim one last time."

My throat was dry; I took another sip of tea.

"They used to love me, on Istiklal I mean. Most of the shopkeepers and I were like friends. They'd call me 'Abi' like I was their big brother, not Chief or Nevzat Bey... Yes, Beyoğlu's Finest Big Brother. It was the late Madam Anahit who gave me the nickname. And I was chuffed, of course. Who wouldn't be? There was a greengrocer in the Fish Market, Sait Usta... We called him Langa Sait because his grandfather had a vegetable garden in Langa. Only Langa Sait ever called me Nevzat Bey. If we'd tossed back a couple glasses of raki at the Cumhuriyet Meyhane on the corner and the conversation was flowing, 'Nevzat Bey' would become 'my friend'. Put a chair down opposite his shop and watch; he set his goods out with a mastery that'd make even a talented artist jealous. Summer or winter, every kind and color of fruit and vegetable imaginable could be found there. So his shop never lacked for husbands whose pregnant wives had a craving. And naturally it stayed open till midnight and beyond. He had a shop overseer by the name of Kasım. A little man in his fifties whose light brown eyes were always full of warmth and who had a smile for everyone. He came from the east of Turkey; his accent was charming and he was overly polite. He'd always insist on treating me to tea or coffee whenever I passed by the shop. He was that respectful, that conscientious. Not just to me, no matter who it was. Everyone in the Fish Market loved him. It'd been thirty years since he came to Istanbul; he'd got himself a cheap place in Tarlabaşı with his two children and was getting by. One of his feet was still always in his hometown though, and he'd go back at least once a year for a wedding, a funeral, or a circumcision.

"When Sait Usta was pushing eighty, he retired to his home; even if he didn't pass the shop on to Kasım, he made the trustworthy man a partner of sorts. One morning I found Kasım waiting for me at the door of the police station. He grabbed my hand and said, 'I'm at your mercy, Chief. Kader is missing. She didn't come home last night. And she didn't show up at her job in the pharmacy this morning, either.'

"I knew Kader. I'd seen her at her little brother Bekir's circumcision. She was a dark beauty, a slender girl with laughing eyes like her father's. She'd also visited me at the station once to report a mugging. We'd had a tea together. She was a personable child and it was a pleasant conversation. So I was alarmed to hear she'd gone missing. I took Kasım back to my office, quickly looked into all the previous night's incidents and had someone check the hospitals, but we couldn't turn up Kasım's daughter. She was twenty years old then so I asked him if she had a boyfriend. Kasım went red in the face and said, 'Of course not, Nevzat Abi! What do you mean? We're not that kind of people.'

"I told him not to worry, that I would find her and, after calming him down and sending him away, I went to the pharmacy where Kader worked. It was a small shop in Büyük Parmakkapı Street. The pharmacist, a woman, asked me who I was and why I was looking for the girl. I introduced myself and explained the situation. 'Kader didn't come in this morning, and we don't know where she is either,' she said. She was lying. She didn't trust me, despite my being police. 'Look, her family is really upset, her mother has high blood pressure...' I started to enumerate, when she asked, 'Did they tell you about Osman?' She didn't get a response from me so she explained. 'Osman was Kader's boyfriend. The two kids have been begging Kasım to let them marry for close to a year. But the man's not having any of it. You see? What would you do if you were in those kids' place?'

"I was relieved. At least I knew nothing bad had happened to the girl. I promised the pharmacist I wouldn't tell her father I'd found her yet, but would talk to her myself first. It was enough for her to give me the phone number for where she was staying. I assured her that Kasım respected me a lot, and that I could reconcile the kids with their family. Otherwise, the problem wouldn't go away. She thought it over for a long time, then finally gave me Osman's number. I called it, and when I told him who I was he got quite a scare, but I explained my intentions were good and I just wanted to help. Kader took the phone. She was in tears and asked me to please not tell anyone that I'd found them. 'My father won't allow us to get married,' she said, agitated. 'He'll do something terrible. We're running away from Istanbul. I'll let you know when we get where we're going.'

"I thought she was exaggerating. That she was scared because she was running away. Running away wasn't a solution; it would just make things harder. And it would be such a shame for Kasım and his wife. Living without knowing what had happened to their daughter. 'Don't tell me where you are staying,' I told Kader. 'But please don't leave Istanbul before hearing from me again. I'll talk to your dad and ring you back.'

"It didn't exactly sit well with her but she agreed. I was at the Fish Market in no time. I sat down on a small chair and told him, 'Order me a coffee, if you will. I have some good news.' Kasım was beaming as he put the order in. I explained the situation. 'The two of them are afraid you'll stand in the way of their marrying,' I told him. 'You have to give me your word you'll let Kader marry Osman.'

"'Kader ran off with that guy?' he griped, giving me a funny look. Frankly, I should have caught on to the anger he was feeling at that moment, but I was blinded by the arrogance doing them this favour had given me. 'That 'guy' is going to be your son-in-law,' I said, making light of it. 'Come on Kasım. You're a gentleman. Promise me you won't raise a hand against them.'

"He didn't say a word but just stared down at the shop floor for a while. Even then, I didn't get it. After a bit, he very suddenly and unexpectedly reached for my hand to kiss it, saying 'God bless you, Chief Nevzat. They don't call you Beyoğlu's Finest Big Brother for nothing.'

"Normally, I should have understood from his tone of voice that he wasn't sincere. But you know, when you play big brother to everyone... There's that incomparable feeling of superiority that helping people gives you. The despicable privilege that comes from being a good person. I didn't understand; I couldn't. Still, was it professional instinct or what Kader had said I don't know, but I wouldn't leave him alone before making him swear to me he wouldn't harm a hair on the kids' heads."

Evgenia's fork fell from her hand as she listened to me. The glow in her eyes had already disappeared and her face was seized with the despair of someone who has sensed impending disaster but knows they can't prevent it.

"Yes, I was relieved. Not just relieved, I was feeling great. Once again I'd done a good deed as Beyoğlu's Finest Big Brother. Once again I had helped people, and bolstered my confidence. And with that eagerness, I called Kader. I explained the conversation I'd had with her father. She wouldn't believe it. 'I'm vouching for him,' I insisted. 'I'll even perform the marriage myself. At the Beyoğlu Registry Office.' Who could resist a favor like that from a goody-goody like Chief Nevzat? The kids finally gave in..."

A lump was forming in my throat; if I talked any more I wouldn't be able to hold back, so I sought refuge in my tea as a remedy. The lump seemed to dissolve. I really didn't need to explain any more. Evgenia had understood. But I felt like if I went quiet now, I'd be doing the young girl whose life I'd destroyed years ago yet another injustice.

"I delivered Kader to her father myself," I continued. "She leaned down and kissed her father's hand out of respect. Kasım didn't react. He just stood there rigid, like a huge stone in human form. That's when I got a bad feeling. Wondered if the man was going to hurt her. I pulled Kasım aside. 'Look, you gave me your word that you won't do anything to Kader,' I reminded him. He smiled. I would understand later, the despair that was hiding behind that forced smile. 'Shame on you, Nevzat Abi. I promised you. Would I ever raise a hand against Kader? She's my daughter after all. Relax.'

"And I did relax. I went home in peace. Had a pleasant evening. The news got to me around midnight. A girl had been stabbed to death in Tarlabaşı, an officer told me over the phone. They'd woken me up, and it never even crossed my mind that it could be Kader. I got dressed and went down to Tarlabaşı. As I got closer to the street where the incident happened, I understood. This was where Kasım's house was. It felt like someone had dumped scalding water over my head, but it was too late. I tried to stay hopeful. Right up until I saw Kader's skinny body, riddled with stab wounds, lying in the middle of the street. Her father had assaulted her as she slept in her bed. She'd thrown herself onto the street, fighting for her life. But her father went after her. He stabbed her, his only daughter, right there in front of the whole neighborhood. I found Kasım sitting on his doorstep, his bloody hands folded in his lap. When he saw me, he stood up respectfully again. 'I'm sorry, Nevzat Abi,' he said, bowing his head. 'I let you down. I couldn't keep my word. God forgives, and I hope you can too.'

"It was myself I never forgave though. Kader's father may have been the one to kill her, but it was me who handed her over to her murderer. I requested a transfer out of Beyoğlu right after that. I couldn't bear to stay in the neighborhood, and I couldn't listen to that Beyoğlu's Finest Big Brother nonsense any longer."

A few tears had hastily trickled from Evgenia's eyes and began to wet her cheeks. I held my napkin out to her.

"I told you it wasn't a nice story."

She took the napkin without looking at my face.

"I wasn't expecting it to be so painful," she said, dabbing at her eyes. She sighed as if in defiance. "I'm sorry. I made you relive something you just wanted to forget."

I attempted a smile but failed, so I reached out and touched her hand.

"Don't be so hard on yourself. Some people are so evil, your curiosity pales in comparison to their savagery."

Evgenia, not understanding what I meant, opened her red eyes wide in surprise.

"Yes, last night, a little further up on the same street where Kader was stabbed to death, another young girl was murderered."

"No, I'm not fooling myself, Inspector Abi. He was also in love with me."

They were sitting on the brown bench outside my office, under the raw light at the end of the station's wide corridor. They were slouched over and looked exhausted, like they'd just come from a long journey. The light really accentuated Sadri's skin, that lovely dark complexion peculiar to the Romani, while the girl with the black headscarf who I guessed was Azize had obstinately pale skin. When Sabri saw me, he immediately took his old black coat off his lap and lay it on the bench, standing up respectfully. He buttoned up the same dark jacket he'd worn the night before and waited for me to approach. The girl was so out of it, she didn't even realize Sadri had stood up. She'd planted her eyes on some random spot on the wall opposite.

I was on the road when I heard they'd arrived. I'd called Ali from the taxi while dropping Evgenia off at her house in Kurtuluş.

"The hostess is here with the clarinetist, Chief. Should we talk to them?"

"Have them wait a bit," I'd said, not wanting to miss out on any details. "I'll be there in ten minutes."

But a garbage truck had slid into a city bus in Osmanbey and we had to wait twenty minutes just for that. By the time we got to the station, a full hour had passed.

"I'm so sorry," I said, holding a hand out to Sadri. "Traffic was a disaster."

An easy-going smile lit up his tanned face.

"Don't worry, Chief. We haven't been here long anyways."

The young girl finally heard us and noticed I'd arrived. She gently stood up and eyed me nervously. On her long slender face, it was her wide olive-black eyes under their thick shapely eyebrows that stood out. She wasn't a pretty girl, but her gaze, her posture and the way she turned her head aroused a feeling of innocence. You know that kind of person who everyone says would never harm a fly? Well Azize was one of those. The night before must have been very hard on her; her face was drawn and there were purple circles under her eyes. But in this state she was more deserving of her name. Azize: saint... She resembled one of those women of faith who had washed their hands of the world. I reached out my hand with a sincere smile.

"Hello. You must be Azize."

She gave my hand a lifeless shake, her fingers like ice.

"Yes," she said meekly. "Yes, Abi. I am Azize."

'Abi', or 'big brother', was like a term of defense for women in the entertainment sector. They used it a lot, for their bosses, their musician friends, some of the old tough guys and for us police. It seemed to encapsulate respect while at the same time showing a helping hand was expected. If a woman like that called you 'abi' it meant 'don't think of harming me, or if you are thinking of harming me, please don't'. And like an 'abi' or 'big brother', I welcomed her into my office.

"This way."

It was hot inside, and stuffy.

"Have a seat wherever you'd like," I said, going towards the window. "I'll open it a bit. You won't get cold, will you?"

Sadri answered with the relaxed attitude of someone who'd been there before.

"No. Fresh air is nice. You saw yourself, our *pavyon* is underground. We're dying of suffocation every night. In the past they even smoked there."

When I opened the window, the street noise rushed in with the chilly air. The papers on the table ruffled gently so I only left it open a crack.

As I went to my seat, I saw Azize and the clarinetist sit opposite each other. Sadri still looked comfortable, but Azize sat cringing on the edge of her chair.

"What'll you have to drink?" I asked, taking off my coat. "And I can order you a cheese toast if you're hungry."

"No, thank you, Chief. We already ate." He looked over at the girl. "Well, Azize didn't eat much really, but..."

A vague cloud of appreciation passed through the young girl's eyes.

"No, thanks, Abi. I'm not hungry."

"Let me order us some tea, then."

Sadri nodded towards the door.

"Thanks, but Inspector Ali got us some. We already drank it while we were waiting."

Before he'd finished his sentence, there was a knock on the door and my assistant's handsome face appeared.

"Morning, Chief."

He seemed so awake, the rascal.

"Good morning. Come on in, Ali. Where's Zeynep?"

"At her computer, getting the reports together," he said, gently closing the door behind him. He looked our guests over, then went and stood behind the clarinetist.

"Okay then..." I said, leaning back in my chair. "Yes..." Sadri kept vaguely smiling with the same friendly expression on his face but I didn't linger on it. I turned to the girl. "Let me first say how sorry I am, Azize."

Her black eyes immediately teared up. Some words poured from her lips, but her voice was so weak I couldn't make out a single one.

"I understand how painful this must be," I said, placing my hands on my desk. "I'm sorry Engin's gone but we have to carry on. If you want to help Engin..."

The moment the name of the man she loved left my mouth, she began to cry. Silently at first, then till she shook. The paternalistic expression on Sadri's face lifted and he was about to tell her to stop, but I signaled for him not to. She needed to cry. We wouldn't be able to talk to her till she got it out of her system. She cried till the tremors began to subside and eventually stopped, then dried her eyes with a tissue from her bag.

"I'm sorry. I can't help myself."

"It's not important," I said, taking a bottle of cologne from my desk drawer and handing it to her. "Breathe this a bit. You'll feel better."

She held a hand out and I poured a generous splash into her small palm. She dabbed it onto her temples and forehead. It must have stung her eyes because she squinted. Her nostrils turned a soft pink color.

"Are you okay now?"

She took a deep breath.

"Yes, I'm good."

"Shall we talk then?" I was trying to stay as far from formality as possible. "Are you ready?"

She didn't want to talk in fact, but she couldn't say no either. What else could she do? She bowed her head.

"I'm ready."

"When did you meet Engin?"

Her eyes misted over again, but this time she held herself back.

"Two years ago, in May..."

She went quiet again. To remember, to recount her memories to men she'd never met before, was hard for her.

"Where did you first run into each other?"

Her black eyes grew emotional with the effects of her memories.

"They came to the *pavyon*, him and Nizam Abi. That woman was with them, too..."

Her brow wrinkled a bit as she said 'that woman'.

"Çilem?" Ali butted in. "Are you talking about Nizam's wife?"

She shrunk into her chair like a child made uncomfortable by a stranger's rebuke.

"You know Çilem, right?"

She turned her black eyes to Sadri as if to say, *for the love of god, help me.*

"Answer the man, Azize," the clarinetist told her. "Why are you being shy? Inspector Ali is no stranger."

She studied the floor for a bit, then swallowed and said, "Yes, I know her. Engin introduced us. She and Nizam came over for dinner..."

Just when I thought she would sing, she shut up again.

I stepped in as the trusty big brother again.

"Her real name was Hacer, wasn't it?"

"Mm... Yes, Hacer..."

"You know they got married?" I explained cheerfully, as though delivering some good news.

She blinked in surprise.

"Married? Nizam Abi married Çilem?"

Finally, she'd snapped out of her trance. Her face even seemed to light up, and yes, she smiled for the first time, showing me the pit in her left cheek. A dimple that made her look even younger than her age.

"Good for them. I hope they're happy," she mumbled.

She was genuinely pleased, perhaps because in her mind she'd pictured it being with someone else. She turned to the man among us who she trusted most.

"Did you hear that, Sadri Abi? They got married. Nizam must be so happy."

"That he must," said the clarinetist. "I wonder what Çilem has to say about it..."

Sadri wanted us to know there was some problem with the relationship. Naturally, Ali took the hint.

"Why do you say that? Didn't they love each other?"

The question was directed at the clarinetist, but Azize took it, since she was sitting across from him.

"They did, but more on Nizam Abi's side... Çilem... I mean, she was a bit..."

When she couldn't work it out, Sadri came to her rescue.

"Black Nizam is a truly ugly man." Since my assistant was standing behind him, he directed his speech at me. "Truly... Not only that but..." He paused a moment then finished his sentence. "He's old... There's at least a thirty year age gap between him and the girl."

263

"Age isn't the issue, Sadri Abi." Azize had come back into the conversation when we'd least expected it. "Çilem was scared. Yes, she was afraid of Nizam Abi."

"Why would Nizam harm a woman he loved?"

"Don't say that. Nizam Abi is insanely jealous. He can't stand anyone's eyes on Çilem. And what with this thing with Ihsan..."

The sentence was only half finished. She'd let something slip that she shouldn't have. Her dark eyes narrowed with misgiving. I tried to put her at ease.

"We know about that. Çilem was with Ihsan before, right? But then she fell for Nizam."

"Fell for, Chief?" Sadri mutinied. "Çilem had no choice in the matter. She's a twenty-three-year-old beauty. Why would she go to that freak show?" Apparently, he didn't think too highly of Black Nizam. He turned his nervous eyes on Azize. "Tell him, Azize! Why are you clamming up?"

"I *am* telling him, Sadri Abi. What else is there?"

The clarinetist frowned.

"Tell him about that night. The night Çilem and him came to your place... What you told me, you know..."

Azize's face went red.

"That's a private matter, Sadri Abi."

"Nothing's private when it comes to murder," I said, trying to encourage her. "A person's been killed, a person very dear to you. What you say may untangle the whole mess."

Her dark eyes were wavering.

"It wouldn't be right. Çilem's a good girl."

"We won't do anything to her," I said reassuringly. "Unless it's directly related to the murder, we won't use what you tell us anywhere. I promise you."

She still wasn't convinced. She chewed her bottom lip indecisively.

"I'm telling you this so you'll catch Engin's killer," she finally said, gathering her courage. "But you promised me, Nevzat Abi. If it doesn't concern the murder, what I say stays here."

"Absolutely..."

She was still uncertain she was doing the right thing.

"God forgive me," she murmured gloomily. "Yes, I met Çilem at the Tarlabaşists Club. At that time Ihsan Abi wasn't fighting with Nizam Abi. We went there with Engin. I saw Çilem in Ihsan Abi's office. She was a pretty girl, really pretty. She'll be a movie star if any directors ever see her. That's how pretty she is. And she's also a nice person, cheerful and kind. We got on straight away. Then there was the falling out with Ihsan Abi. But it didn't hurt my friendship with Çilem. Meanwhile, Ihsan Abi went to jail for possession of an unlicensed gun. Actually, they were going to convert it to a fine, but he had some other court case against him or something so they put him away. After that we started seeing Çilem more often. Engin also knew the situation. He told me, 'You should invite that girl round for dinner one night.' And you know I'm naive, I didn't think anything of it. I asked her over. And while the three of us were eating, the doorbell rang. It was Nizam Abi. At first I thought it was a coincidence but it turns out Engin had planned it. Nizam fell in love with Çilem the moment he saw her. She's so beautiful, who wouldn't? Anyhow, when I saw Nizam Abi at the door, I invited him in, naturally. At first, Çilem was uncomfortable, but then with the wine and whatnot, she relaxed. Nizam was very courteous towards her. He flattered her a lot. Don't be fooled by his ugly appearance, the man knows how to sweet talk. So anyhow, as the night wore on, we looked and saw they'd hooked up."

She'd cut the story short. There were things she wasn't telling us.

"Is that all?" Sadri asked, so we didn't have to.

Azize shot him a look.

"Yes. What else would there be?"

She'd left something out all right, but there was no sense trying to force it out of her. It was plain she was done singing.

"Okay then," the clarinetist snapped, his voice fragile. "If you say that's all there is to it... I only insisted so that we can turn up Engin's murderer."

Azize's face went tense with suspicion.

"His murderer? Was it Nizam who killed Engin?"

He threw up his hands as though losing his temper.

"What do I know if it was Nizam Abi? All the Chief is saying is, tell us what happened so we can find whoever it is..."

"You can trust us, sister," said Ali, stepping in again. It was the first time I'd ever heard him call someone 'sister'. Whether he was speaking from the heart or just trying to loosen the girl's tongue, I couldn't say, but I was pleased with his behavior either way.

"And no one's going to touch a hair on your head so long as you are with us," I said, backing him up. "You should tell us what you know. If you want us to put Engin's killer behind bars, that is."

Her black eyes opened wide in horror and she repeated, "You mean Nizam Abi? Is that who killed Engin?"

She knew only too well the unsightly man wasn't to be trusted.

"It's possible," I said calmly. "You need to help us to figure that out."

She raised her voice excitedly.

"It's because of that woman. It's all her fault. I told Engin not to do it. I told him no good would come of her, but I couldn't make him listen."

Just as she was going to explain, she started crying again.

"What woman?" I said, trying to get her to focus. "Are you talking about Çilem?"

She shook her head violently.

"No, not her... I'm talking about Jale. The woman who ruined our lives. The one who was with Engin and Nizam Abi the first time they came to the Neşe Pavyon."

Jale! The woman whose photo we'd found in the victim's house. *The woman is loaded. But the fool went and fell for that pavyon tramp instead.*

How vulgar the crack about 'that pavyon tramp' sounded now that I was looking at Azize! On the other hand, it was glaringly obvious we had some kind of love triangle here. The innocent-faced girl was the third wheel in this love caravan, yet she'd managed to outshine Jale. She wasn't sure of herself though, or why would she hate her, this woman whose man she'd once stolen?

This meaningless sensitivity wasn't lost on Ali. "She was very close to the victim. Were they still seeing each other?" he asked, trying to sprinkle a little fuel on the fire.

The young girl raised her head gravely. She no longer cared about the tears streaming down her face.

"The woman wouldn't leave him alone... She had a ton of money. She was trying to buy Engin." She herself realized these were insufficient grounds, but she was making a superhuman effort to prove her lover had been faithful to her. She turned her moist eyes on me. "When Engin broke it off with her, Jale proposed a partnership with him. And Engin said to me, 'We'll make a lot of money off it then you and I are off to America.' That's why he put up with the woman. And I put up with it for him. Because one day we were going to leave here. He was even putting the money in my bank account."

Azize's story was getting more and more interesting.

"Why your account?" I pried. "Didn't Engin have one?"

"He did, but he didn't want anyone to know where the money was going."

I remembered the nine deeds in his safe.

"Was he buying buildings with that money?"

"Yes, in Tarlabaşı," she confirmed. "The place was going to go way up in value. That's what Engin said. We were going to make a lot of money, then run away from here."

"Nizam didn't know about this business, did he?"

A look of determined understanding gradually replaced the suspicion in her eyes.

"No. And Engin warned me not to tell him." She'd shaken off her shyness and looked me straight in the eye. "Is that why they killed him? Because he didn't tell Nizam Abi?"

I should've said we weren't even sure yet that it was Nizam, but I didn't. It'd be useful to hear her reaction to the hideous mafia father.

"We'll find out, Azize," I said, with respect for her feelings in my voice. "We'll find out, but let's go back to square one if you don't mind. You were telling us how Engin and Nizam came to the Neşe Pavyon."

She wanted to be sure, to turn her pain into anger and channel it into someone else, to hold someone accountable for her lover's death. That must be why she began to speak more boldly. "Yes, I remember that night well. There was another woman with them. A girl called Violet. One of Nizam Abi's one-night stands. I was on stage singing when they came in.

"One Spring Evening I Met You," the clarinetist reminded her. "Selahattin Pınar's song."

Azize's eyes got emotional again.

"That's right. And it was one spring evening they came. In the beginning of May. When Müslüm Abi heard they were coming, he sorted out a place right in front of the stage for them. Müslüm Abi's our boss; he's a good guy. And he's good friends with Nizam. They were in prison together, to that extent. But anyhow, I didn't notice them at first. The lights get in our eyes, you know. At one point I stepped off the stage because I circulate through the tables when I sing. That's when I saw Engin. The people with him laughed and chatted but he kept his eyes on me. I greeted him with a smile, as my job requires. But he didn't smile or say hi back; he just stared. I'm afraid of that type. They're always trouble later. We need customers who eat and drink, spend money, and then leave. You have to stay away from men who get obsessed. I steered clear of that table, in any case. The evening went like that, and then the next night when I arrived at the *pavyon*, I was met with a bouquet of red roses. I'm not gonna lie, I was a bit jealous, wondering who they were for. It turned out they were for me. And it was Engin who'd sent them. It wasn't long of course, maybe a couple hours, before he showed up again in person, alone this time. He sat at the table from the night before. His eyes were on me again. And he popped three dozen bottles of champagne at my feet. On the one hand I was scared, but I was flattered, too. After the show, he called me to his table and I went over. He introduced himself. 'I met a lot of women in my time, but you are unlike any other. Come live with me,' he said out of the blue. I wasn't as experienced as he was, but no man had ever spoken to me so openly or boldly. To be honest, it was his sincerity rather than his words that affected me. I didn't agree immediately of course, but I was confused. I sat at his table all night, then we left together

268

and he dropped me home in his car. I didn't invite him in, and he didn't ask me for a coffee. Which made me think even higher of him. It meant he didn't see me as a one-night stand. But what was he up to? Did he want to marry me and take me away from the *pavyon*, or just make me his mistress? Yes, in the end he succeeded in messing up my head."

She looked over at the clarinetist again.

"When I couldn't get myself out of the situation, I spoke to Sadri Abi. It's up to you, he said. Do what you feel is right."

"As if you wouldn't do it if I told you not to," the clarinetist mumbled affectionately. "You'd made your decision well before you came to me, girl."

Azize dried her lashes with the tissue she'd scrunched in her palm and continued.

"True. My heart had already made its choice, although I wasn't aware of it. Engin came back every night, and every night he dropped me home. On the seventh night I invited him in. And that's how our relationship started."

"So were you happy?" It was Ali who asked. His voice sounded stern, like he was scolding. I doubted he was intending to upset the girl more. He must have put himself in the position of Azize's big brother. "Did Engin stop seeing other women after he was with you?"

The reverie disappeared from Azize's eyes; the dream was over and reality set in. But she brushed Ali off.

"Yes, we were happy, in the beginning." She sighed as though she were talking about the distant past. "No, I'm not fooling myself, Inspector Abi. He was also in love with me. He was like a new man, brimming with love. At that time I was staying in the building where Sadri Abi is now. In a small flat, with no central heating, no bathroom, and a tiny kitchen. I was bathing at the hamam, if you can imagine. Engin objected to my living in that rat's nest. So I moved into his place."

Sadri had told us Azize had lived somewhere else.

"In the house on Kadın Çıkmazı?"

"No, Engin had another place. On Kurtuldu Street. I moved there. And it really did save me. It had furniture and appliances like a proper house."

"But Engin was staying in the other place," said Ali, putting the question in my mind into words.

Azize's chin began to quiver.

"To protect me. He was afraid he'd be killed at any moment. 'I have a lot of enemies,' he told me. 'We're going to need a lot of money to be rid of them.' It never happened and they killed him."

"Who?" I jumped in. "Who wanted to kill Engin? Come on, Azize, don't hide what you know from us."

"I don't know," she murmured, puzzled. "I swear I don't. He was talking about Italians. They killed his uncle. That's why he came to Istanbul in the first place. They wanted to kill him too."

"Did these Italians come to Istanbul?"

She shrugged in helplessness.

"He never said that. He couldn't go to Europe. He had money in Switzerland. There'd be no issue anymore if he could go there. But he said they'd kill him as soon as he stepped off the plane. That's how scared he was, I mean."

"What about Nizam?" Ali cut in. "How were things between them? Recently, I mean. Was there bad blood between them?"

She gave my assistant the same look of helplessness.

"No, things were always good between him and Nizam Abi. There was no problem."

"Then why didn't you know he got married?" My assistant was asking about a detail I'd overlooked. "Why didn't he invite you to the wedding?"

Azize looked away.

"Maybe he did..."

"Invite you?" Ali persisted. "Wouldn't you have heard about it if he'd invited you?"

"No. Because Engin and I had a fight." She looked up with the relief admitting it had given her and her eyes began to water again. "About a week ago."

"You mean, the last time you saw Engin was a week ago?"

"No, no..."

She shook her head gently from side to side.

"He came to the *pavyon* on New Year's Eve. The night he died... He came to make up. But we fought again. If I'd known..."

270

She started to cry again, sobbing even harder than she had before. And just then, Zeynep walked in. With files in hand, unaware what we were talking about. When she saw Azize, the sobs racking her body, she gave us a puzzled look then quickly put the files on the table and sat down next to the young girl.

"It's all right," she said gently, putting a hand on her shoulder. "It'll be okay."

Azize turned her bloodshot eyes to the stranger sitting next to her. She stared at this woman she didn't know without finding it odd, without surprise, without fear. Our criminologist smiled. Zeynep immediately threw an arm around the girl as her narrow shoulders started to shake and yet another crying fit ensued.

"All right, sweetie. All right," Zeynep continued, stroking her back. "It'll be okay."

They stayed that way a bit. As I watched them, I thought about just how wrong it was to call women 'catty'. Women were the ones who best understood other women. When Azize stopped sniffling, Zeynep gently pulled away.

"Come on," she said, her voice full of compassion. "Splash some water on your face, it'll make you feel better."

Azize didn't object; she got quietly up from her seat. With the assurance of a little girl who'd run into her big sister, she took Zeynep's hand and left the room.

A deep silence hung over the room after Azize left it. The noise from the street sounded much the same as though it were inside. I don't know what Ali or the clarinetist were thinking, but I was pondering what made a woman love a man. Especially a bad one. Did she even know that Engin was a terrible person? She must have known. After all, Jale Hanım had been depositing money into her account. Money from another woman sent to the man she loves. Would any self-respecting person ever accept that? But I was being unfair. This young woman was the last person I should be judging on their self-respect. I couldn't even guess how young she'd probably started working at the *pavyons*. Which of the city's heavyweights had ordered her up like fresh meat, an appetizer at their raki tables. They may even have sold the girl outright to some affluent man. Judging the girl on her self-respect was just cruel. It'd be pretty low to accuse a girl of taking the wrong path when she has no other choice.

"It's disgraceful, Chief," said the clarinetist, interrupting my musings. "Love, I mean. It's scandalous."

Yes, he was caught up in an entirely different matter, our poor Sadri. It wasn't just Azize he felt bad for, I suppose; he clearly had his own broken heart story. Who doesn't? That's probably what he was remembering.

"Were you at the *pavyon* that evening?" I asked, going back to the murder. "I mean when Engin came."

He nodded his head gloomily as if what he had to explain was some tawdry affair.

"I was there, Chief. He barged in like a bull at the gate. Shoved his way through, insulting the waiters as they got his regular table ready for him. He made a big show of popping twenty-three whole bottles of bubbly at Azize's feet. But Azize just ignored him. It's customary for the singer to acknowledge them, to smile even if she doesn't mean it. Azize didn't even look the guy in the face. Engin was seething. He jumped onstage and caught Azize by the wrist. Pulled her off stage mid-song. Müslüm Bey got there before me. Well, he owns the place after all. He took them both back to his office. And as he walked past, he called me in there, too.

"As soon as the door shut behind us, Engin started shouting at her, 'What do you think you're doing? Why are you pretending not to see me?'

"Azize cowered in the corner of the room. She said something along the lines of 'I nodded at you', but he didn't let her finish; he just opened his filthy mouth and shouted, 'Fuck your nods! How many times did I call you and get no answer, and no call back?' Now Müslüm Bey is the prudent sort, he puts up with Engin because of Nizam. But when he heard the swearing, even he couldn't stand for it. 'I won't let you insult my workers in my own place,' he said.

"But once Engin was seeing red... He shoved the man with his right hand and threatened him. 'You stay out of this, Müslüm, or you'll be sorry.'

"If he'd made that move in the *pavyon*, Müslüm would have been forced to pull his gun and shoot him. But with no one but the four of us in that room, he had to take it on the chin. He just told him not to swear and left it at that.

"Engin was shooting daggers, but then decided not to drag it out. He went back to Azize. 'What are you trying to do, girl?' he said, fuming. 'Why are you avoiding me?'

"He was sad as well as angry now. Azize ignored that too. 'I'm not. I just don't want to talk to you,' she told him.

"Engin looked dismally over at Müslüm, then at me. He wasn't comfortable with us there and wanted us to leave, but neither the boss nor I humored him because we couldn't trust him. 'Look, I'm sorry if I messed up,' he said softly, as though we wouldn't be able to hear. 'You know I'm having a hard time of things. I'm trying to put things in order.'

"Azize shrugged as though she really couldn't care less. 'So put things in order then. What's it to me?' she said.

"Then Engin suddenly flip-flopped. He started to beg. Yep, he was begging like a little kid. 'Don't, Azize,' he said, his voice gentle now. 'I know you love me. And I love you. You know that too.'

"Azize started crying then. She said, 'No, I don't.' But she was lying. She was crazy in love with that guy.

"He took his clue from the girl's crying, that bastard. 'Look, you do love me,' he said. 'We were made for each other.' He looked over at us again. He lowered his voice and repeated, 'My life has no meaning without you. I swear it. Otherwise, why would I be here? Why would I humiliate myself this way?'

"Azize had started to go soft. She was sniffling, 'Don't you lie to me.' But it sounded more like she meant 'tell me you love me, even if it is a lie.' That weasel knew exactly what he was doing. He went straight for the jugular. 'I'm not lying, Azize,' he said. 'I swear on my dead mother's grave, I'm not. You know how many women I have around me. None of them mean a thing, there's just you.'

"He'd even taken Azize's hand as he said that. The way he was talking was so sweet even I started to believe him. He'd almost managed to smooth things over, but then thinking the problem was solved, he made a big mistake. 'All right,' he said. 'I did let you down. I broke my promise when I was with that woman Jale.'

"And that comment upset the apple cart again. She pulled her hand away and bristled like a tigress. 'So then you did sleep with her! God damn you! And shamelessly lied to me! What happened to that being slander? To it only being about business. You swore!' she shouted.

"If he'd stayed quiet, let her shout and then begged forgiveness, I think things would've been fine. But the idiot went on the defensive. 'You don't get it... I can't explain. Be patient and it'll all be over soon and I won't see the woman again. There's another story behind this. I can't tell you right now. I swear... Everything I do, I do for us. But just look how you're carrying on...'

"He turned to glare at me and Müslüm again. 'Get out of here, will you?' he said. 'We're having a private conversation.'

"Azize didn't give us a chance to open our mouths. 'You get out!' she shouted. 'Whose place is this anyway? Who do you think you're throwing out?'

"He shouted her name but our girl was beyond fear. 'Get away from me. Go back to your society girl,' she hissed. Engin warned her not to shout. He said she'd regret it. 'So I'll regret it,' she said. 'So what?'

"He was having a hard time holding back, that guttersnipe. 'Look, I'm going to lose my patience,' he started to say. 'You haven't got the heart.' Azize answered, fanning the flames. Maybe if we weren't there he'd have let it go, but with two men there he couldn't. He slapped her. Not heavy though, just light. Instead of backing off, she slapped him back, hard. Which pushed him over the edge, and he went for her like he would a man. Fortunately, we were there to intervene and got Azize away unharmed. But the man went berserk. 'This doesn't end here, bitch. I'm not letting you go,' he threatened.

"Müslüm grabbed his arm and pulled that thug out of the room. I stayed with Azize. The poor thing was in tears. 'You heard him, didn't you, abi? He slept with that woman,' she moaned through her tears.

"I mean, she didn't even care that he'd hit her. All she cared about was that woman Jale. I lost my cool. I wanted to give her a piece of my mind, but it would've been a wasted effort. She was still blindly in love with that hustler. That's why she was so upset. No, Chief, I don't understand this love business. What could a girl like Azize possibly see in a bastard like that?"

I was interested in what I was hearing so didn't interrupt, but Ali butted in with a response.

"A lot," he said. "You can never understand women. I don't find it any big surprise for Azize, but why was Engin so stuck on her? That's what I don't understand. Did he really love Azize?"

275

The clarinetist's lip sagged again.

"I don't know. Engin was right about what he said. He had tons of women around him. All of them beautiful, all charming... And all headed down the same path. Why Azize? I really don't get it either." He looked back at me. "What do you say, Chief? Do you think Engin really loved the girl?"

"It's possible. Affairs of the heart are complicated."

Ali didn't agree at all.

"I think the guy was up to something else. He was using Azize as a cover. Just look how he put her up in his house..."

It sounded reasonable, yet love and reason were two entirely different things. Maybe Engin needed something innocent after all the dirt he was involved in. Or there was still some good in him, even if pushed to the depths of his soul. Maybe Azize was a symbol of that. A flower blooming in a sewage dump. Why not? It wasn't such a stretch for the inner world of men like Engin, that kind of preference. I kept my thoughts to myself. Analyzing the complexities of love wasn't our job right now. It was finding whoever killed our victim, no matter how horrible the man.

"You're right, Ali. We should search the girl's house," I said, putting an end to my assistant's postulating. "Azize won't put up a fuss, will she Sadri?"

The clarinetist didn't show the slightest hesitation.

"No sir, Chief. Why would she? If anything, she'd appreciate it. You're trying to find the man who killed her lover. And even if she does, there's me. She won't break her promise to me."

The sound of my phone put a dot on Sadri's sentence. I didn't know the number. I picked up.

"Good morning, Chief. It's Ihsan here."

It was Dice, and he must have been in a hurry if he hadn't waited for me to call him. I supposed no harm would come from Sadri, but thought it best he didn't know who I was talking to.

"Hello..." I said, without calling him by name. "There have been developments, I guess..."

"You heard? Cemal Abi told me he didn't talk to you yet."

He sounded puzzled.

276

"I don't know the details. Just that there were develop-ments."

"Oh, I understand." His sudden excitement died. "Here's the situation, Chief. This morning I got a call from Çilem. She said she had some important information concerning the murder. She wants to see me. But I wasn't sure. What do you think? Could she know who Engin's killer is?"

It was an optimistic guess; why would a woman who just got married two days ago want to shoot her husband in the foot? And by calling the man's arch enemy, no less? Were they setting a trap for Ihsan?

"Frankly, I was shocked that she called," the gambling den owner continued. "You know, I haven't seen Çilem since that beating incident. I never imagined she'd ever call me."

Maybe Ihsan was setting a trap for Black Nizam and had included Çilem in the scenario. They were exes, after all; perhaps he had something on Çilem... Something that would cost the girl her marriage, even her life... He could've planned it before Çilem and Nizam got married. Killing Engin could have been part of it. Nizam gets me involved in the game and there you have it, the perfect crime. Why else would Dice be chasing me down at this time of morning?

"Go on and meet her then," I said, trying to work out the real reason he'd called me. "What are you waiting for?"

A nervous laugh rang out from the other end of the line.

"I don't trust her... She may be looking for revenge."

"All by herself?"

He got the hint.

"Nizam is probably involved too... I can't say for sure, of course. She could be telling the truth."

Was there a twinge of emotion in his voice or did it just seem that way to me?

"What did she tell you?" I prodded. "Why did you think she was being up front? Did she give you a name or something? Of the murderer, or a suspect, I mean."

"No. She didn't name names. She said, quote, 'I think I know who killed Engin.' "

"She thinks..." I repeated.

He suddenly flared with emotion.

"I shouldn't see her?"

This was getting us nowhere. If it was a set-up, it would be a bigger help to know by who and why.

"On the contrary," I said, choosing to encourage him, "I think you definitely should. But let me know what happens. As soon as possible." I was quiet for a second. "So, do you want any help from us?"

I was expecting him to say yes.

"No, Chief," he answered, proving me wrong. "Thank you. I'll take precautions. Fortunately, we have the muscle for that. I just wanted to let you know the situation."

His voice sounded oddly cheerful. Why was that? It certainly wasn't because he'd spoken to me. I guessed it was because he was going to see Çilem, whom he'd once been in love with, and probably still was. Even her calling had shaken him up.

"In that case, don't waste any time," I said, wanting to put any last doubts to rest. "But I'll be waiting to hear how the conversation goes. Call me right afterwards..."

"Sure thing, Chief. I'll ring you this evening. See you later."

As I hung up, I found Sadri's, as well as my assistant's eyes on me. I didn't let them look away before sticking them with a question.

"How exactly did you meet Azize, Sadri?"

He didn't ask me if I suspected him.

"We met in the *pavyon*," he explained, not the least offended. "She came here from Maraş two, three years back. There's no shortage of cannibals in our world, so the boss entrusted her to me. And I took her home. Back then my mother was still alive, and she was so happy when she laid eyes on Azize. She reminded her of Jenya, as the Bulgarians named her, though we called her Pembe. Frankly, Pembe was darker than Azize, but what could you say, that's maternal love for you. Even if she didn't look a thing like her, she put this other girl in place of her deceased daughter."

It must have been a painful story and I didn't think we should ask, but Ali couldn't stop himself.

"Pembe was your sister?"

278

"Yes, she was." He bowed his head. "She died in Bulgaria years ago."

"I'm sorry to hear that."

"Thank you, Inspector. We lost her in an accident. She was the same age as Azize when she died. If she'd lived, she'd be a grown woman now, married with children. That's life... My mother took it hard, of course. She couldn't erase Pembe from her mind. That's one of the reasons we came here. To get some distance so it would be easier to forget... It got worse; my mother couldn't bear the longing. Last year she passed away. I couldn't go back; we'd sold our house, our land, whatever there was anyhow. What was there to go back to? We do still have friends in Dobrudja, though."

The clarinetist stopped talking when Zeynep and Azize came back into the room. The young woman looked better now. Still, Sadri couldn't stop himself standing up and asking, "How are you? Are you feeling better?"

"My head is spinning, Sadri Abi," Azize murmured in a feeble voice as she sat down in her seat.

"That's no surprise," the clarinetist rebuked. "Your blood pressure's dropped. How many times do I have to tell you to eat something."

Zeynep leapt up.

"Let's get you a sandwich, and a glass of salty yoghurt to wash it down."

Azize grimaced as though the mere thought made her sick. She gently raised a hand.

"No, thanks, Zeynep Abla. I can't eat. If I do I'll just throw it back up. If we went home..."

The clarinetist looked at me, begging understanding.

"Can we go, Chief?"

It'd be a good opportunity for us to search the girl's house.

"Of course you can," I said, as if to indulge them. "Let's let Azize rest a bit, and we'll come round in the afternoon to carry on the conversation. How does that sound?"

My words didn't raise any flags for her.

"Certainly, Nevzat Abi. I'll expect you. I should be recovered by then, I hope."

Zeynep touched the girl's shoulder tenderly once more.

279

"If you don't feel well, we can take you to a doctor..."

Azize was embarrassed, as though she was imposing.

"No, I'm okay now."

As the girl lapsed into silence, Zeynep turned to the clarinetist.

"Did I hear you mention Dobrudja?"

"Yes," said Sadri, with his usual candor. "I was just telling the inspector about the old days."

Zeynep's face came alive with curiosity.

"Are you a Bulgarian immigrant?"

For some reason the clarinetist looked uneasy.

"Yes, why do you ask?"

Zeynep didn't find the man's reaction odd.

"We're Bulgarian immigrants too, or, my family came from there I should say. From Hacıoğlu Pazarcık..."

Sadri's misgivings seemed to scatter.

"Sorry, I get a bit funny when someone asks out of the blue. I can't quite get over that feeling of being a stranger in my own country."

Zeynep gazed at him affectionately as though they were family.

"My father's like that too... If someone asks him if he emigrated from Bulgaria, he suddenly changes color. He says you can never get over the feeling of being an immigrant Balkan Turk... My family is from the village of Sarı Mahmut. Its Bulgarian name is Alekseyevo. What about yours?"

The clarinetist blushed as though he found the situation embarrassing.

"We don't have a village. My family moved to the city years ago. They were musicians. When they couldn't get any food in the rural areas, they packed up and went to the city..."

"It's a lovely place, isn't it?" Zeynep asked wistfully. "I mean, that's what my family tells me..."

Sadri sighed deeply.

"It sure is, ma'am. The land is very fertile. Bulgaria's wheat basket..."

"And you?" asked Ali, turning to the young woman we'd forgotten. "Where are you from, Azize?"

She looked spooked again. Her bloodless face turned even paler but she tried to smile.

"Me?" The hidden dimple appeared in her left cheek. "I was born in Germany. In Hannover... My father left us and ran away to Holland with a German woman. I was four years old when I came to Turkey. My mother remarried in Izmir. We lived in Gaziemir for a while. Then when my mother died..." For fear of rambling, she hurried to finish her words. "When my mother died, I suddenly grew up. I wandered around to various cities. And now, well, I'm here..."

"Couldn't she just be trying to ease her conscience?"

✖

The phone call from Black Nizam came as I was opening the car door. He was probably worried about his nephew Kudret. Or was he calling about Dice Ihsan's scheming with his new wife? I answered with curiosity, but spoke with calm.

"Good morning, Nizam. What's up?"

He tread lightly, figuring I was angry.

"Sorry to bother you, Chief. Things are not so peachy, as you know. There was an attack on the club last night. And our Kudret had to fend them off..."

"Yes, he killed a young girl. Filled her full of holes, the poor thing."

"He got scared, Chief." His voice sounded panicky. "The crowd attacked and they were packing AKs and whatnot..."

His words trailed off into coughing. A smoker's morning fit.

"The Kalashnikov comments came from your nephew," I said, waiting for him to stop hacking. "Nobody else is talking about any rifles. Kudret might be lying to get off the hook."

"No, Kudret doesn't lie, Chief," he began to say, before another wave hit him.

"Anyhow Nizam, it's in the hands of the law. The court will decide your nephew's fate. But I'm glad you called. We need to speak with Hacer Hanım. We have a few questions for her."

The hacking stopped but he couldn't manage to respond.

"If you say you won't give your permission," I continued more sternly, "we'll be forced to bring her in to the station with a court order..."

Suddenly his coughing fits were a thing of the past.

"My permission?" he said humbly. "Don't be silly. We're happy to cooperate. Why don't you come round to our place? You can speak to Hacer and we'll have a bite to eat together."

Nizam lapsed back into that slippery manner of his. He must've benefitted a lot from being in thick with the police, hogtying them with all the favors he'd done them.

"Thank you," I said coldly. "But let's meet outside."

"Certainly, Chief. The club is closed because it's a crime scene... Come to the *ocakbaşı*. It's really calm in the afternoon. The place is on Ipek Street. Yiyen Ocakbaşı. You'll see our sign when you enter the street, just there on the right..."

"Agreed. We'll be there at four."

As I hung up, the side door opened and in one brisk move Ali settled into the seat next to mine. Zeynep climbed in back, as usual.

"Are we going?" I said, to check nothing was missing. "Are we good?"

"Yes, Chief," they answered in chorus.

I turned the key and the old guy's tired engine immediately began to purr. Ali made a fist and gently punched the dashboard.

"Look at that! Your car's in good shape again, Chief."

"Of course he is... He just came from the shop," I answered with justifiable pride. "The motor, brakes, and radiator have all been overhauled. Your friend's been serviced."

"The heat works, too," said Zeynep, from the back seat. "What was that before; so cold it set our teeth chattering?"

I turned and half-jokingly glared at her.

"You say it was cold, but it was this car that got you home in the middle of the night, Zeynep dear."

Our criminologist was taken off guard by the comeback.

"No, Chief, I mean... That's not what I meant."

"What did you mean then?" asked Ali, escalating the banter. "What more could it do? Even with its burnt up oil, dirty carburetor and busted exhaust, it hung in there. It never once left us stranded on the side of the road."

I glanced at his face; the rascal was smirking under his moustache.

"Hmm. So now you are teasing me too, Ali."

He immediately recovered, the scoundrel.

"No, Chief. Would I ever do that?"

But the chirpiness in his voice said otherwise.

Before stepping on the gas, I hung my head with the resentment of the betrayed.

"I'd let you both out right here, but lucky for you these files are urgent." I said, continuing to lay it on thick. "Why don't you ingrates look at the state of your own selves before taking a swipe at my poor car..."

The moment the words left my mouth, I realized I'd put my foot in it. What would I say if they were to ask me what state I was referring to? I'd speak my mind, of course. Say it was easy enough to sit there commenting on my car while still incapable of declaring their love for each other. But neither Ali nor Zeynep got caught on up to what I'd said; the two just laughed it off. That's when I noticed something else. Zeynep was still in her clothes from the previous night. You may say what of it, but our criminologist is very finicky. You don't see her wearing the same thing from one day to the next. Only on nights we were super busy and she couldn't go home would she be forced to carry on in the same clothes. And didn't these two go out together the night before? Did Zeynep not go home? Something akin to jealousy stirred in me, but it didn't last long. I kicked myself for being old-fashioned. The intolerant father went out, replaced by the indulgent supervisor. I hoped they had spent the night together; the two young people deserved happiness more than just about anyone. But I suddenly felt hopeless. Even if the two had stayed in the same house, they'd consider it improper to touch each other. But was that true or were they pulling the wool over my eyes? Acting all shy around me while having a good time behind their naive boss's, back? No, they wouldn't do that. I wouldn't expect that of Ali or Zeynep. Something had definitely gone on between them. They looked happy as clams. And what to make of this contented fatigue in their faces? Just like mine... No, I'd never seen them like this before. The way they looked at each other, even their voices sounded different... Should I ask? But what exactly would I ask? *Hey kids, did you spend the night together?* There was no way.

"Yes, Zeynep," I said, getting serious. "Any new leads since last night?"

After we'd seen Azize and Sadri off, Ali had phoned Jale. The woman met our request for an interview with utmost civility. She'd learned from the papers that Engin had been killed. She was very saddened and wanted to be of help, of course. But she'd be flying to Ankara that afternoon, and unless we could come meet her straight away, it would have to wait till the following day. We'd set off at once so that we wouldn't miss her, taking Zeynep with us so we could stop by the Crime Lab and pick up her results. The assessment meeting we couldn't manage that morning would be held in my faithful old car instead.

"Not so much, Chief," Zeynep began to explain. "We have two important documents in our possession. The first is related to Tidy Tarık. The officers I commissioned found his bank account, with a two hundred thousand lira deposit made one week ago."

"Payoff for killing Engin," Ali immediately speculated.

He'd probably guessed correctly; the individual who deposited the money was most likely the same one to hire Tidy. I searched for Zeynep's eyes in the rearview mirror.

"Who made the deposit?"

"He did, unfortunately," she said, sounding defeated. "Yep, Chief. Tarık brought cash to the bank. Whoever wanted Engin killed must have understood how these things work. He knew how to cover his tracks. But we've determined where Tarık is staying. A big hotel on Sıraselviler by the name of Rikkat. I'll swing by this afternoon. Maybe it'll turn something up."

As the car pulled out of the covered parking lot, I was blinded. With the winter sun on one hand, the glare of the still unmelted snow and the light reflecting off the wet asphalt on the other, it was brighter than a summer day. As my eyes adjusted to the street, I asked, "Did you check the suspects' accounts? If the same amount was withdrawn, we'll have whoever hired Tarık."

Zeynep gently shook her head. The smell of her perfume hit me.

"I just told the boys a bit ago. They're going to take a look at Ihsan's, Nizam's, Jale's, and Nazlı's accounts. They'll check if anyone's taken out the two hundred thousand and we'll get our answers tomorrow."

"We'd better check Azize's too," my assistant warned me. "Since Jale was depositing the victim's money into her account..."

Zeynep didn't think it likely.

"Come on, Ali. That girl couldn't hurt anyone."

So it wasn't just us men; Azize evoked the same sense of innocence in women.

"That's exactly why we need to double check," I said, contradicting our criminologist. "That's the rule, Zeynep. In unsolved murders, you start by suspecting the least suspicious."

"If you say so..." She wasn't at all convinced, but she didn't want to argue. "All right, Chief. I'll give the boys a call and tell them to check Azize's account as well. Incidentally, we've got some information on Nazlı. There's a pretty big file in the political department."

"The political department?" Ali turned his head eagerly. "She was a member of an illegal political organization, wasn't she?"

For some reason he'd taken a real dislike to this Nazlı.

"Not her personally, but Ferhat Çerağ, who the culture center was named after. They studied in the same faculty. Ferhat comes from a family of blue-collar workers. His mother worked in the Tekel brewery and his father was a trade unionist. Ferhat got his leftism from his father. You know they say the apple doesn't fall far from the tree? Well, Ferhat found his father too passive even, and he joined an organization even further to the left. One of those that calls for armed struggle. During student protests, he was detained numerous times for conflicts with the police. And Nazlı was in some of them too."

"You mean they were lovers?" Ali asked excitedly. "Now I understand why she named the culture center Ferhat Çerağ..."

"Actually, the relationship was pretty one-sided..." Zeynep's head was between the front seats as she explained to Ali, eyes shining, "According to a report written by the undercover police who infiltrated the group, Ferhat didn't really care about Nazlı. I'm talking about a report written twenty odd years ago. Nazlı's real concern was unrequited love, not the organization itself. But Ferhat saw her as an element of the petite bourgeoisie. Yep, that's what the officer wrote in his report. But to call Nazlı's father petite bourgeoisie would be an understatement. Hakkı Bey was a full-blown real estate tycoon. He worked as an estate agent. Even more, he rented and sold buildings abandoned by minorities who were forced to flee Istanbul. In Kurtuluş, Balat, Tarlabaşı..."

"That must be why Nazlı opened a culture center in Tarlabaşı," I muttered.

Zeynep didn't hear what I said.

"What's that, Chief?"

"Never mind. Go on."

"I suppose Hakkı Bey was tainted by corruption too. There's a few court cases opened by Rum citizens who emigrated to Greece. But in the end he either won or the cases were dropped. I mean, Nazlı comes from a rich family, not the petite bourgeoisie or middle class. And she was quite a looker when she was young. I saw the photos and I swear she was like a model. Whatever it was she saw in him, she really fell for the leftist. Ferhat was arrested in 1998 in a shoot out. They put him in Ümraniye Prison. Nazlı visited him every week. She wanted to hire hotshot lawyers to get him out, but Ferhat refused, saying they had their own lawyers who were going to plead a political defense. Nazlı was undaunted and made every effort to support the man she loved. But before the verdict was read, all those prisoners who didn't want to go to F-type prisons revolted. It was a huge incident. There were hunger strikes, protests... You remember it Chief; it was called the Back to Life Operation."

I remembered it only too well. The state had been relentless. Dozens of prisoners lost their lives, and there were even security guards among the dead.

"Unfortunately, Ferhat Çerağ burned to death in that operation," Zeynep said, continuing her verbal report. "It was horrific, of course. Nazlı was destroyed. She even got psychological treatment for a while. When she recovered a bit, Hakkı Bey sent her, his only child, to Paris. Under the guise of studying at a private art school, his real aim was to ensure she recovered from the trauma. Nazlı loved France. She didn't join the leftists from Turkey there, but instead forged close relationships with the greens, feminist and human rights groups, that kind of marginal. She came back to Turkey when her mother died and ended up staying here, I guess so her father wouldn't be left alone. Her father also died six years ago, and as the sole heir to a considerable inheritance, she began to carve her own path. As you can imagine, she didn't get involved in any commercial enterprises. She opened the culture center in Tarlabaşı with the money from the real estate and started helping people."

The story didn't convince Ali; he was no fool.

"What do you mean?" he growled. "The woman just opened the center because it was a nice thing to do? You're saying she had no ideological objectives?"

I tried to recall Nazlı's face. The deep lines in her forehead, the wrinkles mercilessly crowding her violet eyes, the brown hair beginning to gray, the prematurely slumped shoulders she tried to hold straight... The woman's pain-stricken, compassionate gaze.

"Couldn't she be trying to ease her conscience?" The words poured from my mouth. "Isn't it possible she just wants to find a bit of peace by doing some good?"

He didn't see the reason in it.

"I don't think so, Chief. Why would the woman have a bad conscience? Why would she hold herself responsible for those kids sniffing thinners? Or Fidan's attack on the gambling den?"

At the last second I noticed the traffic light was red, and I gently stepped on the brakes.

"Because of her father, Ali," I answered, as the car shook to a halt. "Because of the huge fortune the realtor Hakkı made. What was it Zeynep said? The man was dealing in buildings left behind when the Rum went to Greece, leaving all their property and possessions behind. He wrangled a way to acquire the houses of emigrating citizens on the cheap. It would be impossible for Nazlı not to notice this corruption. I think she was genuinely ashamed. Maybe she resented their wealth and wanted to get out from under the heavy burden of this dirty fortune. At the very least she had an idea to use the money for some good. She wanted to help those people who had fallen prey to the dirty tricks that helped him acquire their properties."

As usual, our skeptical policeman wasn't convinced.

"Possibly. But I think the woman looks like more of a militant than a do-gooder. You saw her on the way to that protest. That determined stare of hers. She wouldn't give up unless you killed her. She's committed to her ideals. Don't get me wrong. It's not that I don't appreciate that, but I believe Nazlı has an illegal political group backing her. Maybe even one she created herself. Why not? In that way, she could take revenge on the system for the man she loved. The Gezi Park resistance played right into her hands. She could've formed the Tuesday Group from the kids she recruited from there." He hit his knee gently with a fist. "Of course! Maybe Nazlı had Engin killed. He was already an enemy. They'd already fought. The map of the culture center did turn up in the victim's safe, after all. The woman wasn't born yesterday. Is she so naive she wouldn't know Nizam's men's intentions? Look, she got the whole gang together and attacked his place. Not even Dice Ihsan was that brave. And look how she suddenly appeared at the crime scene last night. Almost the same time we did. Maybe she sent the kids over to Black Nizam's place and was waiting for the outcome. When they fled the crime scene and delivered the painful news, she rushed up there. Isn't that possible?"

Sure it was possible, but I couldn't see the rationale in a woman devoted to the people who loved her taking shelter behind a young girl's death. If Nazlı had thought it right to throw Molotov cocktails into those gambling dens, most likely she would've thrown the first bottle herself. And she didn't fit the usual profile. In this jungle of tired, rundown buildings known as Tarlabaşı, she was a lone woman spending her wealth and resources on society's most down and out. No, even if my assistant's words made sense, my gut said he was wrong. Still, I shouldn't be in a hurry to object. I'd come across some incidents in homicide cases that so defied logic, conscience, and experience that they pointed the wrong way in identifying the perpetrator.

"What do you think, Zeynep?" I said, stepping on the gas again. "Could Nazlı be behind this?"

She cast a glance in the rearview mirror.

"What Ali says fits the circumstances to a tee, actually. A pretty sound scenario could be built on that hypothesis. All the same, this murder doesn't look anything like an assassination planned by revolutionaries. They would have left a message, phoned the papers or something... 'The reprehensible gamblers have been punished for corrupting the people' or 'We will banish all rentiers from Tarlabaşı' or some such thing. Besides that, Engin was killed with a knife. There's no gun around. Last night's Kalashnikovs were probably a figment of the imagination too..." She looked over at my assistant, begging his understanding. "What you're saying is not without merit. I agree that Nazlı should be a suspect. But the reasons I just listed considerably reduce the possibility that she's a killer. I hardly lack appreciation for the woman either. Not just because she helps the downtrodden, but also because she stayed true to her lover. Think about it. Ferhat died and years have passed, but Nazlı is still working to keep his name alive."

"Isn't life more what we imagine than what we experience anyhow?"

⊠

It was noon by the time we left Zeynep and arrived at the apartment building in Cihangir. Jale Hanım had joined the top two flats to make a duplex for herself. The maid hung our coats, politely receiving us, and we followed her up the tasteful wooden staircase to the second floor terrace's glass-enclosed greenhouse. First we caught a whiff of perfume, after which we were met by ceramic pots of delicate orchids and blooming carnations, blonde chrysanthemums and purple azaleas, and a profusion of winter roses. It was a bright place that brought a smile to a person's face... A breakfast table had been laid in front of the large window that overlooked the sea. Jale sat waiting for us, huge sunglasses over her eyes. She must have just finished eating. Plates of cheese, olives, salami, dried meat, honey, cottled cream, and other such things had not yet been removed from the table. She wore a dressing gown the same color as the dark red roses in the beige vase. An alluring robe that exposed half her silicone breasts and opened to the knees of her still shapely legs... When she saw us, there was a twitch in her lips akin to a smile, but she didn't remove her dark glasses, nor did she attempt to stand. She just extended her right hand in the manner of a queen.

"Welcome."

I think she expected us to kiss it, but I settled for a shake. Ali didn't pay it a blind bit of notice.

291

"Bon appétit, Jale Hanım..." I said, as she pulled her hand from my palm. "I'm Chief Inspector Nevzat..."

"So nice to meet you." She was supposedly talking to me, but her gaze was turned on our loose cannon. I guess she couldn't see us well, because she finally removed her glasses. "Why aren't you wearing uniforms?"

"What?" Ali genuinely hadn't understood, but he was bothered by the woman's ogling. He snapped at her. "What did you say, ma'am?"

As she placed the sunglasses on the table, she shot me a look of futility.

"Why are young people so quick-tempered?" She didn't even wait for my response. She just mumbled, her admiring eyes glued to our young officer. "Although... it seems he's more handsome when he's angry."

I immediately took on the role of the sensible middle-aged man.

"This is Inspector Ali," I boasted, with the pride of a father for his son. "We work together."

"Ali, huh? I like men with short names. Though I have to admit, I like them more in uniform."

Ali shook his head to say shame on you. The woman wasn't bothered. She finally turned to me with the flimsy smile of her silicone plumped lips.

"Don't you think so, Nevzat Bey? Men look great in uniform." She gently drummed the table with fingernails painted a shiny black. "Especially the young ones..."

It was hard to say whether she was being genuine or overacting in order to hide her real frame of mind. Either way it was time to put her in her place.

"One of those young men is lying in a morgue right now, Jale Hanım," I said, pulling out the chair opposite her. "A deep knife wound to the heart..."

Things had gone sour, yet she wasn't going to let her dignity be undermined, and she leaned back as if to get some distance.

"You're referring to Engin?"

I gave her a cynical look.

"Anybody else dead these days?"

That world-weary, indifferent expression was immediately wiped from her overmade-up face.

"I... I don't know. I just heard about Engin..."

I was a bit surprised that she'd got so anxious. Ali's question interrupted that.

"When did you last see the victim?"

"You mean Engin?" Her eyelashes blinked. "A week ago... No. No, it was ten days... Something like that I mean."

My assistant didn't mince his words. "Did you discuss the buildings you bought in Tarlabaşı?"

The question hit its mark. Jale's face contorted and her jaw dropped a bit.

"There's no need to hide it; we know you were doing business together."

She straightened up in her chair and pulled the dressing gown around her to try to cover up the breasts and legs she'd left partially exposed. She turned to the maid still standing there.

"Did you ask the gentlemen what they wanted to drink, dear?"

She was obviously stalling.

"Nothing for us, thanks," I said, trying to relay the gravity of the situation. "Please answer the question..."

She turned to the maid, apparently trying to keep her cool.

"It's okay then. You can go."

The maid had sensed something was up and her chubby cheeks had gone beet red. Still, it wasn't her place to meddle.

"As you wish, ma'am," the poor girl said, quickly stepping out of the greenhouse.

"You heard wrong, Nevzat Bey."

Yes, she must have got over the initial shock, because she went on to the counter-attack. However, she was stringing us along and my patience was wearing thin.

"Please, ma'am," I said, cutting her short. "Don't demean yourself any more. We know you sent Engin a hefty sum of money. You were depositing it into the account of a girl named Azize. We can bring you the bank receipt if need be."

Her hazel eyes narrowed and traces of an early defeat appeared on her face.

"How did you hear that?"

"What does that matter, Jale Hanım?" I answered flatly. "You were doing business with Engin."

She lowered her guard, her pride shattered. She stared at the crumbs of bread and cheese on the plate in front of her for a bit.

"We were lovers," she said then, in a voice of surrender. "It's nothing to be proud of. I'm a married woman, but my husband's been bedridden for three years and brain-dead for the last six months. And anyhow our relationship..." She was having difficulty explaining. "How should I say... We had an open relationship. Perhaps you've read about us in the tabloids. And before Rıfat, my husband I mean, suffered a stroke... Anyhow, it's a personal matter... What I meant to say is that Engin and I were lovers, not partners. We weren't doing business together. I was just helping him."

Ali had heard enough.

"It doesn't look like you were just helping a bit. You sent the man a small fortune."

She assumed that aggravating haughtiness again.

"It wasn't so much, my dear... Anyhow, he paid me back every time. In installments, of course." She averted her eyes again. "He'd bring the money over to my house. Deliver it by hand, I mean. So you know, if you ask for a bank statement, I'm afraid I can't give you one."

She was lying through her teeth.

"That's not how Azize tells it." I was the one to cut her short this time. "You know Azize, don't you? This young girl with the baby face? Engin fell in love at first sight. Come to think, you were with him that night... at the Neşe Pavyon."

I was hoping to back her into a corner but my words had an unexpected effect. Her sculpted, penciled-in eyebrows furrowed and her eyes lost their spooked look and blazed. She sat up in her chair as if drawing on some hidden source of energy.

"You believed that *pavyon* slut Azize?

Our genteel host had suddenly turned into a vulgar commoner.

"Yes, Azize Hanım said so," I answered back, emphasizing the word 'hanım'. "Apparently Black Nizam was with you as well, and a woman by the name of Violet."

"That's a lie!" she all but roared from her seat. "That little bitch is lying."

"That's not really fair, is it, Jale Hanım?" I warned her, not because I wanted her angrier so she'd give more away, but because I was genuinely picturing Azize's innocent face before me. "Swearing doesn't really suit a lady like you."

She turned her blazing eyes on me and was going to spill out a whopping retort, or perhaps even swear, then only managed to stop herself at the last moment.

"I apologize," she said, looking away again. "That..." She faltered a bit, as the only adjectives she could muster up were profanity. "That *konsamatris* lured him in with drugs. Otherwise, why would a man like Engin ever give her a second glance?"

"You mean the cocaine," I said knowingly, to try and fish more out of her.

I could have saved my breath. The woman was already itching to spill it out.

"See, you've already heard," she said, her voice eager. "I'd be surprised if you said you hadn't. They're snorting powder day and night, those ones. The girl's ugly nose is going to drop off one day, from blow..."

"Nizam was also using, from what we heard."

Ali's words seemed to spoil Jale's fun.

"No, I don't know about that. I wouldn't want to go falsely accusing anyone. Don't you go getting me into trouble with Nizam Bey."

She must have been terrified of the ugly mafia boss. Maybe that fear was the reason she was willing to send the money to Azize's account. She didn't want Nizam to know she was doing business with Engin.

"But there's a girl called Çilem," she said, grimacing. "Her real name's Hacer... She's Nizam's mistress, and at the same time a friend of Azize's. She's also a smackhead. Maybe they cajoled Nizam Bey in the same way, into these group..." She smirked. "You know what I mean, these group parties..."

Jale let me down. I was expecting the woman to be smoother around the edges, sadder and more devoted to her lover. But it was like she didn't care about Engin's death. As for the jealousy she felt, it stemmed from the battle she was losing to women younger than herself. That's what made her weak. My assistant must have been sharing my thoughts, because he kept goading her.

"We heard that too. They even got together at Azize's house, as a matter of fact. The four of them. Engin, Azize, Nizam and Çilem... And maybe Azize organized the party. But would you look at that; the relationship had a happy ending."

She went quiet, bursting with curiosity, then impatiently blurted out, "What happy ending?"

"Didn't you hear? They got married."

She jerked as if taking an invisible blow.

"Who?" Her voice was panicky.

"Nizam and Çilem..."

Jale breathed a sigh of relief.

"The very day Engin was murdered," Ali said, keeping up the game. "In a modest ceremony on Uludağ Mountain in Bursa."

She shook her head like she was the one betrayed.

"The day Engin died, huh?" I guessed logic and emotion were beginning to battle it out. "So Çilem finally got her way with Nizam then."

It wasn't clear whether she was badmouthing Çilem or feeling sorry for Nizam, but she'd dropped the term 'bey'.

"You don't need to hide it anymore," I said amicably. "We know it was Nizam who got the drugs for them..."

She didn't immediately object, eyeing me over as if to suss out my intentions.

"That's right. Nizam was supplying them," I pressed on. "He has a criminal record; his men were caught with a shipment of heroin bound for Italy... You must have heard Engin's uncle Durdu was also in the drug trade. The Italians had him killed. Durdu was also the one who introduced Engin to Black Nizam, and who sent his nephew to stay with him."

Jale listened in silence.

"Durdu loved Engin like a son and wanted to protect him. Seems he chose the wrong person to do that."

"What do you mean?" she burst out. "Nizam killed Engin?"

This time I watched her a bit, with eyes full of insinuation.

"Isn't that possible?" I asked, before leaning back. "We know Engin was doing business behind his back. And it's common knowledge how ruthless Nizam is..."

She opened her hazel eyes with apprehension.

"Are you talking about the buildings in Tarlabaşı?" She realized she'd implicated herself and tried to fix it. "I mean, the Greek houses that Engin bought?"

"What else? He had nine title deeds on him. And those are the ones we know of. Tarlabaşı is small enough to fit in your palm. You think it's possible Nizam didn't know about them?"

Jale gulped.

"Does he know about me, too? I mean, that I was helping Engin?"

Things were finally falling into place.

"Yesterday we interrogated Nizam. He didn't make any accusations against you, but you know how sly he is. He hides his animosity well, but never forgives a wrong done him. I'd say he's definitely aware of the money you gave Engin. He's just biding his time. He'll wait for things to calm down before settling up with you and Ihsan."

"Ihsan?" she murmured in dismay. "What has he got to do with it?"

Her reaction was surprising. Rather than feeling sorry for herself, it was Nizam's going after another gambler that scared her.

"What do you think?" I said, answering her question with a question. "Why does Nizam want to settle the score with Ihsan?"

She quickly tried to gloss it over.

"How would I know?"

I wasn't going to let her get out of it.

"It seems to me you do know. You sure got a funny look when you heard Ihsan's name."

"It's nothing to do with Ihsan Bey. What you're saying is so horrible... And I've known him for ages... I met him even before my husband got sick. Rıfat and I would go to his clubs together. We had a special friendship with him. I'm aware of the animosity between Nizam and him, of course. So that's why..."

She was definitely hiding something from us but I had no idea what it was. As I was considering putting more pressure on her, Ali beat me to it.

"When did you meet Engin?"

She blinked her long lashes again.

"Two years ago... I don't know, maybe a bit longer. In Ihsan Bey's place. The Tarlabaşists Club had just opened. It was in Tarabya before that. I'm talking about back in his father's day. Then Nizam helped them to move here. There was no problem between the two of them back then. I went there with my husband and we were both immediately taken with Engin."

What was this woman talking about? My young assistant beat me to the punch again.

"When you say you were both taken, what does that mean?"

That risqué look settled into her hazel eyes, although they weren't so daring as they had been.

"Didn't you understand? Rıfat was bisexual. He liked men every bit as much as women."

Seeing the disapproval on Ali's face, she took issue.

"You may find it strange, but Rıfat was a good person." She shook her head as if with regret. "Look, I'm saying 'was'. Even I've lost my compassion. I'm talking like he's dead, but he's still alive. If you can call it living..." Strange, her eyes got watery. She must really love her husband. "Still," she persisted. "Still, I won't pull the plug. I know he'll wake up one day. One day Rıfat will get out of that bed..."

A somber mood descended over the greenhouse. I rushed to prevent my tactless assistant from asking an awkward question about Rıfat Bey's homosexuality.

"Have you got any children? With Rıfat Bey, I mean..."

298

Her wistful eyes helplessly wandered the gleaming Marmara Sea for a while, as if I had mentioned a dream she'd never see realized.

"He didn't want them. He already has two sons. From his first wife, Emel Hanım. When he married me, he didn't want more kids. Though to be fair, before marrying me he sat me down and asked. 'You know who I am, all my faults and weaknesses. Do you still want to marry me?' he said. Yes, he used those same words as he stroked my hair like I was a little girl. I was madly in love with him. 'Of course I do,' I told him. 'But I won't have children,' he said. 'Not because I already have two sons, but because this world's a terrible place and I don't want to bring another child into it.' Hoping to convince him, I told him, 'Don't give up; it'll be better one day.' But he said, 'No, it won't. You're a lot younger than me, and you don't know people. It's never going to get better.' Yes, he was quite the pessimist. How could he not be? His children cut him off because he was marrying me. But his marriage was over. The two hated each other. Even now the kids don't visit their father in the hospital. Despite their owing everything... their villas, businesses, luxury cars, bank rolls... to Rıfat. They never forgave him. Maybe it was the cruelty he saw in his sons that made him not want another child. It's hard to say, but in recent times his pessimism had really grown."

"So the two of you met Engin before your husband got sick then?" Ali, unable to get an answer for the questions in his head, had got stuck on this point. "So then, Engin..." He couldn't quite manage to finish his sentence. "What I mean is..."

She looked disdainfully at my assistant.

"No, Engin wasn't gay. And he never had a relationship with Rıfat."

A blush spread through our mortified boy's cheeks.

"That isn't what I meant."

Jale looked him straight in the eye.

"Yes, it's exactly what you meant. Don't worry though, I'd tell you if they had that kind of relationship. It's not something to be ashamed of, Inspector Ali. People live as they wish."

It'd be up to his boss, of course, to pull him out of the hole he'd dug himself into.

"Anyhow, let's move on from Rıfat Bey," I said, affecting an understanding attitude. "So then your relationship with Engin was still going on. Seeing as how you hadn't cut off your assistance..."

Her eyes got sad again.

"It was... He came round at least once a week. He used to come by more often. Before that girl Azize messed up his head. And don't think the drugs are just a pretext. He really was using cocaine. Whether it was Nizam's men or someone else supplying them, that I don't know..."

She smiled as though she'd read our minds.

"And no, I never use drugs. I tried it once and the veins in my nose split open. We were hard put to stop the bleeding. My nose stayed swollen for two days. I was walking around with bruises under my eyes. I was so scared I swore them off for good. Rıfat used to smoke marijuana to relax but he'd never touch anything chemical." She paused. "I'm telling you all this because you'll hear it from others. So if nothing else you should have the truth." She paused again. She smiled as if making a confession. It was perhaps the most genuine expression she'd worn since we'd come into the greenhouse. "I know, there's no sense in denying it, I'm the one who's been made a fool of in this story." That coquettish sparkle in her hazel eyes was gone, never to return. Her shoulders slumped, and she suddenly became an older woman, though this one was much more candid. "You're right. Engin didn't love me so much. I thought he loved me as much as Azize, however... What's the point; isn't life more what we imagine than what we experience anyhow? But I wish I hadn't been bitten by reality. Azize was that reality."

She reached out and crumpled up the napkin on the table.

"I suppose I don't belong to this era," she murmured. "Men don't understand me. The only one who did was Rıfat, and he's not here with me. He left me in this cruel world and went off to an entirely different one. I thought I'd filled his absence with Engin. But he was so much younger than me. I had fifteen years on him; the same number of years as between Rıfat and me. I thought it was possible but I was wrong. I wasn't as full of love as Rıfat, nor was Engin as naive as me. And I knew Engin would leave me soon enough, because I'd age quicker than he would. I was going to become the insufferable woman. But that unfaithful Engin acted too early, way too early..." She gently shook her head. "I'm sorry. But that's why I made those unflattering comments and annoyed you. Maybe that poor girl is the last person to blame in this business. Azize, the *pavyon* beauty. What an innocent face she has, right? I guess that's what drew Engin to her. What he left behind so long ago, maybe as far back as his childhood, that superfluous innocence."

"Telling mistaken people why they're mistaken, leaning on people who want leaning on..."

✠

The streets were covered in sticky muck. When you stepped on one of the loose stones of Beyoğlu's streets, which they somehow never managed to fix, you'd wind up with mud all over you. That was the worst part of the snow: the melting stage. Everywhere was wet, everywhere sludge, and no matter how hard you tried, you couldn't stay clean and dry.

I sent Ali with the car to pick Zeynep up from the forensic lab. We'd meet at Azize's house in the afternoon. I passed through the back streets and walked towards Istiklal Avenue, on the one hand playing hopscotch on the stones so to speak, on the other thinking about Jale. To be honest, I felt for the woman. Even though I knew she'd lied... Yes, it wasn't just a love relationship she had with Engin. In her own way, the woman had made an investment through buying up Greek houses in Tarlabaşı unbeknownst to Nizam. What really made me sad was her helplessness. She'd lived a life, but she knew it wasn't the life she wanted. Even worse, her vast youth had passed her by as she lived the life someone else wanted. Despite all her money, the properties and possessions, it was the one thing she could never get back now.

"Chief... Chief!"

The kids caught me right on the corner of Büyükparmak-kapı Street where it opened onto Istiklal Avenue. They looked like they'd just returned from war: Keto with his bandaged nose, Piranha with an eye patch, and Musti whose lower lip had exploded from the beating he must have got at the police station. But they didn't give a damn. They stood in front of me with cheeky grins on their faces. I was happy to see them.

"Well, look at the gang of bandits!" I said. "What's up? What are you doing here?"

Keto giggled cheerfully.

"The honest truth or a lie?"

In his own way, he was trying to be sincere.

"The honest truth of course," I said, in a fatherly way. "No lies between us."

"We came out to find some suckers to rob." With a right hand with cotton in its palm, he pointed over to Musti. "We're starving. And also we're gonna celebrate this moron's narrow escape. But you'll understand, we're skint…"

Musti smiled, showing his dirty teeth.

"I was sorry to hear about that. When did you get out?"

The scamp gave me a look like he was up to no good.

"This morning, Chief. They were supposed to let me out before that actually. I didn't steal anything. I just borrowed those instruments. Our musician friends in the coffeehouse misunderstood the situation. When they realized their mistake, they dropped the case."

I gave Piranha and Keto a look.

"And how did these musician friends realize their mistake?"

The street bandit's one eye shone with pride.

"We told them, Chief. That's our job, telling mistaken people why they're mistaken, leaning on people who want leaning on. We went to the coffeehouse and gave them a talking to and the gypsy men immediately came to their senses."

Keto was every bit as much a show-off as his friend.

"Fixing those who want fixing, beating those who want beating. Sorry, Chief, it doesn't sink into their heads any other way."

Whatever I said would be in vain. If there was such a thing in life as a line, these children had crossed it long ago.

"So how did the police let you go? Didn't they say anything about a public prosecution?"

Keto looked at me as if to say, *how naive you are!*

"What are you talking about, Chief? What public? What prosecution? A guy shot a poor little girl to bits last night. And nobody even made a peep. They'll let him go this afternoon, that punk ass."

He was talking about Fidan all right, and he was full of rage.

"Did you know the girl?"

His dirty face got sad.

"Of course I did. Fidan was a good girl." He looked over at his friends. "These guys did too." He gave Piranha's shoulder a hard whack. "This dimwit was in love with her."

The one-eyed boy was embarrassed.

"Fuck off, man," he said, giving Keto a shove. "I wasn't in love with anyone. Quit making shit up..." His one eye, which seemed to accuse everyone, turned to me again. "Don't listen to them, Chief; it's not like that. Fidan was just a really good girl... She'd never hurt anyone. Couldn't if she wanted to. You know those pigeons flying around Taksim Square? Well, she was just like them. Innocent, spooked, and if you got too close she'd fly away... That son of a bitch emptied all his bullets into her." He glared at his friends. "And these jackasses still love that bastard Black Nizam. He can go to hell, him and his murdering nephews too..."

Amazing, it was the first time Keto and Musti hung their heads. So then Fidan's death had affected them too. I gently touched Piranha's arm.

"Come on. Let's take a walk."

Hoping they'd get some money out of me, the three of them came along with no objections.

"How did you know the girl? From Nazlı Hanım's place?"

Musti answered the question. "The culture center? No, Chief, we met before that. In Gezi Park. Fidan was the leader of the group of people who helped us. Fidan and Guerilla Civan... I'm talking about during the resistance... At first those nice men and women were scared of us and I mean, they weren't wrong. Cotton in our hands, bottles of thinners in our pockets, an inch of dirt on our faces... Only Fidan was comfortable around us. And Guerilla Civan. After they took us under their wing, everybody was good to us. They gave us food, and clothing, and medicine... Nobody was going against Civan's word, anyhow."

"And we didn't either," said Musti. "Because Civan had balls. He'd dive right into the police... I saw with my own eyes how many gas canisters he picked up with his own hands and threw across the other side of the barricades. He wasn't afraid of anyone. Of course everybody wanted to be next to him."

It was hard to tell how much of what he said was true and how much exaggeration. They were high, although not so much as last time, and were continuing to huff.

"They really pummeled Kudret and his cousins there on Mis Street. Maybe that's why that son of a bitch killed our Fidan. For revenge."

Was this the fight Kudret had spoken of in the interrogation, I wondered? That brawl where he said they'd saved the policemen's lives?"

"I heard it was Kudret and his cousins who pummeled them," I started to say.

"That's a lie!" Keto shouted. "We were there too, Chief. Kudret and his jackals were running around with döner kebab knives and sticks. But they were afraid to go out in front; they kept coming up behind the cops. They were attacking any university boys or girls they managed to pull in among them. That's when there was a scramble. The police pulled out and these punks ended up all alone in the middle of Mis Street. The people were already fed up, so they pulled these guys in. They beat the shit out of them. And Civan was out in front again, of course. Some of them managed to break free and get away but that dog Kudret landed in our group. They were ready to lynch the punk, and I wish they had. But Civan stepped in and saved that bastard. And then he went and shot Fidan."

"Civan's gonna fuck him up..." Piranha said, full of vengeance.

"And then some," his friend Keto backed him up. "They'll make life in Beyoğlu unlivable for those scumbags..."

Not to be left out, Musti joined the war chorus.

"I hope they call us too."

"What's going on, guys?" I interrupted. "Call you to where?"

They realized their mistake a bit late.

"That's right," I said, stopping all three of them. "Don't hold back or try to hide anything. Tell me; who is calling you and to where?"

"Nobody's calling us anywhere." Keto seemed embarrassed. He'd started walking again and the others caught up with him, so I had to join the caravan too. "What are they gonna do with us, Chief," he griped, as we walked along the wet stones. "Look at the state of us, we're not even any use to ourselves."

"If you *were* useful, where would you go?"

The response came from Piranha, who walked to my left.

"If that bonehead Kudret walks... That bastard who killed Fidan... Civan and his friends are gonna burn down Tarlabaşı. They're gonna fuck up Black Nizam and his nephews beyond recognition. Cricket told us that. They're waiting for the prosecution's decision on Kudret."

Was he repeating an urban legend, or was the Tuesday Group Nazlı spoke of really planning a big operation to avenge their friend's murder?

"Who's Cricket?" I asked nonchalantly, so as not to spook them.

All three of them smiled mischievously.

"Our Memo," Keto explained. "The four of us used to hang around together... He's a few years older than us. Turns out he's smarter too. He gave up the thinner and is working with Nazlı Abla at the culture center. He serves the tea and does all the errands."

"Why Cricket?"

They all laughed in unison.

"Because he can really bounce. Just like a basketball. He gets up to two meters high in one jump. Used to be he'd bounce up into the windows of abandoned buildings when we were searching for a place to sleep. We couldn't get up, but Memo would hop straight in. He didn't leave us outside though; he'd pull us up by our hands. That's how he got the name Cricket. Anyhow, he overheard there'd be an operation. While Civan and Nazlı Abla were talking..."

Their tongues had loosened up, but it wasn't enough.

"Did this conversation take place in the culture center?"

"Yup," said Piranha, wiping his dripping nose with the back of his hand. "We stopped by to get some bread and cheese. He helps us on the sly, Cricket, although this morning we came away empty-handed. Fidan had died so, you know, there was trouble. But anyways, that's when Cricket told us. Civan said that if they let Kudret walk he'd 'stuff Nizam and his nephews into the club and light them all on fire...' Nazlı Abla tried to calm him down, but what could she do? Once Civan sets his mind to it, good luck... He'll fuck every last one of them."

Once again, the angry child had overdone it on the language.

"What happened to not swearing, Piranha? You keep cussing away at everyone..."

He threw up his hands and stomped his feet as if in rebellion.

"What else can I do, Chief? The guys are killing our friends, they're crushing us, they won't let us walk the streets... Are we supposed to just shut up and take it? Don't you think we deserve to cuss at them just a little?"

He'd got completely carried away; there was no use pressing the issue.

"So what does this Civan do? Where does he live?"

All three of them got a mysterious look in their eyes.

"That's anybody's guess, Chief," Keto said, gulping excitedly. "Some people say he's a teacher, some say a poet, and some a terrorist... One of those from the mountains... His nickname is 'Guerilla' after all. It's not clear where he lives. But he's got tons of friends. Everyone respects him. His door is open to all the Kurds in Tarlabaşı. They never have to sleep on the streets."

It was like he was talking about a storybook hero.

"And what does he look like?"

307

The admiration in his eyes grew deeper.

"He's tall, built, and strong... He has eyes like fire. People are afraid to look. And he talks with an accent. Kurdish, that is, like our Şehmo from Siirt. Maybe he's from Siirt too. Who knows?"

"Stop being racist," Piranha snapped. "Kurdish, Turk, or whatever he is, Civan's gonna finish Black Nizam off. Their time in Beyoğlu is up, for both that ugly wife pimper and his nephews."

If what they said was true, we could have a serious situation on our hands. But how could I trust these doped-up kids? I had to talk to Nazlı. Seeing as how she was trying to restrain Civan, she must be against this kind of violence. As I was mulling this over, my phone began to ring. The screen showed Evgenia's name. I had to get away from the kids before answering. I took out another twenty as I had the other night.

"Take it. Go get some food in your stomachs..."

Keto went to snatch it up again, but I pulled it away.

"Not you this time." I held the twenty out to Piranha. "Today you are the leader of the gang."

I didn't let go of it right away.

"Everybody eats their fill."

"Don't worry, Chief."

I warned him one last time as I handed it to him.

"If I hear otherwise, there'll be trouble."

For one second he gave the money between my fingers a snooty look.

"Shame on you, Chief. Am I so low I'd rob my friends of their share?"

Was he going to turn up his nose at my twenty lira? Of course he didn't; he snatched it up the second he'd finished his sentence.

"Don't forget," I yelled out as I walked away, "it's for all of you..."

Keto had already caught his friend by the scruff of his neck.

"Don't worry, Chief. If he tries to give us the slip, I'll rip the food from his belly."

Evgenia had given up by the time I got rid of the kids. I'd have to call her. I pushed the call button and started walking again, across Istiklal Avenue and into Mis Street. The *ocakbaşı* we'd meet Nizam in that afternoon should be around here somewhere. As Evgenia's phone rang, my eyes combed the shops on either side of the street. There it was, at the end. The huge sign was hardly hidden. Yiyen Ocakbaşı... I wondered if by 'yiyen' they meant the word for 'nephew' as it was said in some Anatolian dialects, or if it just came from the word 'to eat'.

"Hi, Nevzat..." Evgenia's sweet voice said, rescuing me from my pointless musings. "Did I catch you at a bad time?"

"Oh, no. I'm free to talk. Go on, my dear."

"What's your situation tonight? I'm with my Aunt Fofo but... She really wants to meet you. What do you say?"

She sounded uneasy. Fofo must be pushing her into this meeting. It was going to be some kind of debut, apparently. I could easily get out of it if I said I was busy, but to be honest I was curious about Fofo, too. And also, I knew it would make Evgenia happy if I met them.

"That'd be great. I'd love to meet her."

"Wonderful!" Just as I'd thought, she was very pleased. "In that case, we'll be expecting you at Tatavla. Come by when you're done."

"Sounds good. I hope nothing goes wrong. Even if it does, I'll definitely make it. I'd just be a bit late..."

"All right." Her voice seemed to flatten. "But don't let anything go wrong. At least not tonight."

"All right, all right, Evgenia. I won't be late. See you tonight."

"Bye now..."

I put the phone back in my pocket as I neared Yiyen Ocakbaşı. The five-floor brick building had been turned into a restaurant as was. Maybe the property belonged to Nizam. From what I could see through the glass door, it was pretty calm inside. Most of his customers must come in the evening. Just as I was about to walk away, the door opened and the suspect we'd interrogated the night before stood there in front of me. Short hair, stubbly beard, and a green anorak with a fur collar. It was him all right, grinning up at me.

"Kudret," I mumbled. "When did you get out?"

The man opposite me chuckled.

"Not Kudret, Chief. Medet."

But of course, it was his twin. They were such spitting images of each other, it was impossible to tell them apart.

"Come on in, Chief," he said, stepping aside. "Let me get you something, my treat."

"No, thanks. I have somewhere to be. I'm coming here at four, anyhow..."

I wanted to cut the conversation short and be on my way but he wouldn't let me go.

"I know. I'm here to get everything ready. How is my brother doing, anyway? You're the one who questioned him, I guess?"

No, he didn't seem like he was threatening.

"Good. When I saw him last he was fine."

He got an impertinent look on his face.

"What do you think? Will he make it back in time for dinner?"

I took a step closer. I looked into his eyes and muttered, "Oh, he'll be back in time for dinner all right. But tonight or in ten years' time, that I can't tell you."

"The greatest achievement of a tyrant is to turn those who oppose him tyrannical."

※

Walking between the buildings waiting to be demolished, their doors removed and frames ripped out, collapsed roofs and caved in walls, I felt like I was in a bombed city rather than the heart of Istanbul. I noticed three women hanging around in front of plates of shiny tin surrounding the buildings. I looked to see if one of them was her, but no, Süleyman's wife wasn't among them. After yesterday's fight, she might not have even come out to work, poor Naciye. I doubted she was unhappy about it. Harem Süleyman may be upset if the money he'd spend on gambling wasn't coming in. Then again, even if Naciye did come out onto the street, it was doubtful she would find any customers this winter afternoon. Business was slow for the three prostitutes; they stood on the corner, tea glasses in their hands, and had started wagging their chins. They were not even thirty years old, but the three had already gone to rack and ruin, much like the buildings. As I passed them, they gave me a momentary once-over from the corner of their eye, then realizing no business would come from me, returned to their conversation. As I made my way down to the Ferhat Çerağ Culture Center, I had to cling to the sheets of tin to keep from getting run over by one of the cars climbing up the sloping street, made excessively narrow by the construction.

"Sir... Sir..." a voice called after me again as I rung the bell over the enormous wooden door.

Why wouldn't they quit following me, these kids? But when I looked over my shoulder, I saw Diogenes, the old man I'd met on Kadın Çıkmazı the night before.

"Hello, Diogenes," I said, smiling. "Are you talking to me?"

He stopped a couple steps away, a huge empty glass in his hand, and was looking me over with a worried expression.

"Tell me, Sir, are you a nationalist today or a police officer?"

The poor thing was making no sense again.

"A police officer," I said.

"Tsk," he said, shaking his head. "That's not what your eyes say, though. No, your intentions are bad. Today, you aren't going to help anyone, not from your own people or your own religion... Today, it won't be the citizens you protect, but the people of your own nation."

Now what did this man mean by that?

"You are one of my nation's people."

"Stop lying," he said, shrinking back in fear. "You don't consider me one of yours. If you had, you would have helped us that day. But you didn't. 'Today I am not a police officer,' you said... We knocked on your door but you didn't open it. And you even dressed your men in civilian clothing and set them on us. You plundered our homes, threw our possessions onto the street..."

He would have kept going but the massive door behind me opened noisily.

"Well, well, Dio. Did you get your tea?"

When I turned my head, I came eye to eye with a teenaged boy, skinny, with disproportionately long legs. This must be the 'Cricket' Memo my kids had talked about. He looked me over suspiciously.

"Did you ring the bell?"

My mind was still on what the old man had said and I couldn't immediately answer.

"I mean, you aren't with Diogenes?" he persisted.

His tone was not at all friendly.

"I'm here to see Nazlı Hanım," I said with authority. "Is she here?"

He didn't even bother to answer my question. In the same challenging voice, he asked, "Who can I say is here?"

"Tell her Chief Inspector Nevzat... She knows me."

The apprehension in his black, almond-shaped eyes immediately gave way to respect.

"Oh, I'm sorry, Chief. I didn't know." He fidgeted then stepped aside. "Come on in, Chief."

I silently slipped in. Before closing the door, he called out to the old man still standing there.

"Well, Dio? Are you coming?"

"Tsk!" He shook his head again. "I won't come in while he's there."

The young man didn't persist.

"Fine, have it your way. See you later then..." He smiled sheepishly as he shut the door. "Sorry, Chief. He's not all there. He's scared to death of the police. Who knows what was going through his head when he saw you." He gestured to the room we'd sat in the night before. "This way, please. Nazlı Abla's in here."

I'd got lucky. I might not have caught her, as I'd purposely come unannounced. I'd wanted to do some kind of raid on this so-called culture center, to see just what was going on.

Nazlı didn't seem surprised to see me. On the contrary, she stood up from the table with a friendly smile as though she'd been expecting me.

"Well hello, Nevzat Bey. I was just going to call you."

"Is that so?" I said, walking over. "What's up? Has there been some development?"

She shook my outstretched hand firmly.

"I'll explain. Why don't you take off your coat?"

I did as she'd said and Memo, waiting only a step behind me, whisked it away.

"Come sit," said Nazlı, showing me to the chair I'd sat in last night. As I settled into it, she stayed standing, giving instructions to the young man trying to hang my coat in the cloakroom.

"Memo, bring us a couple teas, would you?" She paused, suddenly aware of her indelicacy. "I'm sorry; my head's all over the place. I didn't ask if maybe you'd like something else."

I rubbed my cold hands together.

"No, tea will go down well. The sun's out now but it's still freezing."

She turned back to Memo, who'd hung my coat and was standing at attention.

"Memo, dear. Did you catch what I said? Two teas?"

"Two teas..." said Memo, enthusiastically repeating the order. "I just brewed a fresh pot. It's coming right away..."

While Cricket skipped through the doorway and disappeared, Nazlı settled into the chair opposite mine, under a Claude Monet painting depicting the tranquility of a still creek surrounded by colorful plants and flowers. Nazlı herself, however, didn't appear so calm.

"Forgive me, my head really is swimming," she complained once more. "Things are happening so fast."

"No need to apologize. I'd forget too if I was in your shoes."

Her violet eyes grew calmer.

"If you were in my shoes..." She was studying me as if trying to make sense of it. "Why *are* you here, anyway, Nevzat Bey?"

"I can leave, if you want," I said jokingly.

She got embarrassed and looked away for a moment.

"Don't be silly, of course it's not like that... What I meant was, have you heard something new?"

It'd definitely work in my favor to be open with this woman. Unless I was being duped, she'd been honest with me all along.

"Let's call it hearsay. Apparently, there are some people who want to take revenge for Fidan. Most likely the Tuesday Group. They were going to attack Black Nizam's venue. Set Tarlabaşı on fire. They're led by a man called Civan. Guerrilla Civan..."

She started to laugh, silently at first, till gradually she giggled.

"Civan, huh? Guerrilla Civan..."

"Why is that funny?" I grumbled.

She had a hard time composing herself.

"I'm sorry. It's not funny, really. At least not the part about an attack on Nizam's place... The 'Guerrilla' Civan part is a comedy though..." She narrowly managed to stifle another fit of laughter. "No offense, but it looks like your plainclothes officers aren't doing such a great job. Civan Hoca is a teacher here. He's the most peaceful man on the planet. He hurts an ant and he's weepy for days..."

Apparently, she was trying to protect the man. To confuse the sympathetic policeman sitting gentle as a lamb in front of her. But there was no way she was going to succeed this time.

"The most peaceful man on the planet was the one at the frontlines during the Gezi incidents, fighting with police?" I asked ironically. "We're talking about one of the leaders of the protesters here. Someone who picked up gas canisters and threw them back at the police..."

I'll admit my voice had come out louder than normal. But Nazlı began to laugh again as if the subject was incredibly amusing.

"Sorry, sorry..." she said, trying to get control of herself again. "I don't know who told you that, but it's all wrong. Civan Hoca is a teacher employed by the culture center. He teaches the Kurdish women Turkish. It isn't possible he was fighting with any police or anything because one of his feet is prosthetic. But even if it were sturdier, he's not the type to fight with anyone."

Was this woman messing with me?

"Didn't the man used to go up into the mountains? Isn't he Kurdish?"

"Well, that much is true," she said, pulling her graying hair back. "Twenty years ago he went up into the mountains, but he was such a gentle soul he wouldn't even hold a gun. During his first raid, in the middle of a skirmish, he got all dazed. Don't get me wrong, he's no coward... Even when they tortured him, he never gave up a single friend's name, for instance, but he couldn't hurt anyone. He wouldn't flick someone with his fingers, let alone fire a gun. They assigned him to a health services team but he was apprehended during a shootout after his left foot was hit. When his leg got gangrene they cut if off, and after ten years in prison, they let him go.

During his time in prison, he solidified his ideas on passivity which he'd explored in the mountains. 'You can't create an ideal society by means of violence. Because the methods you use will suck you in.' Not my words, I'm quoting Civan. It's what he kept telling the kids during the Gezi Resistance. 'The greatest achievement of a tyrant is to turn those who oppose him tyrannical.' He implored them not to give up on civil disobedience and to never resort to violence. 'Don't throw stones, and no Molotov cocktails. The most effective kind of resistance is passive resistance,' he'd say. Because he knew you could never win a case if you lost the justness of your cause. This is the person you a call a terrorist with blood on his hands."

She made a gesture as if she felt sorry for me.

"I guess you'd better have a chat with the plainclothes police who gave you that report. They are talking about the wrong person. Or else they want to steer you in the wrong direction."

Her words were beginning to get on my nerves.

"There are no undercover police, Nazlı Hanım," I snapped. "This all came from one of your men."

It was nice to see the amused look on her face wither away.

"One of my men?" She looked towards the door and back. "Memo? Our Memo explained all that to you?"

"Not to me, these other kids..."

Her eyebrows furrowed and her broad forehead wrinkled up.

"Those street kids, you know, that also used to stay here? Keto, Piranha, Musti..."

She gave me a funny look.

"And you believed them? Please, Nevzat Bey. Those kids live on another planet entirely. Their lives are so horrific; they use every substance they can get their hands on to escape it. Then come the dreams, nightmares, delusions..."

Could what she said be true? Was it possible these children had distorted reality so much? It'd be easy enough to find out; the tea boy could give us the true story. The same thing must have occurred to Nazlı because she called out, "Memo! Memo, dear, could you come in here?"

Cricket came flying through with the tray of tea in his hands.

"Here I am, abla! And the tea's ready."

When he noticed the unpleasant mood in the room and saw the scowl on Nazlı's face, he realized something had gone wrong and he slowed his steps.

"Come over here. Leave the tray on the coffee table."

He gave me a nervous look, wondering if this cop had got him into trouble. Had he gone through the old files and discovered a forgotten robbery incident, or maybe a mugging? He put the tray on the table but didn't refrain from placing the cups of tea in front of us.

"I brought two sugars, Chief. I don't know if that's enough..."

I smiled to reassure him.

"Thanks, Memo. I don't take sugar."

The young man was going to relax, but Nazlı didn't give him the chance.

"Sit, please."

He swallowed and plunked down in the chair she'd indicated.

"When did you last see Keto and his friends?"

He looked from me to Nazlı as if he was catching on.

"Keto..."

Nazlı stared at Cricket.

"Yes. Keto, Piranha, and Musti..."

The clouds of anxiety suddenly dissipated.

"Oh, that robbery thing," he chirped. "But Musti didn't steal those instruments, Chief. The gypsies gave them to him. The matter was cleared up, anyhow. They let him go..."

Nazlı was really angry that he'd looked at me while explaining.

"Memo, why aren't you answering my question? What do we care about Musti's stealing? When did you see those children?"

He squinted his almond-shaped eyes again.

"About an hour ago," he said hurriedly. "They stop by mornings looking for something to nibble on. I give them the breakfast leftovers..."

Nazlı interrupted him impatiently.

"I'm already aware of that. What did you talk about? Just tell me that."

Cricket got a goofy look on his face.

"What did we talk about? Nothing, just small talk... And there was nothing left to eat, anyhow. The poor boys went hungry..."

Nazlı lost her patience and asked directly, "You didn't say anything about Civan Hoca?"

His eyes opened wide.

"I didn't say anything bad. They killed Fidan... You know you were talking about how there'd be a protest? And I told those idiots, 'Be careful, things could get messy today or tomorrow.' That's all, Nazlı Abla. I swear..."

Not wanting to give the woman the chance to direct him, I immediately cut in. "Didn't you mention Civan Hoca? Explain his views on the matter to the kids?"

He pulled his neck in.

"I didn't say that. Cross my heart, I didn't. I just said I overheard Nazlı Abla talking to him. I swear it, Chief... Those little queers..." It had slipped out of his mouth; his nervous eyes went to Nazlı. "I mean Keto and his friends, they were high, and they probably pulled the story out of their asses..." This time he wasn't bothered by the words that left his mouth. "Yeah, they totally got me wrong, the jerks... Would I ever tell them that, Nazlı Abla? I said I'd do them a favor, those dogs, so they wouldn't get into trouble. Their lives are already fragile; they're gonna get themselves trampled to death."

Nazlı shook her head as if to say *what am I going to do with you?*

"Well then, what were Civan Hoca and I talking about? Explain that to Nevzat Bey. Don't hold back. Tell him everything you heard..." She turned her defiant eyes on me. "I can leave the room if you'd like. You can talk to Memo in private."

She was giving as good as what she gets. I took it on the chin, of course.

"Of course not, Nazlı Hanım. Is there any mistrust between us?"

318

A wry smile appeared on her lips, but she didn't force the issue.

"I brought in the coffee this morning, Chief. Civan Hoca was sitting right where you are now." He pointed at me. "He takes sugar, and Nazlı has hers black. That's when I heard Fidan's friends were really angry. If that degenerate Kudret was set free, they were going to protest. Storm that bastard Black Nizam's venues. The guy has a lot of places around here. Civan Hoca was explaining how he tried to convince them. He was fretting, 'If they don't let Kudret go, the matter will be put to rest, but if that murderer is set free I don't know what we'll do.' And Nazlı Abla said, 'I doubt they'll let him go. They wouldn't be so blatantly unjust.' And that's what I heard." He turned to look at the woman. "Isn't that right, abla?"

She shook her head as if to say *don't look at me...*

"Whatever you heard, just tell him."

"That *is* what I heard. And it's what I told our knuckleheads..." He turned to me again. "I swear on the dead mother I've never met, I'm not lying, Chief. That's what happened..."

The situation was clear; I was paying the price in humiliation for believing those kids.

"Thank you, Memo," I said, reaching out and patting his knee. "You've been a big help."

But my satisfaction meant nothing to him; he looked fearfully over at Nazlı. What if she got angry and tossed him out? The woman didn't give her feelings away.

"All right, Memo," she said gloomily. "All right, you can go."

Cricket grabbed the tray and straightened back up, but he was beside himself trying to figure out Nazlı's reaction.

"Do you want anything else? Water or something?"

"No." With the same authoritarianism, she closed the subject. "You go on now."

He left the room, helpless, taking his doubts with him. Nazlı had already forgotten him.

"Your tea, Nevzat Bey." With a thick finger, she pointed to the steaming red liquid in the tea glass. "Don't let it get cold."

"I owe you an apology," I said, before I picked it up. "The children really misled me."

She didn't wait; she just reached for her tea.

"Well, I was biased too, actually. I blamed the police, whereas the traitor was from within," she complained jokingly.

I wondered if she really would fire Cricket.

"It wasn't his fault. The poor thing was just trying to help his friends."

She took a sip of her tea and set the glass down on the coffee table.

"You're a good person, Nevzat Bey." Her violet eyes twinkled. "I understood that, but you also have a bad side. You're too caught up in your job. You're very opinionated. Who do you think I am, for heaven's sake? An unfeeling, ruthless militant? Some cruel woman willing to risk all kinds of evil for the cause?"

She didn't take anything lying down, this Nazlı. Where she found fault, she smacked you in the face with it.

"Of course not..." I said, finally reaching for the glass in front of me. "I mean, I was a bit worried about Memo. If you fired him, I would feel like I was responsible."

That self-assured smile spread on her pale lips again.

"Did the kids tell you why Memo works here?"

I took a sip of tea.

"No, it never came up. They just told me how the boy can jump, while explaining his nickname."

Before asking if I had time or wanted to hear it, she launched directly into Cricket Memo's story.

"The trees were undeniably talking..."

***

"I came across Memo one spring... In the middle of the night... Must have been one o'clock or so... I had some business to see to that kept me at the culture center till then. I'd been working since morning and I was exhausted. My eyes were burning and my fingers were getting sore. When I couldn't take any more, I turned off my computer. I was intending to jump in a cab and go straight home. But the weather outside was gorgeous. There was an enormous full moon in the sky, and it was cool and balmy, with air like syrup."

As she recounted the story of Memo, Nazlı's broad face shone with delight.

"You know, Nevzat Bey, September is Istanbul's most beautiful season. Particularly on those dreamy evenings... Well, it was one of those. I walked to Taksim to soak it all up. The square was less crowded, but the night owls were still hanging about. Young girls and boys under the full moon, lovers all cuddled up... Everyone was a little tipsy; some were belting out cheerful songs. I slowed down and began to watch all these colorful people around me. It was so enjoyable, like being in a carnival. After that I walked towards Elmadağ hoping to find a taxi, but as I was walking past Gezi Park, a young man crying, 'Help me! Help me!' came flying out of the trees and fell in front of me.

"His skinny frame was shaking like a leaf, his eyes were wide open and he was scanning the shadows of the trees. I thought it was an attack or a mugging, and I looked towards the park, too. Although I had no idea how I'd protect myself when the attack came, I waited with my hands clenched into fists for this faceless thief to jump out from among the trees. But seconds passed, and no one came out. Maybe the attacker had seen me, and got scared and changed his mind. I turned to the boy still using my body as a shield and trembling in fear. 'I guess he got scared,' I said confidently. 'He's not coming out of the park...'

"He gave me a funny look, as if I'd said something odd, then looked me in the eyes and asked, 'Who got scared?' 'Whoever's chasing you, of course,' I mumbled. 'Or is it more than one person? Who are you running from, anyhow?' 'What person?' he said. The horror in his eyes hadn't lessened one bit; he stared into the darkness of the park and explained. 'It's not a person; it's the trees I'm running from.'

"Well, that was interesting. 'Why are you running from the trees?' I asked him. He leaned in to my ear then. 'Because they're talking,' he whispered. 'They keep talking, and talking...'

"A heavy smell of alcohol hit me, and that's when I noticed the scruffy clothes. The young man stood beside me was homeless, not to mention extremely drunk. He'd probably been sleeping in the park. And maybe on that night he'd drunk too much and had a nightmare. But unaware of what was going through my mind, he carried on. 'They are whispering names. Whenever the wind blows, the park fills with their voices. They continually whisper their names, like a hymn, or a prayer...'

"The poor thing must have a screw loose, I thought. 'Never mind,' I said to placate him. 'Let them whisper. They can't hurt you, in any case.' He threw his hands up in desperation. 'Of course they can. They know me. Not just that huge plane tree, but the giant chestnut too. Even those little rose bushes. Yes, even them, the moment a small breeze comes up, they start chattering away.' I knew he was talking nonsense, but I couldn't stop myself asking, 'How do they know you?'

"He answered back without hesitating. 'From last summer. In June.' He pointed to where he'd just come out of the park.

'I was on duty here.' He may have been a drunk, but he sure had a colorful imagination. 'Were you a gardener?' I asked him. He looked offended. 'A gardener?' he rebuked. 'I was law enforcement. Helping the cops. Your average government employee, I mean.' His story was getting more entertaining by the minute. 'What was your job?' I said, to try and appear interested.

"He stared at me with condescension in his eyes. 'Abla, what planet are you from?' he said. 'Only a couple months ago this place was like a war zone. The park was hell...' That's when it dawned on me. He was talking about the Gezi Resistance. So whatever he'd been through this summer had messed up his mind, poor thing. Though I must admit, there was some sense to his fabrication. I got curious as to the limits of his imaginary world and wanted to get deeper into conversation, so I asked, 'What were your job duties exactly?'

"He broke into a sly grin and his rotten teeth appeared. 'I was telling the cops what was going on inside the park,' he admitted. 'It was crazy here back then... Everywhere packed with people, leftists, rightists, religious people, hippies, women, every type you can imagine was here. They beat up a few plainclothes cops inside. That's why the cops were afraid to go in. Inspector Erol Abi from the Beyoğlu Station found me. He's a good guy, Erol Abi. He gives us a bit of cash sometimes, and if we land in jail he has our backs. Well, he caught me on Istiklal Avenue. "You still sleeping in the park, Memo?" he said. I told him, "Yes, sir." He pressed a hundred lira bill into my hand. "Right then. You're gonna come every night and tell me. What goes on in the park, is it crowded, is it calm, who are the ringleaders... You'll report it to me." And that's how my job there started.'

" 'So, you ratted on the protesters,' I said accusingly. The grin on his face froze. 'What could I do?' he said. 'Our government asked for my service...' But when he realized he wasn't convincing me, he brought his friends into it. 'Stumpy Nuri and Balloon Kâmil also did it. In fact, those jerks even took photos of the protesters with the phones Inspector Erol gave them. At least I didn't do that. And that was after the kids in the park helped Nuri a lot. They even took that weasel to see a doctor. He was pissing blood, the little bastard. He had a kidney stone or something. It was thanks to the protesters he got better, and that's the god honest truth. They helped me, too. There was hot food in the park every night. They didn't want money from anyone, everything was free, but everybody was working, no one was slacking off. They were brave kids, really. The police blinded some young guy right next to me. He'd aimed his gas canister rifle right at his face. On purpose, I mean... The kid was a good-looking guy. And now his left eye is gone.' When I asked him, accusingly, why he didn't help the kid, he said, 'I did. Who said I didn't?' He'd raised his voice. 'I carried him all the way to the hospital on my back. I helped the police, but also the protesters. We had no choice; the protestors could be there for a week or, who knows, a month? And then we'd be left with the police again. If I didn't snitch, Inspector Erol would mess with me. He'd make life on these streets hell. You understand?'

"I didn't know how much of what he told me was true. I wasn't so sure an inspector would want help from a man like this, but he sure was good at telling the story. 'So what happened next?' I asked him. 'Was it helpful at least, what you told the police?' 'Of course it was helpful,' he responded with pride. 'They got an hourly report on what was happening in the park. Otherwise, why would Erol Abi slip me another couple hundred?'

"I felt like winding him up. I nodded towards the trees and said, 'But the park's still here. The protesters won. The government didn't chop the trees down.' His face lit up. 'That's right,' he said happily. 'If you ask me, it's a good thing. If they built a shopping mall, they wouldn't let us anywhere near it. The security guards would shoo us away when we got within fifty meters of the door... But...' He suddenly shut up and turned to stare at the trees again. 'But...' he said again. 'Now the trees are tormenting me... Just when I'm curling up under those bushes, just as I'm about to close my eyes, the whispering starts. And the voices gradually get louder... It scares the shit out of me; I swear I'm gonna lose my mind.'

"The effects of alcohol of course, dreams, delusions... 'So go to another park,' I said, trying to calm him down. 'Isn't there anywhere else? Go to Maçka Park... or Fındıklı. It'll be even nicer near the sea.' He shook his head sadly. 'How can I go there, abla?' he complained. 'This park is my home. I can't fall asleep in other parks. I've been sleeping here for five years. Just up there is a magnolia; that tree is like a mother's lap to me. For years I've been sleeping peaceful as a baby under that beautiful smell. Even if I went, other people have already staked their territory. You think they'd let me stay in their space?'

"I felt for the boy. Like Inspector Erol, I pressed a hundred lira bill into his hand. 'Go sleep in a hotel tonight,' I said. 'And come to me tomorrow. I'm at the Ferhat Çerağ Culture Center. Do you know where it is?' 'I know, I know,' he said elatedly. 'On the corner of Sakızağacı Street...' And that's how I met Memo. He came the next day, and I took him on. It wasn't easy for him to adjust of course, and he ran away a few times, but I found him and brought him back. A couple times he came back by himself. Again claiming the Gezi Park trees were talking..."

Nazlı seemed to have finished her story, and she watched me as though expecting some understanding.

"I mean, Nevzat Bey, winning these kids over is like nailing jelly to a wall. I don't go discarding them so easily."

"I get it, Nazlı Hanım. I really get it. And I appreciate your efforts. You really are doing important work. But I'm curious. Does Memo still hear the trees talking? You've taken him to a psychologist, I assume..."

She got a mysterious look in her eye.

"It's a bit complicated. We took him of course, to help him cope with his alcoholism and substance abuse. But the issue of him hearing the trees talk is a bit complicated."

She laughed uneasily.

"It's hard to explain. Maybe when you hear, you'll say I'm crazy too..."

She saw the question marks growing in my eyes and surrendered. "I suppose I'd better explain. You decide for yourself."

I took another sip of tea and listened.

"That night Memo took the hundred lira I'd given him and stumbled away from me. To tell the truth, I couldn't get what he'd told me out of my head. Of course I didn't believe the trees had spoken. In fact, it occurred to me that the boy had made the whole thing up to trick me out of my hundred lira. But I still couldn't help gazing into the park a few meters beyond me. That's when it dawned on me that I hadn't stopped by there since the resistance. Those were hard days; your police attacked without mercy. Everywhere was contaminated with pepper gas, pressurized water cannons around every corner, riot control tanks... They were beating the life out of these young girls and boys with truncheons and wooden sticks. But the demonstrators stood their ground, and Istanbul became a river of people, flowing into the small green space. With each passing day, the number of people joining the resistance grew. One thousand, ten thousand, a hundred thousand, a million... The resistance lasted some forty odd days. In the end, the government caved. Not only did they not get rid of the existing green space, they even planted new trees in the area. But I hadn't seen the park since then, and I felt a strange urge to go in. My feet practically dragged me into the trees.

"When I entered the park, a damp coolness settled around me, the smell of burnt earth, rotted grass... I walked under the dense trees, impermeable even to the bright light of the full moon, and the little wooded area in among all the buildings struck me as a kind of temple. Like the last sacred place in nature we hadn't destroyed. A bird hooted somewhere, I think it was an owl, maybe the last in the city... I stopped and listened, but the sound didn't come again. The wind had died down. I walked down the steps and reached the open area in the middle of the park. For a while I watched the fountain, its water silver under the full moon. It felt very peaceful. I could have sat down on one of those benches and stared at the still water till morning without getting bored. Then I noticed the wind again. You couldn't even call it wind, it was more like a waft, a gentle breeze, that softly blew across my forehead, and through my hair. It was as if all the day's exhaustion left my mind, my body, and flew away. For a moment I felt like I'd become a part of that breeze, the silver pool, the shadowy trees and the moon in the sky. And that's when I heard the voice. It was like a humming, and yes, it was coming from the trees. Was this the same voice the young man had heard? I got goose bumps, but I knew there was no sense in freaking myself out. My mind immediately sought out a logical explanation. It was the wind. Of course it was the wind. And anyhow, it was a hum, not a voice I could make sense of. But on this magical night, my logical explanation immediately fell to pieces. The humming gradually grew clearer, and became the faint voice of a young girl. It began to list the names, one after the other. 'Ali Ismail, Abdullah, Mehmet, Ethem, Mustafa.' Like a prayer, a hymn, or a chant... 'Ali Ismail, Abdullah, Mehmet, Ethem, Mustafa.'

"It scared the living daylights out of me. What was happening? My first thought was that the homeless kid was right; he hadn't been imagining it. The trees were undeniably talking. Without letting up, what's more. Lovingly, respectfully, tenderly as if afraid of disturbing them, it kept repeating the same names. 'Ali Ismail, Abdullah, Mehmet, Ethem, Mustafa.'

"When I looked around, I saw them, on the other side of the pool. Five people, all with their eyes trained on me. That's right, I'm talking about the memorial graveyard. Five faces staring up at me from within their frames. But it wasn't just the photographs there on the green grass, there were five tombstones as well. They were only symbolic, yet they were far more compelling than real tombstones, there under the pale glow of the moon. I went over to them. Looked down at the writing on the tombstones. 'Ali İsmail Korkmaz, Abdullah Cömert, Mehmet Ayvalıtaş, Ethem Sarısülük, and Mustafa Sarı.' The names of the five people whose young lives were taken from them during the resistance to keep these trees from being cut down. I just stood there, not knowing what to do. But the trees, gently swaying in the breeze, continued to list those same names. 'Ali Ismail, Abdullah, Mehmet, Ethem, Mustafa.'

"I wasn't afraid, no, but something was knotting up in my throat and I started to cry. I sat down on one of the benches and cried my eyes out. By the time I left the park, the wind had stopped blowing, and the trees' murmurings had come to an end..."

She looked over at me as if to gage my reaction.

"You must think I've lost my mind, too."

"Of course not..."

"No. No, you're right. I'd feel the same way if someone told me that story. I don't know how to explain it, but believe me, I heard that voice. And when Pera trees whisper, I'm ashamed of my humanity."

It must've been from fatigue, or possibly a prick of conscience, not having visited the park even once since the resistance... She'd probably been feeling some kind of remorse over the people who'd lost their lives. Maybe she was just mixed-up, but what was I supposed to say to the woman now?

"Hi," said a voice, coming to my rescue. "Are you busy, Nazlı Hanım?"

A thin blonde man of average height stood in the doorway, hesitating over whether or not to enter. He wore a dark brown suit with a beige shirt, but had no tie. His face was as slim as his body, the metal-framed glasses were too big for his face and didn't sit well, and under his bony nose, his salt-and-pepper moustache was so long that his lips were obscured.

"Ha! Our terrorist has arrived," said Nazlı, her voice full of amusement. "Come in, Civan Hoca... We were just talking about you..."

He couldn't immediately shake off his shyness, but he still managed to join in the lighthearted banter.

"Nothing bad, I hope."

As he came over, I noticed his right foot had a limp, all right.

"Why wouldn't it be, Hocam? You were introduced to Nevzat Bey as a notorious anarchist. Even worse, I was explaining, a terrorist."

I stood up and shook his hand.

"Chief Inspector Nevzat," I said.

His green eyes staring at me from behind thick glasses, he gave my hand an amicable shake, unperturbed that I was a police officer.

"Nice to meet you, Nevzat Bey, I'm Civan... Civan Asker..."

Yes, he'd said 'Asker' or 'soldier'. It was like a joke, though not wanting to be rude, I didn't laugh.

"Nazlı Hanım was talking about you this morning... Thank you for coming," he said.

He was under the impression Nazlı had invited me here. So once more, her story was confirmed. He sat down in the chair Cricket had vacated. His right leg stayed just so; he pulled it in and put it in place.

"If Fidan's killer is set free, the kids will take to the streets..." He seemed genuinely worried about it. "They're furious... The death of their friend has made them crazy."

Seeing as how he had a rapport with them, Civan could influence them too, but first he'd have to start thinking straight himself.

"Fidan's death is a real tragedy. Anyhow, the suspect doesn't deny that. But attacking the Genuine Tarlabaşists Club with a Molotov is a felony. Molotov cocktails are considered firearms."

He grimaced with helplessness.

They're ignorant, these kids, and they thought no one was in the building. It was written on the door, 'Closed for a funeral'. Their intention wasn't actually to burn anybody; it was to scare the gamblers off. That's why they attacked the Genuine Tarlabaşists Club early in the morning, so as not to hurt anyone..." Seeing me stay quiet, he assumed I'd misunderstood. "I'm not condoning these acts, of course. But when the government doesn't do its job..."

"Anyhow," said Nazlı, cutting in. "We'll analyze the situation later. What do you say, Nevzat Bey, are they going to let Kudret go?"

I tried to convey what I was thinking without mincing my words.

"We finished the interrogation and sent our official report to the prosecutor. I believe the prosecutor will lean towards an arrest, but the final decision is made by the criminal court. If you ask me my personal opinion, I'd say they shouldn't release him. No one had attempted to enter the building... Kudret's previous convictions may be a factor preventing his release. As well as Fidan's having been shot numerous times. But I'm not the judge, and ultimately, the court decides. Of course, Kudret's release is one possible outcome. His lawyer is pleading self-defense. Whether or not he's released, it's what he'll claim. And let's face it, it is a good defense strategy."

"Isn't that sleazy Sacit his lawyer?" Nazlı huffed. "He used to handle my father's lawsuits too, back in the day. That man could burn in hell for hundreds of years and he still wouldn't pay off his sins. But unfortunately, he's also very talented... He knows a lot of people, both among politicians and in the legal system. I hope he doesn't pull a fast one and allow that butcher to go free."

"I hope not too," I repeated. "But even if Kudret does go free, you have to stop these kids from going out into the streets. You know better than I do, Black Nizam is a very dangerous man. His nephews are all raving lunatics. And they're all armed..."

Civan took the words out of my mouth.

"That's what I'm saying, Nevzat Bey. What if you spoke to Nizam? If nothing else, he closes his businesses for a couple days. And keeps a low profile..."

These people genuinely didn't want a conflict.

"That I could do. I'll be seeing Nizam in a couple hours anyhow, and I'll explain the situation. Although how much he'll listen to me is anybody's guess. You can never trust these guys. That's why it'd be more of a guarantee if you could stop these kids."

"Believe me," he said, throwing up his hands. "I've been trying to calm them down since late last night. If it were up to them, they'd have long since gone into action, but I talked them into waiting for the outcome of the trial. If Kudret goes free though, I don't know what we'll do..."

His voice sounded every bit as helpless as mine.

"These young girls who'd fallen prey to the wolves…"

The sun had run riot, beginning to blaze as though it had forgotten it was winter. All around were splashing noises; the snow was rapidly melting on the roofs, the window frames, in all the nooks and crannies on the street, and every so often an icicle fell from the drainpipes of the buildings. If this kept up, by evening Beyoğlu would be completely stripped of its white cloak. As I walked to Azize's house, the coat I wore was becoming a burden. I had to loosen the ash-colored scarf Güzide had knitted for me. Regardless, by the time I came to the building on Kurtuldu Street, I hadn't managed to keep from sweating buckets. Azize's house was exactly the same as her dead lover's. An archetype for Tarlabaşı, it was a three-storey brick building with a hanging bay window. I took a breather in the doorway then pushed the buzzer. Sadri came to the door. He had the same meek look on his face and that perpetual gloomy smile on his lips.

"Come on in, Chief. Your people are upstairs…"

I was aware of that; I'd called Ali when I got to Beyoğlu while I was at the Lades Restaurant having some *kapuska* and *cacık*. I'd invited them too, but those no-goods had already eaten. Once they'd caught an opportunity to have a romantic lunch alone, the two lovebirds would hardly pay any consideration to their old Chief. I hoped he'd at least taken her somewhere nice… But so what if it wasn't? Who cared about food when what mattered was spending time together? Love is all you need. And our boy wasn't such a dimwit as all that. He'd know where to take Zeynep. Come to think, hadn't the rascal just asked me about restaurants the other day? Yes, only a week ago, he'd said, "Chief, you need to give me a lesson on all these fine dining establishments. Beyoğlu's *meyhanes*, the restaurants on the Bosporus, the fish places in Samatya..." So their relationship had already started. I'd be lying if I said it didn't make me feel a bit funny. Why had they hid it from me? I doubted they thought I'd disapprove. Maybe they were just shy... Anyhow, it was their business. I was neither their father nor a relative. They'd tell me if they wanted to, and keep it to themselves if they didn't.

The interior of Azize's house was also the same as Engin's. The door opening onto the entrance, the yellow linoleum floor, the wooden stairs that lead to a wide landing... We went up those stairs which, even though they'd been repaired, creaked with every step we took.

"Here we are. They're in here."

Through the open door, the room appeared exactly the same as the one at Engin's. Looks like our victim was a bit obsessive; he'd revealed his same outlandish tastes in here. A red and white machine-made carpet with a pattern of geometric shapes on a wooden floor and another large red table in the middle with the same two side tables in the same color. Only the sofa and armchairs set was a bit different. The ones at Engin's had been beige, whereas these ones were a pale pink. And there was the same huge LCD TV like a stain on the wall.

My gaze went to my two officers in love, sitting side by side on the pink sofa, busy sipping at the tea that accompanied their patisserie cakes. Azize sat in an armchair opposite them and watched them with drooping eyes. When I entered, all three of them stood up.

"Please, don't get up," I said, motioning with my hand. "I'll go over here."

Sadri must have been sitting in the only empty armchair, and it'd be impolite to take his place. I sat down on the edge of the pink sofa next to Zeynep. The air smelt nicely of perfume.

Zeynep didn't used to wear so much of it, did she? And I think she had a bit of make-up... It suited her but...

"What'll you have to drink, Chief?"

The clarinetist had caught me off guard.

"Umm... No, thanks, Sadri. Nothing for me. I just had a couple of teas..."

"I can make coffee. I'm good at that sort of thing."

"No, no I'm fine." I turned to look at the young woman. "How are you, Azize?"

She just bowed her head and smiled.

"You look better," I said, trying to cheer her up. "Did you manage to get any rest?"

Even though it was her house, she couldn't relax. There was something playing on her mind.

"I couldn't sleep, but it's not important. In any case, I'm not working so..."

I threw my kids an insinuating look.

"I won't bother to ask you two anymore, because you look great..."

A flash of suspicion passed through Ali's eyes and Zeynep's face flushed with hidden misgiving. I didn't push the matter, but instead pointed at the TV.

"Engin had the same one in his house."

The apprehension on Azize's face deepened. She forced herself to try and explain.

"We bought two of them, one for him, one for me..."

I slowly stood and walked to the TV under everyone's bewildered stare. I pulled the apparatus towards me and it popped out about a foot or so. I leaned in and looked at the wall behind it. Just like in the room at Engin's, it was covered with beige wallpaper. I reached out and began to probe the wallpaper. Azize's hurried voice was quick to come.

"What's wrong, Nevzat Abi? What are you looking for?"

She'd stood up and was coming my way.

"I'm trying to find the safe."

I turned and gave her a look as if to warn her not to give me the runaround.

The anxiety in her black eyes was bordering on panic now.

"There's a safe here, Azize. If you don't show it to us, we'll still find it, we'll just lose a bit of time. But if you'll show us..."

"I don't have the key," she said, swallowing. "Engin always hid it in the *cevşen* locket around his neck."

Telling us what we already knew wasn't going to get her off the hook, but I was pleased with her straightforwardness.

"Don't worry. We have the key." I shot our criminologist a look. "You have it, right, Zeynep?"

She answered while opening the massive bag in her lap.

"Just as you instructed, Chief. It's right here."

I turned back to Azize.

"Are you going to show us where the safe is or will we find it ourselves?"

In the place of an answer, she accepted defeat and came over. And I stepped back to let her comfortably reach behind the television.

"Here," she said, pressing firmly on the wallpaper. "Here it is." With the touch of her frail fingers, the wallpapered metal cover slid down and the safe came into view. Zeynep, pulling on her plastic gloves, had already made it to our side.

"Allow me to open it, Chief."

Azize and I both took a couple steps away from the TV. Ali had also stood up, and Sadri watched from his place in amazement, not grasping what was going on. Zeynep turned the key twice, and after a mellifluous clicking, the door of the safe swung open.

A deep anxiety could be read in Azize's listless eyes.

"Do you know what's inside?"

"No," she said, but her face was ghastly pale. "Documents, I suppose... Title deeds and whatnot..."

Turning up the pressure might help.

"Any money, weapons, cocaine?"

She was trembling like a leaf.

"I... I don't know... Engin never told me what he kept in there."

Now she was definitely lying. Meanwhile, Zeynep had opened the cover wide and sank her hand inside. She pulled out the blue files, seven or eight of them, like those we'd seen in Engin's house. As she went to place them on one of the little tables, a few photographs slipped out and landed on the red carpet. I bent down to pick them up and two naked bodies met my eye. One was covered in hair, the other was smooth and youthful. I put on my spectacles. It was Black Nizam's body, the one covered in hair, and the young girl under him had her eyes closed, though whether from pleasure or pain was unclear. The other three photos were different angles of the same scene. I turned to Azize, who had hung her head in shame.

"Is this Çilem, this girl?"

She couldn't take any more. She swooned, and if I hadn't caught her round her narrow waist, she'd have fallen. Ali and the clarinetist rushed over and we carried her unconscious body to the sofa.

"Some water," I called out. Sadri ran and brought some. Zeynep had put all the files down and was massaging Azize's wrists. We wet the girl's forehead and around her mouth. She seemed to come to. Her eyes parted, and when she saw me she shut them again.

"There's no need to be embarrassed," I said in a fatherly voice. "We already know what went on."

She faintheartedly opened her eyes.

"We're not blaming you. We know you were suckered into this."

She cringed and started crying. It didn't last long though; she sniffled and sat up, settling into the sofa with her head bowed.

"Would you like some water?" the clarinetist asked, holding out a glass. "Take a sip. It'll do you good."

"I don't want any..." She wiped away her tears. "It wasn't me. It was Çilem that was suckered into the game..." She sniffled again. "It's that creep Nizam's fault. He forced Engin into it. 'I'm in love with Çilem,' he said. 'You have to help me,' he said. Engin couldn't resist him, and in the end he agreed. You know the situation, anyhow... He invited Çilem round. The poor girl had no idea, and she came over. But I didn't know Nizam was coming either. I swear I didn't. If I had, I would never have got involved in this dirty business. Because I love Çilem. It was like Nizam crashed our party.

But it was too late. At first, when Çilem saw Nizam, she shied away. But after a glass or two of wine, she relaxed. And you know the rest..."

"You're leaving something out," I warned her. "It wasn't just alcohol she was on that night. There was cocaine, too. You all did coke together..."

Her pale cheeks turned red...

"I didn't want to. God help me, I didn't. Nizam pressured us. He was the one who brought it, anyhow. He kept bragging that it was first-rate... I don't like cocaine, but Engin used it. And he would give me pills. Ecstasy and whatnot, you know. They made it seem like we were using it for the first time that night. Çilem didn't want it either, but when I did it, she warmed to the idea. Then we lost control. Or I got drunk I should say, and so did Çilem. I went to the bedroom to sleep. And Nizam took advantage of Çilem's drunkenness... She didn't know what she was doing, poor girl."

I showed her the photo.

"Who took these?"

She shook her head in shame.

"Engin... Engin took them because Nizam begged him too. 'I can't live without Çilem,' he said. 'I have to marry her,' he said. 'With these photos, we'll be able to get her away from Dice. Çilem will be mine. Help me,' he said. Engin wanted to do his boss a favor. And he told me that Ihsan doesn't love her anyway. 'He'll just use her a bit longer then send her on her way, whereas Nizam is in love with her and wants to marry her. It's better for her.' I believed him. And it turned out he was right. You said so yourselves, Nizam really did marry Çilem. It was unfortunate for Ihsan Abi of course. The man's pride was injured. I don't know if he loved Çilem or not, but having your lover be with someone else while you're in prison, and that person being your greatest enemy... It's too much."

This Azize sure was a strange one, feeling sorry for Dice.

"Okay, so how did Çilem feel about it? Did she like Ihsan?"

"Like him?" she repeated, with her wide, child's eyes. "What're you saying, Nevzat Abi? She was head over heels for him! She was in love from the time she was little. Dice

Ihsan was Çilem's father's man... I mean, Çilem's eyes first opened to Ihsan Abi... Like first love... After that disgusting night, she begged me. 'Please, don't let this thing get out,' she said. I swore I wouldn't tell anyone, but would Nizam stop? He sent those photos to Ihsan Abi. The man went off the rails, of course. He beat the living daylights out of her..."

I felt like I was in a Yeşilçam film. A real melodrama. These young girls who'd fallen prey to the wolves and their impossible, innocent love... And the men were also trying everything they could. Just look at Black Nizam. He'd risked all kinds of scandal in order to own the woman he loved. Dice Ihsan was more cautious; I wondered if he didn't really love Çilem. I remembered our conversation from the previous day. Whenever the girl's name was mentioned, silence ensued. No, it was plain that he loved her too but, after seeing those photos, he must have been shattered. The reason Çilem wanted to see Dice was evident now. To pay back, if only in part, the debt she owed a man whose pride was injured and honor destroyed. And in that case, the girl hadn't had any part in Ihsan's going to jail.

"This firearm incident," I said, giving voice to my thoughts. "The gun that landed Dice in prison. Wasn't it Çilem that planted it in his room?"

Her eyes flashed over to the door as if someone was listening to us.

"Nizam's not going to know what we talked about, will he?"

Man, did he ever put the scare on people, this Nizam, meanwhile sitting in front of us with the innocence of the cat that swallowed the canary.

"He'll definitely never know," I assured her. "This all stays between us."

She turned towards the clarinetist.

"Sadri Abi, I love you but please, if what I say gets out, they'll kill me."

Sadri got a sore look on his face.

"Come on, Azize... When have I ever blabbed something you told me?"

She got all coy, like a child sure their mistake would be tolerated.

"Now Sadri Abi, I didn't say... I mean, I just wanted to forewarn you is all."

The swarthy musician's defensiveness immediately passed.

"No need to, my dear. I'd never do you any harm."

She reached out and touched the man's coppery fingers.

"No, you wouldn't," she said, smiling. "I know you wouldn't..."

"One of the people working alongside Dice was really Nizam's man," she continued, feeling all three of our impatient gazes weighing on her. "He's the one who put that gun in Ihsan's desk. Çilem had nothing to do with it. The poor girl cried for days after Dice went to jail, anyhow. Nizam planned the whole thing. A year ago, he proposed a partnership to Ihsan. He told him to give him half his club. Ihsan didn't accept. That's when their relationship soured. 'You can't slip up with Nizam Abi,' Engin used to say. 'You'll pay a heavy price if you do.'" It suddenly occurred to Azize, and she gave me a horrified look. "Was it really Nizam who killed Engin? Because of the Greek houses he bought behind his back?"

"We'll find out soon enough, Azize. What you've told us is of great relevance. So, did Engin give you this man's name? I mean the person who set Dice up."

She shrugged her scrawny shoulders.

"No, he didn't say. And anyhow, he didn't talk much about it. 'The less you know the better,' he'd say. He always tried to protect me." Her dark eyes misted up again. "Engin wasn't a bad man, Chief. His fate was just lousy, like mine. He loved me. Maybe he didn't even know it himself, but he loved me. If you ask me how I know? Well, women just know these things." She turned her pained eyes on Zeynep. "Isn't that right, Inspector Abla? Women just know..."

Zeynep sat there speechless, not knowing how to answer. A mournful silence had fallen over us all; there was only the soft splash of melting snow.

"This landgrabbing could be the cause behind the murder."

⋇

My father always said not to trust the winter sun. Not two hours had passed, but the weather had got very cold. In less than an hour, darkness would fall. Nothing to say about the darkness, but the snow starting up again was a good thing.

"Eight more deeds," Ali grumbled, weighing up Zeynep's briefcase, which he carried in his right hand. "And the nine we found in Engin's house. That makes seventeen!"

We were climbing up Sakız Ağacı to Istiklal, the reverse direction of the path I'd taken at midday... Not counting the naked photos of Çilem and Nizam, no other important evidence but the eight deeds was uncovered in Azize's house. Just some of Engin's documents, useless letters, Durdu's photographs and such... In fact, I was happy about it, that we didn't find any cocaine or a weapon. It would have been torture for the girl, going back to the police station, being questioned again...

"And then there are the ones Nizam bought, right?" said my assistant, carrying on about the buildings. "How many of those?" "Twenty-two..." a red-faced Zeynep reminded him, as the slope got steeper. "And among those were three apartment buildings and two office blocks."

As Ali looked at the ruins of the houses, the paling winter sun made one last effort, spreading shadows onto the asphalt. "What an unsharable neighborhood this has turned into," he muttered.

"Of course they won't share, Ali," agreed Zeynep, trying to avoid stepping in the two little streams of water that flowed on either side. "This is the heart of the city. Real estate values are increasing in Istanbul and still haven't reached a comparable level."

She'd obviously racked her brain over this. I never understood this real estate business either. It was a good thing I didn't. What more could I possibly need than that old house of mine in Balat I'd inherited from my father?

But Ali must not have agreed with me because he blurted out, "What is a comparable level? What determines the price of these houses?"

Despite not having put in the deeds and documents from the safe, whatever was in her grey bag made it difficult for her to carry. She tucked it under her arm and answered.

"Compared to house prices in cities like New York, Paris, and London... In those places a hundred square meters in the city center sell for millions of dollars. Here it's more like three hundred thousand, maybe five hundred thousand... We may be oblivious to the city we live in but Istanbul is a world metropolis." She stopped for a moment and turned her tired eyes on me. "You would know better, Chief. What do those places have that our beautiful city is lacking?"

"The people are lacking." My assistant answered for me. He sounded angry enough to riot. He pointed at the laundry hanging from the lines stretched between the houses. "Look at this scene in the middle of the city center. And it'd be one thing if it was just appearance, but people are afraid to come into these streets at night. The drugs here, the prostitution, the mugging..."

"The poverty..." Zeynep added. "The ignorance, the murders... But it wasn't always like this. It used to be people would put on their nicest clothes to go out onto Istiklal. Presumably, the people living here were completely different. Just look at these gorgeous houses; even now it's obvious..."

I looked around at the unfortunate buildings waiting to be demolished. I thought about the Istanbulites who used to live in these houses, this city of theirs, what they added to our culture. It really did seem the neighborhood was cursed.

Like a town with no shortage of ominous winds after all the pain that was suffered here. The fabric of the city had been meddled with, not just these buildings, but people's lives. This sinister wreckage, this ghetto in the middle of Istanbul, was the price paid for the government's revenge and the mass hysteria. But if I tried to explain that to the kids, they wouldn't understand. And we still had one murder case with two deaths waiting to be solved.

"Anyhow, friends," I said, trying to shake off the terrible effects of Tarlabaşı crashing down on us. "We'll discuss the state of our city later. Let's get back to our investigation. How did Engin die; is it clear yet?"

Our criminologist gently nodded. Despite the weather growing increasingly colder, tiny beads of sweat appeared on her brow.

"Şefik wasn't wrong, Chief. It was a knife thrown from a distance that killed him. One blow. It doesn't appear possible for a knife to sink in so deep from closer proximity. I think the killer was a master at this knife throwing thing. Someone who worked especially hard at it."

"A hitman who uses a knife..." Ali said, expressing his amazement. "Not such a practical means. Unless the man's a psychopath. I mean, unless he takes special pleasure from killing that way..."

"Maybe knife throwing was his profession."

They both turned to look at me.

"Why not, friends? If the man used to work in a circus, for instance. You know, one of those knife throwers. And then he quit and became a hitman."

"The man could have trained himself," said Ali, extrapolating. "I mean, he didn't necessarily have to work in the circus. Maybe he just practiced every day till he became an expert. If we're going to look into Nizam's nephews, we should keep that in mind."

Zeynep shook her head hopelessly.

"I don't mean to burst your bubble, but I did look into Nizam's nephews. Nearly all of them have been involved in crime. Some have committed murders, like Kudret, and others were involved in assaults and robberies. But incidents of injury or death from a hurled knife are nonexistent."

Where Sakız Ağacı met Tarlabaşı Boulevard, two of the female sex workers were still waiting for customers. Seeing them made me think of Harem Süleyman.

"Seriously, Zeynep. What happened with the knife we gave you last night? Sure we know Süleyman, but he had problems with the victim, too. He lost three of his working women to Engin. Not to mention the humiliation... That alone is reason enough to commit murder. Did you detect any traces of blood?"

From the corner of her eye, she looked at Ali, because our overenthusiastic police had insistently objected to this theory the night before. But for whatever reason, he held his tongue now.

"I sent the knife to forensics," said our criminologist. "They're going to compare the measurements to the site of the wound. We'll hear tomorrow, both whether or not there was a trace of blood and if the measurements match up."

My assistant's silence was short-lived.

"With all these suspects," he muttered thoughtfully, "aren't we leaving someone out?"

We were standing there at the crosswalk waiting for a red light to interrupt the relentless stream of traffic flowing past us, both with our eyes on Ali because we couldn't understand what he meant.

"This Sadri," he said, finally spitting it out. "Why is the man so interested in Azize? He's not her father, not her brother. This morning he came to the station with her, and he showed up again this afternoon..."

He was overlooking some details.

"*We* told him to bring Azize to the station," I reminded him. "And don't forget we also spoke to him about searching the house."

"All right, Chief. I know all that but he sure is close to the girl..."

He wasn't wrong to suspect him. Back in the Neşe Pavyon, when Sadri first talked about Azize, it occurred to me that the thin swarthy man might be our killer. But then that possibility slipped my mind. I'm not sure why. Maybe I'd been influenced by the man's oppressed demeanor that so readily accepted defeat. Yes, sometimes it wasn't the people so much as their stories that affected you, and sometimes it was the person. Just how we can separate a person from their experiences was debatable, but separate they were. Life is outside of us, and even if we weren't here, it would flow along on its own. Some people call that fate. Fate. Whoever came up with that explanation did a fine job. Whether or not it's real is irrelevant; the idea of fate relaxes us, allows us to confront disasters, keeps us from losing our minds... Who can resist a sacred scenario written by a higher power? And if you resist, so what? The fragment of our destinies that we can change is so tiny, we mostly just concentrate on staying on our feet in the middle of that raging river. It's hard work, but there are those who've managed to stand up straight, despite the formidable conditions they live under. Well, Sadri was one of those. Getting up and coming here from Bulgaria, working as a musician in that awful *pavyon*, and as if that wasn't enough, trying to help a girl who's surrounded by men who are trouble. Murder somehow didn't fit this scenario. No, in this story, the role of victim suited Sadri more than that of killer. But I shouldn't shrug off my assistants' concerns.

"Let's check out the clarinetist then too, Zeynep," I said, as the red light turned green. "Let's see if we have a file on him."

"You're right, Chief. Leave no stone unturned." As we hurried across the street, she added, "In fact, let me ask my parents. He said he was from Dobrudja, so maybe they'll know."

As we got to the pavement on the other side, Ali held out my trusty old car's keys.

"I left the car in the Taksim parking lot, Chief. Let's cut through here to Istiklal; we'll drop by the Rikkat Hotel where Tidy Tarık stays, on Sıraselviler..."

He was going to the room of the man he'd shot and would be touching his things.

"Come with me if you want," I said, to get him out of a difficult situation. "Let Zeynep check out his room."

He understood the implication.

"Don't worry, Chief. I'm fine." A reassuring smile appeared on his impish face. "Plus, there's no escaping these things; don't you always say to take the bull by the horns?"

What lovely phrases he came up with when it suited him, the rascal.

"Okay then... But when you're done at the hotel, go back to the station. I'm curious about this court decision. Whether or not Kudret will be arrested... I don't want any new deaths in that already troubled neighborhood."

"All right, Chief. I'll head over as soon as we finish."

But that wasn't all. There were things our girl needed to do, too.

"And you concentrate on this Jale, Zeynep," I reminded her once more. "Those seventeen buildings were most likely purchased with her money. Or more precisely, Rıfat Bey's money. The way I understood it, she doesn't want to share her husband's fortune with her stepsons. She may have already calculated getting her hands on at least a portion of it. And Engin was a willing accomplice in the illicit affair. Of course he eventually wanted to take all those buildings out from under her." I pointed at the construction site opposite us. "This landgrabbing could be the cause behind the murder. As you said, Zeynep. There's millions of dollars lying here."

Zeynep stared with great interest at the urban renewal site, as if the killer we were looking for was going to pop his head out one of the stripped windows of these buildings where only the walls remained.

"Don't worry, Chief. I've already sent someone. We're crosschecking all the transactions from Jale's bank accounts against Azize's account."

"All right then. Good luck to us all, friends..."

I left them and diverted into Süslü Saksı Street, with its restaurants and cafes up and down both sides. My watch showed 15:41. I was meeting Nizam at four o'clock. There was no sense in going early. As I considered whether to head up to Istiklal, I saw him. That's right, the author. He stood chatting with someone in front of a small bookshop. He was so caught up in conversation, I could've walked right under his nose and he'd be none the wiser. But to be on the safe side, I ducked into the porch of the cafe on the corner and began to watch him. How could it be coincidence that our paths crossed so much? I wondered again if he was following me. His moving in next to me, his interest in my cases... I'd read a news story two years earlier. A detective novelist in Sweden had murdered three people in order to prove it possible to commit the perfect crime. But come on, this was a family man! He even had a grandson. Why would he take such a risk? Because he felt inadequate? However striking his writing was, whatever interest it generated, in the end it was just a book. The man had never solved a real murder case. All of it fiction, none of it real. Couldn't he have embarked on some crazy adventure to prove himself? To show everyone that he knew this business better than the police, than a killer even? But no, he couldn't possibly be that crazy. What if I were to sit and talk to him face to face? He'd never tell me. And I'd never get rid of him after that. The man already acted like we were family; he'd never leave my house... There you go; it looked like he was coming out... Yes, they shook hands and he walked away from the shop. The man he was talking to went back inside. I wondered if it was the shop's owner. I wasn't going to talk to the author, but maybe the bookseller would have something interesting to say about him.

With the impact of the sharp chill starting to make itself felt again, I approached the bookshop, taking care not to slip on the wet pavement that was already slowly beginning to freeze over. Above the narrow display window, a humble sign read Samarkand Bookshop. As I pushed the door open and went in, I was struck by that smell of books I loved so much. It reminded me of the first floor sitting room in the house where I spent my childhood. The smell of that massive wooden bookcase displaying my mother and father's novels, poetry volumes, and history books. A familiar, carefree voice rang in my ears. Louis Armstrong singing What A Wonderful World... Perhaps that was why he didn't hear me come in, this man who'd just been talking to the author. He was crouched down, lining some books up on the lower shelves. It was obvious he loved his job; he handled the books as though they were sacred objects, like they were living creatures that could be hurt or broken...

"Hello," I said, so he'd notice me. "I wanted to ask you something."

When he saw me, a smile of familiarity spread on his face.

"Oh, hello Chief!"

I couldn't hide my surprise.

"You know me?"

He genially approached me, saying, "Of course, Chief. Who doesn't?" He stuck out his hand. "I'm Kemal. Nice to have you here."

I doubted I was so famous, but I shook the extended hand, of course.

"Nice to be here, Kemal Bey. Seriously, how do you know me?"

He must have found the question meaningless because he shrugged.

"From the murders you've solved, the adventures you've had... You are a hero, Chief Inspector Nevzat."

Good lord, had they serialized our story in the papers without our knowing about it, I wondered? It was entirely possible; I'd have to look into it. I looked back into the bookshop and saw him once again, our author, a grin like a Cheshire cat showing off his white teeth.

"It's for the Spanish release of his book *Patasana*," Kemal explained, when he caught me looking at the poster. "Apparently, they loved it."

Seeing as how we were on the topic, I could safely ask. "What kind of writer is he?"

He gave me a look to say, *as if you don't know.*

"I'm genuinely asking... I'd like to read his book, but I don't know anything about his style."

He smiled in disbelief.

"If you say so..."

This bookseller was every bit as strange as the author.

"That's right; I don't know. I want to know what he writes, and what about."

He nodded towards a desk further on.

"Have a seat, I'll treat you to a tea."

I would have, but there was no time. I had to speak with Çilem.

"Thanks, but some other time. You still didn't tell me what kind of writer he is."

He stayed quiet a bit, that inscrutable smile on his lips, then said, "He's a friend of mine. It'd be wrong to brag." He thought for a moment. "Do you like Selim Ileri?"

"Who doesn't like Selim Bey? My mother first introduced me to his books. My friend Evgenia is crazy about them. She has his latest novel, *Devilish*, I guess it was."

"*Devilish Sense of Disruption*," the bookseller corrected. "Well, he likes Selim Ileri for instance, our detective novelist. I'm not sure if he likes everything he's written, but they're good friends."

"You're right. Selim Bey is a good reference."

"But if you want, I can give you one of his books. You can read it and decide for yourself."

He reached towards a row of books with orange spines, to a shelf apparently reserved for the crime novelist, but I stopped him.

"Thanks, but I have a meeting to attend. I don't accept gifts, but I'll stop round some other time and buy one."

"Murderers kill their own sense of tranquility along with their victims."

※

I was greeted first by the heavy smell of kebab, and then Nizam's smile. As soon as I opened the door, the mafia father's repulsive mask-like face popped up in front of my nose. How did he know I'd arrived? Was he watching from the window?

"Welcome, Chief..."

Whether it was because I believed him to be insincere or what, he didn't seem so likable anymore.

"Thanks," I replied, my smile no less forced than his. "What's up? You been waiting at the door for me, Nizam?"

He chuckled.

"No, Chief, the kids told me they saw you coming up the street..."

Two of his nephews stood behind him, ready to wait on him hand and foot. They were looking down, so as not to appear impudent. I suddenly noticed that everyone had stood up when I came in. By everyone I mean these hooligans, mostly dark, all belligerent young men. Had Nizam gathered every single one of his nephews to the *ocakbaşı*? I guess he was trying to take precautions against an impending offensive from Fidan's friends. Someone must have tipped him off about the potential attack. Or maybe it was just business as usual for these sadistic men. Murderers kill their own sense of tranquility along with their victims.

"Shall we come over here, Chief?"

He showed me to a long narrow table adjacent to a bed of pomegranate-red charcoal that flickered under a large, beaten copper flue. To the right of the fire pit was a flat tray piled high with kebabs waiting to be cooked: with aubergine, tomatoes and onion, in the style of Adana and Urfa, skewers of tiny pieces of meat, chicken shish, every kind of kebab imaginable... I was thinking how I hoped they weren't for me when I noticed another table opposite the fire. *Gâvurdağı*, that finely chopped tomato walnut salad in pomegranate molasses; slices of beef tomatoes, green peppers and cucumbers; fresh parsley, mint, arugula, watercress, and loads of other various greens; plates of grilled aubergines, whey cheeses, and yoghurt with cucumber...

"It's nothing special, but the boys prepared a little something for you," said Nizam, confirming my fears.

"Thank you so much. You've gone to so much trouble but I'm not hungry at all. I just ate," I demurely mumbled in front of the feast table.

He grinned brashly.

"There's always room for more, Chief. You're a brave guy; what have you got to lose?"

I shook my head decisively. "I couldn't, Nizam. Really..."

He was disappointed, but he didn't give up right away.

"Look, don't say I never told you. You can't eat kebabs like this anywhere else..."

I gave the tray of kebabs one more admiring look.

"They look exquisite." I put my hand on my stomach. "But I swear I have no room left."

His two eyebrows, like a cluster of bushes, separated from one another. It was a big let down. He wasn't just aiming to impress me; powerful men are supposed to feed people.

"Some other time," I said, to appease him. "Let's finish this up first."

He appreciated how I talked as if we were on the same side.

"You're right, Chief. Let's finish up this business first. We have quite a dark cloud hanging over our heads."

I took a look round at the empty tables in the room, which got wider as it went deeper.

"Isn't Hacer Hanım here?"

Just hearing his wife's name brought a sweet gentleness to his hard face.

"She'll be here shortly. You know women, Chief. She's a new bride, so she's extra careful with how she's dressed... And she's young." His eyes shone when he mentioned her youth. "I don't get involved. The age we're living in. Women have to be free, of course. She's out shopping, and at the hairdresser's and whatnot. But don't worry. She just called me and she's on her way."

That's when it dawned on me that Nizam's wife must be coming from Dice Ihsan. They were supposed to meet today. I wondered what he'd do if he knew. Her fresh husband, ignorant of what was happening, pointed out the dark staircase on the left.

"Well then, since you're not going to have any food, we may as well go up and talk in the office."

"All right, sounds good..."

He made a show of waiting respectfully for me to go first, and no matter what I did he wasn't going to lead the way, so I gave in and walked ahead. As he followed me, he called out to the coal pit's chef. "Leave the kebabs and tell Sıtkı to start on the tartare."

The moment I'd climbed the first step, the lights came on automatically, and at the same moment music could be heard. It was a song in the *Nihavent* style. The sound must have been coming from speakers hidden behind the plasterboard. I climbed the stairs in time with the music. Photos of colorful foods hung in rows on the walls. *Lahmacun* minced pizzas, eggplant puree with marinated lamb cubes, spicy beef tartare, *gâvurdağı* salad, baba ganoush, garlic and dill yoghurt spread, spiced minced-meat breaded in bulghur wheat... Summer and winter dishes of every variety and all kinds of kebabs... You had to give the photographer credit too, as the photos were lovely. Seeing them really whet a person's appetite. Maybe I'd made the wrong decision by refusing the food. Luckily, the display didn't go on for long; I got to the top of the steps and a room smaller than the one downstairs opened out in front of me.

Nizam turned to the wooden door on the right.

"Allow me, Chief." He reached for the handle on the door near the stairs and pulled it towards him. A man with a shaved head sat at a desk. When he saw his boss, he tried to jump up as though caught red-handed.

"Yes, Nizam Abi..."

The poor guy was so overweight he couldn't manage no matter how he hurried. We were in the middle of the room by the time he'd stood up.

"Come on, Hilmi," Nizam scolded him. "Quick. Get the Chief's coat."

Hilmi wobbled over to me and took the jacket I held out. Giving his best performance, he hung it on a hook behind the door. Meanwhile, in a manner that had become predictable, he pointed me towards the large chair Hilmi had vacated.

"Here you are."

"No," I said, making for the smaller chair in front of me. "Let me sit here. I'll be more comfortable."

In the end, he pretended to lose his temper.

"This isn't right. We prepare a meal and you don't eat it. We try to show you respect, you won't allow it. After a point, it could be considered an insult, Chief."

I was supposed to smile and humor him, but with great solemnity, I pointed to the chair opposite mine.

"Over here, Nizam. Have a seat."

He dropped the insulted act immediately. For a moment a look passed through his eyes, like he had work to do with this damned policeman. But only briefly, and then he sat down in the chair submissively. As he did so, he looked over at the chubby manager who just stood there at the door.

"What are you waiting for, Hilmi?' he lambasted. "Stop gawking. Go on now. Go order us some tea, quick..."

I raised a hand, saying, "Thanks, but I don't want any tea either." Nizam gave me another look of disappointment.

"Not even a cup of tea, Chief?"

"I've lost count of how many cups I've had since this morning. It'll give me heart palpitations."

He sensed my resolve and turned back to the man.

"Okay. No tea then. Go on and pull the door shut behind you."

Hilmi, purple in the face now, let himself out.

"Thanks so much for the preparations," I said, without lightening up. "And for the civility you've shown. But I'm on the clock..."

"But Chief..." he started to object with the same phony decorum.

"Sorry, but no... I am sure your kebabs are delicious. As I said, let's get this business wrapped up and maybe one day I'll eat. I'll need a bill, however, or I won't do that either."

He gave me a look of appreciation so to speak, still wondering exactly what this police *would* want.

"If you don't eat the food Swank Cemal tries to treat you to either, then okay," he said, folding his hands on his chest. "I won't be offended. But if you're treating us differently, then I'll be upset."

He was switching tactics and wanted to place his cards on the table.

"If we have any deficiencies, we can remedy them." He unlocked his arms from his chest and, placing his elbows on his knees, leaned towards me. A foul grin spread across his face. "Don't get me wrong, please... What I meant was I'd also like to be your friend. Like Cemal Abi is. Whatever our end of the bargain, I'm ready to make it happen."

Disgraceful, he was making a veiled bribe offer, insinuating he would protect my interests if I supported him or turned a blind eye to whatever he'd done. Still, it wouldn't suit my interests to immediately refuse. I made it look like I was going along with him.

"Don't be silly. Why would I take that the wrong way?" I locked my fingers together. "Of course we can be friends. Why wouldn't we?"

Nizam was so accustomed to this kind of relationship that he was fooled into believing we'd entered into a secret negotiation. With that temerity, he didn't even hesitate to express his resentment.

"You say that but, Chief, the things you did to Kudret inside..."

The reproach he held in was externalizing as flashes of anger in his eyes, which meant his nephew, that murderer, was quite precious to him. Perhaps he even took what was done to Kudret as a personal insult to himself.

"Why? What did we do?" I asked, feigning ignorance. "He even had his lawyer with him."

He threw his head back as if to say *don't go there.*

"That cop of yours spit in his mouth. Is that any way to treat a young man?"

My expression stayed calm.

"And what would *you* do if someone swore at your mother?"

His face grew pale.

"Kudret swore?"

"Why else would Ali spit in his mouth? Kudret should count his lucky stars that I was there. If I wasn't..."

He didn't want to hear any more.

"All right. I get it. Our dog misbehaved... We have endless respect for our state officials and the police." He said this, but he couldn't manage to shake off his hostility. "But you rode him so hard... The situation is obvious; it was blatant self-defense. They'll let him go when it gets to court, in any case..." He suddenly went all quiet as though he'd let something slip he shouldn't have. "So his lawyer Sacit says, I mean."

"If you're lucky, they won't," I said, shaking my head as though he knew nothing. "And he'll stay inside at least a few months. If Kudret was to get out today, it wouldn't be so good for him *or* you."

His bushy eyebrows joined and his beady eyes disappeared into their sockets.

"What do you mean by that?"

I put on a sarcastic expression.

"Come on, Black Nizam. Don't pretend you don't know. You got that information a long time ago. The friends of that girl you killed yesterday aren't going to let this rest. Every one of them is like a bomb ready to go off. If Kudret is let go..."

His dark face turned yellow with worry but he kept his dignity.

"You think we'll be frightened off by three or four çapulcu?"
I put on a wry smile.

"That I don't know, but last summer in Taksim, those men you call 'three or four çapulcu' forced the government to back down. Hundreds upon hundreds of police deployed here, and they still couldn't cope.

He gave me a blank stare.

"Gezi Park, I'm saying, just look what happened there." Despite all the power of the state, despite all those water cannons and tear gas, who won?"

He swallowed a couple times.

"Are there that many of them, those vermin?"

I curled up my lip as though with helplessness.

"Who can say how many of them there are? They spread some news over the internet and within an hour they've gathered thousands of people. They already have a grudge against you from the Gezi Park events. Fidan's murder rubbed a lot of salt in that wound. Even worse, the kids in Gezi were peaceful, but if armed groups were to enter the equation..."

As the blood drained from Nizam's face, he backed off.

"The Kurds in Tarlabaşı?"

I tried to hide my satisfaction that he'd fallen for my bluff.

"That much I can't say," I muttered. "It could be Kurds or it could be Turks; there are plenty of armed groups in Istanbul... The counterterrorism squads can organize all the operations they want, they still can't quite finish them off."

An inky-black uncertainty came and coiled up in his beady eyes.

"And you're only recently married," I continued, poking at his wounds. "You haven't even got round to the honeymoon with Hacer Hanım. And now this trouble. What's gonna happen if you knock off a couple activists? This time you'll have us all over you..."

Desperation suddenly seized him.

"So then what are we supposed to do?" he asked angrily. His hands were shaking. "We're damned if we do and damned if we don't."

I leaned in as though sharing a secret.

"Close your shops up for a few days." I gestured around. "Your restaurants, your coffeehouses, your clubs, your car parks... Whatever you got. Tell your nephews to make themselves scarce. Grab Hacer Hanım and take a holiday. Go to Russia for a few weeks, for instance. There's no visa or anything. Moscow should be beautiful now."

He was stumped. What I'd said made sense, but he still didn't trust me. Was I playing games with him, as Swank Cemal's man? Or up to something on Dice Ihsan's behalf? Just then, the door opened. A sumptuous smell wafted in, followed by a tall, blonde woman's appearance in the doorway. She wore a sable fur, golden with occasional flecks of black, and her hair, a shade lighter than the fur, was newly coifed. Her wide, emerald green eyes looked boldly out from under thick brown eyebrows, and her ample lips came alive with her tastefully subdued lipstick... Maybe her nose was a bit too wide, but to be honest, that flaw added charm to her face. She was truly a beautiful woman, this Çilem formerly known as Hacer.

The moment he saw his wife, there was no impending danger, nor the murder his nephew committed, no untrustworthy police across from him nor anyone else; he forgot about all of it and all of us, Nizam. His eyes sparkled from deep in their sockets and a charisma spread across his hideous face again.

"Hacer," he said, as if the name Hacer had slipped from his lips a thousand times. He really was madly in love with her, this woman who herself may hate him to death.

"Come in, Hacer."

He kept his eyes on his young wife as if he'd not yet had his fill, but Hacer didn't care one wit about the attention.

"All right," she said, after tossing him a heedless glance. "Good, it's warm in here."

She took off her fur coat, revealing a beige cashmere sweater that clung to her full breasts and a cinnamon-colored thigh-length skirt that struggled to cover her long legs. Fully aware of the effect of her beauty, but not giving a damn about its imposing force, she turned her lovely eyes on me.

355

"Hello, Nevzat Bey." She looked uncertain. "It is Chief Inspector Nevzat, isn't it?"

I stood and held out a hand.

"Hello, Hacer Hanım."

She gently shook my extended hand, her fingers every bit as icy as her stare.

"I prefer you use Çilem."

I smiled, genuinely; beautiful women aroused nice feelings in a person, no matter what anybody says.

"How are you then, Çilem Hanım?"

"I'm fine," the words spilled meekly from her lips. It was apparent she wasn't indulging me any more than she did her husband. It seemed Dice hadn't mentioned me, which meant he still didn't trust the woman. This was good news, although it would prevent Çilem being forthright with me. But then I wasn't sure how much I could trust this attractive woman anyhow. It was plain she didn't like Nizam, but she had no qualms wearing the fur he'd spent a small fortune on. I'd met my share of women who were in love with the comforts their husbands provided, if not the husbands themselves.

"Come have a seat," her husband said, patting the chair next to his. She took her sweet time, hanging her expensive furs next to my cheap overcoat before making her way to the seat Nizam had requested she sit in. Then she stared over at me, yes, as if to say *here I am then*.

"Thanks for agreeing to see me," I started. "You also knew Engin."

She was taciturn as she listened, giving nothing away on her face.

"How did you meet him?"

She smoothed the edges of her beige sweater.

"We met in the Tarlabaşists Club. Engin used to come there quite a bit."

"You worked there too, right?" I said, gingerly coaxing the conversation into more dangerous waters. "With Ihsan Bey?"

"Because of my father," she said with disinterest, as she picked a strand of hair off her skirt. "My father worked alongside Ihsan Bey." She placed the strand of hair into an ashtray on a side table. "You'll understand, they were more like close friends than co-workers. I also worked for a while in Ihsan Bey's place on that occasion."

"I suppose you were there until Ihsan Bey went to prison..." I said, quickly finishing her story.

For the first time, she gave me a nervous glance.

"It had nothing to do with Ihsan Bey's going to jail. I was already planning to leave the club. It wasn't as if I liked the place."

"Anyhow, that's when we met," Nizam interrupted, a relaxed smile spreading on his face. "And after that, she didn't need to work." He reached over and took the woman's hand. "Hacer Hanım became the lady of the house."

The woman confirmed it with a reluctant smile, but she pulled her hand away.

"What went wrong between them?" I asked. "Ihsan and Engin, I mean. They were best buddies up till Ihsan went to jail."

"They weren't best buddies," Nizam began to say.

"Let Çilem Hanım answer, if you will," I said, shutting him up. "You've already had your say."

He rolled his offended eyes away and nervously crossed one leg over the other.

"All right, Chief. As you wish."

I guess Çilem got a kick out of my snapping at Nizam. The iciness in her emerald eyes seemed to crack.

"Ihsan Bey held Engin responsible for the gun found in his club. I mean, he believed Engin planted it. 'He planted the gun *and* informed the police,' he told me."

"He's a lying bastard!" Nizam interjected again. "He's flinging mud, the dirtbag..."

I ignored him and kept talking to Çilem.

"Okay, what do you say? Did Engin plant that gun there?"

A look of uncertainty roamed her eyes.

"To tell the truth, Engin never came by the club. I mean, it would've been impossible for him to put it there."

"Could he have had someone else do it?" I asked, in a thinly veiled accusation against her. "Someone who worked there, for instance?"

Surprisingly, she didn't bite.

"It's possible, but who would do that? Everybody at the Tarlabaşı Club loved Ihsan Bey."

"But someone had to have put it there," I continued to speculate. "Because Ihsan says the gun wasn't his."

"That's true..."

"So, seeing as there's this issue between them, could Ihsan have murdered Engin?"

She looked away, trying with her body language to give the message 'no'. But when she noticed her husband's unblinking eyes staring at her, she preferred to answer, "I don't know, Nevzat Bey... Yes, there was some problem between them, but would Ihsan Bey go so far as to kill him? That much I don't know."

"What is there to know?" Nizam bellowed, beginning to get angry. "Of course it was Ihsan who killed Engin. Who else would it be?"

"What about the hitman in his house?" I put in straight away. "Who hired Tidy Tarık, then?"

He angrily pulled his right leg off his left.

"How should we know who hired him?"

He'd given up controlling himself and his voice. Was he choosing conflict over conciliation?

"Don't get all worked up, Nizam... I'm just trying to figure out what happened."

He huffed in exasperation.

"I know that, Chief. But we've been over this already. What good is it going to do to keep asking?"

"We talked about it with you, not with Çilem Hanım," I said, turning back to the woman.

"You were at Mount Uludağ the night of the murder..."

She was listening nervously, wondering where all this was leading.

"I think you got married that day..."

Before giving Çilem a chance to answer, Nizam pulled a document from his inside pocket and shoved it under my nose.

"Here you are. Take a look; our wedding date is clearly written here. December the thirty-first, 2013... Enough is enough, Chief. Stop breathing down our necks. You think we'd lie to you?"

His dark face had gone bright red with rage and a vein in his forehead was pumping furiously.

"Calm down, Nizam." It was Çilem trying to placate him this time. "Nevzat Bey's just doing his job."

His bushy eyebrows furled. I thought he'd say the conversation ends here, that we'd talk with his lawyer present tomorrow, but he reached into his pocket and pulled out a pack of cigarettes.

"Excuse me, but I'm going to smoke."

I had half a mind to say go outside and do it, but it wasn't going to help to burn this bridge. I ignored him and asked the woman, "Were you surprised to hear Engin was murdered?"

She averted her gaze again.

"More sorry than surprised. I was really sad..."

See, this I wasn't sure about. I seriously doubted she'd get upset over a man who had made her life miserable.

"I knew him," she continued to fitfully explain. "We had some nice times together. He wasn't a bad person, in fact."

Nizam wistfully blew out the smoke he'd inhaled.

"He was a good guy," she asserted. "A brave man. He had a big heart..."

It was the perfect time to drop a hint.

"He introduced you two, didn't he?"

Çilem realized I was alluding to the naked photos and her pale skin flushed, but Nizam had not one iota of shame, he just planted his beady eyes on my face with pure spite.

"Yes, that's right. It was Engin who introduced us, God rest his soul."

We were on the brink of a fight, when at that moment my phone rang, saving my skin.

"Sorry," I said, as I picked up. "Hello?"

"Hi Chief. It's Ihsan... I talked to Çilem. I know who the murderer is..."

You were all that's missing, I said to myself. I watched Nizam from the corner of my eye. He was puffing away on his cigarette. As for Çilem, she still hadn't bucked the effects of speaking to her ex-lover half an hour earlier and was staring into space.

"Great," I said over the phone to the third person in this triangle. "Where are you now?"

"Back at the club."

"Gotcha. I'll be there in a bit. We'll talk in detail there."

He understood I wasn't free and didn't push the subject.

"I'll expect you, Chief," he said, hanging up.

The time had come for me to wrap up this conversation. Otherwise, Nizam and I would lay into each other. I gave the new couple a sincere smile. "Time for me to get going." I held up my phone. "The kids are calling me..." I turned to Nizam. "You were talking about Engin, I guess?"

"Yes, I was saying he's the one who brought us together, god bless him."

There was significance in Çilem's silence, but I pretended not to care.

"It was a lucky thing he did," I said, rubbing my hands together. "Looks like there's nothing left but to wish you all the happiness in the world then."

Nizam froze in bewilderment. When he saw me maintain my silence, he asked with cautious optimism, "Are we through then? Is that all?"

I smacked my hands gently on my knees.

"That's it from me, but if you have anything else to add..."

He took one last drag off his cigarette, this time exhaling with pleasure rather than ambition.

"No, I've got nothing left to say. What about you, Hacer?"

Her brown lashes, thick with mascara, closed over her green eyes, then opened.

"No," she said in a colorless, passionless voice. "What else could I possibly have to say?"

"What wouldn't a man in love do?"

✖

"The man's name was Lütfü. He came from Milan, and as you may have guessed, the Italian mob sent him. They met him in the hotel in Uludağ. Can you imagine the baseness of that man, meeting with the Italian mafia in the honeymoon suite of their hotel? Nizam may have intentionally arranged to meet him outside Istanbul. Just look at the sagacity of that bastard, Chief, marrying on the one hand while putting his affairs in order on the other. He was afraid Engin would spot Lütfü in Istanbul. Because Lütfü used to be one of Engin's men..."

Dice Ihsan was animatedly explaining all this from the table beneath the photo of the bulldog Mualla, lying on its back, legs spread, generously offering up its milk-filled teats to its five little pups. But the real reason for his enthusiasm was not so much the interesting information he'd got as the meeting with Çilem itself. She must have convinced him of her innocence; he'd have already been ready to accept it anyhow. *"What wouldn't a man in love do?"* we could say, to distort a cliché Yeşilçam Cinema catchphrase. Yes, I was quite sure Ihsan loved the blonde woman every bit as much as Nizam did.

"They were talking in the living room of the king suite," he continued, licking his lips. "Lütfü and Nizam, that is. A tête-à-tête. He'd brought along four nephews for protection, but he didn't allow even one of them to stay by his side. He sent Çilem to the next room, too. But the walls were so thin, everything they said was audible. 'The Italians would like to do business with you,' is what Lütfü said. Because when Engin's uncle Durdu died, the shipments of heroin from Turkey were cut off. The men need a reliable supplier. At first, Nizam wanted to stay out of it, but then Lütfü brought up the subject of his being picked up three years earlier. You know that three years ago Nizam was caught with a ship hauling a massive quantity of drugs? The heroin was hidden in limestone, but the police found it straight away as if they'd put it there with their own hands. I mean, someone on the inside definitely snitched. Turns out that snitch was Engin. On his uncle Durdu's orders, of course. Durdu didn't want any suppliers besides himself on the Swiss-Italian route. Naturally, Nizam didn't fall for Lütfü's explanation straight away. 'Can you prove it?' he asked him. Lütfü had come prepared; he laid the Italian police's confidential report in front of him. With that, Nizam lost control. That's just how he is, anyhow. First he just listens without saying much, but once he loses his temper, he's blinded by rage. He doesn't give a damn if the world's on fire or it's raining blood. 'I will fuck that Engin up!' he shouted, pardon my French. 'So then, the uncle and his nephew were playing me. I swear on my name, I will make him pay!' he howled. Çilem told me every last detail. After he'd sent Lütfü away, he didn't recover for a long while. She told me that he went outside for a bit, that he was probably speaking with his nephews. Maybe he called Istanbul to have Engin taken out..."

It was pretty important, what he was telling me, and Nizam may top the list of suspects, but it'd be best not to rush it.

"When did this conversation take place?" I began to peck. "Before or after the wedding?"

It was my asking about the wedding that upset him, rather than my lack of enthusiasm for what he'd revealed.

"After the wedding, just before dinner..."

I had to be sure.

"On the thirty-first of December?"

"Yes," he confirmed. "I mean, six or seven hours before Engin was murdered."

He was staring at me impatiently, as if to ask why I would keep questioning it despite what he'd told me and when everything was clear as day.

"Don't misunderstand me, Ihsan. I believe you. And Çilem has no reason to lie. But I've met Nizam, and he's not the type to murder his closest man over a report like this. He's no risk taker. He'd have to be sure about it."

"He already was," he said, wondering why I couldn't get it through my thick head. "Why else would he snap like that? He'd wait to speak to Engin himself before jumping to conclusions."

"I have my doubts, but let's say that's what happened. He believed Engin was deceiving him. Even then, Nizam is not a man to order the killing of someone who's betrayed him like that. Especially the very person he trusts more than anyone. It's impossible that Nizam would act like that. More likely, he'd kill Engin with his own hands. Or at least want to confront him first. He'd want to see him suffer, the man who sold him out, to see his fear. Or if nothing else, to hear from his own mouth why he'd betrayed him. That's why it's such a weak possibility he had Engin killed."

The wind was gone from Ihsan's sails.

"How can you be so sure?"

Frankly, I understood him. He'd got so close to killing two birds with one stone. With that information, Nizam would be sent to prison, and he'd get back the lover that was stolen from him. But here was this inspector, such a stickler for detail, who had crushed all his hopes by insisting Nizam had no hand in Engin's murder.

"I'm not," I answered, trying to smooth things over. "Nizam is still on our list of suspects. The possibility remains, no matter how slim, that your assumptions will prove true. Men like Nizam are the dregs of society. They come from the very bottom, not to mention the poor guy is no looker. He's seen a lifetime of contempt. And contempt makes a person vindictive. It breeds vengeance. You said yourself he was cruel and full of rage. You can see that in his passion for Çilem, as well. He's used every dirty trick in the book to get her."

I'd touched a sore spot. His face began to change by the second, from shame to anger, ardor to defeat, as if he were experiencing the full gamut of emotions a man in love could have, all at the same time.

"Yes, I know all that, Ihsan. I just saw Çilem not long ago in Nizam's *ocakbaşı*. That's where I was when you called. And before that, I spoke with Azize. The girl told me everything. How the men set that despicable trap, but you made a big mistake too..."

He knew what I meant. He turned to look at our pocketsize Hercules, who stood planted in front of the door. Flea Necmi hadn't left our side since the moment I'd set foot in the Tarlabaşists Club. They'd most likely gone together to see Çilem as well.

"Necmi, wait outside a bit, will you?"

The lightweight tough guy showed no sign of being offended.

"As you wish, Abi."

"What mistake?" he grumbled, as the man left the room. His voice was shrill, like a taut wire. "How did I make a mistake?"

"You made a mistake in sending Çilem away. In playing into their hands..." I explained candidly, as though criticizing a friend I was sure would understand me. "You still don't comprehend that Nizam's problem wasn't getting his hooks into your club? He doesn't need that. The man has enough money as it is. What could he possibly do with your club? It was your lover he wanted. Yes, Çilem... It's pretty plain to see he fell in love with her at first sight. And that is why he wanted to be partners with you. In order to form some kind of relationship with her, or if nothing else, to be near her."

His face tensed up with disbelief.

"Did Nizam tell you all this?"

Paranoia must be something all the men in this underworld had in common, and this fool now suspected I was in cahoots with Nizam.

"Men like Nizam don't share their confidences," I answered back. "And Çilem is his weak spot. He knows the woman doesn't love him. Yes, despite their marrying only a few days ago, he knows it for fact. But he has hope, and without hope he'd have no passion anyway. That's why he never talks about his relationship with her. There's no need to. The girl is with him, in any event. He got what he wanted; he has Çilem. Why should he talk? You didn't stake your claim on her..."

My words were a slap in the face for him.

"Okay but..."

"I know. You're going to say what about the photos. But they gave Çilem drugs. Azize explained everything. Engin had set it up... He did it to win Nizam over because he knew the man had fallen for her... And they tricked Azize too. The poor thing is racked with regret. The real prank's on you, and you swallowed it hook, line, and sinker. Seriously, didn't Çilem tell you all this?"

He squirmed in his seat.

"She told me, of course, why wouldn't she? I didn't believe her..." His eyes seemed to grow moist. "I don't know. I just can't accept that Çilem made a mistake like this. And actually, I'm not entirely wrong. When I went to prison, I warned her. I told her to be careful of that bastard Engin, to stay away from Nizam..."

I wanted to keep my good image of Ihsan.

"The girl is so young..." I said, trying to mollify him. "Sure, maybe she was a bit gullible, going to Azize's house like that. And it wasn't so nice that she stayed there even after Nizam arrived, of course. But at that point, the enmity between you and Nizam wasn't yet out in the open. Maybe she just saw him as a big brother type."

He sadly and gently nodded.

"That's how she'd see him all right. She'd have called him 'Nizam Abi'. And that dirtbag would've addressed her as 'my girl'. Can you believe it? You saw her anyhow; she is young enough to be his daughter. The sneaky bastard, he had other intentions, of course. How could I have known?"

"But you should've known," I said, giving a brotherly warning. "A man can sense it. You should've protected her."

"I would have if I hadn't gone to prison," he said with regret. "It was a trap... And Çilem fell for it. Whatever it was that happened that night..."

"Forget about that night already."

"How can I?" he moaned. "I can't forget about it. I can't get the events of that night out of my head..."

Jealousy sure did eclipse a person's reason. How it blinded us.

"No, no matter what I do, I can't forgive her. Do you think I'm not heartbroken? Today when we met at Tebernüş, the hairdressers, it destroyed me. Çilem was in tears and she took my hand. That's when I understood I'd delivered her to that revolting wife-pimper with my own hands... It was the first time I cursed myself..."

"So, did you apologize to her?"

He gave me a strange look. His sadness turned to anger.

"Why should I apologize? I'm not the real culprit here. Shouldn't Çilem have protected herself? She was weak and she couldn't. Maybe she was confused. Maybe she was impressed by Nizam's wealth. Maybe it really was the effects of the drugs. I don't know. And what does it matter anymore? And anyhow, Çilem's not expecting an apology. On the contrary, she wanted me to forgive her. That's why she ratted on Nizam."

I stared at the poor guy who didn't understand how much he meant to her.

"You are aware of how she jeopardized herself by doing that, aren't you?"

His eyes glazed over and he frowned.

"I know, but while I was in jail..."

His stupidity was beginning to get on my nerves.

"Shut up about that prison, already!" I openly berated him. "Do you love the girl?"

He couldn't answer straight away; he was flustered.

"At one time I loved her..." he finally managed to say. "I know Çilem from her childhood. She's nine years younger than me. I was the first boy she ever kissed. She was in love with me even at that age, and had eyes for no one else... I am very important to her."

The nerve of this guy, bragging to me... I couldn't take much more.

"What about her? Is she important to you."

He averted his eyes again. Of course she was important, but he couldn't even swallow his pride to say it.

"I was wrong about you," I said condescendingly. "I thought you were brave, but you're not..."

Apparently, he'd taken it to heart, the prince.

"That's easy for you to say. What would you have done in my shoes? As Nizam showed every Tom, Dick and Harry those photos. Telling everyone in Tarlabaşı how he was carousing with my lover..." His eyes opened wide. "No, Chief. It's not so simple. However much I may love Çilem, I could never accept that."

"Nizam would have," I glibly replied. "Yep, he would have, because he loves Çilem more than you do. He's a braver, more passionate man than you."

His pupils began to twitch in panic. That frightened child, the one whose father's shadow always hung over him, had taken over. "I've never touched dice in my life," he'd said. Yes, Ihsan wasn't a man for such shady business; neither his mind nor his heart were inclined to deal with such troublesome matters. He was a loving man, who hung cute photos of a family of pugs with dumb looks on their faces on the walls. It wouldn't be right to even compare him to Nizam. It wasn't because he liked it that he kept running this awful business he'd inherited from his father. Was it because he was ashamed, and he knew no other profession? Maybe if he could admit it, if he could face himself, everything would be easier. But I was hoping in vain. Like most of us, Ihsan would continue to live someone else's life rather than the one he wanted.

"You've taken Nizam's side from the start, anyhow," he said, like a spoilsport. "Despite Cemal Abi, you didn't trust me."

"You know very well that I'm not taking sides. Don't go blaming others to cover up your own desperation."

As I got up from my chair, I continued to warn him in the same tone.

"Don't leave town. What you've told me doesn't exclude you as a suspect. You are at least as much a suspect as Nizam is."

He stared at me with hostile eyes.

"Don't waste your energy, Ihsan," I reproached him, before putting on my coat. "You can't win. And if I were you, I'd shut down the club for a few days. The friends of the girl shot by Nizam's nephew are on the warpath. They may try to burn down your place again. It'd be better if you weren't inside."

"The wind sings now our old songs from those places"

⚹

I parked the car in Tatavla's back street, in front of Vaçe Bey's shop, perhaps the last tailor left in Kurtuluş. The shop was closed and Vaçe Bey had gone home. What was he supposed to do when he still heated his tiny shop with a stove? As I shut the trusty old guy's door, the first flake of snow landed gently on my cheek. Was it starting again? I looked up at the sky. No, the clouds were spreading into thin wisps and dispersing, and the full moon was beginning to reign over the fresh night. I remembered my daughter Aysun once saying, as she looked up at a full moon, "It looks like a giant snowball." Such was the mind of a child, finding beauty in every image. Actually, there was an unsettling side to it, the sphere glowing coldly in that deep infiniteness. A side that evoked desolation, abandonment, and death... My phone began to ring and my gaze went from the sky to the ground. I read my assistant's name on the screen.

"Yes, Ali. I'm all ears."

"They let Kudret go." There was more anger in his voice than surprise. "The judge believed everything that gunslinger said. I said if nothing else they'd keep him inside for a few months, but no, they set the guy free. Kill a young girl one day, go for a stroll the next... What a great country."

I hadn't expected them to let him go either, but even so I wasn't surprised. Not to underestimate the judge's role, but

369

Nizam's lawyer Groom Sacit had a long reach, and despite his fall from grace, he knew a lot of people. If the dark-faced mafia father had gone to every expense...

"Anyhow Ali, what's done is done. Let's notify law enforcement and have them take measures in Tarlabaşı. Nobody will be able to hold Fidan's friends back anymore. They'll probably attack Nizam's venues. If nothing else, have them take control there."

"Right away, Chief... We didn't find anything that would help us at the Rikkat Hotel. Not a knife, not anything else..."

He was talking about the place Tidy Tarık had been staying.

"He stayed there for a month. Last week he came back with a man and woman and the three of them had breakfast together. I couldn't figure out who the man was, but the woman fits Jale's description. Tomorrow we'll show the photo to the receptionist."

Jale... I pictured the former beauty who put on the phony arrogance to hide her desperation. Yes, it was entirely possible that Jale had hired the killer. Why hadn't we thought of that before? Engin had probably cheated the woman. After the buildings were in his name, he may have told her she had no claim to them and showed her the door. Jale would have been stuck, with no documentation and no ammunition. Just the empty trust she felt for the man she loved. And it would have been impossible to explain what happened. She couldn't say she wanted to get her hands on a portion of her husband's inheritance before he died. Rıfat Bey's sons would have destroyed her. Perhaps she wanted to hire a hitman to eradicate the problem. Or maybe someone had egged her on. Someone? For example, Dice Ihsan? Of course it'd be Dice Ihsan. Hadn't he said Tarık frequented his club? He could have pushed her to do it, thereby taking out Black Nizam's most trusted man without getting his hands dirty.

"When you go back to the hotel tomorrow, take Dice Ihsan's photo with you. Show that to reception too and let's see if he recognizes him."

"Are you saying Dice was the man with Jale?"

"It's possible, Ali. Let's see what the receptionist says..."

"I understand, Chief. Good night to you then. I'll let you know if anything happens, in any case."

"Please do. Good night, Ali."

As I hung up and walked up the street to Tatavla on this calm Kurtuluş evening, I felt like I was among the crumbling buildings of Tarlabaşı. "People resemble the place where they live," a poet once said. And our legal system, like the places we lived, had grown old and stopped functioning, was beginning to rot and was close to collapsing... Could justice really materialize in this society? Of course Fidan and her friends had committed a crime, but they hadn't even attempted to enter the building... And their aim wasn't to kill the people inside but merely to hassle or intimidate them. In return seven bullets were fired directly at the girl. And now her killer was free. In such a society, could one hope for good? Could you have any faith in justice?

Before I reached Tatavla's door, my phone rang again. It was Nizam calling. So then he was back in a panic.

"Did you hear, Chief?" he dove straight into the subject. "They let Kudret go."

"Congratulations. What more do you want?" I said, wishing him well.

He didn't respond straight away. It didn't seem to warrant a congratulations.

"That police of yours called."

I was confused. Why would Ali call Nizam?

"My assistant?"

"No, Chief. That wimpy Beyoğlu officer... Sami..." His number one conspirator had suddenly become 'my' police. The weasel was trying to protect the man now. "They got wind of where the anarchists were going to gather," he continued. "He told me to be careful. I thought I'd get a confirmation from you."

Our puny little officer was finally good for something.

"I told you," I said, to put even more of a damper on his spirits. "You're in real danger. Don't even think of fighting with those kids. You won't come out on top; it'll be the end of you all. Close up your shops and get out of Tarlabaşı while there's time. And warn your nephews to make themselves scarce tonight."

"We're already doing that. I spoke to all the boys..."

So we'd got to him, Black Nizam. What was it he'd said when we met? "If you don't want to give the angel of death ammunition, you have to limit the number of loved ones you have in this world." But he'd had a rude awakening. He had a wife at stake now. Far from reducing his number of loved ones, he'd connected with someone new, with an incorrigible passion. In defiance of his family, his nephews, and in fact all the written and unwritten rules of the underworld. That's why he withdrew his men from Tarlabaşı without any hesitation.

"Good for you, Nizam," I said, supporting him. "But you should get some distance from Tarlabaşı too, as soon as you can."

"Don't worry, we're in Ataşehir already. I have a house here..."

"Good move. Let me know if anything happens. My phone will be on."

"Thanks, Chief..."

His voice was full of gratitude. I was relieved too, if only a little. Nizam's nephews, encouraged by Kudret's release, could embark on a small massacre this time. At least now there wouldn't be any deaths, and if the activists broke a couple windows or doors, nobody would be hurt. With my mood starting to return, I walked into Evgenia's *meyhane*.

Tatavla was calm. As I pushed open the door with its glazing, I heard the familiar words "The wind sings now our old songs from those places..." It was Zeki Müren singing, an exquisite song by Şekip Ayhan Özışık in the Muhayyer Kürdi style. I was completely free of the tense, untrustworthy weather. This door, with its window, was like a gate of purgatory between life's vulgarity and the elegance of love. Whenever I passed over its threshold, whenever I stepped into this *meyhane*, I was filled with a deep serenity, an indescribable calm. If someone were to ask where is the last spot on Earth that proves the world is a good place, I would immediately answer Evgenia's Tatavla. Actually, it was still empty inside. The tables were all vacant, not a waiter to be seen. As I was wondering where Evgenia had got to, I noticed the elderly woman. She was sitting at a table overlooking the garden. Her eyes, seeming mournful under the moonlight, stared into a plum tree. With her short hair died the color of chestnuts and a rose colored cardigan, she gazed at the tree with familiarity. I'd taken a few steps before she noticed and turned towards me.

"Good evening," I said, going over.

Her bright eyes didn't show any misgiving. She politely stood up. She gave me a once-over with deep blue eyes accentuated by her understated make-up.

"Good evening to you..." She smiled as if we'd been friends for years. "You must be Nevzat."

"And you must be Aunt Fofo."

Her penciled-in eyebrows furrowed with feigned irritation.

"Just Fofo... No 'Auntie' please, all right?" She had very little accent despite having been away from Turkey for all these years. As she resolutely waved a right hand, she continued, "None of these formal niceties, either."

I bowed my head.

"All right then, Fofo. As you wish."

"I wish it like this, because it's more congenial," she said, with the charming conviction peculiar to the elderly. "I refuse to use formalities with the man who swept my Evgenia off her feet."

"I'm with you there," I concurred. "I can't go treating Evgenia's dearest aunt like a stranger."

She let out a cheerful laugh.

"You're a good man, Nevzat..." She held out her small, veiny hand. "I can read it in your eyes. Good for Evgenia, the crazy girl finally made the right choice."

I bent down, took her extended hand, and brought my lips gently down on it. She was thrilled.

"See!" she said, grasping my hand in hers. "See, a true Istanbul gentleman. It's very nice to meet you, Nevzat."

"The feeling's mutual, Fofo."

She looked around.

"Why are we still standing? Let's have a seat."

We sat, and her gaze went back to the thick-trunked plum tree again. Her eyes were so caring, so full of compassion, staring as though in love with the naked body of that tree... She felt my gaze on her.

"She's old," she murmured, keeping her eyes on it. "She's grown old, just like us. Niko planted this plum tree as we were leaving." She turned to me and, squinting, whispered, "You know, my Niko was a partner here."

It was the first I'd heard of it.

"That's right. Yorgo reeled him in. May he rest in peace. My Niko was an angel." She took out her rosary beads. "Yorgo was not bad either..." She threw me a meaningful look. "You never met him, did you?"

"I'm afraid not," I said shaking my head.

She covered the right side of her face with her hand as though she didn't want anyone to see and whispered.

"It's a good thing. He wasn't a bad person, just a little cranky. The things he put Niko through... Yes, I'm not going to lie just because he's dead. May he rest in peace, but you'd have a hard time if Yorgo were alive. I mean Evgenia and you. He'd put you through the wringer. Niko wasn't like that. He was open-minded, with a rich heart..." She turned back to the tree. "It's a damson plum. We emigrated to Athens in the fall of the year we planted it. October of 1964. I thought it would dry up. Yorgo wasn't so interested in trees or flowers. He didn't look after them and wouldn't water them, so I assumed the sapling wouldn't grow. I was wrong about him. He took good care of it. The sapling didn't dry up, and it grew, but it never flowered. Yes, for thirteen whole years it never bloomed... Right up until our first return visit to Istanbul." She sighed and turned to me again. "We were away from our Istanbul for thirteen years... Not because we were scared, but because our feelings were hurt. Well, the tree flowered for the first time that year and produced its first fruit. 'Would you look at that little hussy,' Yorgo said, all jealous. 'Look how colorful she gets when she sees you.' She was all gussied up like a bride, with her red and white flowers..."

She sounded so sad, so sentimental.

"Were you living in Kurtuluş? Before you went to Athens, I mean..."

"No, my dear. Our house was on Kalyoncukulluğu Street... in Tarlabaşı... Do you know the one? From a side street off the Grand Rue de Pera, it winds down to near Priest's Bridge."

Tarlabaşı again. It looked like there was no escape from it these days. If I didn't go to it, it came to me, though I had no complaints.

"I know Kalyoncukulluğu, all right," I said, with a heartfelt expression, as if it had turned out we were kin. "I served there for all of seven years..."

For the first time there was a hint of a stranger on her face.

"Did you know Sezgin? Inspector Sezgin Göçerli?"

Her mood had changed; it was obvious this story wasn't going to end well. I probably shouldn't have gone poking around but my curiosity got the better of me.

"No, I never met him..." I said, trying to make sense of it. "Was this Sezgin stationed in Beyoğlu?"

She was trying to suppress her surging emotion.

"In Tarlabaşı... In the building you were stationed in. He was a good friend. My father looked after his kids. He had two of the sweetest daughters in the world. One was called Ayşe, the other Neşe... My father was a pediatrician. His clinic was on the same street. We all lived together, Turks, Greeks, Armenians, or whoever else was in the neighborhood... Sometimes there was resentment, unwarranted bullying and such, but Inspector Sezgin always protected us and showed us friendship. He'd rush to help us whenever we were in trouble and found solutions for our problems. Up until that terrible autumn... Have you heard about those days?"

She must have been talking about the sinister events of 6th and 7th September... The most shameful days in this city's history.

"I've heard," I said, averting my eyes. "It was horrific, what happened."

"Horrific..." Her eyes were moist. "Yes, horrific... That's the word for it. And we'd had such a lovely summer. The nicest of my life. I was twenty years old and newly in love. I got engaged that July, to Niko... In my Uncle Teo's mulberry garden on Büyük Island. We were so happy, absolutely elated." She shook her head with disappointment. "They ruined the best days of our lives."

"Was your home looted?"

A pain that hadn't lost any of its freshness appeared in her aging eyes.

"Was it looted? It was ravaged, completely ravaged... They killed people, they raped, they dug up corpses from their graves. And they attacked us too, of course. As though they were facing down the enemy. They broke our doors in, stormed into our homes, turned the rooms upside down... They threw all our belongings onto the street and our clothing ornamented the pavements for days. They were so vicious, so hateful..."

I didn't know what to say. My heart was overcome with guilt, as if I had been serving at the same police station at that time and failed to fulfill my duties.

"It's good they didn't hurt you," I said, as some small comfort. "It's good you weren't physically injured."

"We could have been." Her blue eyes flickered nervously as if she were reliving those moments. "Yes, we could have. It was that fear that drove my father to Inspector Sezgin... To ask him to help us. The shops on Istiklal were being plundered, the hordes had turned into wild animals and were attacking people in every street. They painted a black cross on the doors of our houses and our lives were in danger. But Sezgin didn't take a blind bit of notice."

Could the old woman be exaggerating?

"How could that be?" I mumbled. "Did the state police pretend not to notice as all hell was breaking loose?"

A bitterness settled into her worldly-wise face.

"You really are a good person, Nevzat. Yes, even pretending not to notice reveals a human compassion. No, Sezgin didn't pretend not to see. He saw everything, but said he wasn't getting involved. My father told me that later, much later, after the houses and shops were ransacked, after people were beaten and molested, when things had calmed. 'I've never seen Sezgin like this,' he said. As if he didn't even know my father. As if he hadn't knocked on our door in the middle of the night when his little girl Ayşe was burning up with

376

fever. He was so cold, so distant. 'They're going to kill us, Sezgin,' my father told him. 'Our honor, our houses, and our lives are in danger.' Inspector Muavini was unmoved. 'Sorry, Monsieur Leonidas,' he said. 'Today I am not a police officer. I'm a patriot, with a national conscience. I can't help any Greeks.' My father's eyes teared up as he recounted this. He was also an upstanding citizen of this country. He paid his taxes, he'd completed his required military service, he met all his obligations, but this civil servant charged with protecting the citizens just looked at the person stood in front of him as though he weren't human and said 'today I'm not doing my job because you aren't Turkish'."

Diogenes sprang to mind... He'd asked me the same question. "Today are you a police officer or a nationalist?" he'd said. I wondered if the poor thing had experienced the same hatred. Been victim to the same barbarism.

"When in reality, my father had always considered himself Turkish," Fofo continued to pour her heart out. "He was in the church choir when he was young. That experience was why he sang the national anthem so beautifully... In the army, his troop commander gave him an award for it. And he bragged about that award till the day he died, despite everything that happened."

I'd heard plenty of stories about the atrocities committed on this soil and each was more unsettling than the last. People had butchered each other over their differences in language, religion, and race. But hearing about this hate from someone who'd been through it made my hair stand on end.

"I'm so sorry," I said, knowing it was no consolation. "There's a man called Diogenes in Tarlabaşı. I think he went through the same thing..."

"Diogenes? I wouldn't know. I've never heard of him."

"The Saint Constantine Church gave him a place. When we came across him the other night, he was going on about some woman and a girl."

"Oh!" she exclaimed dismally. "You must mean Andonis. Poor Andonis..." She shook her head. "His troubles are like no other's. Such a big tragedy, Nevzat. I hope to God it never happens to anyone else... His wife Katerina and daughter

Nana committed suicide together. Katerina was raped on 7 September, in the basement of their apartment building. Later, she realized she was pregnant, but it wasn't clear whether it was from her husband or the result of the rape. They could have found out if they'd wanted to, but I guess neither of them had the courage. They thought the love they felt for each other would get them through it, but it didn't. Andonis began to drop innuendos about it. Katerina couldn't manage more than five years of his laying blame on her. She was already a sensitive person. I've known her since childhood; she was a neighborhood girl. Still, she did her best to rectify the situation. She tried to insist that they leave that area. She thought that maybe if they moved away from Tarlabaşı, her husband's doubts would also go away. But Adonis wouldn't go. His family had a lot of property and possessions, and he couldn't bring himself to leave. Those doubts that gnawed away at her husband's mind and heart began to drive Katerina mad... Like a tree rotting from the inside out, it ate the woman up inside. And nobody noticed. Then one day she wanted to put an end to this hell she was going through. But first, not wanting her daughter Nana to go through the same thing, she gave her sleeping pills. She put them in her soup, then she swallowed a handful herself. One afternoon they found the two curled up together there on the bed..."

She couldn't talk anymore. She covered her mouth with her hand and a tear spilled down her cheek. I sat frozen in my chair. How dumb. What on earth was I doing asking about this man?

"I'm sorry," I said with regret. "I didn't mean to upset you."

She grabbed my wrist and gave it a friendly squeeze.

"It's not your fault." She seemed to feel a bit better. She took a napkin from the table and dabbed at her eyes.

"How could they do such a thing?" I protested. "Why would the neighbors and the friends on your own street put you through this?"

"It wasn't the people in the neighborhood that did it, Nevzat. We shouldn't blame them. It was people from other neighborhoods. It was one of our neighbors who saved us, for example... Yadigâr Hanım... Her young son Behçet had tuberculosis. He was also my father's patient. As soon as they'd heard what happened, they knocked on the clinic door. 'Why are you staying here, Monsieur Leonidas,' they said. 'Take your wife and your daughter and come to our house.' Yadigâr Hanım hosted us for one whole week. She shared our pain and our grief, and comforted us. She wasn't the only one. There were other Turks, and other Muslims, who protected their Greek neighbors. But some of our other Turkish neighbors, especially the poverty-stricken and ignorant ones, didn't hesitate to take up pitchforks, to ransack the Greeks in neighborhoods outside their own... No, Nevzat, they are not to blame. It's the government who provoked them, who set them on us. If it were up to our neighbors, they wouldn't have let any harm come to us. Maybe there were bad eggs among them, but the majority were good. I'm not just saying that; we really would have lived as brothers..."

She dried her wet cheeks thoroughly with the napkin.

"Look, let me tell you a story. A true story... On Easter Sunday, we used to carry lit candles from the Saint Constantine Church to our houses. We'd light up our icons and form a cross from the soot of the candles in the entrances of our homes. It was a sacred ritual for us. As we tried to get the burning candles to our houses, the children from the other streets would try to put them out. And you know who would help us then? Our Turkish Muslim friends..." She smiled sadly. "But then, just as soon as they'd got us to our houses, those same friends who took pains to protect their Christian neighbors would go straight back out to try to blow out the candles of some other neighborhood's Greeks.

"I don't believe people are bad, Nevzat. I'm pushing eighty, and that's the conclusion I've reached. People are neither good nor bad. We have a devil and an angel inside us. Whichever one we wake up, whichever we nurture, that's the one that captures our soul. If the government of the time hadn't infected its citizens with hatred, these atrocities wouldn't have happened, the devil wouldn't have come to the streets, and we'd have lived on as brothers on this land. Yet, whatever possessed them, they incited unrest, using religion and race as an excuse, and forced hatred into our lives. It started with the Fortune Tax for non-Muslims, continued with the events of 6 and 7 September, and lastly there was the Cypress issue in 1964, after which they tore us from our land. Our households, our mothers' and fathers' graves were here. Our hearts were here but we were exiled. Permanently exiled... So, they drove us away, they kicked us out, but what good did it do? Were they deliriously happy? Did the country progress and the city flourish and prosper? On the contrary, regrettably it went down hill. You see the misery in Tarlabaşı. All kinds of poverty, corruption, and manifold depravities... A monstrosity in the middle of the city, my lovely inner-city district seems cursed. But that's what happens; that's what becomes of a place if you uproot its people who haven't done anything wrong. Can happiness be built on the backs of others' misery?"

"Who is building happiness on the backs of others' misery?"

Evgenia's cheerful voice rang in our ears. She must have thought we were discussing something pleasant; it was hard to see in the dusk. "Oh, I see you are bonding quite well," she continued to tease, not waiting for a response. "Go on, tell me, who are these heartless people stealing other people's happiness?"

I didn't know how to answer that. The idea of also upsetting Evgenia with this painful subject bothered me, but our wise Fofo immediately recovered the situation.

"The ladies of the day, who else?" she said, putting on a sarcastic air. "Yes, I am talking about you, you modern women."

She couldn't bring herself to upset Evgenia either. Evgenia just stared at Fofo, unable to figure out what she was on about.

"It used to be there was a bit of elegance to love, an intimacy..." the elderly woman continued to chastise. "Is there anything like that now? Meet a man, sleep with him three days later... It's like that in Athens and in Istanbul... Is that any kind of love? You have to miss a person, and let them miss you, for it to have any value."

My poor lover, who didn't understand what on earth was going on, looked at me for help. But I had no intention of undermining our complicity.

"I'm with Fofo," I said, mustering all my courage. "Without romanticism, there is no love."

Evgenia was slowly becoming irritated.

"What are you talking about, Nevzat dear? Who is rejecting romanticism and love?"

Fofo didn't even listen to her.

"You're comfortable enough," she continued to scold. "You find a man like Nevzat, you'll sit back and enjoy it."

Evgenia gave an unabashed shrug, realizing she wasn't getting out of this.

"Naturally. Why should I care, in such a fleeting world? I've got my sweetheart; it's enough for me." Then she put the green forest of her eyes close enough to my face to make me dizzy. "Welcome, Nevzat," she said, planting a kiss on my right cheek. "Welcome back. This *meyhane* is not the same without you."

"People become more independent when they get used to losing."

※

Fofo was an amazing woman; one of those extraordinary people who you never regret meeting. She didn't used to be like this. She was more introverted, gloomier. So says her daughter Angeliki. She changed as she grew older. "People become more independent when they get used to losing," she said. It was quite a weighty comment, but I wasn't so sure, because I'd seen plenty of people get more selfish as they grew old.

Yes, she spoke Turkish, Evgenia's cousin, but compared to Fofo her accent was quite heavy. She was like a darker version of Evgenia. Wavy black hair, wide pensive eyes, thin but shapely lips, and maybe a bit slimmer build. Hers was a different kind of beauty. The Mediterranean was in her skin, but she didn't have Evgenia's warmth. She was calm, more demure, and she watched people with self-assured repose. It was the same when she spoke. You would never recognize that she was her mother's daughter. Fofo's glass-rattling laughter was one thing and Angeliki's prim smile quite another... Fofo called her daughter Kula. She'd been married and divorced and had no children, but was planning to adopt when she went back to Athens. I was pretty sure she liked me, even though she didn't show it. Throughout the evening, she looked for excuses to talk to me. With Fofo there, it was nearly impossible. The older woman cut loose, perhaps to drive away the pain of the story she'd explained at the beginning of the evening which, having kicked off with sadness, continued on with frivolity and an abundance of song and dance. Just as Evgenia had said, despite her knocking back one or two glasses of raki, my·fellow Tarlabaşist didn't miss a beat. With the encouragement of the Romani musicians from Dolapdere, she even got up and danced at one point. And she wasn't half-bad for her age, with her belly dancing movements. "One day she's going to die like this," I heard Angeliki say, as she cheerfully applauded. "Without even noticing..." She wasn't criticizing her, it sounded more like she wondered what she'd do when her mother was gone.

"That'd be nice," I said to console her. "Aren't we all going to die anyhow? May God grant us all such a death."

She smiled. "Yes, may God grant us all such a death. With my mother's as late as possible..."

The fun went on right up till I left Tatavla. They even played an old Istanbul folk song as a farewell. The song was about Balat, where I lived. It was where I had to go back to. I wouldn't have left Evgenia at that time of night if she'd had no visitors, but we still had a couple more days of self-imposed separation. Evgenia's guests of honor would go back in two days. As I left, they insisted we come visit them in Athens. Fofo planted two noisy kisses on my cheeks and then turned and gave us a strict ultimatum. "Look, Evgenia. Don't come to Athens without this man, and don't say I didn't warn you."

My gracious lover wasn't at all annoyed with becoming second best. "Don't worry, Fofo. I'll bring him along. What business would I have there without him?"

I was a bit tired of the overindulgent chatter by the time I left the beautiful women. The roads had begun to ice over a bit and, although it seemed to slide a few times, my trusty old car made its way down from Saraçhane to my humble abode safe and sound. I'd just walked through the door when my phone rang. It was Ali again. There hadn't been any turmoil in Tarlabaşı. A large crowd had gathered in front of the Galatasaray Lycée in the early evening to protest the death of Fidan. The riot police didn't allow them to march to Taksim, so there was a press release and then everyone cleared out. No attack took place, nor any skirmishes, and no windows were broken... I guess that meant Nazlı and Civan had convinced the demonstrators.

"Maybe they're waiting for the funeral, Chief," my assistant said, still wary. "We'll have to keep on our toes tomorrow, too."

He may be right, but I was more relaxed now that Nizam had gone away. Perhaps their rivals' pain and anger would ease up a bit if they weren't spotted in Tarlabaşı for a few more days.

"Meanwhile, I think this thing with Jale is conclusive." Ali had saved the biggest bombshell for last. I stopped on the stairs.

"Conclusive how?"

"The day two hundred grand was deposited into Tidy's account, the same amount was withdrawn from hers..."

Yes, the pieces were all falling into place, but I wondered why this information had reached him so late at night.

"How did you find that out? Was it from a reliable source?"

"We got it from the bank. Zeynep delegated the job to Süha, who wrote it in his report..."

Was I missing something because I'd been drinking, or was our addle-brain not able to explain?

"Where is Zeynep?"

"Here, with me..." he said, after a short pause. "We hung out in Beyoğlu a while, worried there'd be an incident. And then we came back..." The blabbermouth almost let it slip that they'd gone to his house, but he recovered. "I mean, I answered first so I wanted to tell you what she said too..."

I got the picture; the two new lovers couldn't tear themselves apart from each other. They were using the threat of an incident as an excuse, of course. For a moment it bothered me, their getting up to something behind my back, but then I remembered that I'd just been kicking up my heels with my lover and her relatives in a *meyhane* till all hours of the night, and it dawned on me how misguided my thinking was. I still didn't loosen up though. We were police, after all, and we had to maintain control.

"Give me Zeynep and let her tell me," I said with a voice of authority. "Everyone has a separate task."

She must have been sweating it, or more importantly, was worried she'd get an earful about her mistake.

"You want Zeynep, Chief?" he continued. "I mean, you need to talk to her?"

"Yes, Ali. Isn't she there? Hand her over. I want to ask her about the transaction. She's the one checking into it so don't you think it'd be better if she explained?"

"Of course. You're right, Chief. Here she is."

After another pause, Zeynep's nervous voice could be heard.

"Yes, Chief?"

I was sorry I'd embarrassed her.

"Hi, Zeynep dear. You all right?"

"Fine, thanks. Just a bit tired." As she talked, the tension in her voice disappeared and she became the Zeynep I knew again. "Luckily, there were no run-ins. But we waited it out just to make sure."

She didn't have it in her to tell me they'd sat in some Beyoğlu cafe or bar, cooing away at each other like doves. And my pushing the subject would be pointless.

"This two hundred thousand Jale withdrew, did you just hear about it?"

"Actually, I found out earlier this evening." Her voice was hoarse again. "This new guy, Sefa... The other day another transvestite by the name of Ceylan was murdered in Kadıköy, and the information he gave us on the timing of the murder was lacking. We caught hell from the prosecutor. I told them from now on they have to notify me both verbally and by email. Well, he blew off the calling me part and just sent an email. I didn't manage to get online till midnight. That's why it's late. But the information is correct. Süha got all the records from the bank. She withdrew the money the same day Tidy got his deposit... The account belonged to her husband Rıfat Gümüşova in fact, but because he's not of sound mind, Jale has power of attorney. She's been using the account herself for the last year."

That was good news, but it wouldn't be of any use on its own. It was crucial that the hotel personnel where Tarık stayed could identify Jale.

"Thanks, Zeynep," I said, and left it at that. "Could you hand me Ali again?"

"Right away, Chief."

The poor girl neglected to wish me a good night, she was so nervous. She was stumbling, her head in the clouds.

"Yes, Chief," came our Beyoğlu Romeo's voice again. "What else can I do for you?"

He was being way too formal, as if he were on duty.

"Well, Ali," I said, to loosen him up. "First thing in the morning, you could visit Tarık's hotel again... with the photos. It's important that the man ID Jale. It's all we have to go on. If he recognizes Ihsan as well, it'll make our jobs much easier."

"I know, Chief. Don't worry. We'll have it all sorted out before you even get to the station."

"That'd be great," I said, keeping it brief. "You go on and get some sleep now. Looks like tomorrow will be another tough day. So, good night..."

"Good night." I was going to hang up when his sweetheart whispered something to him. "Zeynep says good night too, Chief."

I had a hard time not laughing.

"All right, all right. Good night to you both."

As I climbed the steps, I thought about Jale. Yes, she had probably been the one to hire Tarık. But was it over jealousy or being robbed? What state of mind led her to order a person killed? A person she was most likely in love with, no less... Jale must have felt incredibly hurt and helpless. Engin not only broke her heart, he also stole her money. Was any man worth all this? I remembered an exchange I'd overheard in my childhood. "Love makes women beautiful," my Aunt Nihan said, after she'd left her husband and gone chasing after a young teacher. "Wrong," my mother had replied, shaking her head. "Love makes women stupid." I don't know if what my mother said was always true, but it certainly applied to my Aunt Nihan. Three years later, the teacher she'd divorced her husband for fell for a younger woman. "What am I supposed to do, Nihan? I'm in love," he told her, worming his way out of it. What happened to Jale reminded me a bit of my Aunt Nihan's story. And then there was Azize. The third segment of this love triangle. This episode's other heroine. Or should I say victim? Really, who did this Engin love, anyhow? Was the connection he felt to Azize real, or would he show her the door when the time came, just as he had Jale? Yes, Engin was a disgrace, but did he deserve to die? That I wasn't sure of. And we still hadn't found his killer. The hitman hadn't done it, obviously. Somebody had beat him to it. His tardiness was what led to his own death. If he had managed to kill Engin first, he'd probably be lying in a warm hotel bed right now, dreaming about how he'd spend the money he got from Jale, rather than in a freezing drawer in the morgue.

"We are the ones stuck in memories."

"What are you looking at, Daddy?"

She was opposite me, standing at the window's edge. The dark brown curtain accentuated her chestnut hair, and her wide eyes looked out mournfully as though to ask, *When are you mortals' ordeals going to end?*

"Aysun," was all I managed to say. "Aysun, daughter."

It was like she didn't hear.

"What you're looking for isn't here," she said earnestly. "Don't wait for nothing." She pointed out to the dark blue night beyond the curtain. "It's out there, on the street."

She suddenly pulled the curtain back and, with an intense buzz, the blue night spilled inside. New Year's Eve... I thought it was the voices of the revelers, but it wasn't. Was it a prayer from a thousand mouths, or a collective sigh? Or maybe an appeal, a unified bid for mercy.

"Come, look," said my daughter. "What you're looking for is among them."

Without noticing how, I found myself there in front of the window she'd summoned me to. Strange, Aysun was in the middle of the room where I'd been. I felt dizzy. I grabbed hold of the curtain and that's when I saw the crowd. The steep slope of a street was packed with people. You could see their unhappiness, helplessness and despair at first glance. The old and the young, women, children... They lumbered up the slope, their heads bent and a murmur on their lips, a hundred meters below the building we were in. I was suddenly aware we were in Tarlabaşı rather than Balat. So this wasn't our home. Where were we, in that case? I looked back at Aysun, whose face maintained its same expression of compassion, its same grief.

"Who are they, Aysun?" I asked. "Why would whatever I'm looking for be with them?"

She gave me an apologetic look.

"You will have to figure that out, Daddy. I have to go."

I was overcome with panic.

"Don't," I said. I knew something bad was going to happen. "Don't go out there; it's chaos."

A broken smile appeared on her pale lips.

"I have to, Daddy. You know I can't stay here. And my friends are waiting at the door."

I involuntarily looked into the street again. They were standing right there in front of our building. There were three of them, three children. One held a violin, another a *darbuka*, and the biggest of them kept his hands in his red leather jacket. Keto, Musti, and Piranha. I could make out the patch on Piranha's right eye, the white bandage on Keto's nose, even in the darkness of the night. They were huddled together, looking round with their usual indifference.

"How do you know them?" I was about to say, but Aysun was gone. Yes, my daughter had disappeared. My gaze hurriedly swept the room but it was empty. I looked quickly back to the street and there she was with the three children. With heavy yet determined steps, they walked toward the approaching crowd. If they mixed into the crowd, I would never find my daughter again. I hurried down the wooden stairs. As I walked out the door, a pungent odor hit me. Maybe the smell of rotting seaweed. That unbearable stink of algae decaying for thousands of years in the overripe waters of the Golden Horn. A stench so unimaginably old it evoked ancient times. So sharp it was as if an invisible wall had fallen onto the street. I ignored it and rushed to catch my daughter who was about to join the crowd. I could see her straight shoulders as she walked confidently with the boys on either side of her. In a few steps, she would be lost in the peculiar crowd. I took off running after them. As I ran, the smell got stronger and I was having difficulty breathing. My temples were throbbing, my head spinning, and I was feeling sick to my stomach. But I ignored all that; I wasn't going to let my daughter get away. I tried to speed up, stumbled and fell face down onto the wet street.

I saw a pair of bare feet and then, when I looked up, a man dressed in white who stood over me. He held out a veiny hand with long, slim fingers. I took it and stood up. He had a pale complexion, wide eyes, long hair and a wispy beard.

"My daughter." I said, meeting his eyes. "Where is she?"

He smiled, and the night seemed to light up.

"Do not worry." His voice was like a sweet breeze. "Aysun is with us."

That's when I noticed that strange crowd behind him. Old and young, women and children, defenseless and forlorn as though depicted by the brush of a medieval artist.

"Who are you?" I said, looking back at the man. "Where are you going with these people?"

My excitement hadn't affected him at all. He rested his idle hand on my shoulder.

"We are the ones who won't rest in peace."

He was speaking in whispers. I thought he was afraid of someone hearing, but his eyes said otherwise. There was not a speck of fear in his chiseled face.

"We are the ones who were killed," he said, with the placid voice of someone who'd accepted their fate. "We are the ones who were plundered and pillaged and sent into exile. We are the ones stuck in memories, the ones who have lost everything... Together, we are going to where we belong.

I didn't understand what he meant, and anyhow I didn't really care. I just wanted my Aysun.

"Where's my daughter?" I shouted, watching the crowd behind him. "What have you done with her?"

"She's one of us," he said, smiling shyly. "She's also one of the half-finished songs..."

His speaking about Aysun as if judging her bothered me.

"That's absurd!" I shouted, pulling my hand and shoulder away from him. "My daughter has nothing to do with you. Where is she? Where is Aysun?"

His face stayed calm, but he neither gave an explanation nor said a comforting word. He just stared with kindness, compassion and pain. I ignored him. I was wasting time and my daughter was getting further away with every passing moment. If I waited any longer, her fate would be like that of these three children; she'd be enmeshed in the ghost buildings of this pain-filled old neighborhood, on these dark streets, these foul-smelling cul-de-sacs. I'd lose her for good. I shoved the man. He showed no resistance but meekly gave way like a green sapling. I ambitiously dove into the crowd. They gently let me through, just as the bearded man had. I walked among them as though they were grains that hadn't yet turned golden. The gaunt, wide-eyed, sallow people swept past me. They could have lived in any era of history. That's how timeless, how indistinct their presence was. Like the bearded man in white, a look of anguish was in their eyes. A stark compassion, pure benevolence, profound grief... I couldn't understand if it was me they pitied or themselves. And that's what made me angry.

"Out of my way!" I shouted, pushing at them. But there was no need. Before I could touch them, they respectfully parted. A narrow path opened in front of me. A path formed by people on either side. I felt suffocated, and that heavy smell of mold returned. My chest contracted with that familiar pressure. I sped up; I had to get beyond this narrow corridor and away from this smell. I had to find my daughter. I broke into a run. But the same thing happened; as I ran the odor got stronger and I couldn't breathe. My temples were pounding and I was getting dizzy again. As the eyes around me watched with pity, I fell into that dark well again.

The snowflakes falling onto my cheeks brought me round. As I opened my eyes, I could see the snowflakes on my lashes.

"Snow," I whispered cheerfully. "It's snowing."

My joy was fleeting. I remembered Aysun; I still hadn't found her. As I stood up, I realized the crowd had withdrawn. That strange mob had suddenly gone. Not just them but Keto, Musti, Piranha and my daughter. I was alone on the sloping street. As I gazed round at the worn stairs, the rotted brick, the burnt wood and the blackened windows, I heard a noise. What was this? The wind? No, it sounded more like water. A voracious gurgle. Finally, I saw that water was rising in the street where the people had been. Not just rising, it was flooding the lower floors in waves, which swept eagerly along, attempting to swallow the buildings whole. The Golden Horn had overflowed and must now be flooding Dolapdere. If it continued like this, Tarlabaşı would be underwater too, and maybe Istiklal Avenue, even Taksim... Overcome with helplessness, the same question came to mind. Where is Aysun? Was she swept into the flood? As I thought this over, I noticed the water was turning red. It had to be from the dirt and rust in the street. I almost breathed a sigh of relief, but then I noticed the red flecks landing on my face. Was something wrong with my eyes? I blinked. Nothing changed; it was as if tiny red butterflies had covered the sky. It wasn't butterflies though, it was the snowflakes that were red. I felt a rising panic but I pulled myself together, telling myself there had to be a reasonable explanation. It was raining mud. The effects of the wind on the dirt and sand around... That had to be it. And I had to stay calm. I opened my palm to the sky, to try and make sense of it. When the flakes fell onto my hand, they melted, leaving red spots. It wasn't mud, it was darker, and a different kind of red. A tremor of fear passed through me. "Blood?" As the question left my lips, the snow dissolved into rain. Huge drops began to rain down on me in buckets. But they were the same color, that deep red. My hair, my eyes, and my clothes were all bathed in blood. I struggled to get away from the godforsaken red substance, to run into one of the old buildings for shelter. But I couldn't even move. I was stuck in place as though I'd stepped into tar. I looked towards my feet, and saw that the water was rising quickly. I tried again, if only for a few seconds, to escape the water wetting my fingertips. It was impossble; I couldn't move my limbs. The water came up to my throat, my chin, and then as it reached my lips there was the smell of mold again. Everywhere was immersed in that smell, my body, my face, my hair, my breath, even my thoughts... I suddenly realized I was becoming that horrific stench. The red water filled my nostrils, and I had no choice but to cry out in horror.

I was woken by my own scream. I sat up in bed and gasped for air. It was another of those nightmares I sometimes had... I sat still until my breathing returned to normal. When I'd recovered, I rolled over to get out of bed, and that's when I saw it: the picture hanging on the wall in its brown frame. Aysun's big eyes were on me, just like in the dream, looking out as if to ask, *When are you mortals' ordeals going to end?*

"The figments of a novelist's imagination are always worth listening to."

✳

The shadow of the man tapping gently on the car window fell across my face. As I turned to look, my blood froze. It was my own face looking back at me. What was happening? Was I starting to have waking nightmares? It didn't take long for me to realize I'd been mistaken. It was the strange author at the car window. I was annoyed with myself. He was grinning and circling his finger madly in the air. If I'd just had breakfast at home instead of getting my heart set on a cheese toast and tea at the station, I wouldn't have bumped into this busybody.

"Yes?" I said, frowning. "What can I do for you?"

He pointed at the window then started circling his finger again. "Open the window," he said, because he couldn't hear me. I guess that meant that despite the warm shower and strong coffee, I hadn't fully woken up yet. With an irritated huff, I rolled the window down half way.

"Yes, what is it?"

Despite my grumpiness, he didn't look offended.

"I wanted to ask about Bahtiyar's vaccinations," he said politely. "Which ones has he had, I wonder?"

This was what it meant to blush with shame.

"I don't know, really... I don't actually think he's had any. Demir used to look after him before he died. We haven't taken him to the vet since then."

He shook his head, though not with blame or condescension.

"Okay, that's good to know. In that case, they'll start a program for everything he's missing."

That's when I heard Bahtiyar's impatient grunt. He barked sweetly as if to say 'I'm here, too'. I rolled the glass down all the way.

"Bahtiyar! What are you doing, boy?"

He greeted me with a louder bark. I reached out to stroke his head. His fur was soft and he wagged his tail with pleasure, the rascal. Seemed this neighbor I was so down on had taken care of our boy quite well.

"Thank you so much," I said, turning back to the author. "I won't forget the favor."

He immediately started acting like a big man.

"It's nothing, Nevzat Bey. You don't have to thank me. Like you said, Bahtiyar is a friend of all of ours. I was going to stop by this evening, in fact, but you weren't around. I guess you were at Evgenia Hanım's..."

Here we go again. I screwed my eyes up and stared at the man stood there on the pavement.

"I'm sorry, but what does it matter where I spent my evening? Whether I go to Evgenia's or to another friend, what difference is it to you?"

He quickly took a step back.

"I'm sorry. Please don't read anything into it; I was just conjecturing. Of course it makes no difference to me."

Always the same tactic. First a grilling, then if he gets a reaction, he backs off. If he gets none, he delves deeper.

"Look," I said calmly. "I really don't know you. I haven't read a single one of your books. Not that I'm not interested, actually. I like detective stories, and I plan to start reading one as soon as I wrap up this case I'm working on. But I'd appreciate it if you could give me a bit of space. I know your intentions are good. Maybe you're just looking for material for your book, or taking an interest in me in order to create a more believable character, but it puts me on edge. You have to understand, I really don't like this kind of thing. I prefer to live calmly, quietly..."

He listened carefully without taking issue.

"Whatever you say. You're right, of course," he pronounced, with the same gentlemanliness. "Yes, mine is a professional interest. I'm not going to hide it; its because of my novel I'm following you. A purely artistic interest. But if it makes you that uncomfortable, I promise I'll leave you alone... We'll be moving away from here pretty soon anyhow. We're going back to Şişli."

He saw my look of disbelief.

"Really, don't you worry." He got that secretive expression again. "I have a small gift for you to make amends. You'll get it today or tomorrow."

Frankly, I didn't want to forgive him and I didn't want a gift; it was enough that he left me alone.

"Thanks," I said anyhow, so as not to be rude. "And I wish you all the best."

Without dragging it out, I rolled up the window of my faithful old car, turned the key in the ignition, and was just stepping on the gas when he knocked on the glass again. I opened the window before he could sign with his finger.

"Sorry," he began. "You may get annoyed again, but it's the last thing I'm going to say..." He leaned in and all but whispered. "In Shakespeare's play Julius Caesar, a soothsayer warned, 'Beware the ides of March, Caesar.' You know, Caesar was stabbed to death in the senate on March 15th? Well, I feel compelled to tell you to beware the third of January."

It was so ridiculous, what he said, that I burst out laughing.

"When exactly is the third of January?"

"It's today, unfortunately."

No, he wasn't joking. He meant what he said.

"Beware of the third of January, Nevzat Bey... Please don't ask what I mean by that, and don't concern yourself with my source, but at the same time don't brush off the warning. The figments of a novelist's imagination are always worth listening to."

When he'd finished, he walked away with Bahtiyar before waiting for my response.

He had to be insane. Maybe he was after a new game. Whatever he did, he would somehow form a bond with me. No, this author wasn't going to leave me alone. I guess I should have been harsher. I should've openly warned him... "Beware of the third of January" was it? Lord help me, I thought to myself as I stepped on the gas. As my tired old friend lurched forward, the weather suddenly got dark. The sky, bathed in sunlight since I'd opened my eyes, was suddenly covered in inky black clouds as if foretelling some looming catastrophe. I remembered Shakespeare's plays. You know, how without reason a storm breaks, foreshadowing disaster? I shivered. Then I got cross with myself again for letting the strange author get under my skin. The man was slowly losing his mind. I turned from the back streets of Balat onto the main road along the Golden Horn. I leaned in and looked up at the sky through the windshield again. There was no precipitation but the sun, nearly smothered by the blue-black clouds, had lost its golden color and become a big red blob. Where on earth had this writer popped up from so early in the morning? The guy had destroyed my peace of mind. No, I wouldn't be able to relax. I pulled my phone out and punched in Ali's number.

"Good morning, Chief."

He sounded so lively, the scoundrel.

"Good morning, Ali. What's up?"

"We're just getting our things together and will be out of here in a minute. We were looking over the results from Harem Süleyman's knife.... Just a sec, Chief." His voice grew distant. "What did you say, Zeynep? No, the blade had no trace of the victim's blood, or anybody else's. It was clean..."

I won't lie. I was quite happy to hear Harem wasn't our murderer. Maybe he was no pillar to society, but I still wouldn't want the giant to rot in jail.

"Good. What's the situation in Tarlabaşı? Any news?"

"It's calm. So far no reports of any conflicts or disturbances."

I silently thanked Nazlı and Civan again. Black Nizam and his nephews weren't around, so it looked like things were back to normal.

"After we stop by the hotel, should we take Jale into custody, Chief?" Ali asked. "The woman is a suspect, no matter what."

"That's true enough. Even if the receptionist doesn't positively ID her, she still has to account for that two hundred thousand lira. But the woman was on her way to Ankara yesterday, don't forget."

"Oh, that's right. She was supposed to head back to Istanbul later today. She should be here this evening, or maybe tomorrow..."

"Don't worry about it. You go on to the hotel and see what the man has to say. We'll meet back at the station after that. Have you got Ihsan's photo on you? To show the receptionist, I mean."

"Yep, Chief. We pulled it from his file. And it's a recent one, at that. If he's the one who talked to Tarık, he'll recognize him for sure."

"Right, good luck to you then."

"Thanks, Chief. You too."

No matter how dark the sky got, nothing bad was going to happen like that prophet-of-doom author had purported. I put my phone in my pocket and reached for the radio, turning the dial. The car was filled with lighthearted music. The fiddler Tatyos Efendi's *saz* in the *kürdilihicazkâr* style... My pessimism melted away. I tapped on the steering wheel and abandoned myself to the harmony of the music. To think they used to look down on it because it was palace music, when really it had such a lovely resonance. The song changed as I reached the Unkapanı Bridge. The work of a great musician from another minority had begun. It was Udi Hrant's *hicaz* song, and his vocals as well. The program must have been devoted to minority composers. Minorities... I recalled what Fofo had told me the night before. "So they drove us away, they kicked us out, but what good did it do? Were they deliriously happy? Did the country progress and the city flourish and prosper?" No, quite the opposite. It got worse. That great empire extinguished the colors of culture one by one: our music, our literature, our cuisines, our architecture, our clothing, our words... Everything that our lives were made up of just fell away. Our lives were made poorer. The Greeks of Balat, our Jewish neighbors, our mutual friendships, our conversation... And that shadow that occasionally appeared in their faces... All thanks to the sentiments of men like the inspector who'd said, "Today I am not police, but a patriot with a national conscience." Maybe it was wrong to blame him, when he'd been egged on by the racist poison of the politicians and the government administrators... Another song began. The fiddler Sarkis Efendi's unforgettable piece... It was my lucky day; it was hard to come across songs like this on the radio. I couldn't work out the female soloist's voice. As the song went on, my phone began to intrusively ring. I frowned and answered it. Strange, it was Swank Cemal calling. I'd thought he was upset, and was happy to see we were still on speaking terms.

"Hello, Cemal!"

"Thank god I reached you, Nevzat."

There was urgency in his voice. He didn't give me a chance to ask before starting in.

"There's gonna be a fight. They're going to kill each other."

He was talking so fast I couldn't understand what he was saying.

"Where's the fight? Who's going to kill who?"

"Ihsan and Black Nizam, who else? That maniac found out his wife met with Ihsan. He called Ihsan and went mental on him."

"How did he hear they met up?" I asked him, surprised.

"Maybe that hairdresser Tebernüş told him. That's where Çilem met Ihsan yesterday. Tebernüş is a loudmouthed bastard. And he's close to Nizam. When Nizam heard his new wife and his old enemy got together, he went ballistic. He called Ihsan straight away. He told him, 'If you have one iota of manhood in you, I'll be waiting for you at the coffeehouse in Tarlabaşı.' Ihsan tried to take it on the chin, but his rival wouldn't let up. He openly provoked him, saying, 'If you don't come down here, I'll put you in a skirt and have a cuddle with you instead of Çilem tonight."

He must have been blind with rage, Nizam. He didn't give a damn anymore, not about Fidan's friends attacking and not about my warnings.

"So, did Ihsan agree to go down there?" I asked, with one last hope.

"How could he not? If he didn't, he'd never be able to show his face again. Not to mention, Nizam would never leave him alone. He'd corner him somewhere for sure and settle up with him. Ihsan would lose his honor and his life."

Would you look at this. While we were busy worrying about the young activists, the mafia bosses had laid into each other.

"So when were they supposed to meet?"

"Ihsan was just about to leave the club. It won't be half an hour before guns are blazing. I ordered some influential men down to Mizgin's. Nizam will listen to them. But it will take a while for them to get there so it's all up to you and me, Nevzat. If we can delay this confrontation, we'll stop the bloodshed too."

His voice was pleading.

"All right. I'm pretty close to there anyhow. I'm about to cross the Unkapanı Bridge. I'll be in Tarlabaşı within five minutes."

"Thank god. They'll back off if you get there. I'll intervene too. We'll put on a show and keep people from being killed.

"Agreed. I'm on my way," I said, hanging up the phone.

As I dialed Ali again, I looked back up to the sky. The sun was blood red now and the clouds were growing darker and darker as though warning me of the impending disaster.

"The devil has put his own stamp on Tarlabaşı."

I saw Dice Ihsan as I turned the corner. His camel-colored jacket open and his right hand in his pocket, he walked resolutely alongside his most trusted man, Flea Necmi. The three bodyguards I'd met at the Tarlabaşists Club followed two steps behind them. All their jackets were open, in fact, and they each had a right hand in their pockets. You didn't have to be a psychic to understand what they held in their palms. The small square was as dismal as the bullet-grey sky. Still, I was thankful I'd got there before a fight had broken out. I'd been stuck in traffic in Tepebaşı and had almost given up hope, but luckily the jam was a small one and by some miracle the street suddenly emptied out. It didn't look too likely that Ali and Zeynep would get there before me; they'd only managed to get as far as Elmadağ, they informed me in a second call. I couldn't rely on the police teams we'd notified. They'd be there eventually, but the important thing was for them to arrive before the guns went off and blood was shed. Then again, even if Ali had warned them not to go there alone, under these circumstances waiting didn't seem right to me either. I mean, we'd switched roles with my foolhardy assistant this time. What could I do? Every passing minute was strengthening the hand of the angel of death. I hastily floored the gas and turned down Kalyoncukulluğu Street from behind the British Consulate. I ignored the objections of the street's greengrocer and left my car in front of his shop. As the man continued to grumble, I had to flash my badge and tell him, "Calm down, I'll be right back." Rushing into the street next to the Saint Constantine Church, I still hoped to make it to Nizam's coffeehouse before guns were fired. It was no laughing matter; every second counted. I got to the short street in no time, and things were going pretty much as I'd planned. But as I was entering the street that opened onto the square, that poor deranged man suddenly stood in front of me. Yes, Diogenes, whose real name was Adonis. When he saw me, he spread his arms and tried to prevent me from passing.

"Don't go!" he said in a panic. "Don't go. They'll kill you. They killed them, and they will kill you."

His hair was all mussed up and his eyes full of horror. Was I late, I wondered? Had the fight already started and the poor old guy got stuck in the middle? But I would have heard gunfire in that case.

"Who? Who is going to kill me?"

Without raising his head, he gestured toward the square with his eyes.

"That demon... That demon cast out of heaven... He's waiting for you at the heart of the street..." His crazy eyes, looking like they'd pop out of their sockets, stopped on my face again. "Don't you understand, the devil has come to the street. Evil has been set free. There is sin all around... Run away. Don't go in there, whatever you do."

I grabbed his arms and pulled them down to calm him.

"Nothing's going to happen to me." I put on a reassuring smile. "Today I am just police. You understand? Just an officer serving my citizens."

He gave me a look of helplessness.

"It doesn't matter anymore. Whether you are police or a regular person, it doesn't matter. It's far too late. This area's cursed. The devil has put his own stamp on Tarlabaşı. Whatever you do, don't go there..."

I wondered which busybody shop owner or nasty teenager had scared the poor man. But I had no time to deal with that now.

"Don't worry, no one is going to kill me," I said, trying to calm him. "I have a gun. And the other officers will be here soon. Go on. You go on to the church now, Adonis. We'll sit and have a chat later..."

He hesitated as if finding what I'd said odd.

"Adonis?" He shook his head quickly. "No, Adonis is gone. Adonis took his wife and daughter and went to Athens. I'm not Adonis. I'm Diogenes... In search of light..."

He slowly set off.

"You're wrong. I'm not Adonis. He had a wife, and a daughter. They slandered her... But Adonis was a good man. He didn't listen to all the gossip. He grabbed his wife and daughter and went to Athens." He was getting further away. "Adonis was my friend. We lived in the same house and went to the same school. He sends me a letter from Athens sometimes. No, I'm not Adonis. I've never had a wife or a child... They all went off together. The three of them..."

I left the unfortunate man to battle it out with his guilty conscience and rushed off. As I turned the corner, the square unfolded there before me. That's when I realized that nearly every facet of this murder investigation was here. Engin's house was there on my right on Kadın Çıkmazı, Nizam's coffeehouse was a hundred meters up the road, and the Ferhat Çerağ Culture Center was at the top of the street that opened onto the square. Ihsan may also have a house or a building he'd bought around here. I wondered if this would be where the chain of events unraveled. It was impossible to glean from Ihsan's face, as step by step he approached his enemy. I had to admit, the tough guy had more heart than I'd imagined. Maybe my words had had an effect on him. "Nizam loves Çilem more than you do," I'd said. "He's braver, more passionate." But no, no one would go to their death over the sentiments of a chief inspector they hardly knew. Talking to Çilem had emboldened him. His pride couldn't handle being a coward in the eyes of the woman who loved him. His gait was dauntless, his head held up and his eyes focused on some point ahead. Then I saw Nizam, standing at that exact place where Dice was staring, in front of the coffeehouse. He couldn't see me as his eyes were on his enemies. His two favorite nephews were by his side, Kudret, who had been released the night before, and his twin Medet. Strange, hadn't he summoned any of his other twenty-one nephews? Was it because he wanted a fair fight? I doubted that. As far as I knew Nizam, there was only winning; it didn't matter how. For a moment I thought positively, that perhaps he wasn't looking for a fight at all. Was he just trying to intimidate Ihsan and ask him to keep away from his wife? But I quickly overcame the foolish notion; everything had got out of hand. This square would see no compromise without outside intervention. I found it odd that Swank Cemal was nowhere to be seen. Shouldn't he have made it here long before me? And that's when I realized there was no one around besides these eight people who had no qualms about chopping each other to bits.

The market's lights had been turned off, the hardware store on the corner had left its goods out on display and closed the iron bars, the carpenter had pulled down its shutters, the barber disappeared into thin air, and the intercity bus ticket agent had probably not opened to begin with today. Only the coffeehouse where Nizam stood was open. His own venue, where he'd invited Ihsan to come and see him. But he'd chosen to wait for his mortal enemy outside rather than in, for whatever reason.

Hands locked behind him and legs splayed, he waited confidently and motionlessly for his opponent to reach him. There was not twenty meters distance between them, and about seventy or eighty between me and the coffeehouse. I took out my gun and, after loading it, stuck my right hand into my coat pocket just like Dice Ihsan. First there would be an overture, 'you did this and I did that' and such. After that altercation it would be clear whether the hostility would end in battle or conciliation. That's the moment we'd have to intervene. But Swank was nowhere to be seen! If I didn't know him, I'd say he'd chickened out after calling me, but he would never behave so cowardly. He wouldn't run away from a fight even if there was death at the end of it. What could I do? Without him, it looked like I'd be solving this business all by myself. I quickened my steps, but Ihsan and Nizam had already come face to face. They were three, four meters apart now, at best. Their men stood lined up behind them. Ihsan took a step forward, his right hand still in his pocket.

"You told me to come down, well here I am," he said in a sonorous voice. "I'm right here in front of you... Say what you have to say."

Nizam looked Dice over carefully as if seeing him for the first time. It was like a film in slow motion... But his hands stayed behind him; he wasn't a bit impressed with his opponent standing there in front of him.

"Aren't you ashamed of yourself, messing with another man's honor?" he asked, calmly but confidently. "Where do you get off meeting up with my wife? Is that any way for a young man, for a human being, to behave?"

Ihsan didn't take his eyes off his enemy for a second.

"Your wife loves me," he answered, his voice full of vengeance. "I am her first love..."

These were the words that broke Nizam's composure, and he pulled apart the fingers behind his back.

"Shut your mouth!" he growled. "You are a lying sack of shit! Don't you go dragging my wife's name through the mud!"

Nizam's movement had made Ihsan anxious as well. The determination in his eyes disappeared but he didn't back down.

"Actually, it's you who's the liar," he shouted. "You played her, lured her into your web... Çilem never wanted you."

Nizam wasn't the least bit scared. He took another step towards Ihsan.

"She's my wife... She'll be my wife in this world and the next. But you committed a crime, you've sinned, you toyed with someone's honor. And you will pay dearly for it." He was talking less with anger than with the confidence of a judge certain of his verdict. "You will pay for your sins now, but I won't let up in the other world either. I don't know when that will come to pass, but whenever I reach it, I'll see you burn in the most furious corner of hell!"

Ihsan looked at him with loathing.

"I don't doubt we'll meet there. But you'll be there first, not me." All at once, he pulled his hand from his pocket. He turned a large gun, the mark of which I couldn't discern, onto Nizam. "Go on. Talk away."

Things were spinning out of control. I pulled my pistol and shouted, "Stop! Ihsan stop! Don't do it!"

The lines of street warriors facing each other off turned to look at me, the same look of shock in each of their faces. Everybody stood there as if frozen in time. Nizam spoke first.

"Chief, what are you doing here?"

He didn't seem concerned about the gun trained on him; it was more like he was complaining that my presence here had disrupted his business.

"All right, Nizam. All right, stay calm, friends." I turned to Dice. "Ihsan, put the gun down. Let's sit and talk this out like human beings."

Ihsan gestured towards Nizam with the barrel of the gun.

"This guy doesn't understand about being human, Chief. You should stay out of this. It gets solved today. It's him or me..."

Nizam continued to stare at me as if he wasn't hearing him.

"That simpleton Swank called you, didn't he?"

Why was Nizam so fixated on my being here? There were four men opposite him, and it was a matter of seconds before Ihsan would pull the trigger, but there was no trace of fear on his face. He just shook his head hopelessly.

"This dog is right. It gets solved today." He raised his right hand into the air and extended an index finger. "It's him or me," he said, lowering it again. Just then, the gun went off. Two shots in a row. I watched as Ihsan's tall thin frame shook. No, it wasn't his gun that went off. He didn't even get the chance. As he fell to his knees, he turned to look at the closest man to him, Flea Necmi. That's when I saw the gun in the pocket-sized Hercules' hand. No one else had one. Everyone had frozen. Even more shocking to me were the other three bodyguards, who just stood there silently watching him collapse to the ground as if it weren't their boss who'd been shot. Ihsan was the victim of a heinous set-up. A nasty trap laid by his own men. No doubt they were the ones to plant the unlicensed gun as well. It could've been Flea Necmi himself.

He'd also be the one who whispered in Nizam's ear the day before, because he knew about his boss meeting Çilem at Tebernüş' barber shop. Poor Dice. The look he was giving Necmi, whom he'd trusted like a brother, cursing him as the two bullets grew heavier in his torso and death approached. As he watched him, everything that had gone down sank in. Black Nizam had bought out every one of his men.

"Drop your weapon," I said, pointing my pistol barrel at Necmi. "Drop it."

The traitor wasn't sure how to react so he turned to look at his new boss. He would've done whatever Nizam told him to, but it didn't come to that. There was another blast. Ihsan had taken us all by surprise, pulling his trigger again and again with every last bit of strength and rage he had in him. Flea Necmi's half-portioned body flew back one full meter under the affects of the bullets hitting him. Nizam lunged forward and landed a whopping kick into Dice's back.

"Stop!" I shouted again. "Stop, Nizam!"

He turned to throw me a look of hatred, but without giving it a second thought, reached in and pulled out his gun. I wouldn't have another chance to shoot him, and I was ready to pull the trigger when I felt as if a car had smashed into me. I leaned forward as everything around me began to spin. The world going dark... I fell onto my knees as Ihsan had, but I was having difficulty holding my head up. I wasn't able to stay that way long; I gently crumbled to the ground. My eyes were open and I could still vaguely make out what was going on. Nizam didn't waste any more time on me; he took a couple steps back over to Ihsan. He leaned over his rival, and looking him in the eye, said, "You mess with Black Nizam's honor, you die."

He pulled the trigger another three times. I saw Ihsan's skull shatter to bits and blood splattered the hand Nizam held his gun in, painting it red. I tried to sit up. A large foot stepped on my face. A huge boot with mud on the bottom smashing into my right cheek. I looked askance at the face; the young man who'd blindsided me was standing there with a dirty grin. It was one of Nizam's nephews, one of the jackals from the night before in the *ocakbaşı*. He'd probably noticed me when I first came into the square. Nizam's horrid face obscured my view of the young man who had lured me into his trap. He got down on his knees and put his ugly mug right up to mine.

"You weren't supposed to be here," he complained. "Why did you come here, Chief?" The stench of cigarettes from his mouth overbore the smell of blood. "Believe it or not, I liked you. There is something about you that the other cops don't have."

I didn't give a damn about his testimonial. The boot gradually got heavier.

"But I'm afraid I'll have to kill you. You saw me shoot Ihsan." He laughed quietly. "I would spare you if I knew I could solve this with a bribe..." He passed his gun to his left hand and took out his silver cigarette case. He pulled one out. His nephew leaned down and lit it for him. As he did so, he stepped even harder on my face. I felt the bones being crushed. Nizam took two deep puffs on his cigarette. As the smoke rose from his cavernous nostrils, he asked, "What do you say, Chief? Money's not enough to make you look the other way, is it? You won't forget what you saw, will you?" He looked up with futility. "No, you wouldn't. You won't even stoop to lying..."

He took another drag off his cigarette and the smoke twisted up through the small square again. He shot me a look of regret, then settled his cigarette onto his lip. As he took his gun into his right hand and stood up, the words of that peculiar author rang in my ears. "Beware the third of January, Nevzat Bey!" What, was he right? Could he have known I was going to die? I wasn't so upset about dying as I was about that damned author being right.

"No sense in dragging it out, is there, Chief?" the ruthless tough guy carried on. "This is as far as it goes, so farewell..." With one final effort, I looked over at my gun, lying a meter or so beyond me. It wouldn't be possible to reach for it with this big guy standing over me. And just then I saw the silhouettes coming up the stumpy street I'd only just entered.

"Man, isn't that our Chief Inspector Nevzat?"

Was it Keto or Piranha talking? My head was all mixed up so I couldn't tell.

"Holy fuck! What are you guys doing?"

Nizam saw the boys as well.

"What are these little bastards doing here?" he said, turning to his nephews. "Is this how you watch the street?"

His nephews were hemming and hawing to come up with an explanation, but Piranha didn't give them the chance. "Leave the Chief alone!" he cried out.

His voice came out so shrill. Though I didn't have the slightest hope of surviving, a whistling sound could suddenly be heard throughout the square and then a small bird split the ashen sky in two and dove into Nizam's spiky hair. First there was the smell of thinners, after which was a bright flash. And there in front of my eyes, the mafia boss lit up like a torch. A stench of burning hair, flesh, and fabric all at once filled the air. Yes, the fire that had started in his hair had spread over his whole body in the blink of an eye. I looked over and saw Piranha, his red jacket on his back and his right hand clenched into a fist, running over to rescue me with Keto one step behind and Musti bringing up the rear, as usual. But the boys only managed a few paces because that's how long it took the twin nephews to get over the shock of their uncle igniting. Kudret and Medet had already drawn their guns and were firing away in a rage... Piranha was the first to go down, followed by Keto, and Musti just managed to throw himself into the doorway of the building next to him. Thankfully, the nephew stood over me finally managed to come to his senses and remove his foot from my face. Taking off his jacket, he ran to extinguish his uncle. I quickly reached out for my gun and pulled the trigger without warning. Kudret collapsed first, then Medet. The third nephew, seeing where he'd gone wrong, abandoned his dying uncle and went for his gun. I shook my head from where I lay on the ground.

"Don't even think about it!"

At a loss for what to do, he looked from me to his uncle, who writhed on the ground in flames.

"Get down on the ground!" I shouted. "Get down, quick!"

I hadn't actually been talking to them, but Ihsan's three bodyguards, who'd nearly swallowed their little tongues from shock, dropped their guns and lay down along with the third nephew. As they did, I pushed myself up with my left hand.

As the three bodyguards got down, Nazlı's large frame came into view, a baseball bat in her hand and Civan right behind her. The small chair he'd lugged over was now raised into the air as if he was going to bring it down on someone's head. The tea boy, Memo, stood a few steps beyond them. He'd taken a paring knife from the kitchen to come to my rescue as well.

"Nevzat Bey... Are you all right?" Nazlı asked as she approached.

My head was throbbing and I felt queasy, but it was nothing to exaggerate.

"I'm fine... I'm fine Nazlı Hanım."

I turned to where Piranha and Keto had fallen.

"But the kids..."

Nazlı followed my gaze.

"Oh!" Her face contorted and her left arm went limp and dropped the bat. "Oh no, the boys..."

It was a pitiful scene. Piranha had fallen onto his left side, as if the red of his leather jacket had turned to blood, which slowly spread on the pavement of the small square. He must have died before hitting the ground, perhaps with the first bullet. As for Keto, only his curly-haired head was visible. His body was slumped over his friend's just so, on Piranha's right leg, as though he'd found himself a comfortable pillow and fallen sleep. Musti's position was the saddest of all. No, he hadn't been shot, thank the lord for small mercies. He just stood there, staring in bewilderment at the corpses of his two friends.

"Leave it to you men to relate death to love."

✺

Under the dim light of the interrogation room, my head was still throbbing as Jale sat in a chair opposite mine. I should be thankful; our kids had feared it was worse. Zeynep saw I was still sick and got worried there may be brain hemorrhaging. She'd insisted that I stay the night under observation. Ali blamed himself for what happened. When he also pushed the subject, I was almost convinced. Luckily, as darkness fell, the sickness all at once subsided. Otherwise they'd have put me in the bed next to Swank Cemal's. Yes, Istanbul's best-dressed tough guy was in the hospital. He acted just as I'd expected. He hadn't run away, and his only crime was arriving at the coffeehouse before me. Nizam was ready to solve the problem of Dice at its root, so when he saw Swank there he got worried the gig was up and he set his twin nephews on him. The old bird didn't even get a chance to draw his gun. The two young men laid into him hard, this man who was their father's age. They didn't let up till he lost consciousness. We found Cemal in the pantry after it was all over. The poor guy still wasn't himself; he sat all bloodied and cringing in the hole he was thrown into, neither swanky nor handsome anymore. He'd broken two front false teeth and three ribs on his right side. The doctor had seen his situation was serious and ordered a tomography, which luckily had come out clean. He said it wasn't critical and that with bed rest he should recover in a week. What really affected me though was Cemal's words when he woke. "You were way too late, Nevzat."

I wasn't the only latecomer, of course. Ali and Zeynep came minutes after the guns were silent, and after them were the police teams. The wimpy Sami and huge-headed Zeynel we'd seen on New Year's were among them. They had stared at the corpses on the ground in a panic. Two of the men they regularly took bribes off were gone. The officers' faces were overcome with anxiety, especially upon seeing Nizam's charred body. They were wondering if this would make trouble for them. They didn't even dare come over to me.

Nizam had shrewdly distributed his nephews among all the entrances to the streets and we'd picked up nineteen of them in one go. Having bought off Flea Necmi and Dice's other three men, he'd trusted himself so much that he must not have asked them to stay with him, and thought he'd call them if anything went wrong. What went wrong was me, but he didn't take this middle-aged chief inspector too seriously. And I wasn't overly broken up about Nizam, Dice, Necmi, or the two crazy youth having died from my gun's bullets. It would have been better if they hadn't died, naturally, but guns went off and I couldn't prevent it. The kids, however... Those anonymous ghosts of the streets, those unclaimed children for which we were all to blame... Piranha and Keto... Piranha's real name had been Ömer. Ömer Güzelsöz. And Keto's was Kerim Caner. The two had similar stories. A story of children inured to loss. A fact of life that we just met with *How sad!* and then forgot about. The mothers of both worked in a brothel. Yes, Piranha's did also. Maybe that was why he hung out with Keto, to mask his shame... Piranha's father was killed in a blood feud, and Keto's had up and left his son and wife years ago. Both children were abandoned by the closest people to them, and having been discarded by society, they took shelter on the streets. They thought they'd have a chance in these houses where cursed memories run rampant, in this neighborhood abandoned in much the same way they were. But these streets, these dilapidated buildings, only managed to protect them up until this morning... I couldn't get Nazlı's words out of my head, as she knelt beside Keto stroking his

412

curly locks. "We couldn't do it, Nevzat Bey,' she'd said, as tears streamed down her face. "We failed them again."

But life went on. I'd spent the night with a headache, and the following morning we brought in Jale Hanım and her lawyer Batuhan and were still trying to find Engin's murderer.

"You withdrew two hundred thousand lira," I said, trying to ignore the pain that occasionally flared in my neck. "From your husband Rıfat Bey's account..."

"That account is Jale Hanım's too," the young lawyer cut in. He was sitting opposite Ali, and was uncomfortable with my assistant's glowering at him. Before the talk even started, he'd begun to flip his gold-plated pen in irritation. "Yes, Nevzat Bey, there is nothing illegal in her withdrawing that money."

I locked my hands on the yellow envelope in front of me.

"I'm sure that's true. But what concerns me most is not Jale Hanım's withdrawing the money; it's that the same day, the same amount was deposited into one Tarık Seberci's account."

Jale's hazel eyes flashed.

"What? So you are keeping me here over a coincidence?"

"No," I calmly answered. "I'm keeping you here to shed some light on the chain of events leading to the death of ten people."

She shifted uneasily in her chair.

"I see. But what does that have to do with me? My only crime was to pull out two hundred thousand lira. Was I the only one in this massive city of Istanbul to pull out two hundred thousand that day?"

"No," said Ali, joining the conversation. "I'm sure dozens of people withdrew that same amount." He put his right elbow down on the table and stretched an index finger towards the woman. "But you are the only one in this massive city of Istanbul who held a grudge for Engin, knew Tidy Tarık, *and* withdrew two hundred thousand lira."

The proverbial arrogance of this prima donna was raising its head again, but the chubby-faced lawyer came to her rescue.

"Let's say all these assumptions were true, Nevzat Bey." He was speaking to me, as he didn't like Ali. "It hasn't even been established that it was Tarık Seberci who killed Engin Akça. Am I wrong? You still haven't found your killer."

He was right. Ten people had died already but we still hadn't figured out who set it all off by killing Engin. Maybe it was Black Nizam, as Çilem had told Ihsan. Or maybe it was Dice Ihsan himself. All we had were possibilities, just a lot of very compelling scenarios...

I opened the envelope in front of me, took out three sheets of paper, and handed them to Jale. She and her lawyer both had a nervous look in their eyes as they wondered what the papers could be.

"Arslan Yankı..." I went quiet for a moment, to savor it. "You don't know him, Jale Hanım. In fact, you've seen him, but you didn't pay him any mind." I put the paper down in front of her. "I'm talking about the receptionist at the Rikkat Hotel. You went there exactly twice. You met with Tarık both times, once in the lobby and once in the breakfast room. And at both of those meetings, there was a third person with you..."

The confidence in her eyes gave way to panic. I enthusiastically continued.

"Ihsan Yıldızeli, otherwise know as Dice Ihsan. The man who was killed last night by one of his own, Flea Necmi. Ihsan, the owner of the Tarlabaşists Club, the venue where you gamble, that is. And your confidant, perhaps."

The lawyer considered whether or not to object, but when his client stayed silent, he decided against it.

'Yes, Ihsan was a close friend. Close enough for you to talk over private matters with. But more importantly, he was Engin's archenemy. Most probably, he was the one who convinced you to have Tarık kill Engin."

Jale just stared, unsure what to say, but her lawyer quickly recovered from the shock.

"Couldn't Arslan Yankı be mistaken? Dozens of people walk through the door of the hotel daily. How can he be so sure it was Jale Hanım and Tarık meeting there?"

Ali pulled a small envelope from his jacket pocket.

"We had the same reservations, sir." There was a sarcastic ring to the way he said 'sir'. "We thought the man could be mistaken, so we got the images off the hotel's security cameras." He handed a CD to the lawyer. "Give it a watch, and you'll see too." He turned to Jale and gave her an almost flirtatious smile. "You look very stylish in your green coat and gold scarf. Just like a movie star."

The look of defeat in Jale's face grew worse. We'd probably be able to crack her despite the crafty lawyer at her side. "Still all just speculation," her sharp lawyer went on, as if reading my thoughts. "As you said, my client knew Engin Akça, in any case. She wasn't gambling, of course, but it was no secret that she went to the Tarlabaşists Club. Meeting with Tarık doesn't make her an instigator. Moreover, we aren't even so sure Tarık wanted to kill Engin. You found him waiting in Engin's house. Maybe the two were friends. Or perhaps Engin was afraid of an attack, and hired Tarık Seberci to protect him." He shot my assistant a biting glance. "If you'd have taken Tarık alive, we would know what happened."

He was too clever by half, Batuhan, as he made his insinuations. I saw Ali was glaring at him. But we'd do well not to meddle with this young lawyer to the filthy-rich. I butted in, worried my assistant would overdo it.

"That's true, but if that hitman had shot an officer, whoever hired him would never escape our grasp."

A deep silence fell over the room. Jale had begun biting her bottom lip and the lawyer briskly flipped his gold-plated pen in his right hand. Our erratic police watched both of them edgily.

"Why did you meet with Tarık?" Ali asked, breaking the silence. "I assume you weren't ordering flowers for your greenhouse."

Neither Jale nor the lawyer laughed.

"Excuse me?" she said, exaggeratedly raising her right hand to her ear. "I didn't hear what you said."

The lawyer noisily placed his pen on the table.

"You don't have to answer him, Jale Hanım. You can use your right to remain silent."

There was some kind of surrender in this attitude, but the woman watched Batuhan dismissively.

"I know." She calmly blinked her long lashes, then turned her hazel eyes on Ali. "What do you think Tarık Bey and I could have talked about?"

It seemed she'd regained her confidence.

"We ask the questions here," said my assistant, ready to explode.

"All right, Ali," I said, quieting him. I still had hope that we could get Jale to confess, so it would help not to cede just yet. "If you'll let me, I'd love to take a guess as to what you talked about."

She gently stretched out a hand, palm up.

"Be my guest, Nevzat Bey. I'm curious what you have to say, as a matter of fact..."

"Actually, you know what I'm going to say. You discussed the money you'd pay in exchange for killing Engin. And most likely you agreed on four hundred thousand. Two hundred thousand up front, and another two hundred thousand when the deed was done. That's a lot of money. Tarık tricked you. And Dice went along with the scam. I guess when things went wrong with Nizam, he considered using Tarık. Tarık would've accepted two hundred grand in a heartbeat, or two hundred fifty at best... I'm sorry, but they ripped you off." I hung my face so she'd think I sympathized with her. "But really, Jale Hanım, how did you stumble into this? What business have you got with these people?"

She wasn't at all evasive. "People make their own choices, Nevzat Bey," she said boldly. "Most of the time, it's these choices that determine our lives."

Ali shook his head angrily.

"But if you make a choice, you pay the price for it."

A flirtatious smile spread through her perfectly painted lips.

"If I'd committed a crime, I would of course. But I'm innocent." Her face, made younger with make-up, showed no sign of defeat or failure anymore. She turned back to me. "I met with Tarık Bey three times, not two. Twice at the Rikkat Hotel, and once on the terrace at The Marmara Hotel. See, you

416

missed the third. Ihsan was with us all three times because we were thinking of opening a venue together. A gypsy bar. They're a new thing. From the food and music to the decor, the atmosphere, everything is devoted entirely to the Romani culture. And in Tarlabaşı, no less. A sizable population of our Romani citizens lives in Dolapdere, as I'm sure you know..."

As I watched the woman weave this scenario, I'll admit I felt admiration. This Jale was a sharp cookie. Far smarter than her shiny lawyer.

"You know this urban renewal in Tarlabaşı. That entire hovel is on its way out, and new life will be breathed into the city center. Modern life, just as it should be. Distinguished families will move in. And they'll need some new form of entertainment of course. Well, we came up with the project in response to this demand."

"And Tarık was going to what, conduct the Gypsy orchestra?" he mocked. "Maybe with that huge Glock of his?"

She laughed.

"You're a funny guy. Of course I wasn't hiring him for the music. Tarık was going to deal with security. Tarlabaşı is still a bit dodgy, as you know. It'll take some time before it becomes a truly safe place. And that's Tarık's field of expertise. At least according to Ihsan Bey. And I believed him."

Ali kept up his sarcasm.

"So you mean you paid two hundred grand to keep a yet to be opened bar secure."

She looked at him as if to say *What a sweet thing you are!*

"No. Wrong again, sir. I didn't pay a dime to Tarık. I gave the money to Ihsan. I wouldn't know if he gave it to Tarık or not. Ihsan was low on cash, and it wasn't the first time I'd lent him money. Once, my dear husband Rıfat Bey sent him exactly one million lira. It was three years ago or so. Look into it and you'll find the bank statement."

"But you handed him the two hundred thousand in cash," I said, trying to pressure her. "Wasn't it hard to carry so much money?"

She was playing the role of an innocent woman superbly. No doubt she believed the lie herself, just as any good actress would.

"No... Why should it be?" She pointed to the red bag at her feet. "I already carry a suitcase, as you can see."

She looked me straight in the eye and lied, but we had nothing on her to refute what she said. She'd saunter out of here swinging her arms. Nobody could prevent it. "Was Engin blackmailing you?" I asked, to rile her.

The confidence she hid beneath her perfect make-up seemed a bit shaken again. I was expecting her to get angry, and if she lost her cool perhaps she'd give the game away. But no, the woman was a pro.

"Why would he do that?" she said, her expression condescending. "I gave him enough money as it was."

"There's no such thing as enough money, Jale Hanım. You know that better than I do," I said with a cold smile.

My words hit their mark. A flicker of hatred passed through her hazel eyes.

"And how would I know that?"

"From having an inheritance so big you're set for life and will never be wanting."

She knew what I meant, but it didn't bother her.

"You're wrong. I'm not so interested in money. And like you said, I've got enough money to feed seven generations."

"But you haven't got your youth," our merciless Ali continued. "That's why you lost Engin. And that's why you wanted him to die, because that young girl took him from you. If you couldn't have him, no one else could."

Jale kept her cool.

"Poor child," she murmured, looking at my assistant. "Leave it to you men to relate death to love. There's no room for death in the love I feel."

"What about when that love is over?"

My question confused her. She was losing her concentration.

"Yes, your love for Engin was exhausted a long time ago. I disagree with my assistant; I think it's been a while since you gave up on Engin. But he didn't give up on you. Or more precisely, your money. He started blackmailing you. He threatened to tell your stepsons about the buildings you bought together in Tarlabaşı. You got scared the stepsons would strip you of your fortune. Come on, Jale. Tell us how much Engin wanted from you. One million? Two? More?"

Our eyes met for a moment; for a split second she slipped out of her cold, arrogant armor and I thought she'd open up and tell us the truth. But no, she turned back from the brink, though the steeliness in her hazel eyes softened.

"No, nobody blackmailed me. But you're right about one thing. My love for Engin was over." She put on a supposedly mournful air. "As far as killing him goes, the thought never crossed my mind. Murder is such a horrific word. I wouldn't wish death on anyone, especially someone I knew, like Engin."

Batuhan, despite having expended very little effort, seemed pleased with the course of the interrogation up to now and was afraid his client would say the wrong thing at the last moment and ruin everything.

"Shall we wrap this up, Nevzat Bey?" he said, with a triumphant affectation. "It looks like we've covered everything."

He was right. This time we were beaten. No matter what we did, Jale wasn't going to open up to us. I took a deep breath.

"Looks like we did. You're free to go when you want." I leaned confidently onto my elbows. "But we'll be presenting the information we've gathered to the court. Not just about the two hundred thousand paid to Tarık Seberci, but the huge sums sent to Engin Akça, as well. And the ten other victims of this murder, of course. Every last grave detail will be submitted to the court. It'll be up to the judge to decide if there was an attempt on the man's life or not."

Jale, quite sure of herself, began to get her things together.

"My dear deceased father had a saying. A justly chopped off finger doesn't ache."

Ali couldn't stomach the woman's getting away from us.

"This country isn't governed by Sharia Law, Jale Hanım," he snapped. "Fingers are chopped off in entirely different ways here." His handsome face was taut with a feeling of revenge. "For instance, do you think when your husband Rıfat Bey's two sons find out you and these preposterous men are eating up their father's fortune that they are just going to stay silent? Will they just stand there and take it while the inheritance left to them and their dear sweet mother disappears like melting snow?"

The woman's face twisted up and she stared at Ali with loathing. She wanted to answer him but didn't know how. She whipped her head round to look at her lawyer and fumed, "Is that it, Batuhan Bey? Are we through here? Can we go?"

"Is he the killer you've been looking for?"

※

Through all those years of my professional life, if we didn't count my wife and daughter's killers, this was the first time I'd closed a murder file without finding the perpetrators. One by one, we'd interrogated Black Nizam's nineteen nephews, the lawyer Groom Sacit, and Dice Ihsan's three bodyguards. We spoke again with Çilem, Azize, Nazlı, Swank Cemal, and even with Harem Süleyman. The investigation wasn't moving forward an inch; it was just turning around in the same vicious circle. Out of desperation we returned to the previous scenario, the possibility that a hitman had killed Engin. It was Ali's idea. Here's what he said: Tidy Tarık killed Engin in front of the Tarlabaşists Club in order to pin it on Ihsan. From there he went down to Kasımpaşa and threw the knife into the dark waters of the Golden Horn. Then he went to Engin's house with the key he'd got off of Jale because he'd wanted the title deeds. The documents linked Jale to the victim. We came across him as he was searching for the deeds. And that was the end of the hitman. Meaning it was the sinister killer Tidy Tarık himself that kicked off the chain of deaths. And now that he was dead, the fight was over. I could close the file.

It sounded rational, but I still wasn't convinced. It seemed like we were missing something. Some simple detail that we couldn't see despite it being right there before our eyes. Still, it was what my assistant wanted to believe, not because he'd shot Tarik, but because there was no other possibility. The desire for a quick conclusion that could be seen in all impatient people burned away in his mind too. Zeynep was more cautious, but if we could find no other evidence she would also accept his theory. As for me, I'd eventually have to go along with them even if I still had my doubts. But the discussion kept coming back round to Engin's killer. So much so that before going to Zeynep's house at her family's invitation I had to warn the kids.

"Look, the subject is weighing on all our minds, but we will absolutely leave it to rest during dinner. It'd be really rude for Veli Bey and Sakine Hanım."

Zeynep looked unconcerned.

"My parents won't mind, Chief. But you're right. Evgenia Hanım will be there too. Talking murder at dinner won't go over so well."

Actually, I didn't suppose Evgenia would mind either; I knew that however sad she was over the story of Kader I'd explained the other morning, she was dying of curiosity about what I got up to. I was sure our discussion would have her attention, but she wouldn't just stop at listening, she'd also argue her own ideas about who the killer was. Perhaps Zeynep's mother and father would join in too. And there you'd have it, the whole lot of us discussing murder at dinner. But it wasn't as I'd feared. Nobody brought up the deaths, let alone murder. Anyhow, that was how it should be. Our group was closer to a wedding than any death.

On my way to Zeynep's, I stopped by Evgenia's. She was waiting for me outside the exquisite Kurtuluş apartment building, a monument to history where her third-floor flat was. She wore a blue coat and had wrapped a long dark blue scarf round her neck that brought out the color of her eyes. She held a large bouquet of flowers, white and yellow narcissus and freesia. The scent of narcissus and freesia wafted in with her lavender. She was excited, and happy, as it was our first time going to a family dinner together.

Ali also joined us on the way; our fearless officer didn't have the courage to go alone to the house of the girl he loved. In fact, he knew Veli Bey and Sakine Hanım, but for whatever reason this time he was really nervous. Our friend, who hadn't even bothered to dress up for the policemen's ball, now wore a fancy blue suit and even had a red tie around his neck. We found him waiting outside his flat in Beşiktaş holding a huge box of baklava like some improvised object. He had just settled into the back seat when Evgenia teased him. "When are we going to ask the girl's parents' permission to marry her, Ali?"

He blushed like a teenager, our young lover.

"What girl, Evgenia Hanım?" he asked her, with a supposedly innocent look.

"What, is there someone else besides Zeynep?"

"Leave the kid alone, Evgenia," I said, smiling beneath my moustache. "We'll go with him when the time comes, I hope."

He neither confirmed nor denied it, Ali, but that sweet light in his eyes seemed to say it wouldn't be long till he proposed.

Zeynep's humble single-story house was located in the Gaziosmanpaşa hills, on the corner of a narrow street where the smell of coal burned my nasal. A twisted mulberry tree and a tall poplar left to the winter frost in the small garden somehow conjured a feeling of poverty. If my ears weren't deceiving me, I could hear the coo of doves; I supposed one of her brothers must be interested in birds. Zeynep had told me her relatives from Bulgaria had immediately put up three or four story buildings on the land. But her father, more interested in gardens, had left the house as it was. The five-member family met us at the door. Evgenia's flowers were put into a vase and the sweets Ali and I brought were carried off to the kitchen. We lined up in a row near the sofas and armchairs of the small living room. After removing our coats, we'd settled too hastily into our seats, and Ali had landed in the middle. We were like a husband and wife with their son, asking for the girl's hand. Evgenia must have been thinking the same thing, because she occasionally looked over and gave me an impish smile.

Veli and his two sons, Özkan and Serkan, stayed with us. Sakine and Zeynep were flitting about, shuttling back and forth from the kitchen to keep us happy. Özkan and Serkan had their eyes on Ali. Supposedly I was the team boss, though my roughneck assistant was more impressive than his middle-aged boss, even in that timid state. Still, I wouldn't want to be in his shoes. He'd put his hands between his knees and was trying to hide the stress in his face and appear friendly to everyone. After welcoming us to their home, they brought cologne round for our hands. It may seem silly, but traditions like this that were slowly disappearing warmed my insides whenever I encountered them. The sweet smell of lemon cologne filled the small living room. As I brought my hands to my face, I noticed Veli Bey trying not to let on as he studied Ali. I doubted Zeynep had hinted at the idea, but I guess her father was quick on the uptake. After the cologne, a silence seemed to fall, so the older son asked Ali about his gun. What mark was it? Was it a 38 like the one his big sister carried or did he have a bigger one? In fact, this was a subject my assistant could go on and on about, but he surprised me.

"A gun is not something to boast about, Serkan," he said, like a wise man. "I wouldn't touch the thing if I didn't have to."

Good for him, I thought to myself. The boy who'd asked was only sixteen, and his interest in guns probably came from the cheap mafia shows he saw on TV. Zeynep also jumped in to warn her brother.

"Did you hear that, Serkan? I always tell you. Guns, and fighting and breaking things, don't make a man tough..."

It wasn't his sister's words that disappointed Serkan but the scolding from Ali, whom he idolized like a big brother.

"Yeah, but..." he groaned. "You never know who's out there on the street. A man can pull a gun and empty it on you for just bumping your shoulder into him. And then what do you do?"

Zeynep cut in from the head of the table where she set the plates.

"You be more careful. You don't bump someone with your shoulder in the first place. Or let's say you do, then you say sorry. You steer clear of those dirtbags..." She turned and looked at her brother. "Need I say more?"

"Your sister is right," said the prospective brother-in-law. "Let's say you have a gun too. What's going to happen if you

424

pull it? You either shoot the man and wind up in prison or, god forbid, the man shoots you and you wind up six feet under."

If I knew Ali believed what he was saying, it'd bring tears to my eyes. The guy's future in-law was repeating word for word what I'd been telling him for years.

"Nope, Serkan, I'm afraid guns don't suit a tough guy. You wouldn't believe the gunmen we've seen in that world. And what happened? Every one of them chewed up and spit out."

"Couldn't have said it better myself, Ali, son," our rascal's future father-in-law praised him. "We can't get through to the kid. He thinks violence is manliness, when in fact real manliness comes from managing to be a gentleman. Isn't that right, Chief?"

I'd have to break my silence.

"Exactly, Veli Bey." I looked over at Serkan, whose moustache was just beginning to sprout. "If you're that interested in guns, let's go to a shooting range one day. Fire one and get it out of your system. But your dad is right; real manliness comes from being a good person. Beating up on someone who's insulted you, especially with a gun, is not what brave men do."

His eyes, the same brown as his sister's, shone with enthusiasm. He jumped on what I'd said as if he'd only heard the first part.

"All right, Nevzat Bey, so when are we going to the shooting range?"

Evgenia shot me a look although I knew what I was doing.

"We have a case right now. But as soon as it's closed, I'll call you. And maybe Ali will come with us too..."

I'd tried this method three times before, and got a positive outcome every time. These kids who idolized guns, when they smelled the gunpowder and heard the bullets explode on the shooting range – of course I was sly about it and didn't give them earmuffs – they shook in their boots. They chickened out and stopped this pining.

"Well now, let's eat." With Sakine Hanım's cheerful voice, we all stood up. The long narrow table was covered with dishes of food, each more delicious looking than the next. A huge winter salad, two cups of home-pickled vegetables, small bowls of what was also probably home-cultured yoghurt, dark green stuffed vine leaves and light green stuffed bell peppers... First they served a lentil soup. We'd be drinking raki, so I thought it wise not to have much. After that came white beans in a meat sauce and a luscious-smelling rice and vermicelli pilaf. It was the best white bean stew I'd ever had, no exaggeration.

"Delicious!" Evgenia said, beating me to it. "Did you cook this in a clay tandoor pot?"

Sakine Hanım's eyes lit up.

"A master knows her stuff... That's right, Evgenia Hanım. In a tandoor pot, simmered over a low flame."

But I guessed our Ali didn't feel the same. After taking two spoonfuls of the beans, he gulped down a full glass of water. The state of her prospective son-in-law didn't escape Sakine Hanım's notice.

"Is it too spicy?" she asked abashedly. "Did I put too many peppers in it?"

How would he dare to tell the truth?

"No, it's not... I'm just not used to such spicy food."

The poor woman was starting to take it to heart.

"No, really, it's just right,' I said, waving a thumb and forefinger okay sign in the air. "It's delicious!"

"This kid's going to starve if Zeynep makes food this spicy too," Evgenia said, making mischief again.

Luckily, my assistant was busy trying to cool his burning mouth and didn't understand.

"What was that, Evgenia Hanım?"

"Nothing, not important," she said, but Zeynep had heard and snickered.

Her father hadn't caught it either. "It's the style where we're from," he proudly pronounced. "That's how we cook beans in Dobrudja. Sakine Hanım also does a great rice pilaf. She cooks it in pure butter."

As I stuck my fork into the rice pilaf, Zeynep asked about our clarinetist, though I'm not sure what made her think of him.

"Dad, there's this guy named Sadri... a Bulgarian immigrant... Do you know him? He's from Dobrudja. A clarinetist, one of the Romani..."

426

I savored the tastes in my mouth while her father answered.

"A lot of them are musicians. They're very artistic people. Was he from the village of Sarı Mahmut?"

Zeynep reached for the bread basket.

"He didn't say which village, just that he's from Dobrudja and that his name was Sadri..."

"Sadri..." Sakine Hanım repeated, as she filled Ali's water glass. "I don't know the name."

"The Bulgarians gave him the name Sergey... I mean, they wouldn't let them use their real names."

Sakine Hanım wrinkled up her brow.

"There was a gypsy called Sergey... But no, it can't be him. You remember, Veli? He was in the papers? He killed his sister..."

Veli gave his wife a blank look, but I remembered the clarinetist saying his sister had died in an accident.

"This Sadri's sister also died." My assistant ignored his burning mouth and jumped in. I guess like me, he had begun to carefully follow the conversation. "But his was killed in an accident."

"Sergey's sister also died in an accident."

This Sadri's story was getting more interesting by the minute. Ali continued to pick away at it.

"But he didn't kill her, did he?"

"He did, but not on purpose, of course. It was an accident, as I said." She shrugged her shoulders, as if surprised we were so interested in the subject. "Still, I don't think it's your Sadri. He wasn't a musician, Sergey. He threw knives."

Ali and I nearly fell off our chairs.

"Threw knives?"

Veli interrupted his wife, thinking she'd explained it all wrong.

"Not like you think, Nevzat Bey. In the circus... I remember now too. It was all anyone talked about for days. But that was a long time ago. A couple years or so before we came to Turkey." He glanced at his wife. "Isn't that right, Sakine?"

"No, it was one year before. We went to Edirne the following year, in May, remember?"

"That's right," said Veli, gently smacking his forehead. "I forgot. Anyhow, he was a knife-thrower, Sergey. A strapping young man, too. Eyes sharp as an eagle's, strong arms, long fingers... His nickname was even 'Knifer'. They were from the village below ours, from near Mehmet's... His mother wove baskets. All the women in that village were basket-weavers, and all the men musicians. Fathers, sons, and grandsons. But Sergey had a different calling. As I said, he worked in the circus, in Shumen. It paid better..."

It had shaken us all to the core, this information falling into our laps when we least expected it. If what was going through all our minds was true, it meant we had our murderer.

"What exactly did he do in the circus?" I asked. "I mean, how did he throw these knives?"

Veli continued with the appetite recalling the past had given him.

"You know the routine. One person stands up against a wooden board and the other stands opposite them and throws knives. I saw the show twice. He could nail a fly from five meters back. The Bulgarians would never have let him work in the circus if he weren't so skilled, anyhow. He was just that talented, Sergey. He got so carried away, he was doing the show with his eyes closed. But that much confidence is not a good thing." He looked at his son. "A knife is a weapon like any other; it's no joke. One day his hand shook, and the knife lost its way and sank right into the poor girl's heart..."

"Oh no!" our tender-hearted Evgenia put in. "What a terrible pity!"

The truth was out, but I wanted to be sure.

"Was the girl's name Jenya?"

Sakine sadly confirmed it.

"Yes, that's right. Jenya. She was an innocent seventeen year old. What a beautiful girl she was... They buried her in a wedding dress." She looked us in the eye one by one with suspicion. "Why are you all so quiet? And why the strange looks?"

None of us could say a word; Ali, Zeynep and I just sat there frozen at the table. Evgenia was the first to catch on.

"Or is it... Is he the killer you've been looking for?"

"Love has nothing to do with goodness."

※

Sometimes life was like that; out of the blue, you'd get a tip. A door would open when you least expected and all the mystery behind a murder would spill through. That is what happened on this occasion. What started off a pleasant meal had turned into a professional investigation thanks to information we'd come on purely by chance. It'd ruined our nice dinner party, of course. I made my apologies and left their home. Evgenia went back to Tatavla, and I took Zeynep and Ali and made my way to the Neşe Pavyon. As I passed under the red neon lights and went down the short steps, I heard an old song that tugged at my heartstrings. I stepped through the low doorway and the voice got even louder. On the stage, under the spinning balls of light, a full-figured, scantily clad woman sang this hicaz song. Although her voice was nothing to write home about, it was moving that she sang so from the heart.

There weren't many customers in the *pavyon*; only three of the tables were full. The seven men among the three tables were all quite drunk. Naturally, they didn't give a damn about the song; they were busy ogling the *konsamatris* nearby, waiting for their chance to grope at the women. The five women sitting at tables against the wall waited despondently for more customers. Azize wasn't among the tables of men or the waiting hostesses. It must have meant she hadn't started work yet. As soon as we walked in, the women began to make eyes at us, but then seeing Zeynep with us they got confused and stopped putting the moves on. I was taking a look around when a young waiter popped up in front of us. Unlike the women, he didn't have an issue with Zeynep.

"This way, please." He indicated one of the tables in front of the stage. "You can sit up close to the performers."

"We don't want a table," said Ali, his tone imperious. "We're police."

The pushy expression on the waiter's face withered. After his shock had passed, he began to search for someone in the darkness. That's when I saw Sadri. He sat in the middle of a five-man group of musicians on stools behind the singer. He was in a black suit again, his white shirt turned lilac under the blue light, with the same slumped shoulders and mournful expression. Suddenly there was a huge man in our way. Standing tall and also in a black suit, his hair cut short and dark moustache turned up slightly at the ends, he watched us with the wide-eyed apprehension of a wolf sniffing danger.

"These gentlemen are police," mumbled the inexperienced waiter. "They don't want a table."

The tension in this behemoth's eyes gave way to concern, though he tried to hide it.

"Is that right? Well... welcome." He held out a hand. "The name's Müslüm. I'm the owner."

"And I'm Chief Inspector Nevzat," I said coolly, shaking the extended hand. "We're here as part of an investigation."

"Nevzat Abi!" His voice sounded excited. "So it's you, Chief! So sorry, I didn't recognize you in the dark..."

The man knew me, but I couldn't place him. I took another look at the face in the shadows but it was futile. In the end, he realized my predicament.

"Come on, Chief. Did you forget? 'Slash' Müslüm. From the Kristal Pavyon. They shot my partner Şükrü..." He threw Zeynep a shy look. "You must remember old 'One-Bollock' Şükrü, Chief..."

I remembered; their place had been in Tepebaşı. One night after midnight there had been an attack on the *pavyon* and Müslüm was the only eyewitness. 'Bucktooth' Sabri had committed the murder. In those days he was one of the most vicious dogs around. But Müslüm wasn't scared in the least, and he'd stood firmly behind his testimony. Of course this show of bravery could have just been because he'd had a part in Şükrü's murder...

"Wow, Müslüm!" I said, giving him a friendly pat on the shoulder. "I didn't recognize you in this darkness either."

His concern left him and he appeared to be happy to run into me.

"Let's go back to my office."

My gaze went to the stage, where poor Sadri sat completely unaware of what was happening and continued to accompany the singer.

I doubted he'd see our sitting in the boss' office as a chance for him to escape, but I still thought it wise to play it safe. I pointed to one of the empty tables.

"I'd rather sit back here."

Müslüm looked from the stage back to me, understanding something was up. Still, he didn't object.

"As you wish. Let's go over to this one on the left here. It gets less noise." He turned hastily to the young waiter. "Get this table set up. The Chief will drink raki..."

I gently touched his arm.

"Not tonight, Müslüm. Let's take a rain check."

He paused again. He didn't want to talk in front of the waiter so he sympathetically put in, "You're on duty, you mean. All right, but you can have tea, I assume."

"How about a coffee?" I asked. I had a slight headache.

"And we'll have instant coffee," my assistant said. "Isn't that right, Zeynep? Instant?"

It appeared things had moved along in their relationship; Ali was giving Zeynep's drink orders now.

The table Müslüm showed me to was behind a massive column. I supposed he put his poorest customers here. For us it was ideal, however, because very little sound made it back here. Once he'd settled in, the owner of the place was ready to have his curiosity satisfied.

"So, Chief, what brings you here? I hope everything's okay."

"Like you don't know," I said, leaning back. "Why do you think?"

"Because of Engin?"

"He was here the night he was murdered..." I said, getting straight to the point. "Having a go at Azize... You were involved in that altercation too, in fact."

He shook his head as if revisiting an unpleasant memory.

"He was here all right, but it was no altercation. He attacked the girl. His problem wasn't with me, but Azize. The guy was psycho. He was obsessed with the girl. But he was seeing other women at the same time."

"Jale?" Ali cut in. "Did you know her?"

Müslüm grimaced.

"Those people are bad news... The woman had a finger in every pie, and her husband was a weirdo, anyhow. The man had a stroke or something and disappeared, and she started to come here on her own. In the beginning, she would come with Engin. Engin was eating her money, as you can imagine."

Müslüm's voice was interrupted by a feeble clapping sound. The singer's show was over, and it was the *konsomatris* applauding their colleague rather than the customers. The buxom woman bowed all the way to the stage floor for men who wouldn't even stoop to listen to her. As the singer climbed offstage, the musicians began to shuffle. Apparently, they were taking a short break.

Müslüm, noticing my eyes riveted on the clarinetist, asked innocently, "Are you here for Sadri?"

Instead of answering, I just gave him a look. A heavy, sorrowful look that left no room for discussion.

"What do you mean? Sadri...?" He almost swallowed his tongue from the shock. "Our Romani killed Engin?"

No one at the table answered and it finally sunk in. He brought his fingers up to his mouth and I thought he was going to tug at his moustache, but he changed his mind and lowered his hand to the table.

"It's not like it's never crossed my mind, but I just couldn't picture him doing it." His voice sounded crestfallen. He looked over at Sadri, who was stepping off the stage. "I told him to forget about the girl... I guess that means he didn't listen. It's such a shame; he'll die in prison, that man."

Sadri saw us, but he couldn't be sure, so he shielded his eyes with his hand. He recognized me first.

"Chief..." As he attempted a smile, he noticed Ali and Zeynep. He froze, then recovered his smile and made his way over, dragging his feet. "Welcome..."

Müslüm got up silently from his chair.

"Come here, Sadri. Come sit," he said, hiding his sadness. "I have some business to tend to."

He gave his boss a look of thanks.

"Cheers, Müslüm Bey."

Nobody spoke at the table for a while. Not even Ali opened his mouth.

"You came for me, didn't you?"

Yes, it was Sadri who'd broken the silence.

"We came for you," I said, my voice mournful. "We've come to take you in."

He wasn't alarmed, nor did he deny anything.

"How did you know?"

"You gave yourself away," I said sadly. 'I'm a Bulgarian immigrant,' you said. 'From Dobrudja.' I nodded towards Zeynep. "Her mother and father know you... Or more precisely, they heard about what happened to you. I mean with Jenya, or Pembe... The accident your sister was in."

He pulled his right hand off the table as if he didn't want us to see it and placed it into the darkness of his lap.

"So that's how you knew..."

"Yes, that's how we knew..."

It was quiet again. The drunk customers' dissonant laughter made it to our table. As they got louder, the silence at our table became unbearable. In our line of work you needed to have empathy, but his lack of emotion was even too much for me. It'd be good to continue the questioning.

"That night... I mean the night of the incident. You said you fought with Engin. He attacked Azize here, didn't he?"

He calmly nodded, as though the incident didn't involve him.

"That's right... That's what I said. He'd done it before, but I never saw him as angry as this. I think he was on drugs or something. He was hitting the girl so brutally, not considering how it'd end. And he was shouting curses at us. I didn't care about that, but as I left the room he threatened Azize, saying, 'This doesn't end here. I'm not going to let you go, you whore!' I panicked. Not for myself but for Azize. I thought he really was going to kill her. He'd never spoken like that before. I pictured Azize dead before my eyes... the coffin, the graveyard, her being buried in a wedding dress just like Pembe... No, I couldn't allow that to happen. I left Azize alone in Müslüm Abi's office and went out. I went to the kitchen... took out the sharpest knife I could find, the one that fit my hand best... The musicians were on a break anyhow, so I rushed out into the street. It had only been a few minutes since Engin had left. I walked one direction first but couldn't see him. The sound of people celebrating the New Year was coming from Taksim Square, but I couldn't hear Engin's footsteps. I rushed up the street the other way. I'd got a few hundred meters when the icy air took my breath away. I was about to give up when I saw him. He was walking quickly, angrily... I matched my steps to his, tried to breathe like him. With every step, I was bridging the distance between us, but then he noticed. I knew it from the way he slowed down, from the way his ambition let up. I also knew he had a gun, so I had only one shot at this. If I couldn't kill him, Engin would definitely kill me. I saw his right shoulder move; his hand was going for his gun. He was going to turn and shoot. I stopped and weighed up the knife in my hand, raised it level to my head and waited. A couple more steps and he also stopped. As soon as he did, he turned towards me with his gun, and that's when I threw the knife. The gun just hung there in the air, and I don't know why, but he smiled at me before falling on his back to the ground. I went over; his eyes were still open but he was already dead. I was happy he hadn't suffered much, at any rate. I grabbed the knife and hurried back here, then washed it off and put it back. The music was about to start so I got up on stage, sat in my chair and picked up my clarinet." Sadri sighed deeply. "Maybe I wouldn't have done it if I'd thought it through. Or I wouldn't have been able to. Because I'd have understood Engin wasn't going to kill Azize. He was in love with her, too. Yes, though he didn't know how to love, he was in love with Azize."

"And you? Were you also in love with Azize?"

Ali had asked the question in earnest with a mix of sadness and curiosity. Not like a police officer, but like a young man affected by the story he'd heard.

"Love!" A bitter laugh spilled from Sadri's lips. "Love?" he murmured to himself. He couldn't work it out, or maybe just wanted to brush it off, who could say? He looked over at me. "What is love, Chief? You've been around the block. What is it?"

The question caught me off guard. I laughed too, and my laugh came out rather awkwardly as well.

"I don't know... Caring for something and not being able to reach it? A desire for something you can't obtain? I don't know. Maybe it's wanting someone by your side... But everyone has their own special recipe for love." My gaze went to our two young police officers. "Isn't that right? It's different for everyone, love..."

Even though it hadn't been my intention, they thought I was dropping a hint and averted their eyes. I was embarrassed. More than embarrassed, I was mortified, and of course I clammed up. But Sadri didn't.

"She reminded me of my sister," he muttered. "Not her appearance. I don't know if it was the look in her eye, the bend of her neck or the way she talked, but there was something about her that reminded me of my deceased sister. And that helplessness... The way she was facing the world alone... How she stared innocently into your face... I don't know; I don't think mine was love. It wasn't right what I did. I killed a man. But anyhow, love has nothing to do with virtue. If it did, Azize would have left Engin a long time ago. She wouldn't have gone and thrown herself in front of his house, saying, 'Please, don't leave me!' the first time that guy beat her up. No, love is not a good thing. If you ask me what it is, I can't tell you, but it's not good..." He turned to me as if asking for help from an old friend. "Actually, I was going to come turn myself in. I swear I was, Chief. And explain everything I'd done, like I did just now... I decided to come clean on that very night. It made no difference to me whether I lived on the inside or the outside. But when I saw the look on Azize's face when she heard Engin had been killed, I got scared. Azize was still madly in love with Engin. I was afraid if she found out I'd killed him, she'd hate me. You understand; it's a very human emotion. Azize is the only one in life that I value. To have her hate me... Okay, maybe it was a stupid line of thinking. Because she'll still hate me now... Well, let her. What can I do? As I said, Chief, love doesn't understand virtue so well. Love has nothing to do with goodness."

"Beyoğlu's Finest Big Brother"

✳

The snow had started again. Quietly and sparsely, the flakes were being scattered over Beyoğlu. Although I'd left home to go to the station, I'd been walking for a while on Tarlabaşı's streets. Sadri would be taken to the prosecutor's office today and I wanted to be with him. Nobody else would come but us, and maybe his worldly-wise boss Müslüm would send one of his men to put a few lira into his pocket. No, Azize didn't want to see Sadri. Our killer had been right; when she learned he'd murdered her one and only love, she first went into shock, then cursed the impoverished clarinetist to the heavens. She wouldn't forgive him any time soon. Maybe one day when she grew old, very old, as she cleaned the toilets in a brothel in one of the smaller cities, she would understand that Sadri was the only one who truly loved her... Or perhaps she would never understand and would hate him till her last breath, this musician who'd taken the life of the man she loved. I won't hide it; I feel closer to those who have lost than those who have won. There is much more compassion in what they've been through, much more pain. To understand this, you only need look at the tragedy of Sadri. Yes, even though he'd murdered Engin, this sinewy-fingered, droopy-eyed man was this story's real victim. Beside his innocence, Azize's purity would be no cleaner than the glass in the windows of these derelict buildings. Yes, these desolate buildings, this infamous district that we laid waste to with our hate and our mass hysteria, these murders, this evil, this market where human flesh was sold... I suppose that's why I steered my faithful old guy into the side streets. To see one last time this ghost neighborhood in the heart of the city, to fathom it and feel its curse.

I'd parked my car in front of the Tarlabaşists Club, there where Engin was killed, where the bloodstain on the pavement had long since faded. Then I headed all the way down to Kadın Çıkmazı, to where Ali had shed blood, and took a spin round the little square where the big battle had broken out. My heart was aching as I thought of Piranha and Keto once again. I thought about Dice, Nizam, Flea Necmi and the two young nephews whose lives were taken by my bullets. They'd been born into the wrong lives, as the wrong people... I didn't stop by the Ferhat Çerağ Culture Center, which had taken Musti under its wing again; I didn't have the guts to look into those violet eyes of Nazli's, shadowed as they were by grief. I'd come to the street of the Genuine Tarlabaşists Club. I looked down at the ground where Fidan's slender body had been; there was no sign of any murder committed there either. I hurried away. I wanted to take a long walk, breathe a bit, maybe distance myself from everything that had happened... As if I could escape...

"Chief! Chief..."

I was used to it now. Somebody was always calling out to me on these streets. I turned round and saw the bookseller. That strange novelist's friend. He was standing in the shop doorway, giving me a friendly wave. The man was polite enough, but I didn't have the patience to chat with him now.

"Hi, Kemal Bey..." I said, keeping my distance. "How are you?"

I was trying to maintain my civility while escaping, but he wouldn't allow it.

"I have something for you... Somebody left it."

Where did that come from? I wouldn't be able to get away at this point so I made my way to the bookshop. I shook the snow off my coat in front of the shop, then went inside.

"What is it?"

With a mysterious smile on his lips, he held a book out to me.

"Your neighbor's latest novel... It just came out today."

So then, this was the bothersome writer's latest attempt at forming a relationship. "He could have dropped it at my house," I muttered discontentedly. "I do live right next door."

"He was going to, but I insisted," he said, being protective of his friend. "You remember you said you were going to stop by? Well, I asked him to leave it with me, and he humored me."

I took the extended book.

"Anyhow, thank you."

He pointed at the book.

"He signed it for you."

Yeah, what an honor... As if I cared about his autograph. Not wanting this to drag on, I answered flatly, "How lovely." I settled the book under my arm without even looking at the cover. Then I held my right hand out to the bookseller, who stared at me without losing that mysterious expression of his. "I'm sorry, Kemal Bey. I have somewhere I have to be. Always on the run, you know."

This time he didn't insist.

"I understand. When you're free, I'll be expecting you."

I hurried out of the shop and around the corner into Mis Street, where I stopped and took the book out from under my arm. I took a quick look at the cover. All at once, the book's title jumped out at me. *When Pera Trees Whisper.* I took my glasses out of my coat pocket and placed them on the tip of my nose, then hurriedly turned the page:

"Looks like the killer acted faster"

✖

It is a policeman's nightmare, New Year's Eve. That night when everyone else is laughing and having a ball, happily dancing away, means some horrific hours for us; a dark, bloody, never-ending nightmare that starts in the afternoon and goes on till the first day of the year grows light. There's always an incident; it never fails. Somebody always fires a gun, somebody draws a knife, somebody murders somebody... Up to now it has always been like this, and it will be like this forevermore. This is the reason holidays have been revoked and the whole force is on edge. While some people are out living it up in fancy restaurants and night clubs, or others at home with their families and loved ones, we police will greet the new year with our so-called little celebrations in our boring stations, all of us in bad humor, or worse. All of us hypervigilant due to the announcement that will come over the radio. Strangely enough, tonight the time has flowed by without any noteworthy incidents save the occasional injury, or one of those disgraceful molestations seen every New Year in Taksim. Maybe tonight would be an exception and no one would kill anyone. Maybe the murderers would put their business on hold for tonight... Just as hopes were beginning to rise, the announcement came, as Ali, standing, was nibbling at the last crumbs of the raspberry cake left forgotten on the table and I sipped at my coffee... Right at that moment, the transmitter relayed the New Year's first murder. A male body had been found in Tarlabaşı.

GLOSSARY

There is a tradition among Turks of using titles, or familial relationship names, to address people who are not actually relatives. These titles are used as a sign of respect, alone if you do not know the person and tacked on after a person's given name if you are familiar with them.

Hanım– Similar to 'madame'

Bey – Similar to 'sir'

Abla – Big sister

Abi – Big brother

Teyze – Aunt (for an older woman)

Amca – Uncle (for an older man)

Usta – A term used for a person who has mastered a craft or is exceptionally skilled at their trade

Hadji – An honorific title given to a Muslim who has completed the pilgrimage to Mecca

Cacık: a cold soup made with yoghurt, cucumber, and mint

Çapulcu: a Turkish word, roughly translated as 'riffraff' or 'looters', that was re-appropriated by Gezi Park protestors to mean 'a person who fights for their rights' after being used derogatively by Turkish Prime Minister Erdoğan during the Gezi Park Resistance in June of 2013

Darbuka: a goblet-shaped drum held under one arm and struck with the hand

Döner: a type of kebab where meat is cooked on a vertical rotisserie and sliced into thin pieces before serving

Gavurdağı: a tomato-based salad of finely chopped vegetables with pomegranate molasses and walnuts

Kokoreç: grilled sheep's intestines

Konsomatris: a woman employed by a pavyon to entertain the male clientele and encourage them to buy drinks

Kapuska: a traditional stew which takes its name from the Russian word for cabbage

Lahmacun: a round, thinly rolled piece of dough topped with spiced minced-meat and onions and oven baked

Meyhane: a traditional bar/restaurant in Turkey and the Balkans where people drink raki accompanied by an array of mezes and often Balkan or Turkish music

Meze: small side dishes served alongside alcoholic beverages, similar to Spanish tapas

Ocakbaşı: a traditional restaurant where meat is cooked over an open fire pit and served with an array of smaller dishes and alcohol

Pavyon: an exorbitantly expensive adult entertainment club where men go to watch female vocalists perform and chat with 'hostesses', both of which may or may not be prostitutes

Saz: a traditional, long-necked stringed instrument similar to a lute

Syrtos: a popular Greek folk dance